THE
WING
MAN

To my new best friend, Jackie!

Hope you enjoy this book!

Natasha.
A.

THE
WING
MAN

Natasha Anders

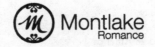

Montlake
Romance

Text copyright © 2017 Natasha Anders
All rights reserved.

Published by Montlake Romance, Seattle

www.apub.com

Amazon, the Amazon logo, and Montlake Romance are trademarks of Amazon.com, Inc., or its affiliates.

ISBN-13: 9781503943155
ISBN-10: 1503943151

Cover design by Eileen Carey

Printed in the United States of America

I dedicate this book to my wonderful mother, Freda, for her strength, positivity, and unwavering spirit. Rest in peace, Mommy. Words cannot express how much I love you and how much you mean to me. I'll miss you every single day for the rest of my life.

CHAPTER ONE

Mason Carlisle sucked in a bracing breath of icy cold air, and then, ignoring the heavy pool of dread that settled in his stomach, stepped into Ralphie's Pub. A wall of humidity and noise slammed into him and stole the clean air from his lungs in an instant. He hadn't set foot in this place in over a year; it wasn't really his scene. Not anymore.

"Hey, Mason. Long time, buddy. What can I get for you?" the heavyset bartender said as Mason sat down at the end of the bar. Mason dipped his head in greeting and cast a glance around the unusually full local pub. He couldn't recall ever seeing the place this busy before, and he wondered what the occasion was.

"Just a beer, thanks, Ralphie," he said. "It's really pumping in here tonight."

"Yeah, hey? A hen party." Ralphie pointed his double chins toward a corner of squealing, giggling women, and Mason frowned. Ralphie's wasn't the sort of place to attract hen parties—or *women*, for that matter—so their choice of venue was perplexing to say the least.

"Who's getting married?" Mason asked, running a hand over his stubbled jaw, absently noting the need for a shave. He wasn't particularly interested in Ralphie's answer but was killing time until his brother, Spencer, showed up.

"Andrew McGregor's girl, the pretty one. Marrying some fancy rich guy."

The local veterinarian, Andrew McGregor, had three daughters, and just about every guy in high school—Mason included—had had a crush on the pretty one, Dahlia. Daffodil, the cute, older one, had been in Mason's class. He recalled her being obnoxious and sarcastic. He didn't really remember much else about her or the other, youngest one.

Mason didn't particularly care to dwell on McGregor's girls right now; he was more interested in where the hell his brother was. Spencer had begged Mason to join him at Ralphie's and now couldn't be bothered to show up on time. If not for the fact that Spencer was going through a rough spot after his separation from his long-time girlfriend, Tanya, Mason would have ditched his ass and headed home. He had a dog that needed walking, a six-pack that wanted drinking, and a classic eighties action movie to watch.

Yeah, all things considered, he'd much rather be at home.

A scandalized squeal coming from the corner had him swiveling his head instinctively to the rowdy crowd of women just in time to see a *huge* green dildo being passed around.

"Seriously? That thing looks like the Hulk's cock. Talk about placing unrealistic expectations on a guy. I hope her groom can compete." Spencer's voice came from behind him, and Mason turned to glare at his brother.

"You're late," he groused.

"Yeah, sorry," Spencer said, rubbing his hand tiredly over the nape of his neck. "A couple of tourists came in for some hiking equipment. It was a big sale; I couldn't just close up shop." Spencer owned a successful sporting goods store in the center of town.

"So why'd you want to meet?" Mason asked, cutting to the chase as he took a thirsty pull from his beer. "It sounded urgent."

"It is . . . I need a favor, Mase." His brother looked so damned serious that Mason sat up straight, alarmed.

"Anything," he promised, somewhat rashly.

"They're having Lia McGregor's hen party here tonight," Spencer pointed out unnecessarily, and Mason spared an impatient glance at the gaggle of giggling women before slanting his gaze back to his brother.

"Get to the point, will you?" he prompted, and Spencer shrugged.

"That kind of *is* the point," he muttered, his voice so low Mason barely heard it above the chatter of the crowd and the overloud laughter of the women in the corner.

"I want to spend some time with Daff tonight. You know I've always liked her, and if she'd given me the time of day back when, I would probably never have hooked up with Tanya. I was too damned stupid to really try in the past, but I won't let the opportunity slide by again. The McGregor sisters hardly ever hang out in the same places we do. This could be my last chance."

"Yeah, they don't hang out where we do because they think they're too bloody good to spend time with the likes of us," Mason scoffed. "Spence, we're hardly their type. They go for the preppy guys with the right backgrounds. A guy like you wouldn't stand a chance."

The Carlisle brothers had been the rebels at school, the troublemakers from the wrong side of town. They had both long since outgrown that reputation and, despite their tough upbringing, had made successes of their lives. Spencer, with a rugby scholarship in hand, had graduated debt free. After a relatively successful amateur rugby career, he'd gone on to obtain his MBA and had returned home a local sports hero, capitalizing on his reputation by opening his sports store.

Mason, in the meantime, had used his dual South African and UK citizenship to join the British military. At just nineteen, Mason had been better at soldiering than he'd ever expected, and after only a year in the military, he had undergone the grueling selection process for the

Special Air Service. After leaving the SAS five years later, he had, to the hilarity of his former brothers-in-arms, used his "abs of steel"—so hard-earned in the SAS—in a short-lived and embarrassing underwear modeling career.

He still cringed when he thought about it and preferred to wipe that year of his life from his mind.

"Look, I have to grab this opportunity," Spencer was saying urgently. "I'll regret it forever if I don't try, Mase."

Mason peered at his brother for a moment before shrugging and waving toward the women with his beer bottle.

"So go for it," he said. "I'm not stopping you. In fact, I have no idea what this has to do with me. Am I supposed to hold your hand? Applaud when you score? What?"

"You know how close the sisters are. Dahlia's distracted by her friends, because it's her hen night, but Daff probably won't allow herself to be diverted by me if the other one is left to fend for herself."

"And you want me to what?"

"Talk to her."

"Her who?" Mason asked, genuinely confused.

"The *other* one, Daisy . . . distract her. Flirt with her, pay her some flattering attention. Daff will—"

"See right through that," Mason completed with a snort. "That's the dumbest plan you've ever come up with, Spence, and that's saying a lot, considering your history of dumb ideas."

"Come on, Mason, you can be convincing. You're great with women. She'll be so flattered to get some attention from a stud like you that she'll probably fall all over herself for the opportunity to hang out with you."

"I'm kind of insulted on this chick's behalf, Spencer. You're being a dick."

"It's Daisy McGregor," Spencer dismissed. "She's used to it."

"Doesn't make it right." Mason was a little disgusted with his brother's attitude. He couldn't believe that people actually treated the poor girl this way. She was a McGregor; she couldn't be *that* bad. And if she were, it was still no excuse to be an asshole to her.

"Come on, Mase, please. It's Daffodil McGregor. I've been half in love with the girl since high school."

"Man, this is just all kinds of wrong," Mason muttered, running an agitated hand over his head. He kept his hair cropped military short. Seven long and eventful years after leaving the army, and it was still hard for him to wear it any other way.

"I'm asking you to be my wingman, bro," Spencer pleaded. "I've never asked you for anything before. Well, hardly ever . . . but this is important to me."

"It's not going to work."

"But can we at least try? There's no harm in trying, right? If they shoot us down, so be it, but I really need to try."

Mason stared at his brother for a few long moments. That bitch, Tanya, had really done a number on him. Spencer had always been a steady guy, had loved Tanya with everything in him, yet she had cheated on him with just about every available guy in town. Worse, after Mason had returned from England, she had tried to seduce him as well. Luckily Spencer had discovered her infidelity before Mason had been forced to tell him about it. But he still felt like a douche for not warning his brother about Tanya before Spencer caught her in bed with two guys at the same time. And it was because of that guilt that he now found himself nodding in response to the plea he saw in his brother's eyes.

"So what's the plan?"

"Well, they're still busy with the hen party thing—no boys allowed—but according to Ralphie's intel, Lia has to leave the party early, so they'll probably be winding down soon. Daff, the other one, and a few of the ladies will be staying on a bit afterward, so that's when we should make our move."

Mason thought this was all a bit skeevy, but he folded his arms over his chest and nodded, keeping his discomfort with the entire plan hidden behind a blank mask. A thought occurred to him, and even though it pained him to ask, he felt he had to.

"Spencer, if she rejects you, that's it, right? You won't persist?" His brother looked wounded that he had even asked, but Mason had seen enough crazy shit in his lifetime to feel that the question was warranted, even if the guy he was asking was his brother. Spencer had been through so much with Tanya that Mason wasn't sure if any of his brother's hatred for the woman had bled over into his dealings with other females. He hoped not, but one could never be certain.

"I like her, and I just want a chance to prove that to her," Spencer said. "I won't go all crazy stalker on her, Mase. Come on."

Mason held his hands up and shrugged.

"So which one is Daisy McGregor?" he asked, changing the subject as he glanced discreetly over at the women.

"You serious?" Spencer gaped at him, and Mason lifted his shoulders again.

"It's been years since I've even thought of the McGregor girls. And I don't think I've exchanged a single word with the youngest one. Refresh my memory."

"In the corner, next to Dahlia."

Mason subtly scrutinized the woman he hadn't noticed before. She seemed to be hiding in that corner, completely overshadowed by the beauties sitting at the table with her. She didn't appear to be interacting with them much and kept looking down at her phone. Mason wondered if she were chatting with someone or keeping an eye on the time.

She seemed as interested in being here as Mason was, which was not at all. It piqued his interest, and he diverted his attention back to his beer.

"You're in, right?" Spencer asked, and Mason hesitated, directing another quick look over at the woman in the corner.

"Sure, why the hell not?"

⟿

Daisy McGregor sat in her corner, quietly sipping her drink while listening to the avid gossip of the other women around the table. She really wished she was at home, cuddled under a blanket in front of the TV with her sweetie, but her sister was getting married. Daisy loved her sisters and would do anything for them, even if she sometimes felt like she had nothing in common with them.

"Mason apparently sold his stake in the security business last year. For *millions*." Sharlotte Bridges, one of her sisters' friends, said in a stage whisper, referring to the younger Carlisle brother. The women had been all abuzz since spotting the two men at the bar. Mason Carlisle was something of a unicorn around these parts: a mythical, wondrous, and beautiful creature.

"Can you believe how well the Carlisle brothers have done?" Zinzi—another *friend*—hissed.

"Look at them." Shar sighed, dropping her chin into her palm and making googly eyes at the two huge, gorgeous guys seated at the bar. "They're so freaking hot."

"You've always liked the bad boys, Shar," Daisy's sister, Daffodil, said, giggling.

"Well, yeah. Who wouldn't? They can be so . . . *imaginative* in bed." Shar grinned.

"How would you know? It's not like you've ever dated a *real* bad boy," Zinzi pointed out skeptically. "And that Mason—from soldier, to model, to bodyguard of the rich and famous—he might be a little too much for you to handle."

"I bet I could get one of those two in bed," Shar said, and Daisy sank farther back into the recesses of the booth. She really disliked Zinzi and Shar, and she couldn't understand why her sisters were friends with them. They were totally superficial and materialistic. Shar, the gorgeous blonde who was taking bets on whether she could seduce a Carlisle brother, was *married*, for cripes' sake. Granted, her husband was three times older than her and rumored to have mistresses on four different continents, but he was still her husband. They could both practice a little bit of discretion, at the very least.

Zinzi, the daughter of a phenomenally wealthy philanthropist, had dated princes and politicians but routinely slept with her drivers, bodyguards, and fitness instructors. But God forbid she ever openly date one of them. Now Lia seemed to be following them down that same path. She was marrying Clayton Edmondton III, heir to the Edmonton Diamond Company and pretentious asshole of note. Daisy couldn't stand him, and she knew Daff didn't care for him either. But Lia firmly believed that she was in love, and nothing her sisters said—or Clayton did—would change her mind. It was painful to sit back and watch Lia make such a huge mistake with her life, but to protest too much would be to alienate her completely.

The other women were still oohing and aahing over the Carlisle brothers, and Daisy couldn't help but slide a glance over at the two men. They were definitely good-looking guys, both tall, dark, strapping specimens of hotness. Spencer had the heavy build of a rugby player, not an ounce of fat on him, just big and brutish and entirely savage looking.

But while Spencer merely *looked* savage, Mason Carlisle exuded menace and danger from every single pore. He was more sparely built than his older brother and a couple of inches shorter than Spencer's six foot three, but while Spencer was thick with muscle and seemed to possess brute strength, Mason's power and strength had a lethal grace. He was perfect, absolutely perfect. And even if Daisy weren't already familiar with his eight-pack, his beautifully strong shoulders, tight butt, and perfectly sculpted legs—thanks to those revealing underwear ads—she would *still* have known that utter perfection lay beneath that gray formfitting Henley and those faded blue jeans.

But not for all the chocolate cake in the world would Daisy ever let on that she found either one of the brothers attractive. The women would all—with the exception of her sisters and their childhood friend, Tilda—tease her mercilessly and cruelly, knowing that she didn't stand a chance with either man. Daisy was well aware of her so-called shortcomings, and she was resigned to them, but that didn't mean she would ever give this bunch of bitches any fodder to chew on.

So she remained hidden away in her corner, pretending to laugh at their stupid comments and have a blast while they played their silly little hen party games in a venue that they had chosen because they wanted to "live dangerously." Please, like Ralphie's was *such* a dive. It was just a regular sports bar, but it was so far removed from these women's lives that to them it probably seemed like the ghetto.

Daisy sighed and reminisced about a time when her family had been just normal. A bit more well-off than some, but normal just the same. Their father was a *vet*, for God's sake. You couldn't get more ordinary than that.

Normalcy had fled after her parents had joined a snooty local country club when Daisy was ten and her sisters thirteen and fourteen. Daisy had watched the other women in her family go crazy after that. Everything became about the right clothes, the right makeup, the right jewelry, the right men . . . and because she would rather hang out with her father and the animals, Daisy found herself drifting apart from her mother and sisters. Her father was as baffled by the transformation as Daisy, and together father and youngest daughter weathered the storm of shopping and pretentiousness that became their new norm.

The other women were moving on from their previous topic of conversation and were once again focused on Lia's party.

"This one next." Nina Clark, one of their long-standing—and more likable—family friends held up a tiny gift bag. Lia peeked into the bag and squealed when she saw what was hidden beneath the tissue.

"Don't act all coy, you're *so* using those on your wedding night." Nina laughed as she took a sip of her rum and coke. Everybody had been disappointed upon discovering that Ralphie's wasn't the type of establishment to serve frothy, pretty cocktails. In fact—after the women had delighted in inundating their shy young server with orders of "screaming orgasms," "slippery nipples," and "blowjobs"— Ralphie himself had hastened over to curtly inform them that he didn't serve exotic cocktails and they would have to order beers or hard liquor.

"Show us," Zinzi demanded, and Lia lifted a pair of furry pink handcuffs and a satin blindfold to the squealing delight of the other women.

Daisy winced and once again eyed her gift, which lay at the bottom of the pile. She had somehow missed the fact that they would be doing naughty gifts only, and Daisy knew that her present would go down like a lead balloon. She glanced down at her phone for what felt like the thousandth time tonight and willed time to speed up. Lia had a late dinner with her fiancé and his parents tonight and had to leave at eight. It would be awesome if eight o'clock rolled by before Lia opened Daisy's present, but her luck was never that good, and she watched nervously as her sister reached for yet another gift from the shrinking pile in the middle of the table.

"What the hell is that?" Tilda asked from the other side of the table when Lia pulled the gift out of the bag, and Daisy was grateful her friend had asked because she had no idea either. It was a weird, alien-looking silicone thing, and Daisy couldn't quite figure out what it was for.

"Cock ring," Shar educated smugly. "It vibrates for his pleasure and has a little rabbit attached for hers."

Lia, who had been as red as a tomato for most of the evening, blushed even more, and Daisy felt her own cheeks heating in sympathy. This evening had certainly been . . . educational, to say the least.

There were only two gifts remaining now, and Daisy cast another desperate look down at her phone. Five minutes to eight. Lia let out yet another scandalized squeak and lifted the crotchless panties with matching demi bra and garter set that Tilda had given her.

"Oh my God, Tilda, those are so naughty." Daff sniggered and Tilda grinned.

"I figure they'll thrill the hell out of Clayton Edmonton the Third," Tilda said drily.

"Best have a killer wax job done on the lady garden before you wear these," Zinzi advised. "A full-on Hollywood."

"Ugh, I hate going fully bald; it's so creepy," Daff said, wrinkling her nose. Daisy heartily concurred with her sister's sentiment but didn't say as much, knowing it would only drive some of the other "ladies" present to express surprise that Daisy even tended her "lady garden."

"Ooh, one more," Shar cooed as she lifted the huge box from the center of the table. She directed a smug little smile at Daisy, and the latter curled her fingers into the palms of her hands as she realized that Shar—tonight's "events coordinator"—had deliberately not told her about the gifts. What a spiteful cow. Daisy had no clue why Shar and Zinzi disliked her so much, but they had always gone out of their way to make her feel like a total idiot in public.

"It's eight o'clock, Lia," Daisy said, properly speaking for the first time all evening. "You have to get to your dinner with the Edmontons, don't you? My present isn't important. You can open it at home."

Lia, despite the company she kept, was a sweetheart, and even though she didn't quite "get" Daisy, she was loyal to a fault. Unfortunately that trait worked against Daisy in that moment.

"Nonsense," Lia said in her sweet voice. "I've been dying to see what's in this box all evening. A few more minutes won't do any harm. I can't very well leave my baby sister's gift unopened, can I?"

"Yes, you can. I don't mind," Daisy said, and Daff glanced at her sharply as if picking up on her desperation.

"Yeah, Lia, we can open it later," Daff chimed in, and Daisy slanted her a grateful look.

"But we're all really curious now," Zinzi said with a sharklike grin, and Lia nodded, her mind made up, before tugging the bright-red ribbon off the box. Daisy sank back against the sticky leather seat of the booth and kept her face expressionless as her sister tore off the wrapping and then glanced down into the box.

"Oh," Lia said blankly as she lifted one of the practical fawn-colored hiking boots from the box. She stared at it for a long moment. "This is . . . nice."

"It's for your honeymoon," Daisy explained bleakly. "Because you guys are going . . ."

"Oh, *Daisy*," Lia said softly, a beautiful smile lighting up her face. "How thoughtful. Thank you."

Lia and Clay were going on a hiking and horseback honeymoon in Peru, which had surprised the hell out of Daisy because Dahlia was *not* into the great outdoors. The idea must have been Clay's, and Daisy just wanted to get her sister something to help her prepare for an adventure Lia was totally ill-equipped to deal with.

"Guess you didn't get the memo about the gifts," Zinzi pointed out with a snide little smile.

"Shut up, Zinzi. I think it's an awesome present, and I wish I'd thought of it," Daff said. "Lia's going to need that and more for the honeymoon from hell her future husband has planned."

"I think it'll be romantic," Lia said defensively. She was always sensitive to even the slightest hint of criticism aimed at her precious Clayton.

"It will," Daisy soothed, shooting her eldest sister a warning glare, causing Daff to roll her eyes.

"Anyway, I really love the boots, Daisy." Lia wrapped her arms around Daisy's shoulders and hugged her. "So sweet. Thank you."

"Hmm," Shar purred. "So practical. But you're a practical kind of girl, aren't you, Daisy? Not one for all the naughty frivolities of the evening, I suppose? Well, that's to be expected, of course. Lack of experience and all that. I hope we haven't embarrassed you too much?"

"Jesus, Shar, must you be such a cat?" Daff asked in disgust.

"Anyway," Lia intervened quickly when it looked like Shar was about to retort. "I must be off. Thanks for a lovely evening, ladies."

Zinzi and Shar got up too; they had been trailing after Lia like lapdogs lately. The news of her engagement to one of the most eligible bachelors in the region had made them latch on to Daisy's middle sister even more tightly. It was sickening to watch them fawn all over her, when both Daisy and Daff were fully aware that either woman would stab their sister in the back in an instant. Zinzi and Shar had never meant to stick around after Lia left the party, and the other women knew that, which was why they had arranged to stay a bit longer after the hen party disbanded. They wanted to have some real fun, which was almost impossible with Zinzi and Shar around.

Everyone said their good-byes, and lots of air kisses were exchanged. Daisy received a hug and kiss from Lia, but the two other women simply "overlooked" her in the flurry, which Daisy didn't mind at all. The remaining women watched the trio leave and then sat down with huge grins.

"Why do we hang out with those two again?" Nina asked and a chorus of "dunnos" followed.

"Habit, probably," Daff said. "But after this wedding, I think I'll be spending less time with them. They're becoming worse. I'm sorry they were such complete bitches, Daisy."

Uncomfortable with being put in the spotlight so abruptly, Daisy shrugged.

"They're not worth getting upset over," she muttered.

"You're always so Zen about stuff." Tilda sighed, taking a sip of her drink only to discover that it was empty. "Anybody up for a round of tequila shots?"

When the group responded with high-pitched whoops, she grinned and summoned the waiter over.

"Let's get this party *started*," Nina yelled and turned every male head in the place when she jumped up and did a little hip-thrusting dance to go with her words. Someone behind the bar cranked up the music, and after a few more shots, all the women were soon dancing exuberantly. Daisy groaned and tried to hide in her corner, downing her shot in a desperate gulp. This was so not her scene. The other women, after trying to coax her out of her seat, gave up and swanned off onto a makeshift dance floor and were all happily bumping and grinding away with a few of the younger guys in the bar.

"You don't dance?" A deep, dark voice suddenly intruded from almost right beside her, and she yelped and looked up . . . and up . . . and *up* to the tall man standing on her left. He was propping up the wall next to the booth, his back and shoulders resting against the wooden panel as he stood with one knee bent and his foot braced against the wall. He was staring down at Daisy with a slight smile. She shook her head rapidly, trying to dispel the haze from several tequila shots and a flaming black Sambuca as she tried to figure out why the heck *Mason Carlisle* was standing here talking to her. All the head shaking resulted in a spell of dizziness and nausea as the alcohol rebelled against the movement.

"Mind if I sit?" he asked, his deep voice rolling over her like a wave of warm honey. He didn't wait for her to reply and sat down anyway, moving around the table to sit in the spot Lia had vacated. None of the other women had noticed him at their table yet and were chatting and flirting with guys on the dance floor.

"You're Daisy McGregor, right?" She nodded stupidly in reply to his question. Why was he here? This was so weird. "I'm Mason Carlisle. I went to school with Daffodil."

"I know," she said, her voice finally returning. It sounded rusty and unused, but at least it was functioning again.

"So how have you been, Daisy?" he asked, taking a long, thirsty pull from his beer. She watched his throat work as he tilted his head back to drink and was riveted by the way his Adam's apple bobbed with each swallow. Why was that so sexy to her? Probably the tequila.

"I've been good," she finally responded after he lowered the bottle and stared at her with those penetrating forest-green eyes of his. His lashes were dark, long, and spiky, and she was fascinated to note that she could differentiate between each individual lash. Gorgeous.

"And your sister's getting married, I hear. Who's the lucky guy?" Why did he want to know about that? Was he another in the long line of men who had fallen into despair when he'd heard about Lia's engagement? How very disappointing and predictable of him. She cleared her throat and was irritated to find it parched in the presence of this overwhelmingly gorgeous man. In an attempt to dispel the dryness, she snagged the glass closest to her and downed the contents, which caused her to wheeze, cough, and blink away tears. Amused by her reaction, Mason picked up the glass and sniffed it.

"Scotch. Neat, if I'm not mistaken. Hell of a drink, not quite what I expected from you."

"What were you expecting?" she asked, her voice full of challenge. Why was she so offended by that comment? It wasn't even her drink.

"Wine?" The last word emerged on the closest thing to a sneer she could manage, and he shrugged as he carefully replaced the glass.

"Well . . . yeah."

Daisy discreetly nudged her half-full glass of white wine away and lifted her chin rambunctiously.

"I've had tequila shots and flaming Sambuca tonight, so a little Scotch is like mother's milk to me."

"Of course," he said, obviously fighting back a grin. "I'm sorry for not realizing that immediately."

Daisy paused and pinched the bridge of her nose sheepishly, acknowledging that she was being a bit silly.

"Okay, it was awful. I didn't really know what was in the glass," she admitted and saw his eyes light up in appreciation of her honesty.

"Yeah, I'm not a big Scotch drinker myself," he confessed.

"I thought it was a *man's* drink," she pointed out, and he lifted his powerful shoulders comfortably.

"Guess I'm not the man I thought I was." She scoffed at that response and gave him a pointed once-over.

"Mr. Super Soldier slash Underwear Model slash Bodyguard to the Stars not the man he thought he was," she mused, and he grimaced.

"How the hell do you know all that about me?" he asked, clearly astonished.

"You're joking, right? The town has a website dedicated to your accomplishments," she said, taking a casual sip of her wine to swallow down her laughter at the appalled look on his face.

"What?"

"Oh, you didn't know?" she asked. "It's plastered with pictures of you in those tight boxer briefs. And in uniform, of course, and there are a few of you in a tux, hulking behind that princess at the Cannes Film Festival last year."

"I . . ." He seemed at a loss for words, and even in the dimly lit pub she could tell that his face had gone bright red. "That's . . ."

She covered her mouth and doubled over as she finally allowed her laughter to escape.

"Oh my God, the look on your face!"

"It's not true?" he asked, looking half relieved and half annoyed at her.

"No, of course not," she said between unladylike snorts. Her eyes were streaming, and he sat back, folding his arms across his impressive chest as he eyed her with an inscrutable look on his face. When her laughter finally died down, he handed her a napkin.

"Your cheeks are wet," he explained when she looked up at him questioningly. "From your tears of laughter at my expense."

His delivery was so deadpan that she sniggered again and grabbed the napkin to dab at her flushed, damp cheeks.

"I'm glad I amuse you," he said, quirking an eyebrow.

"I'm sorry, I couldn't resist. You looked so horrified."

"How *did* you know all that stuff about me?"

"Come on, it's a small town . . . everybody knows everything about everybody, and the Carlisle brothers were always fodder for gossips anyway." She winced and then shook her head. "I'm sorry, that didn't come out right."

"No worries. I know what you mean. After all, the McGregor sisters were the talk of the town on occasion too. All the guys wanted to date"—his voice petered out as he realized what he was about to say, and he stumbled over the last words—"you girls."

The delivery was so lame and unconvincing that Daisy laughed.

"You mean my sisters?"

"Uh . . ." He seemed at a loss for words, and she grinned.

"Don't worry, I haven't spent all these years under any illusion that the men in this town see me as anything but the *other* one. The pretty one, the cute one, and the *other* one, right? That's what they call us?"

He kept his own counsel, taking another almost desperate gulp from his drink while remaining stubbornly silent.

"I don't mind." She leaned over and patted his arm, unable to believe that she was initiating contact with him, but she couldn't resist it. "It's better than being called the *ugly* one." His arm tensed beneath her hand, and his eyes snapped up to meet hers. He looked so pissed off that she lifted her hand abruptly.

"Has anybody ever called you that?" he growled, and she understood—hopelessly charmed—that he was seriously offended on her behalf.

"Well, no. Not that I know of," she said, and he gave her another long, penetrating look before dropping his gaze down to his beer bottle. He had looked so dangerous in that split second that Daisy had no doubt that if she'd said yes, he would have found whomever had insulted her and done something very nasty to them. A notion that was both ridiculous and flattering.

"So what have you been doing since leaving the glam bodyguard job?" she asked, and he shook his head.

"It wasn't that glam," he said, gracing her with a gorgeous smile. "Most of the time I had to do stuff like hold a certain pop princess's hair out of her face while she puked, or stand around for ages while a very well-known actor got fitted for hairpieces . . . or pick up the shit of a spoilt starlet's pampered pooch. And for the most part, it was mind-numbingly boring."

"I don't suppose you can name names?" she asked, dropping her chin into the palm of her hand as she watched him.

"Nondisclosure agreements," came his succinct response, and she thrust her lip out in a pout and then immediately sucked it back in as she wondered what the hell had prompted the reaction in the first place. Daisy didn't pout, preen, or primp for a man. It wasn't her style, and—according to her mirror—it looked ridiculous on her. Was she flirting with this guy? With *Mason Carlisle*? She didn't even know how to flirt. Was it just instinctive after all?

Who knew?

"What's going on in that head of yours?" he suddenly asked, looking genuinely interested.

"Why'd you come over here to talk with me?" she deflected, lifting her gaze to his and surprising a flash of something—was that *guilt*?—in his eyes.

"I was just curious," he said. "Wondered why you weren't out there dancing with your friends."

"I don't dance," she confessed.

"Everybody can dance."

"Well, I didn't say I *couldn't* dance. I said I *don't* dance."

"Why not?"

"Because the only dance I truly excel at is the chicken dance. Every time I attempt to dance like an adult, I always bust out some stupid chicken dance moves and wind up embarrassing my dance partners."

"You're shitting me again, right?" he asked after a beat, looking honestly uncertain.

"Nope." She kissed her index finger and crossed her heart with it. "God's honest truth. If I went out there right now, I'd start flapping about and doing that ridiculous butt thing."

He burst out laughing, the sound so genuinely amused that Daisy couldn't help but smile at the belly-deep laughter coming from this intimidating-looking man. Now it was his turn to wipe his streaming eyes, and when Daisy silently offered him the napkin back, it just set him off again. The sound was starting to draw attention from people at the other tables and booths. Daisy tried not to notice how astonished they all looked to see him sitting there with her.

His laughter eventually wound down to just a few rumbling chuckles, and he shook his head and stared at her for the longest time.

"Do you want to go someplace quieter to talk?" he asked, his voice still carrying a trace of laughter, and she glanced over at the group of women who were tossing speculative glances in their direction.

"We're talking now," she pointed out.

"I suppose so." He took another swig from his bottle, but upon realizing it was empty, signaled one of the overworked young waiters to bring him another. "So we'll stay here then."

"You don't have to sit with me. You now know why I don't dance. Curiosity appeased, right?"

"Thanks, dude," he told the waiter with a nod when the guy brought his beer. He scratched at the edges of the label on his beer bottle with his thumbnail before refocusing his attention on Daisy and responding to her previous comment. "I have no one else to talk with."

"Weren't you here with your brother?" she asked, looking around for Spencer Carlisle and lifting an eyebrow when she saw him out there dancing with her group. "He's got some moves."

"Yeah," Mason agreed.

"Why don't you join them?"

"Nah, I'm okay where I am. I'm enjoying our conversation. And I don't dance either."

"Don't? Not can't?" she asked sharply, and he grinned.

"Yep."

"Why not?"

"I never discuss that on the first date. That's second-date material," he said, and her eyebrows leapt up.

"This isn't a date, though," she reminded him, and he took another swig of beer before shifting those big shoulders uncomfortably.

"Yeah, only because you won't go someplace quieter with me." She laughed incredulously at that bit of nonsense. Had her world just taken a turn into crazy town? Because this made no sense. Why was she having "date" conversations with this man?

"Maybe I missed something here," she said, circling her finger in the space between them. "Or maybe I'm drunker than I thought because this conversation stopped making sense about two minutes ago."

"I asked you out," he said, and she blinked, before laughing.

"Guys like you don't go out with girls like me," she ridiculed.

"Well, not if you're going to have that attitude," he said, looking almost angry.

"Take a look at all of you, and then take a look at all of *me*." She rolled her eyes, and his jaw clenched.

"I've been looking at you for the last half an hour, and up until *this very moment*, I saw a smart, funny, entertaining woman with whom I wanted to spend more time," he said, his voice so low she barely heard him over the crowd and the music. "That was before the self-pity, though."

"Self-pity? I was being realistic."

"Fine, don't go out with me!"

"Fine! I *will* go out with you," she rejoined, and he looked completely confused.

"Wait, what?"

"Come on." She grabbed her jacket. "Let's go."

"But . . ."

"Where do you want to go? What's open at this time of night?"

"MJ's?" he suggested, still with that confused look on his face.

"Perfect. Let's go."

CHAPTER TWO

Mason couldn't remember the last time he'd been so confused, amused, entertained, and just plain gobsmacked by someone. Daisy McGregor was not at all what he'd been expecting. He'd spent the last thirty minutes completely bemused by her. He glanced over at Spencer, who was trying—and failing—to chat with Daff. The woman appeared to acknowledge his presence with the occasional shimmy in his direction but didn't seem to have much to say to him. Mason felt kind of sorry for his brother, but hell, he had tried to warn the guy.

Mason looked up at Daisy, who had jumped to her feet and grabbed her coat, and he wondered at the impulse that had driven him to ask her out to MJ's. He wasn't attracted to her, but he for damned sure wouldn't mind talking with her a little longer. He was enjoying their exchange so much that he was almost resentful of the thumping music and loud background noise in the pub, which made it hard to hear her clearly. So he had suggested they go someplace quieter and had even used the dreaded *date* word. He shouldn't have referred to it as such; it fostered expectations.

It would *definitely* give her the wrong idea. And while Mason had been forced to do a lot of shitty things in his life, he had never deliberately hurt a woman, and he feared that this path would only lead to pain for Daisy McGregor. She was too damned nice to be hanging out with a guy like him. He had tried the long-term relationship thing and decided it wasn't for him. These days, he tended to fuck and flee, and maybe that made him an asshole, but the women he usually associated with knew what to expect from him. They were happy enough with the short-term arrangements he preferred. Somehow, he didn't think Daisy McGregor was the kind of woman who indulged in that type of fleeting sexual encounter. Still, he was committed to this now and had to see it through, so he beckoned the waiter over and quietly requested the bill, asking the guy to include Daisy's drinks on his tab.

"My drinks have been covered . . . Hen night," she elaborated for the waiter, who nodded his understanding. "Anything in addition to that will be taken care of by my sister. The bombshell in purple over there."

"No problem, ma'am," the guy responded and then asked Mason to hold on for a couple of minutes while he retrieved the bill.

Mason and Daisy stood waiting without speaking, the ease of the last few minutes suddenly replaced by a weird tension and awkwardness that told him she was as uncertain about this so-called date thing as he was. Mason was thinking of ways to back out gracefully when Daisy, with the forthrightness that he was beginning to recognize was stock in trade for her, just came out and said exactly what he'd been thinking.

"This probably isn't a good idea. I won't hold you to it," she said with a rueful smile, and he noticed her dimples for the first time. They were cute as hell.

"What do you mean?" he asked perversely, despite knowing exactly what she'd meant.

"I mean going to MJ's with you is a dumb idea; we should both just head home."

"I don't think it's a dumb idea, and you're not getting out of it that easily." Mason was aghast to hear the words cross his lips, and he wondered why the hell he had uttered them when he basically agreed with everything she had just said.

"I'm just saying that we've probably exhausted all topics of—" He interrupted her before she could finish her sentence.

"Nonsense. We're going to MJ's."

"Anybody ever tell you that you're incredibly bossy?" she asked, not doing anything to disguise the irritation in her voice, and he grinned.

"All the time."

"Fine, but I'm calling it now, this is probably the worst idea in the history of the world."

"Anybody ever tell *you* that you have a tendency to exaggerate?" he fired back at her, and she shoved her dark-rimmed glasses back up her nose and rolled her eyes.

"About a billion times a day." He grinned at her response. The waiter returned with his bill, and Daisy excused herself to go to the powder room.

"Hey, Daisy," he called as she turned away from him. She stopped and glanced back over her shoulder. "No ducking out the bathroom window."

She snorted and waved her hand dismissively before walking away.

"I'll wait outside," he said as she headed toward the back of the pub. She held one thumb up to signal that she'd heard him but didn't look at him again.

Mason settled his bill, leaving a hefty tip for the grateful waiter, and grabbed up his leather jacket before heading out the door. He stood just outside the pub, facing the empty street as he listened to the muffled sounds of laughter and music coming from inside. Riversend had a population of only about three thousand permanent residents. It was very much a summer tourist destination, and the quiet little town went into hibernation during winter. There was no nightlife to speak of, and most people commuted to the larger outlying towns for work every day. Mason appreciated the tranquility of the place so much more now than when he was a restless, borderline-delinquent kid. And even though the years away had defined his character and broadened his worldview considerably, it was good to be home. Back when he was a kid, he had felt trapped, but now—knowing that he could leave any time he wanted to—he felt a sense of belonging.

Aside from the bustling pub behind him and the bright light coming from the always-busy MJ's farther down the street, the tiny town's main road was quiet. Riversend was sleepy and peaceful and—after years of violence and craziness—exactly what Mason needed.

It was a brisk late May evening, and he could see his breath misting in front of his face. The cloud of steam was reminiscent of smoke and made him yearn for one of the cigarettes he had given up more than a year ago. He shoved his hands into his jean pockets and swayed back and forth on his heels as he continued to wait.

The music and chatter increased in volume as the doors swung open behind him, and he turned with an expectant smile on his face, which faded somewhat when he saw his brother's large frame silhouetted in the doorway.

"Hey, where are you off to?" Spencer asked, stepping out on the sidewalk with Mason; the door didn't swing all the way shut behind him, and the noise bled out into the peaceful night.

"Heading over to MJ's with Daisy," Mason replied.

"Seriously?" Spencer asked with a slightly incredulous laugh.

"I'm hungry."

"Mase, I appreciate you coming out here tonight, but you don't have to do that."

"Do what?" Mason asked with a frown, confused.

"You know what." Spencer grunted, closing the gap between them slightly as he stepped closer. "I know I asked you to keep the other one distracted . . ."

"Her name's Daisy," Mason corrected irritably.

"Yeah." Spencer waved the correction aside impatiently. "Whatever. Look, I know I asked you to keep her distracted, but taking her out? That's going above and beyond, Mase. I don't think Daff's that interested, so you don't have to do this. Go home and catch that movie; I know that's what you'd prefer doing anyway. You're probably bored out of your skull by now. Sorry about this, man. But like I said, I had to try, you know? It's just a shame you had to waste your time with the other one while I did so."

It was a shitty thing to say, and Mason was about to tell Spencer exactly that when he noticed a pair of earnest eyes behind a pair of unflattering dark-framed glasses peeking up at him from behind his brother's broad shoulder.

Fuck.

She was so damned short that she had actually managed to come up behind Spencer without Mason noticing. And—damn it—were those tears sparkling in her eyes? He felt like a total shit now and glared at his brother for a moment, before brushing by him and following the woman as she quickly turned away and walked up the road at a brisk pace. He heard Spencer swear behind him as his brother realized that Daisy had overheard him. Mason shot him a warning glare over his shoulder and held up a hand to prevent him from following.

He caught up with Daisy in a few short strides and took hold of her elbow to halt her movement. She went taut but stopped and glared up at him fiercely from behind those heavy frames. They were beneath a lamppost, and he could see every emotion in that expressive face. She looked equal parts angry and resigned.

"Look, you shouldn't have heard that," he began roughly as he agitatedly rubbed his hand back and forth over his scalp and wondered how the hell he had gotten into this situation.

"It's nothing I haven't heard before. I'm the ugly one, remember?" she asked, without a trace of bitterness or self-pity in her voice. In fact, she sounded remarkably calm. "But that's okay because being pretty isn't everything, since 'a brain is *just* as important as good looks.' And 'at least I'm *clever.*'"

She used air quotes to make it obvious that she was parroting someone, and he shoved his hands into his jacket pockets and felt his brow lower as he considered the casual cruelty those supposedly well-meaning people had subjected her to. She wasn't even that bad looking. She just needed to do something with her hair, maybe. Put on a little makeup . . . dress better . . . lose a few kilos.

He appraised her seriously. Her hair was crazy; he couldn't tell if it was up in a bun or a ponytail, but whatever it was, most of the curly, mouse-brown strands seemed desperate to escape their confinement. She had a round face, a dab of a nose that her heavy-looking black-framed glasses kept sliding down, which meant that she was constantly peering at him from above the rims. Her deep-gray eyes were nice, big, and luminous and surrounded by thick, dark lashes and dark, arched eyebrows. She also had round cheeks, those adorable dimples he had noticed earlier, and a bit of a double chin when she laughed. He liked her lips; they looked soft and were naturally pink and lush. Surprisingly kissable lips set in a round, otherwise ordinary face.

The woman also appeared to have absolutely no dress sense; she was wearing a flannel shirt combined with a pair of snug faded jeans that clung to her shapely, if somewhat ample, butt rather sweetly. He couldn't tell much else about her figure beneath the oversized shirt and boxy bomber jacket—who even owned bomber jackets anymore? He thought they'd all been left behind in the nineties, where they belonged.

She seemed to have bigger boobs than one would expect from a woman who was five foot three at most, but he couldn't tell for certain.

Okay, he had to admit, she was a bit of a train wreck. Still, it had to suck to hear that the only thing you had going for you was your brain.

"Look, obviously the MJ's thing isn't going to happen now," she said matter-of-factly. "I think I'll just head straight home. I'm tired anyway." Mason felt a pang of regret at the wariness he now saw in her. Gone were the humor and sharp wit of before, and in their place was an obvious reluctance to lower her guard any more than it had already been lowered.

"How are you getting home?" he asked.

"Walking, it's not that far."

"It's a mile out of town," he protested. "I can take you."

"Nah, it's really not that far, and I could use the exercise, right?" she asked, sending him a crooked, self-effacing grin that just about did him in. How often did she demean herself just to prevent others from doing so?

"I'll take you," he maintained.

She sighed. "Look, Mr. Carlisle—"

"Mason," he interrupted.

"Right. Just because I overheard your conversation with Spencer doesn't mean you have to try and make up for it. You were being his bro, right? His wingman or whatever. He's always been interested in Daff; I remember him sending her really bad poetry in high school."

"You're shitting me! He did?" Mason asked, momentarily distracted. He couldn't have been more surprised if she'd told him Spencer had donned a tutu and danced ballet.

"I memorized one," Daisy said, that wicked grin making a welcome reappearance. "Want to hear it?"

"Hell yeah!"

"Okay, hold on, let me think . . ." She held her thumbs up to her temples and swayed slightly before lifting her head and meeting his eyes. *"Daffodil. Tell me you will . . . be mine. Your smile is like gold and like diamonds your eyes do shine. I'll love you forever and forget you never."*

Mason paused a beat before doubling over and clutching his middle as he went off into gales of laughter.

"Oh Christ," he groaned after a couple of minutes of gut-busting laughter. "After that you *have* to let me repay you with a ride home."

Daisy stared up at the painfully handsome man standing in front of her and considered his offer. He really epitomized masculine perfection, all six foot one of him. He had a gorgeous, lean body, combined with ruthlessly short golden-brown hair that she knew was wavy and thick when it was longer. He had a perfect square-cut, cleft jaw, which was currently bristling with stubble; high cheekbones; chiseled, bow-shaped lips; and straight brown eyebrows set above those gorgeous forest-green eyes she had admired earlier. The only thing that spoiled all that visible perfection was the thin, vicious scar that slashed through his left eyebrow—stopping just shy of the outer corner of his eye—and the slightly crooked nose. All this male gorgeousness was incredibly distracting and muddled her thinking.

Daisy knew she really had to get away from him and away from this stupid pub. If it hadn't been for Lia's hen party, she would never have ventured into town tonight. She hated having to deal with people socially.

And sure enough she'd had her stupid feelings trampled as usual. After all these years, one would expect her to have a thicker skin, yet people still managed to upset her with their snide little comments. But Mason Carlisle had hurt her in a brand-new way tonight. He had crept beneath her usually stalwart defenses and made her believe he was genuinely enjoying her company and honestly wanted to spend more time with her.

God, she was such an idiot!

She should have known when he approached her tonight that it was too good to be true, should have known he was getting her out of the way so that his brother could flirt with Daff. It was the story of her life, after all—she was fodder for wingmen. But she had allowed herself a brief moment of fantasy. Mason Carlisle had never been nasty to her, hadn't really paid her much attention at all, to be honest. They had been years apart in school and moved in completely different social circles.

Naturally all the girls—including her sisters—had had a crush on the Carlisle brothers in high school. Who wouldn't? They were blessed with an overabundance of good looks, were star athletes, and had the appeal of being just a little too rough and wild for the good girls, which had made them irresistible. It still did. And just once, Daisy wanted to see what it felt like to be the center of a beautiful Carlisle's attention.

And it had been . . . wonderful, until she'd discovered his true objective. High school all over again.

"Come on, Daisy," he prompted again. "Let me drive you home."

"Okay," she said, reluctantly. He clearly felt bad. He had obviously never meant for her to find out about his deception. Maybe he would leave her alone when he got the guilt out of his system.

"Great, I'm parked just around the corner."

He had a wholly masculine vehicle; a very rugged Jeep Wrangler, which was caked with mud and looked like it had seen a lot of serious adventuring.

"How'd you get it into such a state?" she asked, struggling to keep the awe out of her voice.

"I've been doing a lot of camping and off-road traveling since my return. This baby has been up north to all the major national parks and over countless mountain passes . . . she's a good car," he said as he patted the square bonnet of the black Jeep appreciatively.

"So you haven't *really* been in town a lot since returning to the country?" That would explain why people hadn't seen him around much.

"Nope." He tugged open the passenger door and gave her a hand up as she awkwardly climbed into the aggravatingly high car. She had grown up around similar vehicles but had never really mastered the art of climbing into one with dignity and grace.

"Sorry it's nothing fancier," he muttered apologetically as she gave a quick glance around the inside of his car. He shut the door and was in the driver's seat seconds later. His delicious, clean, and crisp masculine fragrance enveloped her as he shut himself in with her. "And I apologize for the smell."

She flushed, grateful for the dark. How had he known she was appreciating his scent, and why would he apologize for it?

"No need to apologize," she said quickly.

"I took my dog, Cooper, for a run on the beach this morning, and he can never resist going in for a dip, even though it's colder than a witch's . . . uh . . . *boob*. That's why it reeks of wet dog in here."

Wet dog? All she could smell was Mason, but now that he had mentioned it, she did detect the underlying scent of eau de soaked pooch.

"I barely smell it," she said honestly, clicking her seat belt into place. He followed suit and started the car without saying anything more.

"You're going to have to refresh my memory," he said as he started up the car. "I can't quite remember how to get there."

A little puzzled by that statement—why would he ever have known how to get to her house in the first place?—Daisy shrugged and proceeded to give him directions to her small home on the outskirts of town. There were no other words between them for the next five minutes until he pulled to a stop outside her place.

"This isn't the farm," he observed lamely as he sized up the neat little house, with its perfectly cut pocket-size front lawn behind a wrought-iron fence.

"God no," she muttered, self-consciously playing with the zipper of her jacket. "I couldn't continue living there with my sisters and their constant well-intentioned attempts to dress me 'properly' or paint makeup on me while I slept."

"Wait, they actually did that? The makeup thing?"

"Yep, I once woke up with my left eye glued shut because my sisters had botched up the fake eyelash application."

"You must sleep like the dead," Mason observed in a wobbly voice, clearly struggling to conceal his amusement from her.

"I've been known to sleep through a plane crash or two." She nodded.

"So why don't you just let them get it out of their systems? Let them make you over or whatever?"

"What do you see when you look at me?" she huffed impatiently.

Mason considered her question as he peered at her in the scant illumination provided by the moonlight sifting in through the car windows. How the hell was he supposed to answer that question without getting into a shitload of trouble?

"A woman?" He ventured tentatively after a long pause, and even in the dim light he could see her rolling her eyes.

"A short, dumpy, and frumpy woman. No amount of makeup or clothing will change the first two, and as for the latter . . ." She paused, and Mason thought he caught a glimmer of yearning in her moonlit eyes. "Let me put it this way: I'm a bridesmaid at Lia's wedding."

"Yeah?"

"So are Daff, Sharlotte Bridges, Zinzi Khulani, and Nina Clark. Basically, most of the women you saw at that table tonight. Lia has found a bridesmaid dress that manages to flatter everybody. Everybody, that is, except me. I look completely ridiculous and—yes—frumpy in the stupid thing. So you see, it doesn't matter what they put me in, I always look the same." She said it so matter-of-factly and with such a lack of bitterness that Mason could only stare at her for a long moment; her gray eyes looked colorless in the moonlight, her crazy brown hair managed to catch the faint light, and the bits that were sticking up looked like they had tiny shards of moonbeams trapped in them.

"I'm sure you look . . ."

"Uh-uh." She held up a stern finger. "Don't! No empty platitudes between us, Mason Carlisle. I like that we now know where we stand with each other. No misunderstandings. You're the wingman. I'm the ugly girl."

"Come on, Daisy. Don't call yourself that," he chastised uncomfortably.

"Anyway," she said, brushing aside his comment, "do you feel, like, super guilty about everything that's happened tonight?"

"I do," he said, a small frown indenting his brow as he wondered what would come next. He had felt seriously punch drunk and wrong-footed from the moment he'd met this woman, and it made him both uncomfortable and ridiculously lighthearted. He liked her unpredictability and her offbeat sense of humor, and truth be told, despite his expectations to the contrary, he hadn't been bored once this evening.

"So I've given this some thought—well, okay, I've only just thought about it, but I think it's a fabulous idea—and I was wondering if you would consider being *my* wingman?" The blunt question shocked him, and he stared at her uncomprehendingly for a moment as he tried to process her words.

"What?"

"I was hoping you'd feel guilty enough to do me a favor and consider being my wingman," she elaborated, which didn't really clarify anything at all.

"I'm not sure I understand," he admitted. How could he be *her* wingman? How would that even work? Like in the traditional sense. Did that mean . . . "Wait, are you . . . are you *gay*?"

He watched her lips crook up at the corners and her mischievous eyes lit with laughter, and he liked that he could make her smile again. It eased his guilt somewhat. Not *much*, but it was a start.

"No. I'm not gay. I don't mean *that* kind of wingman. Lia's getting married. Remember?"

"Yes?" God she was confusing. And interesting . . . very, very interesting.

"So I need a date. Someone who'll deflect the inevitable well-meaning comments about how at least I have my brain and don't need a man to support me or whatever else people have to say to me this time. Seeing me show up with a ripped, good-looking guy like you will confuse the *hell* out of them, and while they won't believe for an instant that we're seriously dating, at least it'll shut them up while they regroup. Leaving *me* to enjoy my sister's wedding in peace."

"Uh . . ." Mason wasn't sure what to say. On the one hand, he did feel terrible about the way things had gone down tonight and wanted to make it up to her. On the other hand, weddings and monkey suits and rich snobby people just weren't his scene. Then again, it could be entertaining as hell to see how this sharp, witty woman dealt with those people at her sister's wedding.

"Free food, drink, and lots of hot women for you to ogle," she said in a wheedling tone of voice, and he felt himself grinning at her.

"I don't ogle other women when I'm out with someone," he corrected. "But free food and drink? I think that's worth the price of admission."

"Seriously?" she squeaked, looking genuinely shocked by his words, and his grin widened when he comprehended that the little fast-talker hadn't been half as confident as she had let on.

"Sure, why the hell not?" It was only after the words had left his mouth that he realized that they were exactly what he had said to his brother before falling down this particular rabbit hole.

Daisy was stunned that he had agreed but even more surprised that she had asked him in the first place. She wasn't sure where this idea had come from, but as she'd continued chatting with him, it had seemed like an ideal solution to a problem that had been looming in her immediate future. At least she knew exactly where she stood with this guy. He was good looking, seemed fairly personable, and he had already hurt her—more than she would ever have believed possible from someone who was a relative stranger to her.

She liked him a lot, and that's probably why it was so painful. But she was angrier with herself for being hurt by something that—in retrospect—should have been completely obvious from the moment he'd approached her. She'd never give him the opportunity to hurt her again, and that's why she would be perfectly safe with him as her wedding date. She had been inoculated against his charm thanks to tonight's farce. Her heart was safe in his presence.

"When is this thing?" he asked, knocking her out of her reverie.

"Exactly two weeks away," she said. "It's a weekend thing, on the Wild Coast, so you'll have to pack a bag."

"We should be seen together before then," he said. "To make our romance seem a little bit more realistic."

"I didn't say we would pretend to be romantically involved," she said, alarmed. "No one would believe that."

"They won't if we just showed up together without warning, but if we appear to be dating for a couple of weeks beforehand, it would seem more plausible."

"I don't want it to seem plausible," she protested irrationally. "I just want a date for the wedding."

"Look, I feel shit about tonight, and this is the least I can do. But if I'm going to do it, I'll for damned sure be doing it right. We're having dinner at MJ's tomorrow night."

"No, that's not necessary," she said vehemently.

"I say it is. It won't be of any benefit to you if I'm seen as some bastard who just carries on a one- or two-night stand with a woman and then dumps her immediately afterward."

"*I* could be the one doing the dumping," she pointed out, and he stared at her levelly for a long while, remaining insultingly silent in response to her statement. Okay, so nobody would believe Daisy had done the dumping after just one weekend together. Maybe his idea had merit. Appear to be dating for a bit—no matter how unlikely it seemed—and that way their inevitable "breakup" would appear a little less humiliating for her.

Mason didn't know why he was pushing this. He should consider himself lucky that all she wanted from him was one weekend. But, despite all her protestations to the contrary, he knew that she had been hurt by the evening's revelations. He figured this would help her salvage some pride and ease his conscience a bit in the process.

She mulled over his words for a long moment, before nodding to herself as she obviously made up her mind about something.

"Okay. MJ's. Tomorrow night."

"Great," he said, flashing her a smile, before getting out of the car and rounding it to help her out of the passenger side. He walked her to the front door, and a dog started frenziedly barking on the other side of it.

"Thanks, Mason," she said while she fumbled for her keys. "I'll see you tomorrow night."

"I'll pick you up at seven."

"Right."

They stood there awkwardly for a moment before Daisy turned away and unlocked the door.

"So . . . bye," she said, but he didn't respond, he just kept staring at her. He was freaking her out a little. Why was he just standing there? She cleared her throat, stepped into her house, and, with a quick apologetic smile, shut the door in his face.

"Hello, Peaches," she greeted her excited toy Pomeranian. "Did you miss me?"

She bent to pat the affectionate white furball before straightening to peek out of the peephole, wondering if Mason had left yet. He was slowly making his way back toward his car, and she ignored her dog's faint whines for attention as she watched him throw another lingering glance back at the front door before getting into his car.

Daisy heaved a sigh of relief and turned around to slump against the door. She listened to his car engine start up and then grow fainter as he drove away.

What a weird evening. She slid down the door and sank onto the floor, finally giving Peaches the welcome she deserved. The dog was in raptures as she wriggled into Daisy's lap and laved her face enthusiastically.

"Ugh, enough, Peaches," Daisy finally decreed after the dog's tongue managed to squirm up one of her nostrils. She shuddered and set Peaches down before levering herself up from the wooden floor.

She shrugged out of her heavy coat and casually tossed it over the coatrack along with her shoulder bag.

"I'm not sure I made the right decision tonight, girl," she informed Peaches conversationally as she moved through the tiny living room to the open-plan kitchen. Peaches trotted faithfully along behind her. "I mean, I'm not exactly sober, am I? It's never wise to make big decisions when you've had one too many."

She glanced over at Peaches; the little dog had jumped onto the sofa and was staring at Daisy with a tilted head, looking for all the world like she understood every word. Daisy sighed. She needed a few more dogs, a couple of cats, and possibly a hamster or two before she could be considered a *true* spinster, but having full-on conversations with her dog certainly was a step in that direction.

Still, it beat talking to herself. Which was exactly what she had found herself doing after moving into her own house and before getting Peaches. She preferred talking to the dog; it just seemed less . . . sad.

Her thoughts turned back to the situation with Mason Carlisle. Propositioning him the way she had tonight was so far from her usual behavior that she couldn't quite bring herself to believe that she'd done it. And that he'd agreed to it.

There was no way they were going to be able to maintain the dating façade. Nobody would believe it for a second. She would contact him in the morning and call the whole thing off. And she was confident that once he had time to think about it, he'd be relieved to get out of the obligation.

"So I'll call him tomorrow," she told Peaches as she turned to the kitchen to put the kettle on for some tea. "And that'll be the end of it."

CHAPTER THREE

Someone was knocking on Mason's front door at a seriously ungodly time of the morning, and it was setting Cooper off. His Lab mix was downstairs barking at whatever crazy bastard was trying to break down the door. The knocking, combined with the barking, made it impossible for Mason to ignore the unwelcome caller.

"Yeah!" he yelled as he pushed himself out of his nice, warm bed and tugged on his sweatpants. He hissed when his feet hit the cold floor and let loose a stream of profanity that only grew more creative as he thumped his way downstairs.

"Coop, quiet," he growled, and the dog immediately obeyed and sat on his rump, keeping his eyes trained on the front door. Mason yanked the door open and glared at Spencer, who was standing with his shoulders hunched against the rain, holding two giant paper cups of fragrant coffee.

His brother shoved one of the cups into Mason's hands before pushing his way inside and heading straight for the kitchen. Mason glared at Spencer's back, taking a sip of the coffee and slamming the front door pointedly before following the other man. Cooper was happily greeting Spencer, who had seated himself at the island in the center of the room. The guy was more than a little wet but didn't seem to notice it.

"What the hell do you want, Spencer?" Mason asked impatiently, sitting down next to him. "It's not even six yet. It's freezing outside, and I'm hungover because *you* dragged me out last night."

"Did Tanya ever hit on you?"

Whoa. Mason, who'd been about to say even more about his brother's ill-timed visit, felt his mouth slam shut.

"Why are you asking me that?" he asked, monitoring Spencer's reaction carefully.

"After you left last night, I ran into Graham Price, remember him?"

Mason vaguely recalled a guy about Spencer's age, good with cars or something.

"Yeah?"

"Graham was drunk and congratulated me on my breakup with that treacherous skank, said she hit on everything with a dick. I mean, it wasn't news to me, I know that she cheated on me. Saw it with my own eyes. But suddenly every guy I know has a story about how she hit on him and how lucky I am to be rid of her. And it got me thinking . . . every guy I know has a story. But not you. You never once said anything—good or bad—about her, and I was just wondering, you know. Did she ever hit on you?"

"What difference would it make if she did or didn't?" Mason asked cautiously, hating that bitch for putting him in this position.

"Well, you're my brother, and I reckon you would have warned me about her if she'd ever put the moves on you, right? You wouldn't have let me just go on seeing that cheating bitch?"

Shit.

"Yeah, she hit on me, Spence," Mason admitted, taking a deep sip of his now-lukewarm coffee, and watched his brother's shoulders tense as he absorbed the blow.

"Why the *fuck* didn't you tell me, Mason?" Spencer asked, seething frustration in his voice.

"I was going to, I was trying to figure out how, but then you caught her with those guys and everything went to hell. Telling you at that time would just have poured salt on the wound and telling you afterward seemed unnecessary. You'd already heard about her from other guys, hearing it from me wouldn't have made any difference. It would only have hurt you more. You get that, don't you? I didn't want to make it worse for you."

Spencer didn't say anything; he kept his gaze focused on his coffee.

"I feel like such an idiot," he confessed after a long silence. "I thought she was the one, man."

"I know."

"So last night was a colossally stupid idea." The abrupt change in subject threw Mason, and it took a moment for him to regroup.

"Things didn't go too well with Daffodil McGregor, did they?" he asked with a slight grin, and Spencer huffed.

"I don't know, man, at times she seemed to really enjoy dancing with me, but afterward it was like she didn't even know I was there," Spencer said.

"Pretty much like it's always been, then?"

"Yeah, sorry again for saddling you with the other one."

"Daisy," Mason reminded, and Spencer nodded.

"Yes, her. I felt like a bit of an asshole when she overheard our conversation," Spencer admitted, and Mason's brow lifted.

"Only a *bit*? Spencer, the whole messed-up situation didn't sit right with me from the beginning. She's a nice lady; she didn't deserve any of the shit we piled on her last night."

"I said I was sorry," Spencer grunted defensively, and Mason swallowed down a surge of irritation. His brother was a clueless idiot, but he was a *hurting* clueless idiot at the moment.

"To me. Not to her, and she's the one who deserves the apology."

"It's not like I'll see much of her again. Like you said last night, the McGregor sisters don't run in our circles, and that one is the least sociable of the three, so we're even *less* likely to see her."

"About that." Mason absently patted Cooper's head, which was resting on his knee, while the dog stared up at him with slavish devotion. Having never had a dog of his own before, the last year with Coop had been eye opening. It was awesome having a buddy to hang out with during the day but also wholly uncomfortable being the animal's whole world. For someone who had never had anyone or anything so defenseless depend on him before, Mason still felt somewhat awkward in his new role of sole caregiver to a dog.

"About what?" Spencer prompted, and Mason's train of thought came back on track with a bump.

"You'll likely be seeing a bit more of Daisy McGregor than usual over the next couple of weeks. I've agreed to be her date to her sister's wedding."

"*Daisy* McGregor's date?"

"Yes." Mason took another sip of his—now cold—coffee and grimaced before setting it aside. He got up and moved around his kitchen, getting a pot of coffee brewing, while keenly aware of his brother's eyes boring into his back.

"Why?" Spencer asked, the word a study in perplexity.

"Because she asked me."

"Even *after* overhearing the conversation between us? The chick must be more desperate than I thought."

"She's not desperate." Mason found himself defending Daisy, even while admitting to himself that maybe she had been a little desperate to make the proposition in the first place. "She's just . . . clever. This way she has a date for her sister's wedding but without any commitment or emotional entanglements."

"I'll be damned." Spencer's voice sounded almost admiring. "She used your guilt against you, didn't she?"

Mason turned to face his brother, trying to keep his expression as neutral as possible.

"You want some breakfast? Bacon and scrambled eggs?"

"I could eat. So how will this whole wedding date business work? I mean, people will know right off the bat that it's just a pity thing on your side."

Mason didn't respond to that, he grabbed the eggs and bacon from the fridge and got busy preparing breakfast.

"Unless she doesn't care that people will see right through the charade?" Spencer speculated.

"Don't worry about it," Mason said, irritated with his brother's persistence. "It's not your concern."

"I feel kind of responsible," Spencer countered. "I mean, it's my fault you got mixed up with her in the first place."

"It is," Mason agreed with equanimity, while vigorously beating the eggs before dumping the lot into a pan. "But I'm fully capable of taking care of myself, and I wasn't coerced into doing this. So don't worry about me; little Daisy McGregor is hardly a threat to me."

"Little." Spencer sniggered and Mason glared at him.

"Stop being such a shallow dick, dude. No more snide comments about her; she's going to be my sort-of girlfriend for a couple of weeks, and I expect you to be on board with that. Got it?"

"Sometimes you're still such a soldier," Spencer groused, pouring two cups of coffee from the now-percolating machine and placing a mug on the counter closest to Mason. "Barking orders like a general."

Mason thought about that before acknowledging to himself that he would always be a soldier. It was ingrained, and he had felt most useful and most alive when he was fighting side by side with his brothers-in-arms. That said, it wasn't a lifestyle he could, or would, be able to maintain. It came with too much emotional baggage, and if Mason hadn't left the service when he had, it would have claimed the entirety of his soul.

He divided the eggs and bacon between two plates and slapped one down in front of Spencer, before picking up his coffee and joining his brother at the island again. He casually tossed Cooper an extra piece of bacon, which the dog downed in one gulp before immediately looking up for more.

"That's all you get," Mason chastised. "And that's only because we're jogging it off later. Go lie down."

The dog gave him a reproachful look before slinking off to the kitchen rug and lying down, keeping a hopeful eye on the eating men.

"You're going jogging in this weather?" Spencer asked, and they both glanced out the kitchen window to the torrential downpour outside. It had been threatening to rain for days and had finally started sometime during the night.

"I've run in worse," Mason responded succinctly.

"Seriously?" Spencer looked both impressed and horrified. "Care to elaborate?"

"No."

Spencer cast him a curious sidelong look before shrugging and forking down more of his eggs and bacon. The men ate the rest of their meal in silence.

⁓

"Good morning, Thomas," Daisy greeted the young boy with a huge smile. "How's Sheba doing today?"

"Good, Dr. Daisy. See?" He pointed to a spot just above the small brown dog's tail, indicating the healing patch of skin there. Just a week ago the patch had been crusty and seriously inflamed. Sheba, indeed, looked to be on the mend.

"Oh, you've been taking good care of her, Thomas. Well done." The boy beamed at her praise, and she gave the little crossbreed dog a cursory once-over to ensure no other problems.

"Keep using the ointment until it's finished and bring her back to me in a month, okay? And we'll see if her fur grew back." She was happy that the dog seemed to have overcome the mild case of mange that had been developing. "Don't forget to keep her out of the sand and make sure her bed is clean and dry."

"Yes, Dr. Daisy." Thomas nodded, his thin shoulders squaring as he practically bristled with pride that the doctor trusted him with the task. He was only about eight and had showed up a week ago at the free animal clinic that Daisy and her father ran every Saturday at the *Inkululeko* informal settlement just outside of town. The boy had been distraught that his beloved pet was in distress and, while his mother waited outside, had carried Sheba in himself and explained the problem in the most adult way he could. Daisy had respected him enough to respond to his seriousness with equal gravity.

Patient after patient followed Thomas. They were always slammed at the clinic, and despite the bad weather, today was no different. The workload kept Daisy and her father busy the entire morning, with barely a word spoken between them as they administered vaccinations, took care of minor ailments, and caged a few of the more serious cases in their van for further treatment at her father's veterinary practice in town. They treated everything from cats and dogs to cart horses, goats, chickens, and even a cow. By the time they closed shop they were exhausted, filthy, and smelly.

"You coming around for dinner tonight, Daisy?" her father asked as they climbed into their van.

"Uh, no," she said, thinking about her "date" with Mason Carlisle. Something she had successfully managed to push to the back of her mind while she was working. She was still considering canceling it, but the later the day got, the less likely it seemed that she would do the sensible thing and save herself some embarrassment.

"All the wedding stuff getting to you?" her father asked with a grimace as he carefully navigated the muddy dirt road that led back into town. "Don't blame you. If I have to hear one more conversation about bouquets and shoes, I think I'll lose my mind."

"I have an appointment," Daisy mumbled, trying to keep her flush under control.

"A what?"

"A . . . a thing. An appointment," she said. Grabbing her bottled water, she took a thirsty gulp and focused her attention on the passing scenery. The narrow dirt road was lined with thick forest on either side, but once they hit the tar road just outside of town, the view opened up to include ocean. It really was a gorgeous part of the world. It wasn't called the Garden Route for nothing.

"An appointment? On a Saturday night?" Her father sounded confused, and she sighed.

"It's a casual thing."

"With Tilda?"

"No. I have more than one friend, you know?" she huffed, and he threw her a quick look, surprised by her curt response. Daisy avoided his gaze and dragged out her phone for the first time that day. She never had time to check it while she was at the clinic. Her eyebrows flew up as she registered the insane amount of messages and missed calls—most of them from Daff and Tilda.

The messages were all similar:

So what did you and hunkalicious Mason C get up to last night???? *CALL ME.* That one was from Daff.

Tilda: *OMG!!! Did you REALLY leave with Mason Carlisle last night? Whaaaaat? Details ASAP!!!*

Another one from Daff: *Did you see him naked? Did you shag his brains out? You dirty, dirty girl!! I. Am. SHOCKED!* Daisy snorted at that one. Daff knew that Daisy was awkward around men and that she was unlikely to even have kissed Mason Carlisle.

She shook her head and pocketed the phone again, not in the mood to read any more of the crazy messages.

Her father had gone quiet after she'd snapped at him, and feeling guilty, Daisy opened her mouth to apologize, but he spoke before she could.

"Do you have a date, by any chance?" Daisy nearly swallowed her tongue in shock.

"I . . . *what*? Why would you think . . . who told you that?" Her father threw her another one of those sharp, assessing glances that never seemed to miss much.

"Daff was very chatty at breakfast this morning. She said something about Mason Carlisle?"

"Daff was up for breakfast this morning?" Daisy asked, stalling and genuinely surprised. Her sister always took full advantage of the weekends and never missed the opportunity to sleep in, especially after a night out.

"She was just coming home, I think," her father said with a shrug. Ah, well that made more sense. "So . . . Mason Carlisle?"

"We were just talking."

"And he's the one you're seeing tonight?"

"Maybe. I haven't decided yet."

"The whole world has seen him in his underpants," her father muttered, and Daisy's lips twitched. Of *course* that would be the first thing on her father's mind. "What kind of man parades around in his underwear in public?"

"He's also a decorated soldier," she reminded him.

"Then there was that nasty business with him and that drug addict pop star last year."

"That was just rumors." Daisy hoped. There had been speculation in a number of the gossip rags that a certain pop princess regularly did drugs with her bodyguard, after which they had depraved orgies.

"Hmm, Tim Richards still insists to this day that the Carlisle brothers were the ones who vandalized his store twenty years ago." This town had a long and unforgiving memory.

"He never had any proof of that, Daddy," Daisy said, and her father shrugged again.

"So do you like him?"

"Daddy, he's a friend. Well, more like acquaintance really. Nothing more."

"You know I only want what's best for my girls." So why was he okay with Lia marrying Clayton? She knew her father didn't like the guy and she couldn't understand why he hadn't revealed that to Lia. She was about to ask him when he drew the van to a stop outside her house.

"Be careful around that man, sweetheart," her father said. "He has seen and experienced things that you can't even begin to comprehend. And all that war and death can do irreparable damage to a man's psyche. I doubt he'd be great boyfriend material."

His words made Daisy pause. Mason seemed as well adjusted as the next guy, but her father was right, the man had seen combat, and Daisy had to wonder how much of Mason Carlisle's affability was just a front.

"Don't worry, Daddy. Nothing's going on between us." It was sweet that her father would even think that a guy like Mason Carlisle would have any romantic intentions toward Daisy. She was vanilla and he was decadent fudge with roasted almonds, caramel swirls, chocolate sprinkles, and a cherry on top. But her father was her father, and he thought his daughters were all beautiful. The fact that Daisy was his not-so-secret favorite made him even more protective over her.

She leaned over and planted a kiss on his craggy cheek.

"Have fun with Mom and the girls tonight. I hear they're fine-tuning the place settings. It's going to be a big night."

He grimaced comically.

"Why do *you* get to sit out of these things?" he groused, and she laughed.

"Because I have 'nothing of value to contribute,'" she quoted good-naturedly. She had deliberately cultivated that image early on, knowing her sisters and mother would inevitably start leaving her out of any and all wedding planning. Suggesting pizzas for the menu and trifle for dessert had been the last straw as far as Lia was concerned.

"If you can't be serious about this, then I don't see how having you here is of any benefit at all." Lia's complaint after Pizza-gate. And that had

been that. Daisy was included in the bridesmaids' stuff but now thankfully managed to avoid anything else wedding related.

"If I resorted to your dirty tricks there'd be tears and hysteria." Her father sighed, and Daisy grinned.

"Face it, old man, you're in it for the duration. Have fun." She grabbed her bag and left the car with a cheeky salute. She watched him drive off before turning back to her house. Immediately the situation with Mason Carlisle sprang to the forefront of her mind again. She wouldn't call it off. She'd meet him and tell him face-to-face to forget about her stupid idea.

It seemed like the mature thing to do. Just a shame that her stomach was flipping around in crazy circles at the thought of seeing him again and this time without the comforting filter of a nice alcoholic buzz to bolster her courage. She couldn't very well be tipsy every time she saw him, and without that little bit of so-called Dutch courage, she feared she would become a tongue-tied moron around him. Just her usual self, really.

She sighed as she let herself into the house, picking up her excited dog as she made her way to the living room.

"Did you miss me, Peachie Pie?" she asked her dog, in what she knew was an obnoxious high-pitched baby voice, but she was quite unable to help herself. "Did you miss me? Peachie Pie wants some walkies? You do, don't you?"

Peaches was practically wriggling herself out of Daisy's grip in her excitement, and Daisy put her down for fear of dropping the squirmy dog.

"I'll grab a shower, and then we'll go for a walk, okay?" The rain had let up for a bit, but judging by the gunmetal-gray clouds still brooding above the town, it was just a temporary reprieve. Luckily Peaches didn't require much exercise, so a quick walk around the block would do the trick.

Daisy had a fast shower and changed into slouchy gray sweatpants, a pair of neon-pink Wellingtons, a fleecy hoody, and a raincoat to match the Wellies. She clipped on Peaches's harness and leash, and they were good to go.

Sadly, Daisy's idea of a quick walk around the block was immediately scuttled by Peaches, who stopped at every random bush, pillar, and post to have a sniff. It was an exercise in frustration, and her dog seemed completely oblivious to both the cold and the impending downpour.

"Come on, Peaches," she implored for the umpteenth time when, approximately halfway around the block—about fifteen minutes from home—the first fat droplets of rain began to fall. Turning around would be pointless since it would take the same amount of time as just continuing on.

Peaches glanced up at Daisy before dawdling on, sniff-sniffing her way along at a snail's pace. The rain was getting heavier and—horribly—some of the icy water had found its way down the top of one of her boots. The wind was starting to pick up too, and Peaches, *finally* realizing that she was wet, cold, and uncomfortable, stopped walking completely and trotted back to Daisy to be picked up.

Visibility was practically nonexistent as the rain began to sheet from the sky. Daisy remained on the grassy verge of the sidewalk, trying to stay well away from the street in case any cars came along. She wanted to avoid being splashed or run over. Both equally unpleasant prospects right now. But most people knew better than to be out in this weather, and only two cars had passed her since she had started on this rash endeavor.

She tucked the shivering Peaches closer to her chest and trudged on for another few minutes, when she heard the sound of an engine coming up behind her. The car didn't slow down, and *naturally* there was a huge puddle right beside the road at the exact spot Daisy happened to be passing. The car was going at such a speed that it didn't really matter how far away from the road she was, she was still completely soaked by the disgusting muddy water.

"Oh, *come* on!" she seethed and muttered a few choice words under her breath. She glared at the back of the car and frowned when the brake lights came on as it slowed down. When the reverse lights flashed on, she had a moment's panic as she imagined a psychopath kidnapping her before the car got close enough for her to recognize it as Mason Carlisle's Jeep.

The feeling of relief didn't last long as she faced the reality of seeing him again. While looking like a drowned rat. Lovely.

The Jeep drew abreast of her. The passenger window lowered, and she stared into the adorable face of a yellow Labrador retriever mix. The lolling, grinning face distracted her for a brief moment before Mason's voice drew her back to reality.

"Daisy?"

"Oh, Mason, hey." She strove for casual, difficult when she knew she probably looked completely ridiculous.

"What the hell are you doing out here in this downpour?" He was incredulous.

"Just taking my dog for a walk. It wasn't raining when we left." She watched his eyes drop to her feet and then continue searching.

"What dog?"

"Uh . . . Peaches." She drew her tiny dog out from beneath the protective cover of her coat, and the shivering animal immediately snarled at the bigger dog. The Lab's reaction was comical; he yelped and dove to the floor in front of the seat and cowered beneath the dashboard.

"Jesus, Coop. Stop embarrassing me." Mason sounded so completely disgruntled that Daisy couldn't help grinning as she tucked Peaches back under her coat.

"Anyway . . . I'll see you later," she said with an insouciant little wave and started to wade off in the direction of her house.

"Daisy, get in the car," Mason commanded.

"We're nearly home."

"Coop, in the back," he ordered, and the Lab complied without hesitation. Daisy was impressed by the dog's level of training.

"Daisy, *get* in the car," he said again, in the exact same tone of voice that he had just used on his dog, and she immediately bristled.

"It's not necessary."

"Seriously? You're going to be pointlessly stubborn? Why?"

Good question. Daisy heaved a sigh and acknowledged that she really had no reason *not* to get into the car other than her own pride and vanity, and Mason Carlisle cared about neither. He was just an acquaintance offering her a lift home, and she was turning this friendly, meaningless gesture into a *thing*.

"I didn't want to inconvenience you," she said as she opened the car door. He seemed to accept her half-truth.

"Nonsense, we're headed that way anyway." Daisy clambered into the seat gracelessly, and when her half-frozen fingers fumbled with the seat belt, he reached over to help, enveloping her in his warmth and masculine scent. As he fastened it for her, Peaches's wet little head popped out from beneath Daisy's coat, and she took a nip at Mason's fingers while he clipped the belt in.

"No!" he growled at Peaches, and her dog reconsidered her attitude and licked his knuckles instead. He raised his startling green eyes to hers, eyebrows raised quizzically. "Is this thing *really* a dog? It looks like a half-drowned hamster to me."

"Sh," Daisy hissed. "You'll hurt her feelings. She's a toy Pom. Give her a break; she's drenched and not looking her finest right now." The same could be said for her owner, and his eyes seemed to warm with laughter as he acknowledged her unspoken words.

"Coop's wet too," he pointed out. "And he still looks like a dog."

"Well, Coop has natural good looks; sadly it doesn't come that easily to Peaches."

"Well, she's a feisty little thing, so hopefully she knows that a big personality is as attractive as all the other surface fluff."

Daisy wasn't at all sure they were discussing the dogs anymore, and she wasn't comfortable with the perceived subtext. She loathed being told that she had a good personality, and that was what it felt like Mason was doing here. Girls with "good personalities" never got the guy. They were never the romantic leads. They were always just the comic relief and the best friend. Daisy was so sick of being that girl, and she would rather not hear that Mason Carlisle saw her in the exact same light as everyone else.

Then again, she could be reading too much into his words, and he could just be talking about Peaches.

"She's cold," she said, changing the subject abruptly. "We should get her home and dried off."

"Of course," he said after a weighty silence. "We'll have you home in no time." He pulled away from the curb, and the short drive to her house was conducted in silence. When he slid to a stop in front of her gate a couple of minutes later, she smiled at him.

"Thank you so much. In this weather, it would probably have taken us much longer to get back home."

"Always a pleasure."

"We're lucky you came along."

"I'm sorry about splashing you back there; I wasn't expecting any pedestrians out in this downpour. I wouldn't have seen you if not for all that pink."

"Why were *you* out in this?" She couldn't contain her curiosity anymore, and the question just slipped out.

"Cooper and I went for a run on the beach. We would have gone earlier, but I decided to wait until the rain let up a bit." He went jogging in *this* weather? On the beach? Who did that? Even if it wasn't raining, it was still cold and windy. Conditions weren't ideal.

"Jogging on the beach? But it must have been pretty rough out there."

"Yeah, there's a helluva storm surge. I cut our run short because I was concerned Cooper would try to take a dip and be pulled out to sea." Daisy shuddered at the thought. "He stayed well away from the water's edge, though. I mean, he usually loves the ocean, but I think it freaked him out today. Still, I wasn't going to take the risk, so we left just before this downpour started."

"Well, Peaches and I both thank you for your timely rescue."

"Coop and I are always happy to rescue pretty damsels." She screwed up her nose at that.

"Cooper's been hiding from Peaches since the moment we climbed into this car," she pointed out, glancing back at the dog. He was pressed as far back as he could get and giving her some serious whale eye. As if sensing his fear, Peaches poked her tiny black nose out and kept up an unrelenting series of kittenish growls. Poor Cooper looked terrified.

"Peaches, behave," Daisy admonished. "I'm sorry, she's usually a lot friendlier than this. She loves other dogs and loves people, but she must be in a bad mood because of the weather or something. I've never seen her behave like this before."

Mason looked skeptical but refrained from commenting.

"So, I'll pick you up tonight at seven?" he suddenly said, and Daisy blinked at him for an uncomprehending moment.

"Uh . . ." She was aware of her mouth opening and closing and knew she probably looked like a fish out of water. "About that . . ."

"Don't you fucking *dare*," he interrupted, his voice mild despite the profanity, and her mouth snapped shut. "No backing out, Daisy."

"But it . . ."

"Seven. Let's see how tonight goes and reevaluate after that, okay?"

"It was a stupid idea."

"Maybe. But I'm still happy to do it and make it convincing. If nothing else, we'll have a nice evening out and that'll be the end of it."

"Okay." It was far from "okay," but she'd set this whole stupid thing in motion, and now it felt like a runaway train that was building momentum as it headed toward a brick wall.

"Great." He watched while she climbed out of his stupidly high car. "See you later."

He continued to observe as she walked up the path and unlocked the door, and when she turned to wave at him, he drove off with a cheerful honk of the horn. It was only when she was inside that she realized that she should probably have insisted on driving herself tonight. That way she would be in control of what time she left.

Just another stupid mistake to add to the long list of colossal mistakes that she had made over the last twenty-four hours.

~~~

After blow-drying Peaches and taking another shower to warm herself up, Daisy finally succumbed to the inevitable and called Daff back. Her sister's messages hadn't let up at all, and having her phone buzz every five minutes was aggravating.

"Daisy?" Daff sounded out of breath when she answered her phone, and Daisy frowned.

"Are you jogging?" What was it with people running or walking in this weather today?

"What? In *this*, are you crazy?" Her sister was still puffing slightly.

"So why are you out of breath?"

"I was doing Pilates. Stop trying to distract me and tell me what happened between you and Mason Carlisle last night."

"Nothing. We talked and he gave me a ride home. He's a nice man. Very gentlemanly."

"And that's all?"

"What did you expect me to say? He brought me home and we . . . we did it like monkeys all night long?" Daisy blushed when, after pausing for a beat, her sister roared with laughter.

"Did you really just say 'did it like monkeys'?" Daisy's jaw lifted defensively. Daff could be so obnoxious sometimes.

"I said what I said," she muttered, her voice brittle, and Daff, sensing her embarrassment, tried to tone down her amusement.

"You need to lighten up, Daisy Doodle," she teased, using the family's embarrassing nickname for Daisy.

"I would if I wasn't the constant butt of your jokes." Okay, Daisy knew she was being a bit unfair; Daff didn't usually make fun of her. At least not maliciously. It was always just good-natured sibling ribbing.

"I was just teasing you," Daff said, wounded.

"I know." Daisy sighed. "I'm sorry, Daff. I've been a little oversensitive lately. PMS probably."

"So what *was* all that with you and Mason Carlisle last night?"

"We chatted for a bit, I said I was going home, and he offered me a lift. That's the extent of it . . ." She paused again, thinking she should embellish on that, especially since she was about to be seen in public with the man again in just a few hours' time.

"Oh." Daff—bless her heart—sounded disappointed. "He seemed really into you."

"We are going out to dinner later," she informed reluctantly and winced when Daff squealed.

"Oh my God! *Seriously?*"

Daisy shifted uncomfortably before reiterating, "It's just dinner."

"Dinner with *Mason Carlisle*! Shar is going to absolutely shit herself with envy."

"I don't care what Shar thinks."

"What are you going to wear?"

"It doesn't matter."

"Oh, but it *does*! Lia and I will be over in half an hour to help you get ready."

"No!" Daisy snapped. "It's not like that. It's nothing romantic. It's just dinner. Between friends. I don't want you and Lia blowing this out of proportion. I'm wearing jeans, and that's that."

"Half an hour, Deedee." Yet another nickname—an abbreviated, equally horrific version of "Daisy Doodle."

"Daff, *no!*" She should have known her sister would make a big deal out of this. "I don't need your help."

"See you later," Daff said cheerily and hung up before Daisy could protest any further.

"God." Daisy squeezed her eyes shut and resisted the urge to throw her phone across the room. She settled on shaking it instead and screaming in frustration, surprising Peaches out of a snooze. Maybe if she changed out of her comfy sweats and into something dressier before her sisters got here it would dissuade them from *once again* trying to "pretty her up."

The thought spurred her into action, and she leapt up from the sofa to dash into her bedroom and frantically throw something on.

When Daff, Lia, and their *mother* showed up exactly half an hour later, Daisy was hot and flushed but dressed and ready for her dinner.

"You all wasted your time," she said by way of greeting. "I don't need your help. I'm dressed already, see?"

"Darling, if there's one thing I have told you time and time again, just because a woman is dressed does *not* mean that she is ready," her mother admonished, leaving a trail of Joy in her wake as she swept past Daisy.

"What she said," Daff said smugly, leaving her own expensive vapor trail to mingle with her mother's as she also brushed past a bemused Daisy.

"Hi, Daisy," Lia greeted with a warm hug. Her middle sister had always been the sweetest, most eager to please of the three daughters. She never saw the bad in manipulative people like Shar and Zinzi and allowed them to walk all over her. Lia's sweet naïveté was also why Daff, and even Daisy, despite being the youngest, felt protective over her and had tried to curtail the whole Clayton thing back in its nascence.

"Hey, Lia," Daisy greeted, returning the hug.

"Sorry about this," Lia whispered. "I tried to stop them, but you know how they get."

"Yeah."

"Thank you again for the boots. They were my favorite gift. I don't think I'll use any of the other stuff," she confessed with a blush.

"Not even that gigantic green dildo?" Daisy asked, raising her voice slightly.

"Sh!" Lia covered Daisy's laughing mouth with her hand as she darted a frantic glance around to see if their mother had overheard, but the older woman was busy fawning over Peaches. The dog was doing her crowd-pleasing, guaranteed-to-get-her-cuddles, two-legged jig. Daisy's mother, Millicent, was eating it up with a spoon. The older woman adored animals. She didn't even mind dogs and cats shedding all over her designer dresses.

"Oh, aren't you too precious for *words*," her mother enthused and played right into Peaches's manipulative little paws by scooping her up and giving her a cuddle. She turned to Daisy, Peaches's fluffy face squished up against her left cheek, and was immediately back on task.

"So, it's probably too much to hope that you've bought yourself a dress or two recently," the older woman said with a resigned little sigh.

"I have the dress I wore to Nana's funeral, but I'm not changing. I think I look okay for dinner with a *friend*."

"Daisy, don't be difficult, and Nana's funeral was five years ago; that dress will be both dated and too small."

"Ouch, Mom," Daisy retorted without much heat.

"I don't see why I have to pull any punches; you've put on a few pounds since then." Daisy wasn't going to argue; she had gained a couple of inches around the thighs and bum, but she was pretty much the same weight she had been since high school. She had always been plumper than her sisters, and her mother tended to focus on that a little too much sometimes.

"Jeez, Mom, she still looks exactly the same," Lia said, and Daisy could have hugged her.

"Which isn't necessarily a *good* thing," their mother stated, and both Lia and Daisy sighed. There was just no winning with her. "A woman's look needs to evolve, become more refined and more mature."

"Mom, I'm a vet. My clothes suit my way of life."

"Sweetheart, you're not a vet twenty-four seven, no matter what your father says. You're allowed to have a life."

"Look, save this intervention business for a worthier cause than dinner with Mason Carlisle. The guy's just a friend. I promise, when I find someone I'm romantically interested in, you'll have free rein"—she paused a beat as she thought about that and then added—"within limits. But this is really not the right occasion on which to waste all that makeover mojo."

"At least run a comb through your hair."

"A comb can't get through this mess," Daisy snorted, and both Lia and Daff giggled.

"Oh, for goodness sake!" Their mother handed Peaches over to Lia and forcibly grabbed hold of Daisy's elbow.

"Ow! That hurts," Daisy protested as her mother dragged her toward her bedroom. The older woman—despite being as thin as a rail—was at least four inches taller than Daisy's five three, and she used that height difference to her advantage. Her other two daughters had inherited her height and her body, while Daisy took after her paternal grandmother.

"Sit down, Daisy," her mother said as she pushed Daisy down toward the bed. She was using her no-nonsense "Mom voice," and Daisy knew arguing would be futile. Her sisters had trailed them into the room and were both watching with interest as their mother picked up a brush and dragged it through Daisy's thick curls.

"*Ow!*" Daisy winced again when the brush snagged in her hair. Her mother gentled her movements and began to soothingly stroke the brush through Daisy's hair. Her mother had always known exactly how to handle Daisy's uncontrollable curls, and the gentle tug of the brush brought her back to her childhood.

"You have such lovely hair," her mother said softly. "But you never do anything with it. Braiding it or tying it up does it a disservice."

Daisy shrugged. "It's an uncontrollable mess. And it takes way too long to fix it, so it's easier to just put it up. I need it out of my face for work anyway."

"Yes, but you're not going to work now, are you?" Daff piped up, and Daisy glared at her. As far as she was concerned, her oldest sister had committed the ultimate sin in calling their mother, and Daff knew it too. She returned Daisy's glare with an unrepentant grin, and Daisy—refusing to be charmed—focused her attention on Lia, who at least looked sympathetic.

"So tell me more about this young man of yours," Millicent McGregor said as she continued to brush Daisy's hair with long, hypnotic strokes.

"Oh, for God's sake. He's not my young man," Daisy muttered. Her mother tugged one of her curls sharply, and Daisy sucked in a pained breath.

"Don't take the Lord's name in vain," the older woman reprimanded.

"Sorry." The word was surly, and Daisy sighed inwardly, disgusted that she always allowed her mother and sisters to drag the latent teenage drama queen out of her.

"So what's he like?"

"I don't know. I've only had one conversation with him. But he wanted to . . . to discuss his dog with me." The lie tumbled over her lips without thought, and her mother's brushing stopped for a millisecond before she continued on.

"But he can do that during office hours," Lia pointed out.

"I got caught in the rain this afternoon, and he gave me a ride home. We were talking about his dog, and he suggested we continue the conversation over dinner." Oh *God*, where were all these crazy half-truths coming from? Daisy wasn't exactly a master of subterfuge, which made her plan with Mason even more insane. She would never be able to keep up the pretense.

"So you see, it's more like a business dinner or something. No need to get all dolled up."

"Daffodil, hand over your hair clip," her mother commanded, ignoring Daisy's words, and Daff reached up and tugged a pretty, ultra-feminine floral crocodile clip from her hair. Her sleek hair, which had been held out of her face by the clip, slid forward like a silk curtain, and Daisy sighed in envy. Her sisters both had perfect hair. Naturally.

"There," her mother announced happily as she stepped back. "Lovely."

Daisy glanced at her reflection in the mirror, and her jaw dropped. How did her mother *always* do that? It hardly seemed fair that no matter what Daisy tried, she couldn't work the same magic on her own hair. It looked like such a simple fix too: her mother had dragged back the hair that usually just hung on either side of her face and pinned it back, while at the same time twisting it into an exotic, slightly off-center loose knot. The rest of her hair feathered down in soft, dreamy little curls that made her round face look a little less plain.

"Now we can see your pretty face," her mother said fondly, her expression softening as she gently stroked one of Daisy's cheeks before stepping back.

"Next we need to do something about this top," she said, immediately back to business. She took a step back and perused Daisy from head to toe before gasping in horror. "Oh, good grief, Daisy! Are you wearing one of your father's shirts?"

"Men's shirts are all the rage now," Daisy said, pretending indifference, when really she was mortified. She had grabbed the first thing she could find, and she now saw that it was one of her dad's shirts. She often borrowed his shirts if she went to her parents' place for dinner after work. God knows she couldn't fit into her mother or sisters' clothes.

"It's an old flannel shirt," her mother said. "And it would probably have been repurposed into a dust rag by now if you hadn't taken it."

Daff was riffling through her wardrobe and making disgusted sounds as she went through Daisy's clothes.

"These are all awful," she said, and Lia and their mother both went over to have a look.

Humiliated and getting more than a little pissed off, Daisy had finally had enough.

"I know you all have good intentions, but I'd like you to leave now," she said sternly, but they ignored her and just continued to mutter among themselves as they went through her personal things.

"Hey, *enough!*" Daisy's eyes widened in surprise when she heard the unfamiliar voice bellow in fury. Wow, was that really *her?* She sounded awesome. No-nonsense and a little scary in a cool take-charge kind of way. It definitely got everyone's attention, and their heads—even Peaches's—all swiveled toward her in unison.

"Please leave. I'm sorry that I'm not *pretty* enough or skinny enough or well-dressed enough to pass your exacting standards. I'm sorry I'm such a disappointment to you all." She sucked in a deep breath and softened her voice but was unable to keep the wobble out of it. "Look, I love you guys, and I know you mean well, but I'd appreciate it if you were all gone by the time Mason gets here."

It was entirely against Daisy's nature to speak out against her sisters and mother. It was easier to just let them have their way and then quietly go back to doing things her own way . . . This—whatever *this* was—felt liberating and terrifying.

Her sisters and mother hadn't deliberately set out to make her feel inadequate, and their advice and criticism over the years had always been well intended. But none of them ever considered how hurtful they were being, and Daisy had simply *allowed* them to treat her that way, to make her feel that way, and she knew that was on her. But she was twenty-seven years old, a partner in her father's veterinary practice, independent, and self-sufficient, and it was time she stood up for herself.

But her sisters and mother all looked so shocked and distressed by her uncharacteristic outburst that Daisy immediately forgot her resolve to stand up for herself and fled to the en suite. She locked herself in like the little coward she was and sank down on the commode while she listened to the other three women quietly murmur among themselves.

"Daisy, we're leaving," she finally heard her mother say through the closed door. "I hope you have an enjoyable evening . . ." There was a long pause, and she heard her mother sigh through the thin wood of the door. "I—I love you sweetheart. I'll see you soon."

Daisy screwed her eyes shut and swallowed back a sob. She felt awful and was about to call out when she heard her bedroom door click shut. Peaches's mournful little howl a few moments later confirmed that they had left the house. Daisy crept out of the bathroom slowly, half expecting Daff or Lia to be waiting for her in the bedroom. But they weren't, and Daisy had never felt lonelier.

She unbuttoned the stupid shirt and tore it off before sinking to the edge of the bed and dropping her face into her hands as she considered the repercussions of her little meltdown.

CHAPTER FOUR

It was still raining when Mason rolled to a stop in front of Daisy McGregor's small house. He sat there for a long moment, feeling strangely nervous about the evening ahead. He wasn't sure exactly what to make of this woman. She was oddly compelling. He knew she was going to back out of last night's drunken proposition and figured it would be for the best, but at the same time the little ruse would be a welcome diversion for him, and God knows, Mason needed to get out of his own head for a while.

He rubbed a hand vigorously over his buzz cut, a nervous habit that he'd developed after joining the army, before inhaling deeply and dashing out of the car to the front door.

He shook his head as the dog started up a cacophony just inside the door. He heard Daisy frantically try to shush the animal, but the little puffball only barked louder.

Daisy looked flustered when she opened the door, and he grinned down into her flushed face.

"Hi. I'm sorry. She gets a little carried away . . . *Peaches!*" The last word emerged as the dog actually made a dash for his ankle.

"Stop that!" Mason made sure *his* bark was louder and more authoritative than the dog's, and she backed up in confusion, hiding behind Daisy's legs when Mason stepped over the threshold and into the small lobby.

"Nice place," he said after giving the cozy living room a look around. She had a way with colors that made the place seem warm and inviting.

"Thanks." She hovered awkwardly at the front door, obviously not having expected Mason to come inside. "Would you like a drink or something?"

The question lacked some serious conviction, and he knew that having him in her home, sipping a beverage like some proper fucking gentleman caller, was the last thing she wanted. Perversely it made him feel suddenly *very* thirsty.

"Yeah. What you got?"

"Coffee, tea, some soda."

"Coffee, thanks."

"I only have instant," she said, and he shrugged, sidestepping her to peruse the wall of framed photos behind her.

"I'm not fussy," he said absently as he studied a photograph of Daisy and her sisters. They all had the same pretty eyes, the same clear skin, and the exact same smile. Daffodil and Dahlia had sleek brown hair a shade darker than Daisy's crazy curls, and they were both slender and tall, while their baby sister was significantly shorter with less-fashionable, lush curves. The photograph was at least five years old, and Daisy's figure had ripened a bit since then, her hair was longer—she looked less like a brown-haired Little Orphan Annie.

He sensed her hovering behind him before she headed to the open-plan kitchen, Peaches trailing anxiously in her wake. Mason kept his eyes on the photos. They told the tale of a happy family, lots of smiles, laughter, family pets, and outings. A life without hardship, a life of privilege and upper-middle-class wealth, a stark contrast to Mason and Spencer's upbringing.

Their father and mother had been less successful at the parenting thing. The old man had been in and out of jail for petty crimes, and their mother was a functioning alcoholic. While Mason's parents had cared about their children in their own dysfunctional way, the boys had been left to their own devices much too often. And after their mother's death, money was scarce, and both Spencer and Mason had been guilty of shoplifting food because there often wasn't enough money for basics like bread and milk. They were lucky not to be caught; their lives would probably have turned out quite differently if they'd been arrested for shoplifting.

Mason shrugged off the sudden bout of melancholy, tucked his hands into his jean pockets, and turned to face Daisy. She had her back to him as she moved around the kitchen, and he found himself absently checking out her round, lush ass in those slightly-too-tight blue jeans. She was also wearing a simple long-sleeved black top, nowhere near as baggy as the other stuff he'd seen her in so far, and he was surprised to see the distinct nipped-in waist that gave her a full, curvy hourglass figure. She was built like a fifties bombshell—a particular weakness of his—with generous extra padding distributed attractively in the butt, thigh, and boob area.

She turned to face him, and he noted, for the first time, that the front of the top was some kind of V-neck wraparound thing that tied around the waist. It did fabulous things for her cleavage. Man, Daisy McGregor had killer tits, and Mason shifted uncomfortably when his cock went unexpectedly hard at the sight of her plump chest. She had a magnificent body, and he didn't think Daisy or anybody else really appreciated that fact. He walked toward the island that separated the kitchen from the living room and placed himself behind it, grateful that it was high enough to keep his crotch out of sight. He was stunned by this unexpected development. He liked the woman, but he hadn't expected to find himself turned on by her. He needed time to process this information and time to get his rampant dick back under control.

"Sugar or milk?"

"Black. Thanks." Thankfully his voice was passably normal, just a little gruffer than usual. "You look nice."

"Oh. Thank you." She blushed, and he was fascinated by the way the color crept up over her chest, into her neck, covering her cheeks and tinting the tops of her ears. A full body blush. He wondered where the rosiness originated from and figured that the only way he'd ever know was if he made her blush while he had her naked and pinned beneath him. He choked a little at the thought, which wasn't helping his hard-on go down in the slightest.

She placed a mug on the marble countertop in front of him, and he sat down on one of the high barstools, still careful to keep his lower body out of sight. She had fixed herself a cup of tea and stood awkwardly on the other side of the island, fiddling with the infuser.

"I like your hair like that," Mason observed and was delighted when the comment caused another one of those all-over blushes. He did think her hair looked pretty. How did women achieve that effect? It wasn't up, it wasn't down, but it was somehow both. It was a mystery to him, but it looked good on her, and the wispy tendrils that framed her face and trailed down her neck suited her.

"Thanks."

There was a long, awkward silence while he sipped his hot coffee and she continued to nervously dip the infuser in and out of the hot water in her mug. She didn't seem to know what else to do with her hands, and she had her gaze fixed on that tea as if her very life depended on it.

Mason kept his attention on her downbent head and wondered what it would take to get back the relaxed, charming Daisy of last night.

"You going to drink that?" he asked after a few more moments, when it became apparent that *she* wasn't going to be the one to break the silence. His voice startled her into dropping the infuser, and they both watched it plonk into the hot water, chain and all.

"Damn it," she whispered and sighed deeply before raising her wary eyes to meet his.

Here it comes. Mason braced himself for the words he could practically see forming in her head.

"This is not a good idea."

"We'd better get going," he said, ignoring her statement and keeping his voice jovial as he handed the coffee mug to her. "I made reservations."

"You did?" She seemed flummoxed by his words, but he didn't give her time to think about it, and before she knew it he had her bundled into her coat with her handbag over her shoulder. Mason waited by the front door while she settled Peaches. He had swiped an umbrella from the stand in her foyer and courteously escorted her to the sleek and sexy BMW i8 crouched like a waiting leopard in the driveway behind her Renault.

"Is this your car?" she asked as she took in the dark interior of the car while he buckled himself in.

"Yes. I like to use it for special occasions." He loved this car and grabbed every opportunity he could to drive it. Not that he often did. It seemed ostentatious to speed around their tiny town in this electric beauty, and he couldn't exactly take it on his off-road adventures, so he had driven it a mere handful of times since he'd indulgently purchased it just a year ago.

"This isn't exactly a special occasion." Her negativity was starting to get on his nerves, and he gritted his teeth before responding.

"Allow me to decide for myself which occasions I think are special," he just *barely* refrained from snapping at her, and she was silent for so long, he wondered if some of the impatience he was feeling had managed to creep into his voice after all.

"Are we going to MJ's?" she asked, and he gave her a quick look, trying to read her expression in the dim light.

"Yep."

"You don't need a reservation for MJ's."

Aaahh. Mason felt his lips stretch into a grin.

"I was wondering when you'd pick up on that."

"Why'd you say you had reservations?"

"I'm hungry and wasn't in the mood to stand there having yet another ridiculous discussion with you about whether we're doing this or not."

——

Daisy didn't respond to that, averting her gaze out of the passenger window instead. The roads and sidewalks gleamed wetly beneath the pale streetlights as rain continued to torrent down. She tried not to think about how good Mason smelled, how she was completely enveloped by his scent, how she wanted to lean closer and just inhale him all in. Okay . . . so maybe that last one was a little creepy, but heck, the guy smelled amazing. And he looked absolutely breathtaking too. He was wearing faded jeans and a gray Henley under an open black, waist-length down coat, with a furred hood. He wore his clothes with an ease that Daisy kind of envied. He gave ordinary clothes a sexy, chic masculine appeal that she hadn't ever seen any other man achieve. She felt positively frumpy next to his splendor.

He parked as close to MJ's as he could on a Saturday night, which, despite the wet weather, was still about five doors away. He reached for the umbrella and told her to wait, while he leaped out of the car and dashed around to her side to open the door for her.

Daisy wasn't used to such chivalry from the opposite sex. They usually dove to assist her sisters, leaving Daisy to open her own doors and carry her own shopping. This was a complete novelty. He raised the umbrella above her head and made sure she received the lion's share of the protection it offered. The left side of his body was wet when they reached the restaurant entrance. He held the door open for her with one hand while he shook the umbrella vigorously with the other.

MJ's was jam-packed as usual, and Daisy's wet glasses fogged up the second the hot air hit them, making it hard for her to see. She reached up to remove them, while Mason took a light hold of her elbow and followed one of the staff who led them to an empty table in the middle of the floor and informed them that their waitress would be right with them.

He dragged a chair out for Daisy, and feeling both self-conscious and flattered, she slid into it. She wiped her glasses, and by the time she had them back on, he was already seated opposite her. A quick glance around the room confirmed that there were a lot familiar faces around and that some of them were quite openly staring at her and Mason.

"Man, I haven't been to MJ's in *years*," Mason was saying. "I think the last time I set foot in this place was as a dishwasher."

Mason used to bus and wash dishes here. He must have been close to eighteen at the time. And while she would never admit to it now, a fourteen-year-old Daisy used to come to MJ's hoping to catch a glimpse of him. He hadn't noticed her, though. In fact, he hadn't really paid attention to any of the girls who had tried to flirt with him back then.

"It hasn't changed at *all*," he said, shaking his head ruefully. "It's like it's still stuck in the early twenty-ohs."

"Nothing much changes in Riversend," Daisy said, and his eyes smiled into hers, sending her tummy aflutter again.

"Yeah, I noticed. I was gone, what? Twelve, thirteen, years? And everything is exactly the same. I mean Mr. Kane is still the principal of the high school, for God's sake."

"How do you even know that?" she asked.

"Spencer. He's often invited to give motivational talks to the kids. Can you believe that? Old Man Kane hated us, and now he's asking Spencer to talk to the students? Apparently he wants me to speak to them too."

"And will you?"

"I don't know. It's not my scene. What do I have to say to a bunch of teens?" He looked uncomfortable and more than a little embarrassed at the thought.

"You've done really well for yourself, Mason," she said. "And you came from such humble beginnings. A lot of the students come from similar backgrounds. You and your brother could inspire them to do more with their lives."

"It wasn't anything special. We worked hard. I had three jobs, and I saved every cent I earned so that I could afford the airfare out of here. That meant no dates, no social life during my entire adolescence . . . no kid wants to hear that."

"They might not want to hear it, but it's *exactly* what some of them need to hear."

He cleared his throat and fiddled with the salt and pepper shakers, before reaching for the menu.

Their young waitress drifted over to their table.

"Oh, hey, Dr. Daisy," she greeted when she saw Daisy and then stared at Mason with open curiosity. "Do you want your usual drink?"

"Hello, Thandiwe," Daisy greeted the teenager with a friendly smile. "I think I'll have a glass of your house red tonight."

"Make that a bottle of your best Pinotage," Mason said, and the girl nodded, her riot of beaded braids bouncing pertly. She was a pretty girl, with a warm smile, and one of those troubled teens Daisy had just been talking about.

"Okay, I'll be back in a few minutes with your wine and to take your order," Thandiwe said, and Daisy nodded.

"So what's your 'usual' drink?"

"I'd rather not say; it's embarrassing."

"As embarrassing as the chicken dance?"

She snorted and shook her head. "Nowhere near as bad as that."

"So come on, tell me."

71

"Virgin piña colada," she confessed, keeping her eyes on the red-checkered tablecloth and wincing when he laughed.

"A little rum never hurt anybody," he said.

"'A little rum' leads to a lot of rum leads to the chicken dance."

"Seriously?"

"Don't ever watch my parents' twenty-fifth wedding anniversary DVD. It's . . . epically awful."

"Hell, you shouldn't have told me that," he said, an element of unholy glee in his voice.

"I doubt you'll ever get to know them well enough to see the horribly embarrassing family DVD collection, so I think I'm safe enough," she said smugly.

"Challenge accepted."

"It wasn't a challenge."

"I'll be the judge of that."

"Mason . . ."

"Your wine," Thandiwe said, interrupting what was proving to be the most frustrating and entertaining conversation Daisy had had in a long time. The girl popped the cork on the wine with a flourish and decanted a portion for Mason, who took a sip before nodding at her to go ahead and pour.

"Are you ready to order?" Thandiwe asked, reaching into the kangaroo pouch in the front of her black apron and pulling out her notebook.

"Not quite yet," Mason told her with a smile, and she nodded.

"Just call when you need me," the girl said before flouncing off to a neighboring table.

"So was I mistaken or did the lovely Thandiwe call you *Dr.* Daisy earlier?" Mason took another appreciative sip of his wine and stared at her with those beautiful and unsettlingly penetrating eyes of his.

"I'm a vet," she said, trying to remain unaffected by that all-seeing gaze of his.

"No shit? That's great. Just like your dad, huh?"

"Yes, I can't remember ever wanting to be or do anything else. I spent my childhood tagging along behind my dad as often as he'd let me, and when I was a teen, I helped out in reception. I've only been a qualified veterinarian for a year now and in partnership with my father."

"And? Is it everything you thought it would be?"

"It's hard work and often gut-wrenching, but it can heartwarming and rewarding as well. I started a free clinic at *Inkululeko* about six months ago, and it's my favorite part of the week. I feel like we're really making a difference with that clinic. We run it on Wednesdays and half days on Saturdays. We're always slammed on Saturdays, but I love it."

"You worked today?"

"Yes. That's why I was stuck walking Peaches at such an impractical time."

"And what do you do for fun, Daisy McGregor?" he asked with a smile, and Daisy's breath caught when she noticed the sexy dimple winking at her from his left cheek.

"Uh . . ." She lost her train of thought, distracted by the dimple. And she tried to gather her thoughts as she fought to regain her composure. "Nothing much, really. Work takes up a lot of my time right now, what with us still trying to get the clinic properly running and funded. When I do have a moment to spare, I bake."

His eyes flared with interest.

"Yeah? Like cakes and stuff?"

"All kinds of cakes, biscuits, pies . . ."

"I happen to like pies," he said without subtlety, and Daisy laughed.

"I'll bear that in mind."

"I'm partial to cakes and biscuits too."

"I'm sure you are." She giggled, and he returned her smile.

Daisy McGregor might not be the cute one or the pretty one, but she sure as hell was the adorable one. How nobody else could see that was beyond Mason. He wanted to keep that wide, gorgeous smile on her face, but it was already fading to be replaced by her more habitual earnestness.

He saw their waitress, Thandiwe, approaching and shook his head slightly to indicate to her that they weren't ready yet, before lifting the menu.

"All this talk of confectionaries has made me hungry," he confessed as he perused the menu. His eyes widened as he stared at the all-too-familiar items listed on the laminated paper. "This menu is still *exactly* the same."

"I know."

"*Exactly* the same, Daisy," he repeated, waving the plastic card in front of her face. "Seriously, and I don't just mean the content. I'm almost sure this is one of the actual menus they had when I was working here. See this water stain?" He pointed to the blotch beside the *M* in MJ's. It was on the paper that was sandwiched between the thin sheets of plastic and had to have been there before the menu was laminated. "I know I've seen it before. How have all of you not *died* of boredom yet?"

"Most of the younger people leave as soon as they're old enough. They move to Knysna, Plettenberg Bay, Port Elizabeth, or sometimes further afield to Durban or Cape Town. Or in certain extreme cases . . . the UK." The last was said with a pointed glance over the top of the menu, and he grinned again.

"And why didn't you leave?" Especially since the people in this town were so set in their ways, they hadn't even noticed that she was a captivating woman in her own right who didn't deserve to be forever unfavorably compared to her sisters.

"I went to university in Pretoria, but I always wanted to come back here and join my dad's practice. Still, that taste of independence was what led me to move out of my parents' house and buy my own place.

My sisters are so content living there, and I get so—" She stopped talking abruptly, and he wondered if she felt guilty about whatever she'd been about to say. She did seem fiercely loyal to her family. She put down her menu and folded her hands over the piece of plastic. "I already know what I want to order."

It was a pointed change of subject, and he allowed it only because he really was famished, and he didn't want to push her in case she clammed up. As it was he was just grateful she hadn't again started talking about how going ahead with her plan was a bad idea.

He waved Thandiwe over, and they placed their orders—pasta *arrabbiata* for Daisy and a rare steak with baked potato for him—before he turned his attention back to his dinner companion. Her hair was starting to slip out of that knot and beginning to resemble a soft cloud around her face. The heat from the place added a becoming flush to her cheeks.

"What about you?" she asked, and he blinked, startled out of his perusal of her pretty face.

"What do you mean?"

"What do *you* do for fun? Especially now that you're back in our boring little town. I can't imagine you'd find it that interesting being back."

"You'd be surprised," he muttered under his breath. He was finding her more and more fascinating with every passing moment, but he didn't think she was quite ready to hear or believe that. "I haven't been in town long enough to get bored yet. I've been on the go for the last year. I like camping, hiking, off-roading, parasailing, and I do a bit of surfing when it's not fucking freezing." He paused and then winced. "Sorry, all those years in the military with a bunch of crude guys didn't do much for the vocabulary."

"And what are your plans now that you're home? Do you intend to settle down here? Stay permanently?"

He fiddled with the stem of his glass as he considered the question.

"Not entirely sure, really."

His answer surprised Daisy. Mason Carlisle struck her as a man who always knew what he wanted and when he wanted it. The indecisiveness seemed out of character. "After selling my half of the company, I thought I'd try something I've always wanted to do."

"Which is?" she asked, lifting her glass for a sip of wine.

"Nothing."

She choked on her drink and squinted at him.

"What?"

"I've always dreamt of being rich enough to do absolutely nothing," he elaborated with a sheepish grin. "Granted, I was about seventeen and working those aforementioned three jobs when I wished for this, but I thought I'd give it a go."

"And how's it working out for you? Doing absolutely nothing, that is?"

"Honestly?" he asked, dipping his head and looking up at her through those gorgeous eyelashes of his. She found the almost shy gesture incredibly appealing and fought back another one of her embarrassing blushes.

"Yep."

"It's boring as hell. I've always had something to do, and all this leisure time is driving me crazy."

"Well, you've kept yourself busy with the hiking and climbing and stuff, so you haven't been completely idle."

"But that was fun and unproductive, and for someone like me, it's damned near decadent to be able to do anything I want, without any sort of regimen. I've lived my entire life according to a schedule, sometimes mine, mostly someone else's—so this just feels"—he stopped as he searched for the correct word—"wrong. It feels wrong. And I feel selfish."

"You've spent your life helping others, Mason. Cut yourself some slack." She would have continued if Thandiwe hadn't chosen that moment to bring their food. Mason looked a little relieved by the interruption, and once their bubbly server had left, he very determinedly changed the subject.

"Ah, now this is one thing I'm happy remained the same," he said with an appreciative sigh, after giving his steak a long and lusty look. "The food at MJ's has always been awesome, despite the lack of variation in the menu."

"Or maybe *because* of it," Daisy suggested. "Why change something that's working perfectly fine in the first place?"

"Touché," he said, before slicing off a sizable chunk of the—much-too-rare-for-Daisy's-liking—meat and shoving it into his mouth. He groaned, leaned back in his chair, and closed his eyes as he chewed on his meat. He looked incredibly sexy and—quite uncharacteristically—Daisy found herself wondering if he showed this much enthusiasm and sensual appreciation during sex. She would assume so. Mason Carlisle just seemed like the type of man who did nothing by half measures. He enjoyed every sensual, physical, and cerebral aspect of life. The type of man who took action and went after the things he wanted, rather than standing on the sidelines watching all the important experiences in life pass him by.

He opened his eyes and caught her staring, her fork halfway to her open mouth, and Daisy quickly averted her eyes, despite knowing that it was already much too late to pretend she wasn't completely riveted by him.

"Sorry, I appreciate good food a little too much sometimes. Bad table manners, I know." He was smiling as he spoke, inviting her to share his self-deprecating humor. She forced an answering feeble smile in return, but her expression froze at his next words. "I'll be on my best behavior at your sister's wedding, though. I promise not to act like a starving man at a banquet and embarrass you."

Embarrass her? A man of Mason Carlisle's caliber couldn't even begin to grasp the concept of embarrassment. But, that aside, it was time to address the elephant in the room, and Daisy sighed as she placed her fork neatly on the side of her plate.

"Mason, I really appreciate the fact that you were—*are*—willing to help me out like this, but the inherent dishonesty of it is making me feel really uncomfortable, and I don't think I can, or even want to, go through with it."

He said nothing, kept his focus on his plate as he sliced off another piece of steak and speared some steaming potato along the way as well. He shoveled the contents of the overburdened fork into his mouth and watched her closely while he chewed. He ate like a man, no delicacy or artifice about him. He washed the food down with some wine and sucked at his teeth before finally making a noncommittal sound in the back of his throat. It sounded like a lion's purr and unsettled Daisy more than she was willing to let on.

"So you're uninviting me?"

"Well, I mean, it wasn't like it was an official . . ."

"*Daisy?* I thought that was you!" The loud, overly sweet voice had the same effect on Daisy as fingernails on a chalkboard, and she girded herself to face the owner of that voice.

"Hey, Shar," she greeted with more of a grimace than a smile, but Shar had already dismissed Daisy and her laser-like focus was pinned entirely on Mason.

"And look who you have with you. Mason, how wonderful to see you again!" She leaned over, probably giving Mason a generous eyeful of her exposed cleavage, and kissed the air on either side of his face. "It's been *years*! I thought I saw you last night, but I was out celebrating my friend's hen night, you know."

She then, to Daisy's annoyance, dragged up a chair and sat down at their table, turning her body toward Mason and completely excluding Daisy from their exchange. Mason casually continued to eat, saying nothing, but staring at her in interest, occasionally allowing his eyes to stray down to her breasts and then back up to her lovely face. His expression was inscrutable, making it hard for Daisy to figure out what he was thinking.

"What have you been up to? Are you home for good? What brings you to MJ's tonight?"

Mason's eyes, for the very briefest of moments, slid over to Daisy, and he cleared his throat before putting his knife and fork down. He leaned back in his chair, draping one arm over the back and angling his body toward Shar's. The woman leaned forward, anticipating his reply, since—with the shift in his body language—she now had his entire focus. Feeling hurt and slighted, Daisy cringed—wishing she could just sink into the floor and disappear. Anything to avoid this.

"Date." The word was concise and didn't exactly invite further conversation. Shar's eyebrows rose, and she laughed delicately.

"A date?" She glanced around the restaurant as if expecting to see someone appear, before she allowed her eyes to rest on Daisy. "You mean with our little *Daisy*? Well, that's new. Daisy doesn't date, do you, sweetie? Too busy with her cows and chickens to bother with men. But bless you for getting her out and about. We don't see enough of you around town, Daisy." She raised her voice in that condescending way ignorant people had when they spoke to deaf or mentally challenged people. Daisy gritted her teeth, knowing from experience that responding would only delay the unpleasant encounter and invite further bitchiness. "I've been telling your sisters you should get out more. Get a little more exercise, you know? Good for the *body* and soul."

"Lady—forgive me, I'm not exactly sure what your name is—but I'm trying to sweet-talk Daisy into a second date, and you're kind of ruining the moment," Mason said, plastering an amiable grin on his face while he kept his voice soft and pleasant. "I'm a patient guy—sometimes I'm even a nice guy—but I can't say I appreciate the interruption. Now if you don't mind? Daisy and I have some acquainting to get back to."

Shar gaped at him in visible shock, her mouth opening and closing unattractively as his words sank in. Daisy had clapped her hand over her own mouth in disbelief halfway through his charming little put-down. Nobody dismissed Sharlotte Bridges like that. Daisy's eyes swiveled to Shar to see how she was taking it, and she could see that Shar's shock was wearing off and her eyes had gone cold with malice.

"I guess you can take the man out of the ghetto but—no matter what his achievements—you can never entirely eradicate the stink of his origins from him," she hissed.

"Wow, really?" Mason's grin disappeared, and his eyes went frighteningly icy. He looked so dangerous in that moment that even Daisy felt a little uneasy. "You're going to pull this elitist bullshit? In this day and age? Don't be ridiculous. This is getting tiresome, lady. Why don't you shove off back to wherever the hell you came from and leave us to enjoy our evening?" He dismissed her with a careless wave and refocused his attention on Daisy, who was having a hard time keeping the mixture of awe and horror she was feeling from showing on her face.

Shar was too concerned with her image to create a huge scene, and she aimed a fulminating glare at the wide-eyed Daisy before turning and stalking back to her table, where a few of her usual toadying minions sat eagerly awaiting her return.

Mason shook his head and went back to his meal as if the interruption hadn't occurred.

"That was . . ." Daisy's voice petered. There was really nothing she could think of to say about what had just happened, and Mason shrugged.

"That chick's a bitch; why did you allow her to muscle in on your territory like that?"

"What do you mean my territory? The table?"

"No, Daisy, I mean *me*," he growled. "We're obviously here together, and you allowed her to force her unwelcome way into our conversation."

"Well, I didn't know if you wanted to speak with her or not. I don't have any rights over you or any control over with whom you choose to speak."

"Hmm." He shrugged. "You were irritated by the interruption. I could see it in your eyes. So why did you let her walk all over you like that?"

"I don't know," she said, shaking her head hopelessly. "Habit, I guess."

"You *always* let her treat you like that? Like you don't matter? What the fuck? Why?"

"I don't know," Daisy repeated and swallowed back a lump in her throat as she considered his words.

"And she'll be at the wedding?"

"She's one of the bridesmaids."

"Are the rest of them like that too?"

"Some of them, yes."

"Why is your sister even friends with a viper like that?"

"It's a small town, and Shar is very influential."

"I don't give a fuck if she's the pope's daughter; she was always a bitch, even back in high school, and I never could figure out why people allowed her to have so much power and sway over them."

"So you *do* know who she is?"

"Of course I do, but do you think I'd give her the satisfaction of knowing that? I never liked her."

"She's very beautiful."

"So's a blue-ringed octopus, but it can still kill the hell out of you."

"A blue-ringed octopus?" She couldn't quite contain her giggle. "I don't think she'd appreciate being compared to an octopus."

"Daisy," he said, his voice serious and his eyes level, and she put her elbows on the table and leaned forward in interest. She was shaken when his eyes dipped to her cleavage for a long—wholly appreciative— moment. When his gaze came back up to meet hers, it had a smolder in it that made Daisy feel hot all over. His voice had roughened slightly, and it made his next words sound way sexier than he probably intended. "I'm not allowing you to uninvite me from that wedding. We're going. Together. Got that?"

"Yes."

"Great." An awkward silence descended over the table, and she could hear Shar's voice from across the room. Horrible words like "human trash" and "ignorant, uneducated jocks" drifted over the general hum of conversation clearly meant for them to hear, and Daisy winced in embarrassment.

"I'm sorry about Shar. The things she said were . . ."

"Why?" he interrupted. "Why be sorry? You're not the one who said them. I've met loads of chicks like her in my lifetime. Spoilt bitches who want to 'slum' it with the soldier or the bodyguard but would never been caught dead with them in public. Hell, I've even fucked—sorry—my fair share of them. I know exactly what they're all about."

"Still—"

"Don't ever apologize for other people, Daisy. Unless"—a fleeting expression of doubt crossed his face before it settled into handsome impassivity—"unless that's why you changed your mind about the wedding. Because you think I'm not good enough."

"What?" Daisy laughed outright at that. "Seriously? That's the most ridiculous thing I've ever heard. You're a great guy, Mason. A nice man. Attractive and interesting. You—"

"Let me stop you right there." He held up a hand and shook his head. "I'm not *nice*, Daisy. If I was *nice*, if I was halfway decent, I'd let you back out of this wingman scheme."

"So . . . so why don't you?" She wasn't sure she wanted to hear the answer to that question but couldn't prevent the halting question from slipping out.

"Because I'm a selfish asshole."

"I don't understand."

"You're the nice one, Daisy. Sweet, kind, fun, entertaining. I like hanging out with you. But after the newness wears off, you won't like hanging out with *me*, and that's why I should have let you call this thing off. But that's not going to happen, because I'm enjoying myself, and regardless of whether this is the best thing for *you*, it's what I want. And when I want something, very little can stop me from getting it."

"I still don't understand."

"You will." The words were said in such a grim voice that they sent a shudder down her spine. "Now eat up and then tell me everything I need to know to make Operation Wingman succeed."

Mason watched as Daisy nibbled her lower lip while she considered his words. She sighed softly—her lovely chest rising and falling gently in the process—and removed her glasses to pinch the bridge of her nose. He had tried his utmost to keep his eyes above chest level this evening, but he knew she had caught him looking a couple of times. He was trying to maintain a calm and friendly demeanor, but the truth was, his body had been on a low simmer for most of dinner, and he was finding it hard to focus on what she was saying when all he wanted to do was taste those full, soft-looking lips and slip his hand inside the low *V* of that top.

She replaced her glasses and lifted those gorgeous gray eyes to meet his.

"There's not much to know except that people are going to have a hard time believing this charade," she grumbled, and he hit her with the sweetest smile in his arsenal—the "panty dropper" as his army mates called it—and reached across the table to lay one of his hands over one of hers.

"Trust me," he crooned, lifting her surprisingly delicate hand and turning it palm up to trace the lines with his index finger. Her breath caught, and his smile widened even further as he slathered on the charm. "They'll believe it."

He dropped a kiss into the center of her palm and folded her fingers down until they were curled over the spot he had marked with his lips. Her skin was incredibly soft, and damned if his lips weren't *actually* tingling after the brief brush against her soft, fragrant flesh. *Tingling*, for God's sake. What kind of bloke would ever confess to feeling tingly? And yet here he sat, with tiny starbursts of sensation popping and fizzing all over his lips.

Her breath came in ragged gasps, and he was fighting to keep his own breathing under control after the unanticipated impact of that brief, intimate caress. He had to be very careful here. This wasn't a reaction he had foreseen at all. Take her to the wedding, make her feel special, treat her like a princess, and job done, conscience assuaged. He liked her, wanted to spend time with her and enjoy her company, but sexual attraction shouldn't have factored into the equation at all.

"See?" he muttered, resisting the urge to clear his throat, knowing that doing so would only draw unwanted attention to the hoarseness of his voice. "I can lay on the charm as convincingly as the next guy."

Too convincingly. Daisy surreptitiously dragged her hand beneath the table and rubbed her palm against her jeans, hoping the roughness of the denim would eradicate the lingering sensation of his warm lips from her flesh. If they were going to do this she *had* to remember that this was all pretend, that Mason Carlisle's overwhelming charm—no matter how convincing—was not real. It would be so easy to forget that fact, so easy to buy into their little deception and become the victim of her own dumb plan.

"So, are we doing this thing?" he asked, refilling their wineglasses. His hand seemed a little unsteady, and his voice sounded thicker than usual. Daisy briefly wondered about that before shrugging the tremor off as Mason readjusted his grip on the bottle and dismissing the gruffness she had heard in his voice as her imagination. Especially since he sounded perfectly normal when he prompted her again moments later, "Are we?"

Daisy took a fortifying sip of her wine before inhaling deeply. She thought back to all those other family events, Lia's engagement party, Shar's behavior just minutes before, and considered the impotent anger, frustration, and resentment she'd felt with every well-meaning auntie patronizingly informing her that her parents were so lucky to have her to look after them in their old age. Showing up with Mason Carlisle on her arm would definitely make them pause for thought. A smile tilted her lips as Daisy imagined the looks on their faces. Then there was Shar and her ilk . . . Mason had been a wonderful balm on her bruised ego earlier, and while Daisy knew she had to fight her own battles, Lia's wedding probably wasn't the place to start doing so. She briefly considered his strange warning that he wasn't nice, not quite sure what to make of it. She scrutinized his face carefully, but no trace of that earlier broodiness remained. His current expression seemed aloof, but his eyes were warm and gently encouraging.

"Yes. Let's do it," she decided with a firm nod, and Mason's lips stretched into a wonderful grin, one that showcased his dimple beautifully.

"No more wishy-washy bullshit, Daisy. No more changing your mind. Got it?"

"Yes, sir," she said, giving him a little salute, and he shook his head.

"That was the worst salute I've ever seen in my life," he chastised.

"How do you do it in the British navy, then?"

"Army," he corrected.

"Sorry, army."

"Easy, palm facing outward, index finger just on the brow. See?" he demonstrated with a smart and snappy salute that impressed her more than it should have.

"You must have looked really handsome in your uniform," she breathed appreciatively, and he chuckled.

"Don't tell me you're one of those women who goes sappy at the sight of a guy in uniform?" Not any guy, just Mason. Daisy figured she'd melt into a puddle of unrequited lust if she ever saw the man in uniform. But she wasn't about to tell *him* that.

"The navy uniform is kind of sexy," she admitted with a grin, and his brow furrowed.

"I was in the army," he reminded, with that inborn male arrogance that told her he assumed that she must have made a mistake.

"Yes, so you said. Pity. You would probably have looked quite nice in navy whites."

He winced and then laughed.

"I walked right into that one, didn't I?"

"Totally."

"You don't often see them in whites, you know? They usually muck around in something less glamorous."

"Ssh." Without thinking, she lifted her hand and placed her fingers over his lips. Then self-consciously snatched them back when she realized what she had done. Damn it! Just when she was getting over that kiss too. Her gesture had effectively silenced him, and she watched in fascination when the tip of his tongue ran over the same spot her fingers had just been. As if he were sampling her taste.

She shook herself, a little irritated to be thinking such ridiculous thoughts, and focused on their conversation.

"Don't destroy the fantasy," she admonished, embarrassed by the unfamiliar throatiness of her voice. A tiny smile kicked up one corner of his mouth, and his eyes narrowed.

"What fantasy?"

"The, uh . . . the navy thing. You know?" *Shut up, Daisy,* her inner voice shrieked, *shut up!*

"What does this navy fantasy guy wind up doing to you exactly?"

"Nothing." She shifted uncomfortably.

"So he just stands around doing nothing? Lame."

"I just think it's a flattering uniform, that's all," she said, trying to insert some firmness into her voice and take command of this crazy conversation.

"I could borrow a buddy's navy whites," he suggested with a wicked grin. "And wear them for you. But I'll probably do a hell of a lot more than merely stand around modeling it."

Don't ask!

"Like what?" *Crap!*

"I'll probably start with a slooooooow strip tease." Daisy was captivated by his eyes; they were staring into hers with scorching intensity, and she was finding it hard to breathe. Her mouth was bone dry, and she took another desperate gulp from her glass.

"I'm surprised you'd know how to do that," she croaked. Why wasn't she putting a stop to this conversation? It was unlike any other discussion she had ever had in her life, and she wasn't sure if she wanted it to continue or end.

"What? A striptease? I've seen it done enough times. It seems pretty easy. Put on some sexy music, do a hip-swaying, raunchy dance, and strip. But make it last, build anticipation . . . reveal only a *tiny*"—his hand drifted to the top button of his Henley and popped it—*"sliver"*— another button.

Daisy's eyes were fixed on the smooth, tanned skin peeking through the tiny *V* he had created at the base of his throat, and she swallowed heavily. Her breath came in rapid pants while her entire body felt as if it was on fire.

"Of skin"—another button. How could a man's *throat* be so sexy? Oh God, she could see his clavicles now. She wanted to run her tongue over them. They looked so strong and masculine. What was happening to her?

"At a time"—a fourth button slid free of its hole to reveal the tiniest portion of his chest. She could see the slightest sprinkle of light-brown

hair, and she absolutely ached to run her hand over the silky-looking stuff, to feel the velvety texture of his glorious skin beneath the palm of his hand. She ran her tongue over her dry lips and swallowed again.

"You okay, Daisy? You're looking a bit flushed." His hands dropped back to the table, and Daisy stifled a groan when she realized that the impromptu little demo was over. She glared at him; he had done that deliberately, the *bastard*. He had known exactly how he was affecting her and had teased her mercilessly nonetheless. Daisy didn't know what game he was playing with her, but she didn't like it.

"It's a little hot in here, that's all," she lied, and he allowed the untruth to go unchallenged, merely nodded his acceptance.

"It is a bit uncomfortable," he said agreeably.

CHAPTER FIVE

Mason felt like a bastard. Why had he done that? He couldn't explain his motivation even to himself. All he knew was that he enjoyed teasing her and that he had pushed them both way too far with that stupid little strip show. Her pupils were still *huge*, only a sliver of gray rimmed them; her breath came in huffs; her hands were trembling; and she still had that delicious rosy flush highlighting her cheeks. God, she was sexy when she was turned on, and all Mason wanted was to get her someplace private and fuck her senseless. But if ever a chick had "complicated" stamped all over her, it was this one, and Mason knew that any sex with her would come with way too much baggage, and he sure as hell didn't want her enough to have to deal with any emotional crap.

He preferred quick, easy, and uncomplicated, but the Daisy McGregors of the world wanted hearts and flowers and commitment—he shuddered discreetly at the thought—with their sex. Best to steer clear. He'd be better off going to a woman like that Shar bitch for his sex. A shame she left him cold.

Still, he hadn't had more than one hookup since getting back from London, and that had been nearly eight months ago. Jerking off was getting old, and he figured he was way overdue for some fun between the sheets with a pretty, flirty thing who wouldn't expect much more than a roll in the hay from him.

Sadly, because Riversend was so small, he'd have to venture further afield for his sex. God knew he didn't want the whole town knowing whom he fucked. That was the one drawback of being home, everybody knew everyone else's business. He had to ask Spencer where the prime pickup spots were around these parts.

He cleared his throat and tried to regroup his thoughts and felt like a total shit all over again when he glanced over at Daisy and saw that she was having a hard time meeting his eyes.

"So tell me everything I need to know about this wedding," he invited, wanting to get them back on task. She looked up, and he could see the relief in her eyes at the change of subject.

"Well, it's going to be a big deal: a destination wedding, with an *intimate*"—she used air quotes—"rehearsal dinner at the venue. Very sophisticated and elegant; Clayton's parents insisted."

Something in Daisy's voice alerted Mason to the fact that she wasn't too impressed with her future in-laws, and his eyes narrowed.

"Tell me about the groom."

Daisy shifted uncomfortably. She didn't like Clayton, she didn't trust him, and she hated the way he made her feel. His comments about her body when nobody else was listening, so subtly insulting but couched beneath layers of bonhomie, had set her teeth on edge from the very beginning. The way he crowded her space when he spoke to her, the "accidental" brushes against her breasts when no one was looking—usually followed by insincere apologies and jokes about how her chest was hard to avoid— and the times he patted her butt with seemingly casual affection. He made her skin crawl, and she avoided being alone with him as much as possible. She hated the fact that Lia was marrying him but didn't know how to verbalize how she felt.

The last time his hand lingered a little too long on her waist, she tried to confront him about it, and he had blinked at her innocently, affected surprise, and made her feel like she was reading way too much into the "affectionate" and "brotherly" pats.

"You're hardly my type, Daisy doll," he had guffawed. *"Maybe you're the one harboring less than sisterly feelings toward me. After all, it's not uncommon for a younger sister to covet what her older sister has. But I'm a taken man, sweetheart. So don't read too much into my hugs. I'm just trying to be brotherly."*

"Daisy?" She blinked in response to Mason's gentle prompt and shook her head slightly as she came back to the present. "Where'd you drift off to?"

"Nowhere. Sorry. I was just trying to think of how to describe Clayton Edmonton the Third to you."

"That's a mouthful." He chuckled, and she grinned.

"He insists on always being introduced that way."

"Well, that tells me a lot more about him than you could possibly imagine," Mason said.

"Really? Such as?"

"Such as the fact that he's a pompous ass for one." Daisy snorted in response to that, and he grinned. "Go on, tell me I'm wrong."

"I can't," she confessed with a helpless laugh. "That was pretty much spot on."

"You don't like him much."

"I don't like him at all," she corrected, and his gorgeous eyes went somber.

"Any particular reason? Aside from him being a pompous ass?"

"He's not good enough for my sister. And I'm pretty sure he'll wind up hurting her, but how do I tell her that when he's been nothing but charming and loving to her?"

"And less than charming to you." How the heck was he so astute? Or was she just that transparent? It was a little unnerving.

"Somewhat."

"In what way?"

"That doesn't matter."

"It does to me." His green eyes pinned her to the spot, and she felt unable to even blink. "And more importantly, it does to you."

"It's just little things really." She didn't want to tell him about Clayton's creepiness. What if Mason dismissed her fears as her imagination too? Clayton was good looking and successful and engaged to Daisy's very beautiful older sister. Why would he even look twice at dumpy little Daisy? So she settled for vagueness, not wanting to see the disbelief in his eyes if she told him the main reason for her dislike of Clayton. "I don't believe he'll be good to her."

"Have you tried telling Lia how you feel?"

"Yes. Both Daff and I have. But it's hard to put a damper on all that happiness. She seems genuinely in love with him, and whenever we say even the slightest negative thing about him it hurts her."

Well, Mason could kind of relate to that; after all, he'd avoided telling Spencer about his bitch ex-girlfriend for similar reasons. But then again, they'd already broken up and telling Spencer would have achieved nothing, while it seemed like Dahlia McGregor was on the verge of making the biggest mistake of her life. Mason for damned sure wouldn't have kept his mouth shut if Spencer and Tanya had stayed together.

"Okay, so the groom's a douche bag, anything else I need to know?"

"His best man, Grier Wentworth Patterson, is an elitist snob who thinks that anybody from an even slightly lower income bracket is there only to serve his drinks and pander to his needs."

"Charming."

"Most of his other groomsmen are cut from the same cloth. I met some of them at Lia's engagement party," Daisy said and tried to keep her tone neutral as she thought back to that party. Shar had let it "slip" that the guys had drawn straws to see who would be partnered with Daisy. The toxic cow had then held a hand up to her lips in faux regret and tittered that she "hadn't meant" to reveal the demeaning information. Of *course* she hadn't.

"They're all going to want to foster a friendship with you," Daisy warned, and Mason grimaced.

"What the fuck for?"

"Well, look at your résumé, Mason. From war hero"—he snorted at that, but she ignored him—"to underwear model, to bodyguard for the stars, to millionaire playboy. They'll be wetting themselves to get chummy with you."

"What? A ghetto rat like me? How goddamn flattering." He sounded anything but flattered, and Daisy bit her lips to keep from laughing at the sheer disgust that clouded his words.

"It'll do wonders for their street cred."

"Street cred? *Street cred?* What does that even mean?"

"These guys think they're God's gift, and you've become something of a celeb around these parts. They're going to want to induct you into their ranks."

"Like a cult?" he scoffed.

"Yep," Daisy affirmed with a little grin, secretly entertained by how off-putting he seemed to find the notion. She had no idea if anything she'd just said were true, but it was fun to watch him squirm.

"You're bullshitting me again, aren't you?" he asked with suspiciously narrowed eyes, and she giggled.

"Of course I am. How would I know what that sneak of weasels are thinking?"

He chuckled and then trumped her. "Don't you mean that crevice of assholes?" Her eyes widened, and she burst into laughter, immediately drawing attention to their table.

"Oh, that's good," she chortled, and he grinned again.

"I would have gone with forest of dicks, but forest sounds too damned impressive."

"A d-dribble of dicks?" she suggested, still laughing, and that set him off.

"Jesus woman, that's just *wrong!*" he chastised between hearty chuckles.

"But effective . . ."

He flashed her another one of those devastating smiles and proceeded to ask her about the other bridesmaids, her sisters, and her parents. He had such an easy manner about him, that she found herself opening up to him unreservedly, which was unusual for her. They laughed often, and Daisy knew that they gave the appearance—to anyone who happened to be observing—of a couple enjoying each other's company immensely.

"So are you busy tomorrow?"

His change in subject was so abrupt that Daisy answered without thinking. "Not really."

"Great, I'll pick you up at seven."

"Wait. What? Seven? In the morning?"

"Yeah. Dress warmly and comfortably." His words barely registered because she couldn't quite get past the time.

"The sun isn't even up at seven yet."

"Yes."

"I'll be asleep."

"No, you won't, you'll be awake, because I'll be picking you up at that time."

"Why? What could you possibly want to do that requires getting up at the butt crack of dawn on my one and only day off?"

"You'll see," he said mysteriously, and her eyes narrowed.

"I won't be able to see much of anything with my eyes closed," she groused.

"Drink lots of coffee; you'll be fine." She eyed him speculatively for a moment, wondering what he was up to. She knew that this was just another part of the pretense and knew she had to play along, but that cravenly part of her was once again pleading with her to back out. She tamped it down firmly. There would be no backing out from here on out.

She just had to keep that first night front and center when dealing with Mason. He was good at pretense, he had spent time charming her, entertaining her, making her feel liked when all he had been doing was clearing the way for his brother to flirt with her sister.

And tonight again, while Daisy had been genuinely enjoying herself, he had been putting on a show for Shar and everybody else. Which, to be fair, was exactly what Daisy had asked him to do. She just hadn't expected him to be so convincing.

"Do you want to get some dessert? Or maybe head over to Ralphie's for a drink?" Daisy was enjoying the evening so much that she hadn't even noticed she'd finished her meal and that the dinner crowd at MJ's was thinning. She cast a look around, surprised to note that the restaurant was nearly empty.

"No, I think I should head home. Especially if I have to be up in the early hours of the morning."

"It's not that bad," he chastised. She didn't respond, merely gave him a look, and he grinned.

"Trust me, you'll change your tune when you have to deal with predawn Daisy in the morning," she warned, and he chuckled before signaling Thandiwe and asking for the bill.

After he had settled their bill, waving aside any attempt from Daisy to pay half, he took her arm and led her out into the cold night air. It had stopped raining, so they had no need of the umbrella, but it was freezing cold, with a sharp, blustering wind that cut right to the bone. Still the air had that crisp, fresh after-rain smell, and Daisy inhaled deeply before settling into the car.

The drive home was short, and when they got to her place, he wordlessly got out and assisted her from the car. He tucked her hand into the crook of his elbow and led her to the front door.

As they stood in the darkened doorway, the peaceful silence shattered by Peaches's excited yapping, Daisy stared up into his unreadable features and wondered how one ended a fake date properly. Handshake? A polite thank-you and a quick escape through the door? An invitation in to coffee?

Although that last one strayed dangerously close to normal post-date behavior.

"So . . . thanks," she ventured, fumbling with her keys as she struggled to unlock the door. He took the keys from her and efficiently unlocked it for her. She took them back with another mumbled "Thanks."

"You're welcome." The words were silky and murmured directly into her ear. She hadn't known he was leaning in so close, and the feeling of his warm breath on her cold skin completely disconcerted her. Her hand dropped to the door handle as she prepared to remove herself from the uncomfortable situation. But when she tugged at the door nothing happened, and she was confused for a moment, until she looked up and saw that he had a hand flat against the wooden surface, easily preventing her from opening it.

Convinced that he didn't know that he was blocking her way in, she turned to face him and saw his teeth gleam in the pale light spilling out from her living-room windows.

"I can't open . . ." Her voice faded when he leaned in even farther, his bulk making her feel small and more than a little trapped. She tensed, her heart speeding up and accelerating her breathing in the process. What was this? If she didn't know better, she'd think he was going to kiss her, but that was a ridicu—

Her frantic thought processes ground to a screeching halt when his lips dropped to hers. It wasn't a demanding kiss—in fact, one would be hard-pressed to call it much of a kiss at all. It was just a light press of his lips on hers. Sweet, chaste, and incredibly confusing. Their lips were the only point of contact between them, and Daisy froze in shock. Not entirely sure how to respond to this.

She felt his mouth—those soft, velvety lips—stretch into a smile against hers and she resentfully wondered what he found so amusing about this. Was he making fun of her? Was this just some elaborate joke on his part?

It was her worst fear come to life. That this interesting, intelligent, likable, and very good-looking man might find her a source of amusement and pity like all of the other men around here.

His body shifted, and she went even more rigid, ready to flee if he said even one hurtful word. But all he did was bring his warm, callused hands up to cup her face. He lifted his lips, ending the passionless, innocent little kiss.

"Relax." The word brushed across her lips delicately, and her brows lowered as she pondered the gentle command. She wasn't given long to think about it before his lips were pressed to hers again, and this time there was nothing chaste or ambiguous about the kiss. It was *hungry*.

His lips parted hers, and before she knew it his tongue was there, a living, ravening thing, a restless flame, demanding more than she knew how to give. She moaned and melted against him, opening herself up to him, her own tongue tentatively stroking against his. Answering his insistent demand for more.

He groaned and his body folded around hers, pushing her against the door as her front was pressed up against his chest. She felt none of the cold winter air, and the rain—which had started up again—didn't stand a chance of touching any part of her because Mason was there, jealously hoarding her senses for himself. He was all she could see while his scent surrounded her and his warmth and hardness enveloped her, making her feel safe and protected. The rich taste of him, coffee mingled with mint, intoxicated her. And she was deaf to anything but the sound of his breathing and his soft moans.

In those long few moments, Mason Carlisle was her entire world. Nothing else existed outside the circle of his arms, and Daisy gave herself up to him entirely.

Mason knew he had to stop this. He was getting too carried away. Too wrapped up in Daisy McGregor. What a delightful little armful she was—soft, warm, and sweet-smelling—with a tart, irresistible tongue that he wouldn't mind sucking on all night long.

It was that thought—the recognition that if he did not let her go right now, he'd seduce his way into her bed—that drew him up short. He took one last, hungry taste before reluctantly easing away from her. She was trembling, which made him immensely thankful, because that meant she couldn't feel how badly he was shaking too. His hands dropped from her face, and he instantly missed the feel of her soft skin. He stepped back and put an inch of space between them and immediately sucked in a sharp breath when the frigid air intruded where before there had been only heat.

Her eyes finally opened, so huge they just about swallowed her face. "Why did you do that?"

Hell if I know, Mason thought wryly, and he stepped even farther away from her, shoving his hands into his pockets, hoping to disguise his erection but succeeding only in making himself more uncomfortable when he brushed against his primed and oversensitive cock. He bit back a curse and wasn't thinking clearly when he answered her question.

"Rehearsing." He regretted the lie the moment he said it, even more so when he saw her instant emotional retreat.

"Right." Her breathing was still unsteady, and the word sounded soft and shaky. He had hurt her.

Shit.

"Thanks for tonight. I enjoyed it." She hesitated before adding, "I mean, it went well, didn't it? Laid the foundation for the wedding and stuff."

"Yeah." And then, because he had to be honest and he couldn't leave her thinking that the whole evening had just been about their stupid charade, he said, "I enjoyed it too."

"Oh."

"So," he said, clearing his throat casually and trying to pretend his balls weren't turning an icy shade of blue. "Wear that fetching pink waterproof ensemble you had on today. And the Wellingtons are a definite requirement. Bright and early. Seven."

"Got it."

"You'd better get inside before your dog strokes out."

Finally tuning in to her surroundings once more, Daisy realized that poor Peaches's bark had ascended to a pitch high enough to break glass. She grimaced and fumbled with the doorknob again.

"Okay. Good night." She pulled the door open and retreated, shutting the door in his face just as he was saying his own good night.

Peaches went into raptures, and she absently stooped to pick up the wriggling, whimpering dog. Her face got laved, but she barely noticed as she peeked through the window and watched as Mason paused to flip up his hood before slowly ambling to his car.

She moaned and pressed her forehead against the windowpane after he drove off. She needed the shock of cold to snap her back to reality. She was going to have to be better at this. Kisses meant nothing to a sophisticated, experienced man . . . she had to develop a thicker skin and build up a tolerance to those inebriating caresses. She couldn't fall apart every time he kissed her or touched her. Their charade would call for a lot of that kind of thing over the next few weeks, and Daisy was going to have to put on her big-girl panties and deal with it.

Peaches had settled down and now lay snuggled in Daisy's arms; she breathed an occasional contented sigh, and Daisy kissed the dog's fluffy head affectionately.

Her phone beeped, and she put Peaches down to get it from her bag. It was a text from Daff: *Can we talk?*

Daisy groaned as she thought about the way she had left things with her mother and sisters earlier. She really didn't want to have this talk right now.

Tired. Tomorrow, okay?

She made her way to the bathroom to run a bath and was undressed, wearing nothing but a robe, by the time her sister responded again.

Okay. Sleep tight.

Yeah. You too. She added a smiley face to show that she wasn't angry anymore and then set her phone aside and sank into her warm, fragrant bubble bath with a sigh.

She tried to clear her mind and not to think about Mason and how much she liked him. He was doing her a massive favor, and developing a crush on the guy would only succeed in making things awkward. She wasn't a silly teenager; she could get over this.

⌒⌒

Her phone rang at six twenty the following morning, and Daisy groaned while she fumbled for it. Peaches made a protesting sound and snuggled even closer.

"Yes?" she snapped when she managed to get the thing to her ear, but it continued to ring. Aggravated, she stabbed at the screen and repeated her terse greeting.

"Rise and shine, Sleeping Beauty." She immediately recognized Mason's sexy, raspy voice.

"Oh my God," she mumbled. "What do you want? It's the middle of the night."

"It's a gorgeous day, and you're missing the best part of it." Did he have to sound so relentlessly upbeat? And what was that sound? It was loud and persistent and . . .

"It's pouring, Mason!" She held her phone away from her ear and angled it upward so that he could hear the thundering downpour. The move made no sense since he was probably well aware of the rain. She brought the phone back to her ear. "Can you hear that?"

"I can *see* it," he said, amusement lacing his voice. "I'm looking out at it from my kitchen window."

"If ever there was a day to take a rain check, this is it." She sat up in bed, ignoring Peaches's aggrieved whine, and pushed her tangled hair out of her eyes. It was still completely dark, and she had to lean over to click on the bedside lamp.

"It'll probably ease off soon."

"Mason, this rain is so epic it won't be stopping for another forty days and forty nights."

He laughed. "I'll be over at seven, see you then."

"No, Mason . . . *wait*." The absolute silence that greeted her frantic exclamation told her that he'd hung up and she tossed the phone aside and lay back down with a groan. She dragged the warm covers over her head and cuddled Peaches closer. The man was crazy. Days like these were made for lazing in bed with a good book, or getting comfy in front of the TV and binge-watching *The Walking Dead*.

Well, she had no intention of getting up until the last possible moment. By her estimation she could lay around for another twenty minutes before getting up and getting dressed.

The doorbell woke her, and she blinked in confusion before swearing when she realized that she'd fallen asleep again. Peaches was up and heading for the front door, yapping all the way, and Daisy leapt up and yelped when her feet hit the cold tiles. Jeez, she should really get some underfloor heating installed. She slid her feet into her comfy slippers and shuffled toward the front door where Peaches was putting up a tremendous fuss. She hissed at the dog to be quiet, but Peaches ignored her and continued to do her best watchdog impersonation.

A quick glance out of the front window confirmed the identity of her visitor, and she dragged open the door, only in that instant recognizing that she wasn't looking at her best.

"Seriously?" he commented drily when he saw her. Peaches appeared to recognize him and stopped barking immediately. Mason stepped into the house, smelling of wind and rain and bringing a gust of seriously cold air in with him.

"I'm sorry. I fell asleep again," she muttered defensively.

"That's not what I meant," he said. "I don't think I've ever seen an adult in a onesie." She flushed bright red. She should really have dragged on a robe before answering the door.

"It's warm," she retorted.

"It certainly looks warm," he agreed. He prowled—it was the only word she could think of to describe that predatory walk of his—toward her, and she backed up defensively, but he dodged to the left and circled around her.

"What are you doing?" she hissed, turning to face him.

"Getting the full three-sixty effect. Love the bunny tail and the matching slippers. Very *avant-garde*." She covered the tail with her hand, seriously embarrassed. She should have gotten up and dressed after his call; she had only herself to blame for this humiliation.

"I'll get dressed," she muttered, and he grinned.

"You do that. Peaches and I will make some coffee."

"Uh, do you mind letting her out into the yard; she needs to do her business."

"No worries." He stooped to pick Peaches up and ambled into the kitchen, looking way too at home for a man who had only visited once before. He made her small house feel even smaller, and she hurried into her bedroom, feeling awkward and unsure of herself.

She brushed her teeth and dressed as quickly as she could, not comfortable with the idea of him roaming around freely in her home, and when she rejoined him less than ten minutes later she scanned her living room and kitchen anxiously. Sure enough, there was a balled-up pair of socks in the corner of her sofa and—worse, *so* much worse—a bra draped over the back of the same sofa. The very piece of furniture on which Mason had chosen to make himself comfortable, and if his self-satisfied grin was any indication, he had placed himself there deliberately.

He had one arm stretched out on the back of the sofa—his long, elegant fingers inches away from her lacy pink bra—with an ankle crossed over his knee and a mug of steaming hot, deliciously fragrant coffee resting on one hard, denim-clad thigh. God, he was absolutely gorgeous as he sat sprawled on her couch looking way too confident and way too sexy.

She watched as his fingers began to tap rhythmically against the upholstered fabric of the sofa, and her eyes darted up to meet his. His grin widened. He seemed to know that her gut reaction was to snatch up her underwear, and his eyes were challenging her.

"The coffee smells good," she said, striving for insouciance and failing.

"Plenty more where this came from," he said, nodding toward her kitchen, and she headed for the coffeemaker and poured a mug of the rich brew while she told herself that it was *just* a bra. Mason had surely seen more than his fair share over the years. Still, she was sure he was used to dainty little A cups. Hers were C heading into D territory, embarrassingly big for someone of her height. At times she looked and felt like an overstuffed pigeon.

"So, what's the plan?" she asked, taking an appreciative sip of the fabulous coffee. Why couldn't she ever seem to get her coffee to taste like this? She very carefully sat down on the edge of the couch, putting as much space between them as possible, while desperately trying to figure out how to remove her bra from his line of sight.

Mason could tell how much Daisy longed to snatch up her pretty pink bra, but to her credit she was doing an admirable job of restraining herself. She was trying very hard to be casual about it, but her fiery blush betrayed her, as well as the constant shift of her eyes back to the fetchingly draped undergarment. She would be horrified to know that he had picked it up from the seat, catching a whiff of her sensual fragrance as he did so, and arranged it over the back of the sofa, fully intending to unsettle her. She was charmingly easy to embarrass. Most women wouldn't be at all perturbed by something as innocuous as a bra on display, but Daisy McGregor had enchanting old-world sensibilities, and Mason was enjoying them to the fullest.

"Before I answer that," he murmured, "I want to know what *those* are." He nodded toward a small display cabinet in the corner. It was filled with the oddest collection of ornaments. Weird little caterpillars: glass, ceramic, porcelain, wood, and plastic worms. Most were dressed like people, tiny wormy people smoking pipes, reading books, even dancing. It was more than a little strange.

"My caterpillars," she supplied awkwardly.

"What are they for?"

"I collect them."

"Why?"

"Because I like caterpillars. I started collecting when I was thirteen, and honestly . . . I think I actually bought only twenty of them myself." Twenty too many, if you asked Mason. "The rest are gifts from family and friends." Jesus, there were well over a hundred creepy little people caterpillars in that cabinet. Talk about enabling someone, her family took the cake.

"So where are we going?" she asked, deliberately shifting the topic back to what it was before, and recognizing the stubborn glint in her eyes, Mason allowed it. The caterpillars were a bit out there for him, and he was happy to let it go.

"You don't want to be surprised?" he asked, answering her question with one of his own, and if her narrowing eyes were any indication, she didn't appreciate his evasiveness.

"I don't really care for surprises."

"You don't? That's too bad. What if I told you I had a surprise for you in my pocket?" Her eyes widened, and she made an incredulous half-laughing, half-snorting sound as her gaze drifted south. Mason burst into laughter as she projected her thoughts as clear as a bell. His laughter startled her eyes back to his, and he grinned at her.

"*Not* the pocket I meant, but I like the way you think," he teased and watched as her face did that slow burn thing again. He patted his chest, and her eyes were drawn to the breast pocket of his plaid flannel shirt. "This pocket."

She seemed to forget her embarrassment as her eyes flared with interest.

"What kind of surprise?" she asked, her voice steeped in skepticism.

"The good kind." Her teeth worried her succulent-looking lower lip while she eyed his pocket with a mixture of wariness and curiosity. God, that lip . . . the more she nibbled at it the fuller, pinker, and more moist it became. He longed for another taste of those plump lips but viciously tamped down the urge to drag her into his arms and kiss the holy hell out of her.

"Show me," she said, after a great deal of deliberation. He leaned toward her, close enough to smell the fresh fragrance of her shampoo.

"Come and get it." He expected her to retreat at the challenge, but she surprised him when—after one last nervous nibble at her lips—she reached out toward his pocket. His breath snagged and his heart stuttered in his chest when he felt her questing fingers hesitantly dip into his pocket. The first tentative foray didn't yield any results, and she dug in a little deeper, creating friction on his hypersensitive nipple. He unsuccessfully bit back a groan, and her eyes snapped up to his, her face so close he could count each individual freckle on her nose and see the pale-blue striations in her gray eyes. He shifted his coffee mug a little to the left in an effort to conceal the growing bulge in the crotch of his jeans and fought to keep his face impassive and his breathing even. Her eyes dropped from his, back to where her small hand was fumbling around in his pocket, and the tip of her tongue crept out as she focused on what she was doing. There was an adorable little wrinkle of concentration between her eyes as she managed to snag what was in his pocket, only to drop it again. She finally managed to get a proper grip on it and dragged it out with a triumphant whoop.

Daisy stared down at the item in her palm in confusion. She still felt hot and flustered by his nearness and that damned delicious scent of his, so her brain was a bit delayed, but she couldn't for the life of her figure out what it was she had in her hand. It looked like an earring, a really ugly earring. It was spherical in shape, weighty, and seemed to be made of lead. She turned it over and bent her head to examine it more closely.

"It's a sinker." Mason's warm breath stirred her hair as he spoke, and she repressed a shiver at the intimate sensation.

"What do you use it for?"

"Fishing."

"Fishing for what?" she asked stupidly and looked up just in time to catch a grin flirting with the corners of his mouth.

"For fish."

"I don't . . ." Her words faded as comprehension dawned and horror replaced confusion. "No."

"The blacktail are really biting at *Kleinbekkie* this week," he said, and his complete butchering of the Afrikaans word, which meant "small mouth," momentarily distracted Daisy. It was endearing how bad the pronunciation was, and she guessed his grasp of the language was probably as terrible as hers. *Kleinbekkie* was the smaller river mouth just outside town, and it was a popular local spot for fishing, picnicking, and surfing. "I thought we could catch some for lunch."

"No. This is why I hate surprises, see? This is the worst surprise ever."

"It's actually more an IOU at this point," he confessed, and she glared at him. He wrong-footed her at every turn, and she had given up on understanding him.

"What?"

"You're right, the weather is too damned terrible for fishing today. I was hoping it'd clear up a little overnight, but—while *I* wouldn't mind going out there today—it's not ideal for a novice. So I figure we'd take a rain check on the fishing and do it some other time."

"Try never."

"Come on, Daisy, you'll like it."

"Doubtful. And if you knew the weather was too bad for fishing, why did you drag me out of bed at this ungodly hour anyway?"

"I thought we could do something else."

"Like what?"

"Dunno."

"You're a very frustrating man."

"So I've been told. What do you want to do today? And don't say go back to bed."

"Well, I'm awake now, aren't I?" she pointed out huffily.

"Want to go somewhere for breakfast?"

"Nothing's open yet," she groused, and he shrugged.

"Not here, but I know this great place about forty minutes away."

"That's pretty far; if we just waited forty minutes, we could go to MJ's."

"We were at MJ's last night." He looked a little annoyed by her suggestion, but Daisy definitely did not want to be confined in a car with him for that long. Not with the crazy awareness and tension simmering between them. Okay, so the tension and awareness were probably totally one-sided, but why put herself through unnecessary stress?

"I thought the point was to be seen around town together."

"People will see us coming and going together, and they'll wonder. *That* is the point. We want them to speculate. If we're always out at MJ's putting on a performance, it'll start to look unnatural."

"I suppose you're right," she conceded, and he reached over to tweak a curl, but his hand lingered and he wrapped one of the strands around his finger, his knuckles brushing across her cheekbone in the process. She stilled at his touch, telling herself that it wasn't a big deal. Still, the gesture felt alarmingly intimate, and he must have thought so too because he quickly withdrew his hand and resumed tapping the back of the sofa.

"Trust me, Daisy."

"I'm trying."

They were quiet for a long moment, the only sounds coming from the howling wind and rain outside and Peaches's light snoring from one of the armchairs. Daisy finished her coffee as quickly as she could and reached out to take his empty mug before getting up to carry them to the kitchen. In the process she "accidentally" pushed her bra off the back off the couch. She ignored Mason's knowing chuckle and rounded the couch to pick up the bra before retreating to the kitchen with mugs and underwear safely in hand.

"We should hit the road soon," he said, stretching lazily as he spoke, and she nodded, shoving her bra into the junk drawer to retrieve later, before rinsing the mugs. "I hope you're not scared of bikes," he said, as he leapt agilely to his feet. Daisy paused in the act of drying her hands on a tea towel and stared at him in dismay.

"What?"

"Motorbikes. I hope you're not . . ." His voice tapered off, and a snort escaped. His shoulders started shaking before he started to guffaw, huge "heeyucks" that had him folding his arms over his middle and doubling over. If he started slapping his thighs, Daisy would have to find a way to comprehensively kick his ass. "You . . . you should see your face."

"Glad I amuse you," she said stiffly. Not like she hadn't been the butt of someone's stupid joke before. He sobered almost immediately and took a couple of steps toward her.

"Hey, come on. I wasn't . . ."

"I take it you weren't dumb enough to ride a motorcycle in this weather?" she asked, and he shook his head.

"Daisy." He lifted a hand as if to touch her, but she stepped out of reach and turned away.

"I just have to see to Peaches's food. Feel free to wait in the car."

"Daisy, come on . . ."

—

Shit. He hadn't meant to offend her; he just liked her prickly and prim reactions sometimes. But this wasn't prickly or prim; this was something else. He'd hurt her . . . *again.* And he wasn't entirely sure how. He watched her gracefully move around the tiny confines of her kitchen and felt awkward as hell. Did he really need this kind of grief in his life? Why the hell was he putting up with her shit anyway? He couldn't figure it out. He couldn't figure *her* out.

"Look, I was joking, okay? I didn't mean to offend you or upset you." She stopped moving, her back still to him, and sighed before throwing back her head and staring up at the ceiling. For some kind of divine intervention perhaps? Who knew with her?

She turned to face him, her pretty eyes strained.

"I may have overreacted a bit, it's just . . ." She paused, and he gritted his teeth in exasperation.

Just what? Jesus, and she called him frustrating.

"I've been the butt of someone's joke too many times to count."

"Oh." *Oh.* Fuck.

"I'm stupidly oversensitive sometimes. I just thought you were . . ." *Different.* She didn't have to say it. The unspoken word hovered between them, and Mason swore beneath his breath.

"I'm an asshole," he muttered, trying—and failing—to keep the defensive tone out of his voice. "I told you that last night. But in this case the assholery was unintentional. Daisy, I didn't mean to make you the butt of my lame joke. I enjoy your reaction to my teasing; you're cute when you get all grumpy and righteously indignant."

Her eyebrows furrowed. "So the fishing thing wasn't serious?"

"Nope. That was totally serious. We're going fishing as soon as the weather clears."

"But *why?*"

"Because I think you'd like it. And when we go camping, you and Peaches will love roughing it in the wilderness." Her eyes widened, but something in his expression must have clued her in because her face cleared almost immediately.

"You're teasing me again. Right?"

"Only partly. No way in hell will we be taking Peaches camping with us." Another small frown from her, but by this time he was openly grinning, and a shy, sweet smile blossomed at the corners of her mouth.

"Stop that," she grumbled good-naturedly.

"Now you're getting it, babe."

They left a few minutes later, and despite knowing that he'd only been pulling her leg earlier, Daisy was relieved to note that he had indeed arrived by car. The BMW. He wrapped a protective arm around her shoulders as he hustled her to the car, keeping her shielded from the wind as he opened the door for her.

"Hell of a day," he said breathlessly when he slammed his way into the driver's seat. He switched on the ignition, and she winced when hard rock immediately blasted from the speakers. It was so loud, she could practically see the windows vibrate.

"Shit. Sorry." He turned down the sound to a less glass-shattering setting, and she was able to recognize the guitar solo from Lynyrd Skynyrd's "Free Bird." The guy had good taste. "You can change the playlist if you want to."

"That would be sacrilegious!"

He shot her a shocked glance before refocusing his attention to the road. "You appreciate a bit of classic rock, then?"

"Who doesn't like 'Free Bird'?"

"Only all of my ex–lady friends. I think it was a little too old for them."

"Great music never ages. Pick your ladies more carefully next time," she advised. She curled up in the huge seat and gazed out as they passed through Main Street. It was after eight by now, and most of the businesses were just opening. She spotted a few familiar faces, and Mason was driving well below the speed limit, which allowed pedestrians to pause and admire his car before glancing up to check out the occupants. Luckily the rain had let up enough to allow them all a good, long look. She grinned and waved saucily at a few of the stunned faces that recognized her.

"Having fun?" Mason asked, and she nodded enthusiastically.

"This is awesome. I feel like passing royalty or something. Oh, that's Mrs. Turlington," she said, giving a happy little squeak when she spotted the town's most notorious gossip. "This will be all over town by lunchtime. This was a great idea, Mason."

"Glad you're finally developing an appreciation for my genius," he said with a self-satisfied grin, and she rolled her eyes.

"Wipe the smug off your face, mister. It doesn't become you." He laughed outright at that, and as they reached the end of Main Street, he revved the engine a bit before picking up speed and leaving Riversend behind.

CHAPTER SIX

Mason snuck a few glances at Daisy's profile as she stared out at the scenery. She was surprisingly familiar with a lot of the older songs on his playlist. She occasionally hummed along and seemed to have a preference for the Queen ballads. Mason had a hard time keeping a straight face when she unexpectedly belted out a hilariously off-key accompaniment to "Bohemian Rhapsody," complete with screeching guitar solos and all. He didn't even know if she was aware of it—but it was fucking adorable. When Prince's "Purple Rain" came up, she bounced excitedly in her seat and looked at him.

"I love this song!" And once again with the off-key lyrics. This time, Mason joined in, leaving his inhibitions on the side of the road and enjoying himself thoroughly in the process. He never sang along with his tunes, preferring to just listen and enjoy . . . but as he sang, his voice sounding rustier than a two-hundred-year-old nail, he found a freedom of spirit that he couldn't recall ever having before.

—

"This is so wonderful. I never knew it was here." Daisy stared out at the rustic log cabin tucked away in the forest like a perfect little fairy-tale cottage. It even had smoke curling from a fieldstone chimney. If not for the discreet sign above the door—"Le Café de la Forêt"—she would have thought it was a private residence instead of a restaurant.

"It's a bit out of the way, usually only frequented by hikers and campers."

"Is that how you know about it?"

"Nah, an old buddy of mine owns it."

"Army buddy?"

"No." Daisy was fascinated by the tinge of red suddenly highlighting his sharp cheekbones. "Modeling buddy."

"I didn't know one made *buddies* in the modeling industry. I always imagined it being quite cutthroat."

"Nah, the male modeling industry is just one happy family of outstandingly good-looking guys. All getting along, bromancing or romancing—depending on one's proclivities—having sing-alongs and danceathons. It's awesome, nothing cutthroat about it at all." He unbuckled his seat belt as he spoke, ignoring Daisy's helpless giggles, and reached over to unbuckle hers as well.

"Come on, you're going to love Chris, he's an awesome guy and a freaking great chef."

"He's a chef?"

"He was modeling to pay for culinary school." He exited the car and rounded the front to open the door for her. She still couldn't get used to that, and when he held out his hand, she couldn't do anything but place hers in it. She tried—unsuccessfully—to gracefully swing her legs out of the car, and he assisted her with the gentlest of tugs.

He didn't let go of her hand once she was out and instead tucked it into his elbow as he led her to the front door of the picturesque cabin. The rain had let up a great deal since that morning, and it was drizzling slightly, creating havoc with her curly hair by frizzing it uncontrollably.

Her glasses steamed up when they stepped into the warm, rustic interior of the restaurant, and Daisy inhaled appreciatively. The place smelled of baked bread. It was warm and homey, and she immediately loved it.

"Do my eyes deceive me?" a deep male voice boomed dramatically, and they turned to face the most amazing-looking man Daisy had ever seen in her life.

"Close your mouth, Daisy," Mason instructed mildly. He reached out, gripped her chin between his thumb and forefinger, and gently shut her gaping mouth.

"Mason Carlisle, *mon ami*! What a pleasure this is," the tall, well-built, beautiful man with absolutely perfect facial bone structure said. Straight nose, sharp cheekbones, luscious mouth, chiseled jaw, and intense eyes, combined with absolutely flawless ebony skin. His shaved head just made him look even more classically beautiful. For a man like this to be hidden away in such an isolated place seemed a total waste.

"You're . . ." Her voice failed her, and she cleared her throat and tried again. "You're Christién." Of course she recognized him. He had been the male equivalent of a supermodel, and to find him here, practically in her backyard, was just surreal.

"Ah *oui*. I am. And who are you, *ma petite*?" His French accent was so sexy. He was Congolese, she remembered reading that somewhere. She wondered how he had wound up in this tiny corner of Africa. She would have expected him to live in Paris or Milan or somewhere equally cosmopolitan.

"I'm, uh . . . I . . ."

"This is Daisy McGregor."

"You're as pretty and fresh as the flower you are named after, *ma belle*." Daisy giggled like a giddy teen. The sound was so bubbly and adolescent it completely threw her, and a self-conscious hand flew up to her mouth as if to force the foolish sound back in. Mason's face was completely unreadable. Nothing there, not even the constant little amused smirk that he usually wore around her. He always looked like

115

he found her endlessly entertaining. She hadn't really known that until she now noticed its absence.

"Mason, it's been months, nearly a year, if memory serves." He then launched into some excitable French, and Mason completely stunned Daisy by responding in the same language. She hadn't known that he was multilingual. Then again, there was so much that was still a mystery about the man, and for all his seemingly laid-back attitude around her, she didn't think he'd be very forthcoming about his private life and past. Not with her. Their relationship wasn't the kind to inspire confidences from him.

"But we are being rude. Forgive us, *ma petite*." Christién suddenly switched back to English, and taking Daisy by complete surprise, he placed his hands on her shoulders and tugged her toward him to plant a kiss on each cheek.

Whoa! He smelled almost as good as Mason.

"This is the way of friends who have not seen each other for many months. But I have a new friend now. *Oui?* Come, sit. You must eat. You have the glorious look of a woman who enjoys her food very much, *non?*" The observation, coming from anybody else, would have been considered an insult. But Christién said it in such an overtly admiring voice that it couldn't be construed as anything other than a compliment.

The place was empty, which was unsurprising, considering how far away from everything it was. And since it wasn't advertised anywhere that Daisy knew of, she immediately worried about the economic viability of Christién's business.

He ushered them to a gorgeously crafted round wooden table, with padded spindly-legged chairs. The place was beautifully furnished. All the woodwork was stunning and obviously bespoke. More people should know about this place.

As she sat down, she reached for the beautifully bound menu, but Christién snatched it away.

"*Non.* You will eat a special meal. Nothing you can find on this common menu." She doubted very much that there was anything remotely common on that menu, but she allowed him to take the decision from her. Mason was watching her keenly, that inscrutable expression still on his face, and his intense stare was starting to make her uncomfortable. Christién ensured that they were warm, promised to be back with something to drink, and left them abruptly alone.

"I love it here." She sighed, breaking the long and awkward silence that had descended over their table. Mason made a noncommittal sound and toyed with the place settings.

Daisy's fingers absently traced over the detailed scrollwork carved into the wood, and his eyes dropped to watch the movement, his gaze disturbingly intense.

"So your buddy is pretty famous," she observed, her voice laced with amusement, and Mason shrugged.

"You seem a little starstruck."

"Well. The guy's a supermodel. Wasn't he voted the sexiest man alive like three years in a row? And he modeled for Calvin Klein, Alexander McQ—"

"I'm aware of his résumé," Mason interrupted. "I just didn't think it was the type of thing you'd be conversant with."

"Why? Because I'm not a fashion plate and outstanding beauty like my sisters?" The words were defensive, and Mason sighed.

"No. Because it's a lifestyle I figured you'd find frivolous and beneath you."

What?

"I'm not sure I understand."

"You're an educated woman, you have a proper career. I just thought you had weightier things to think about than models and stuff." The last word trailed off self-consciously as Daisy gaped at him in absolute astonishment. "Daisy, you're the smartest woman I've ever dated. You're not like the others, who would get giddy over shallow shit like this."

"We're not dating," she said, a little astounded that she had to actually remind him of that fact.

"You know what I mean."

"I'm not entirely sure I do."

⌁

Mason wasn't sure he knew what he meant either. He had just been weirdly disappointed when Daisy had not only immediately recognized Chris but had instantly started fangirling over him. It didn't fit with his image of her. She was the brainy girl; she was supposed to be better than that. She shouldn't care about superficial crap like this, and yet she'd been nearly speechless at the sight of Chris. He definitely didn't like the way she had gone gaga over the other guy. Mason liked how slightly in awe of him Daisy always seemed. He thought back to the obvious little crush she seemed to have on him that first night before she had discovered the truth. He'd enjoyed her fascination, even though he had known it wasn't something he could encourage. Still, to now see some of that infatuation transferred onto Chris stung . . . more than a little. He wanted her attention and focus on him alone.

"Never mind," he dismissed, his voice rough, and he cleared his throat self-consciously. "It's not important."

"So you and Chris worked together?"

"Not at all. He did a lot of the catwalk stuff. Very much in demand because of that flawless bone structure and skin of his. He was in the big leagues, and I was small fry. I modeled mostly body shots for catalogs and magazines. I was shamelessly used for my hot bod. This mug of mine wasn't special enough for anything else."

⌁

He rubbed a rueful hand over his square, stubbled jaw as he spoke, and Daisy had a hard time believing there was anybody out there who didn't think he was absolutely stunning. Sure, Christién was gorgeous, but Mason had a rugged masculine appeal that the other man, with his too-perfect features, was lacking. While she could stare at Christién all day, Mason was the one who made her feel weak-kneed and hot under the collar. Not that she would ever reveal that fact.

"Chris and I ran in the same circles, and at one point were rivals for the same woman."

"Ah, the beautiful and talented Gigi," Christién supplied as he placed a couple of steaming mugs of something delicious-smelling in front of them. Daisy wrapped her cold hands around the hot mug and inhaled deeply. She could smell both cinnamon and chocolate infused with something else.

"Drink up, *ma petite fleur*. It is my own recipe. You won't be disappointed. So, Mason was telling you about the time we were both infatuated with Gigi?" He clutched a hand to his chest and sighed, the sound steeped with longing and tinged with more than a little melodrama. "Gigi. So beautiful and so treacherous. She loved having us compete for her affections, and in the end, after we were like snarling dogs after the same bitch, she threw us over for a woman."

Mason chuckled, took a sip of his drink, and then shut his eyes as he savored the taste.

"Chris and I found ourselves in the same little *osteria* in Milan, nursing our wounded egos at the bar," he said. "We started talking and discovered how much we actually had in common. We've been friends ever since."

Daisy made a noncommittal sound, dying to ask for details. He'd revealed so much and yet so little. What exactly did the two men have in common? Other than similar tastes in women and a background in modeling? She was desperate to ask but not sure she had any right to the information. She took a sip of the hot drink and moaned involuntarily. Gosh, it was good.

"This is delicious." Chris gave her a smug grin, and after thumping Mason on the back, he excused himself to prepare their meal.

"Why did you decide to stop modeling?" Daisy asked, deciding to leave the topic of women and vice behind.

"I think the more pertinent question is why did I start," he corrected. When he didn't elaborate, she felt compelled to prompt him for more.

"Well? Why did you start modeling, then?"

"It was just after I'd left the army. I was bumming around, feeling a little disconnected from civil society. Everybody else seemed so . . . normal. And I wasn't. I was staying with a friend, sleeping on a mattress in his living room, doing the odd job here and there. The plan was to join the army, see the world, get a degree on their dime. The reality was, I saw the worst of the world, and I didn't have time to get that degree because it turned out that I had *other* more valuable skills and the army wanted me to hone those particular talents before anything else. So I gained a skill set that was useless in normal life and that put me in pretty much the same boat I was in before I left Riversend. Waiting tables. Doing delivery work. Odd jobs. I was working at a trendy restaurant in Soho when an older guy slid his card across the table and told me to contact him if I ever got sick of waiting tables."

He shook his head and laughed in a self-deprecating way before raising his eyes to meet hers. Daisy was completely riveted by his story and trapped beneath that piercing gaze.

"I thought he was hitting on me. I'd had a few guys offer me money to suck their co—" He coughed, catching himself before saying the word. "Sorry. Anyway, a few older guys offered me money to do stuff with them. Older women too. And I would have dismissed Bernie as just another one of those guys, if one of the waitresses hadn't spotted him giving me the card. She told me that he was a big deal in the modeling industry and that I should follow up and see what he had to say. I called him the next day, and he asked me to come to his office and lined up a few jobs almost immediately." He shifted his broad shoulders awkwardly. "Modeling never sat well with me. It's not my kind of thing. But within three months the money made it worth my while. Like I said, I was never in Chris's league. But I did all right."

He had done more than "all right." Daisy had seen him in so many magazines and advertisements during that year. Prominent brand names in some of the bigger fashion publications. He was being modest, and she knew it was because that chapter of his life embarrassed him. Which was ridiculous when he had been such a success at something he'd essentially been half-assing. In truth, Daisy didn't think the man had ever experienced real failure. Everything he decided to do, he excelled at. Which was rather extraordinary for a guy who came from such humble beginnings.

"And how did you get into the bodyguarding business?" She propped her elbows on the table and rested her chin in the palms of her hands, wriggling a little in her chair to get comfier.

"I went to an industry party. Lots of rich and famous around, and I spotted one of my buddies." He grinned. "Army this time. He was shadowing this old lady. At first I thought he'd got himself a sugar mama, but there was something in his stance that made me pause. There's a thing we do—soldiers, that is—when we first walk into a room. We assess. We look for potential threats, exits, barricades, anything that can help us if the shit hits the fan. It's instinctive. But Sam was doing more than that; he looked like he was on active duty. He never once relaxed. He noticed me immediately, of course, acknowledged me with a nod, and then went back to hulking over his little, old—obviously stinking rich—lady."

"Sam Brand, right? Your business partner?" Daisy breathed. He gave her a speculative look.

"You know a lot about me." Daisy fought back her blush as she considered her response to that observation. She stuck with mostly the truth.

"Just what I've read in the tabloids. Besides, it's *Sam Brand*." She put enough awe into her voice to divert him from the truth, and he glared at her.

"I'm starting to think you're just using me to get to my friends."

"Well, can you blame me? Have you looked at them lately?"

"They're just guys. Besides . . . Sam's gay."

"Really?" Surprise made her almost shout the word, and Mason sighed before moving his shoulders uncomfortably.

"No. Not really," he admitted with a wry grin. "He's as straight as an arrow. But you'd hate him. He's a prick with women."

"It's not like I'm ever going to meet him. So I'm allowed to fantasize."

"Here we go with the fantasies again. What's he doing? Standing around, flexing his muscles?"

Affronted, Daisy said the first thing that popped into her head. "Nope, he's doing that slow strip tease we talked about last night . . ."

"Unoriginal." Mason scoffed. "The bastard's stealing my sexy moves."

"And," Daisy inserted loudly, while holding up a finger to shut him up, "I'm mirroring his every move! His top comes off . . . *my* top comes off. His pants for my skirt. His socks, my bra!"

Mason knew she was being the Daisy equivalent of risqué, and he found her sweet for trying, but he was more than happy to seize control of the conversation again.

"Yeah? A pink bra? Lacy?" She knew exactly what he was referring to, he could see it in the embarrassed wash of color high on her cheek-bones as well as the increased pace of her breathing.

"No. Not like that at all. Pink is much too girlish and innocent for the occasion. This one is black, with red lace, made not for support but for seduction."

And just like that, little Daisy McGregor felled him. The thought of her full breasts straining against the confines of a sexy, barely there bra was ridiculously hot. He could picture the soft, pretty mounds overflowing at the top, eager to be released, quivering and ready to spill into some lucky bastard's willing hands. Pink tips distended and begging to be tasted.

Kissed. Licked. Suckled.

Mason was hard in seconds, and his own breath came in jagged pants as he fought to bring himself back under control.

"Matching panties, of course. With little red bows at the sides." He bit back a groan at her words. The woman was killing him. She was utterly destroying him, while casually swinging her feet back and forth like a schoolgirl and taking appreciative sips from her warm drink. The higher-than-usual pitch of her voice and her slight breathlessness were the only indications that she wasn't comfortable with this role of femme fatale and that the whole conversation was well outside of her comfort zone.

Despite that—or maybe because of it—her words were a huge turn-on. Largely innocuous though they were. It was Mason's own imagination, filling in the blanks, that was doing the real damage here. If she knew the thoughts racing through his mind right now, she'd bolt. So he did his level best to even out his breath and slouch even further down in his chair in an effort to conceal yet another hard-on.

It was becoming an embarrassing habit by now.

"Well, hell, we're going to have to start calling you Dirty Doctor Daisy from now on." He grinned lazily. "Your fantasies are showing some improvement. Definitely heading into PG-13 territory."

To his own ears, his voice sounded strained, but she huffed and tossed a napkin at him, clearly not finding anything amiss. He deftly caught the napkin and leaned forward to pinch her cheek, like some creepy affectionate uncle. He had to keep her oblivious to his inconvenient attraction to her. If she knew about it, and he acted on it, she would wind up getting hurt. Sex for her would be an emotional act; for Mason it was a basic animal need. He would break her heart, and Mason didn't think he'd be able to handle the massive amount of guilt that would go hand in hand with breaking her heart.

"So what happened after the party?" she asked, and he frowned, confused.

"What?"

"After you saw Sam Brand with the old lady?"

"Oh." Shit, that conversation felt like forever ago. He'd forgotten that her fantasy was supposedly constructed around Sam Brand, and suddenly he fucking hated the thought of her fantasizing about taking off her clothes for Sam.

Logically he knew the whole thing had been made up on the spot, but the fact that Sam was the leading man in that little scenario made Mason feel downright murderous. He picked up his mug, viciously controlling the slight shake in his hand, and took a measured sip of the rapidly cooling drink, desperate to get his thoughts in order before replying to her question.

"Sam called me the next day, gave me some shtick about prancing around in my underwear, before telling me that he was working for a personal protection company. He didn't agree with some of the company policies and was thinking of branching out on his own. Wanted to know if I would consider giving up my pretty-boy gig for some real men's work."

He snorted at that last thought. *Men's work.* The four badass women they employed would happily—and efficiently—kick Sam's ass if he ever said anything like that in their presence.

"I said yes so fast I nearly sprained my tongue. We went into the business as full partners. Luckily, both Sam and I had connections—Sam from his previous jobs and me from the modeling industry—and built a client base from there. We had a staff of twenty elite close protection officers in a year and became a recognized and trusted brand within eighteen months."

He shifted his shoulders; he wasn't comfortable talking about himself, but Daisy had once again dropped her chin into her palms and was staring up at him over the tops of her glasses. She looked like a curious little owl, with her hair haloing wildly around her face, and despite the distinct lack of anything seductive in the pose or in her expression, Mason crazily wanted to kiss her again.

Maybe it was because she looked so damned interested in everything he had to say. It was flattering. Intelligent women like her tended to put him into one of two categories: dumb jock only good for a fuck, or arm candy . . . only good for a fuck. He was accustomed to being overlooked and underestimated. He was often dismissed as nothing more than a good-looking, brainless slab of muscle, a henchman to keep the bad guys at bay. Clients appreciated his appearance because the wealthy liked to surround themselves with beautiful things, and that was all he'd been to them: a functional ornament, there to look pretty but be scary. He sure as hell hadn't minded the no-strings sex that came along with the territory. Clients were strictly off limits, of course, but their friends most definitely were not.

Still, it had rankled to be dismissed as nothing more than a moron with big muscles and a low IQ.

"*Gorgeous, isn't he? Poor dear is frightfully good looking but unfortunately quite dull-witted. Then again, it doesn't take much brainpower to jump in front of a bullet, does it?*" That comment, from an aging pop diva, still stung, and it hadn't even been close to the worst he'd heard. But he'd been starstruck when he met her and disillusioned very soon afterward.

"Why do you want to know all of this anyway?" Irritated by his lapse into melancholia, the question came out a bit more abruptly than he intended. "We're supposed to be focusing on you and the wedding stuff."

"Isn't it better if we each know something about the other? More believable?"

Yeah, that made sense. And kind of disappointed him a little. He wanted her interest to be genuine, and wasn't that just perverse as hell?

Get it together, douche bag! the general in his head commanded.

"I suppose you're right. But seriously, enough about me. Tell me more about you."

"We covered that last night."

"Surely there's a lot more to know about you?"

"I'm pretty boring," she said with a self-deprecating grin. "I knit in front of the TV on Friday nights. Nothing earth-shattering there. You're the one who has partied with princesses and politicians."

"Hardly partied. That was all work."

"Even the modeling parties?"

"Especially those." He grimaced as he recalled that scene. Sex, drugs, alcohol . . . and a shitload more drama than a frickin' telenovela. While he was modeling *he* might as well have spent his Friday night knitting in front of the TV, he had been that far removed from the party scene. The only reason he had been at that party, the night he'd reconnected with Sam, was because Chris had needed . . . He nearly choked back a laugh as he remembered. Chris had needed a wingman.

Because, of course he had.

As if on cue, Chris bustled back with a basket full of freshly baked, delicious-smelling bread, which he placed on the table between them. Daisy's eyelids slid to half-mast, and she moaned as the warm, tantalizing aroma drifted upward. She reached for a slice and bit right into it.

"Oh my God, this is amazing," she said around a mouthful of bread, and Mason grinned at the lack of artifice. He grabbed her hand and pulled it toward him and tugged the remaining piece of bread from her fingers. With his teeth. He didn't really think about the intimacy of the impulsive act until his lips brushed against the tips of her fingers.

And then he couldn't prevent himself from compounding the colossal error in judgment by giving her skin the tiniest of flicks with his tongue.

—

Daisy snatched her hand out of his hold, folded it into a defensive fist, and cupped her other hand over it, cradling her fist to her chest like an injured bird.

Chris whistled slowly before pointedly retreating.

"Don't *do* things like that," Daisy hissed, and Mason shrugged, his expression maddeningly unperturbed.

"I just wanted a taste of the bread," he explained, and she glared at him.

"There's a basketful of the stuff right in front of you. I'm placing a moratorium on all the pretend PDA when we don't have an audience. And while we're at it, I want no more of that practice kissing either."

His hand hovered above the breadbasket as he perused what was on offer, taking his time with his selection while he kept her waiting for his response. He finally chose a slice exactly like every other slice in the basket and methodically ripped it apart, dipping chunks into the provided assorted preserves.

"You want this all to look good when it comes to showtime, right?" he asked between bites.

"It's making me uncomfortable," she confessed without thinking. Her words stilled his hands, and he gazed at her for a long moment.

"I make you uncomfortable?"

"The situation does. And the touching . . . and stuff." Her voice petered out, and she cleared her throat awkwardly. His eyes narrowed as he kept her pinned beneath his gaze for a moment longer.

"I'm a tactile guy. It's natural for me to casually touch someone when I'm talking to them."

"It is?"

No. It was complete bullshit. He didn't go around sucking people's fingers, or brushing his knuckles against their cheekbones . . . he wasn't wired that way, but he could think of no other way to divert her from the fact that he was a touchy-feely fucker around her. And her alone. How could he explain that to her when he couldn't make sense of it to himself?

"I'll try to curb my natural instincts. But I can't make any promises. It's what you signed up for when you asked me to be your fake boyfriend."

"Fake date. Not fake boyfriend. There's a difference."

"Other people won't see it that way. If they're not used to seeing you date, they're going to assume that this is serious between us."

"What makes you think they're not used to seeing me date?"

"Oh, I don't know, maybe the fact that you've roped me into doing this for you?" Her teeth nibbled at her soft lower lip as she considered her words. Mason's eyes dropped to that lip; her teeth were making little white crescents in the soft flesh, which almost immediately darkened into a deeper shade of red when the teeth moved on to a different location. It was distracting as hell, the tug and release of her teeth on that soft, juicy-looking lip. How was he supposed to concentrate on this conversation when she was doing that?

"Stop that!" Daisy jumped at the sudden harshness in Mason's voice. Why did he look and sound so angry?

"What?"

He reached over and *shockingly* dragged his thumb down over her lower lip, tugging it from between her teeth and brushing the pad of his thumb over the sensitive surface.

"Stop biting your lip."

"It's a nervous habit."

"I make you nervous?" His brows slammed together, making him look even scarier, and she shook her head.

"No. Yes . . . I mean, maybe a little." He reached over again and his thumb gently rubbed back and forth across the surface of her bottom lip, one end to the other, and it felt . . . much too good. For a brief, crazy second she leaned in to his touch before sanity reasserted itself and she pulled her head back and out of reach.

She sucked her lip into her mouth, trying to rid herself of the residual sensation of his rough thumb so gently caressing her skin.

"Don't do that again." Her voice was a hoarse whisper, devoid of the commanding edge she'd hoped for.

"I can't make any promises," he muttered, and she sighed impatiently. He was just being difficult again. "I start having X-rated visions when you do that thing with your mouth."

"Stop being a smart-ass, Mason. I'm serious."

She thought he was kidding. She'd probably head for the hills if she knew that he was as serious as a heart attack right now. He forced a grin and shrugged.

"You're getting a little too good at reading me."

"You're making it easy," she said with a dismissive wave of her hand.

Chris chose that moment to return, holding two plates of the most beautiful-looking food Daisy had ever seen.

"I present to you, my version of twice-baked goat's cheese soufflé with an accompaniment of arugula, fig, and roasted almond salad." He placed the plates in front of Daisy and then Mason with a flourish.

"It looks amazing and smells even better," Daisy enthused, her mouth already watering as she stared down at the perfectly baked soufflé, next to a beautiful, fresh-looking salad, on a plate garnished with artistically sprinkled tiny purple and yellow flowers.

"Bianca," he called to the sweet-faced young woman hovering behind him, and she shuffled forward to place a couple of flutes of brightly colored drinks in front of them. "Mimosas with my compliments. Enjoy."

"Thanks, Chris. Looks good," Mason said, and Daisy sent him a disbelieving look. His returning gaze was perplexed, and Daisy sighed. Men were seriously clueless sometimes.

"It looks more than merely *good*, Chris," she corrected, and Mason made a sound that was somewhere between exasperation and laughter.

"You already said that," he pointed out.

"One can never receive too much flattery," Chris said calmly. "But I'll leave you to enjoy the fruits of my labor. Bon appétit."

He left with a flourish—she guessed he was the type of guy who added flourish and flare to everything he did—taking Bianca along with him.

"You could have asked him to join us," Daisy admonished, picking up her fork and sending another admiring glance down at her plate. It was almost criminal to eat something so beautiful.

"He wouldn't have," Mason said, having no qualms about completely destroying the work of art on his plate. He had two huge bites down before she even had time to gently prod her quivering soufflé with her fork. "Besides, it's bad form to just insert yourself into someone's date."

"Mason."

"Yeah, yeah, not a date," he said from behind a mouthful of salad. "Got it. Point is, Chris doesn't know it, so bad form."

Daisy took a small amount of the soufflé onto her fork and sighed when the rich, tart flavor burst across her taste buds. She couldn't *quite* contain the tiny moan of appreciation that slipped out. Her eyes slid shut to fully appreciate the taste.

Fuck me! I'm in such deep shit here. Mason paused, his fork hovering halfway between the plate and his mouth. Did she have to look like she was having an orgasm? It was just a soufflé, damn it! It tasted eggy and cheesy and shouldn't make anybody look like they were coming. He could damn well give her a real reason to look like that.

He shifted in his seat in an attempt to alleviate his discomfort. He and Spencer really had to go cruising for babes soon. This was getting tiresome.

"So, a few logistical issues to work out," she said prosaically after a few more moany, breathy bites. "I'm driving to the Wild Coast; everybody else is heading there a day earlier, but I'll be finishing up some last-minute stuff at the practice. It will be the first time the locum goes to *Inkululeko*, and I want to go over a few of the more serious ongoing cases with him. I'm not sure when you want to leave—"

"With you." No question about that. She was the only reason he was going in the first place, and he for damned sure didn't want to spend any more time with those bitches her sisters called friends than was absolutely necessary. "We can take turns driving. And just to be clear, we're taking the BMW."

"Oh, that's not necessary."

"Yes, it is. I'm not going to be stuck in that little toy car of yours for nearly seven hours." She seemed to think it over before shrugging and nodding. There was a lull in the conversation as she made love to a slice of fig, and he diverted his gaze and guzzled down his entire mimosa in a single gulp.

"Anyway, I think the hotel may be fully booked already, but I'm looking in to reserving a room for you at a nearby lodge."

"We'll share." She looked scandalized by his words, and he pretty much felt the way she looked, not sure where the hell the suggestion had come from.

"We will *not*."

"Are you sharing with one of your sisters? Or maybe one of those other bitches?"

"No."

"Great. I'll take the sofa."

"Mason, absolutely not."

"And just to be clear, I'll be paying for my half of the room."

"No, you don't have to. I asked you to do this; I'll pay. But for a separate room. In a different hotel."

"And how will that look? Like we're platonic friends. And not even close platonic friends since I'll be in a completely different hotel."

"It'll look like I'm not easy."

"Nobody will think you're easy. Two weeks from now we'll be well past our third date. Everybody will assume we're sleeping together anyway. And I'm paying for my half of the room. End of story."

"Mason . . ."

"I won't lay a finger on you, promise." He considered that for a moment before amending, "Well, not unless you want me to."

"I won't want you to." She looked pissed off now, which was disappointing because it meant that she was done eating. Which meant no more sex show. He supposed he should be grateful for that, considering what a state it was putting him in, but he couldn't help but feel a tiny pang of loss.

"Daisy, in all seriousness, it's your best move. It'll shut them up for years," he said, trying to inject some earnestness into his voice, even though he wasn't entirely sure he had her best interests at heart.

— 

"I'll think about it," Daisy conceded, even though she couldn't believe she was actually considering the idea. Sharing a room with him for two nights didn't seem like the sanest course of action.

"Great." He speared a fig from her plate, having demolished his own meal in record time, and bit it in half, before offering the other half back to her.

"No," she refused, while he held the fork less than an inch away from her mouth.

"Are you sure?" he asked, brushing the fig along the closed seam of her lips. She sighed and opened up, tugging the sweet fruit from the tines of the fork. The guy really seemed to have no concept of personal space or inappropriate public displays of, well, if not affection, then familiarity.

"So what kind of things do you knit?" The mundane question surprised her, and the genuinely interested expression on his face absolutely floored her.

"Easy stuff. Scarves and hats."

"Guy I knew, Kyle Quincy, used to knit to pass the time."

"Model?"

He grinned, stealing another fig off her plate and once again offering her half. She took it without thinking twice, too interested in his story to make a big deal out of it. "Soldier."

"Seriously?" She couldn't even begin to imagine some macho soldier-type hulking over a pair of knitting needles.

"Yep. Big bastard. He used to sit around knitting these dainty little baby things for his sister and later for his wife."

"I'm not going to lie, I find that both bizarre and awesome."

"Quincy was an awesome kind of guy."

"Was?" She watched the open grin fade from his face to be replaced by shadows and turmoil.

"Yeah. He was KIA." He fiddled with his fork and kept his eyes downcast. "Left behind his wife and two-month-old baby girl. Linzi." A fleeting smile graced that mobile mouth. "We gave him hell over that name. I mean, who names a kid Linzi Quincy?"

"I'm sorry."

He shook his head and met her eyes, the distant look on his face replaced by something warmer. "It was years ago. Shit, Linzi is probably around eleven or twelve now. Hard to believe. I haven't thought about Quincy in years."

Daisy didn't believe that for a second. Something told her that he thought about his fallen brothers-in-arms every single day. "Well, if Quincy was knitting baby clothes, then he was probably a lot more skilled than I. That's next-level knitting for someone who can barely finish a scarf."

"I'm sure your baking is pretty damned awesome," he said, and she shrugged.

"Nothing compared to Chris's bread." She was surprised by the sudden snap of impatience in his eyes.

"Why do you *do* that? You're constantly selling yourself short, and it's annoying as hell. Chris is a trained chef; it's his job to make excellent food. But I'm pretty sure your baking is a thousand times better than his amateur veterinary skills."

Mason was heartened by the shy smile that bloomed on Daisy's lips and the slight glow of warmth in her cheeks.

"I'm sure it is too. His mediocre attempts at a routine vaccination would most likely pale in comparison to my zucchini-and-bacon bread."

"Dear God," he whispered in awe. "That's an actual thing?"

"Yep."

"How soon can you make one for me?"

"I'll call you the next time I bake one," she reassured.

"No, you're baking one *for* me. You're not giving me a slice from a bread that you just happened to bake."

"I'll consider it," she teased. He enjoyed it when she felt comfortable enough to tease him; it gave her eyes a saucy, naughty glint that was about 20 percent charming and 80 percent cute.

"Consider this; I'll be annoying and persistent as hell until I get my bread."

"And that's different from the usual you, how?"

"Bake that bread and you'll never have to find out."

She laughed, and he relished the way her face lit up and her eyes crinkled at the corners, those gorgeous plump lips opening to reveal her straight white teeth. She had a piece of arugula caught in her teeth, and Mason found even that adorable as hell, though he knew that she would be mortified to learn about it.

—

Daisy was genuinely sad to say good-bye to Chris an hour later. He had joined them at their table about half an hour before they left. Bringing coffee and rich chocolate cake to top off the perfectly decadent meal that Daisy knew she couldn't afford to indulge in. Especially not a mere fortnight before squeezing herself into that sausage casing of a bridesmaid dress. She didn't think she would ever be this comfortable and familiar with Christién Roche again. She might frequent his restaurant in the future without Mason, but she'd be just another customer.

Chris almost immediately dispelled that belief when he hugged her and said, "You come back any time, *ma petite fleur*. We will eat and drink and converse like the old friends we will soon become. *Oui?*"

"I'd like that so much," she breathed, delighted by the invitation. And then even more delighted when—instead of the traditional double air kiss—he planted a great, smacking smooch right on her lips.

She was a little dazed when Mason led her back to the car and incoherent for the first five minutes of the drive home, barely registering anything Mason said. She only tuned back in when he pulled the car to the side of the road and turned off the engine.

"What's going on?" she asked.

"Oh, back with me again, are you?" His voice was steeped in sarcasm.

"I mean, the guy *kissed* me, Mason. Did you see that?"

"Yeah, I saw it. Didn't impress me much."

"Well, it wouldn't; you're not into him at all."

"And you are?"

"He smells nice and his lips are soft and very . . ."

"Oh, for Christ's sake . . ."

He wasn't going to listen to her rhapsodize about Chris's lips, for fuck's sake. Sure, the guy had laid one on her but had kept his eyes on Mason the entire time, clearly hoping to get some kind of reaction from him. And if he had prolonged that kiss a second longer he would have gotten Mason's reaction right in the teeth. Not cool, man.

Now, only wanting to shut Daisy up about Chris's dreamy lips, Mason cupped a hand around the nape of her neck to tug her closer, using his thumb to tilt her jaw up and her face toward him. He grunted in satisfaction when he had her lips angled exactly right and planted his own mouth over hers. Screw Chris, she'd forget about his lips in . . .

Jesus, her mouth is soft. He sighed and leaned in closer; she tasted even better than he remembered. Tart, sweet, and savory all at once. His thumb was stroking idle patterns down her throat, and he lifted his free hand to cup the other side of her jaw, sweeping both thumbs down the soft skin of her throat and pausing at her pulse points to enjoy the crazy fluttering of her heart. His tongue demanded entry, and she opened for him, her own meeting his with delicate, shy flicks. He wanted more, needed more, craved more. He fucking *deserved* more.

His breathing was out of control, and he was embarrassed by the hungry, primitive sounds coming from him as he deepened the kiss, one hand going to the back of her head and grabbing a fistful of that gorgeous hair before tugging and exposing her pale throat to him. His mouth moved down over that delicately scented column, farther down to the hollow where her neck met her shoulder, and lower still to the gentle slope of her breast. She was making her own breathy sounds, the same sexy noises she made while she was eating. God, he had *known* that she would sound exactly like this when she was turned on.

His hand moved down, burrowing its way beneath her layers of clothes until flesh met flesh; he found the ripe curve of her breast and toyed with the laced edge of her bra, until he lost patience and fully cupped the sweet, soft mound. It filled his hand perfectly, the hard nipple burning into his palm like a hot little coal. He flexed his hand experimentally, catching the nipple into his contracting palm and was rewarded by the guttural sound of pleasure that caught in the back of her throat. She arched into him, and he lifted her breast, lowering his head toward it, desperate to get that sensitive peak into his mouth even through layers of clothes.

One of her hands was cupped around the back of his head, pulling him toward her, while the other clawed madly at his back. He could feel the scrape of her nails even through his thick shirt. He couldn't get close enough, the seat belt restricting his range of movement, but before he could attempt to unfasten it, the sound of an air horn blaring as a truck shot by the car—close enough to rock it slightly—sent them both flying to their respective corners. Mason swore softly, and then put a little more effort into it, until the only sounds they could hear were the rain pattering on the roof, their heavy breathing, and Mason's very prolific range of curse words.

Daisy had both hands pressed to her lips, her huge eyes—magnified by her askew glasses—peering at him owlishly over her fingertips.

He owed her an explanation. But what could he say after that performance? He had a huge erection—there was no hiding the thing from her—and he knew she was aware of it by the way she was very pointedly keeping her eyes on his face. So much for keeping her oblivious to his attraction to her.

He finally ran out of English swear words and launched into French, which was only fair since it was Chris's fault that they were in this position.

CHAPTER SEVEN

Mason had kissed her, *properly* kissed her, and seemed to regret it almost immediately afterward. So why kiss her in the first place? And he wasn't unaffected by it. Even with her peripheral vision she could see how *very* not unaffected he was. He was still breathing heavily and swearing. Well, she assumed he was swearing, since he had moved on from French to something that sounded like Arabic—and he was quite determinedly not making eye contact with her. He was doing that thing, where he ran his hand over his scalp. She had recognized it as a nervous habit the first time she'd seen it, and judging by the number of times he was doing it now, he was *very* agitated.

He finally switched back to English.

"Okay, so I'm really competitive," he said, which was literally the last thing she expected to hear from him in this moment. "And when you were going on about Chris and his lips . . ."

His voice trailed off, and it didn't take a genius to put two and two together.

"Oh." *Wow.*

"So it wasn't really about you. Well, it kind of was. But not really." Yeah, surprise, surprise . . . it was never really about her. What a—a *jerk*, seriously! One minute he's chastising her for selling herself short, and the next he's proving to her once again that she had reason to do so.

"I see."

❧

Damn it! Of course she believed this line of bullshit; the woman had very little self-esteem, so *naturally* Mason had to go and reinforce the low opinion she already had of herself. But he honestly did not see how telling her that he couldn't keep his hands to himself around her would improve the situation at all.

He wanted to fuck her, get her out of his system, and move on. But it always came back to not wanting to hurt her. Even though he seemed to fail at that time and again. Judging from the look on her face right now, he'd done it again.

Yeah, he was a real fucking prince among men, wasn't he?

There was nothing more to say. He turned the key and restarted the car, and the music kicked on. A more current playlist this time, but she kept her eyes fixed on the wet green world sliding by, not even tapping a foot to the beat.

As for Mason, well, it was another five miles before his erection finally subsided, and the feel of her hard, hot nipple faded from his palm.

❧

The drive home felt like it took forever, while in reality it was only half an hour. The rain had let up when he finally brought the car to a stop outside her little house.

"I'm sorry. I was a bastard," he said, and she was startled by the subdued words. His first since the kiss.

"You were." His lips twitched at her easy agreement.

"I'm not really used to being friends with a woman," he admitted. His eyes gleamed with sincerity, and she chewed her bottom lip thoughtfully before remembering his reaction to it earlier and immediately stopped.

"We barely know each other; I'm not sure we're actually friends." He looked a bit taken aback by her frank assessment.

"I enjoy your company. I like talking to you and hanging out with you. I think we have the beginnings of a pretty good friendship, Daisy."

"Mason, you're a great guy. Anybody else would have called me crazy when I first brought up this stupid idea and called it a day. But when this is over, we won't see each other again, we won't hang out, we won't be friends. That's the reality of our situation. And I'm okay with that."

I'm not. The words hovered on the tip of Mason's tongue but he swallowed them back. He had caused enough damage and confusion for one day.

"Let's just see this thing through and be done with it," she continued, and he nodded.

"Dinner tonight?"

"I usually have dinner with my family on Sunday."

"I'll take you."

"Boundaries, Mason."

"What about them?"

"You're overstepping them again."

"You're going to need me there."

"What makes you think that?"

"Think of all the questions they'll have. Do you really want to lie to your family? Or would you prefer me to be there to deflect the questions and do the lying on your behalf?"

"Lying by omission is just as bad." The crazy situation just kept getting worse and worse.

"I'll be there to watch your back, Daisy."

"It's my family, Mason. They're the ones who watch my back."

"Yeah? Seems to me they're the reason you were driven to this course of action in the first place."

That made her pause for thought.

"Maybe I should just avoid Sunday dinners for the next couple of weeks."

"You can have dinner at mine. I'll cook."

"Oh my God." He was missing the point entirely. She pinched the bridge of her nose, trying to ward off the headache that was starting to build behind her eyes.

"Well, you're going to need a reason for bailing on dinner with your family, aren't you? So what's it to be, dinner with your family with me as your wingman? Or dinner at mine, just the two of us. And the dogs, of course."

This wasn't quite the nightmare she'd been expecting. Dinner had gone off quite smoothly; it helped that her mother and Daff were still treading on eggshells around her, which had led to restrained and polite dinner conversation, even though she knew they were both dying to unleash a torrent of questions. Lia wasn't at home, which had also helped a lot. After dinner, Mason and her father retreated to the comfortable living room for coffee, her father gently quizzing Mason about his combat experience along the way, and Daisy knew her reprieve was over. So much for watching her back; Mason and her father had kicked off a generational bromance from the very moment they had been reintroduced, and now they had both abandoned her to her mother and sister.

"For the record, I never thought you weren't pretty enough," her mother fired the first salvo without warning. "And while I always thought you could stand to lose a few pounds, it was because I was concerned about your health."

Daff said nothing, merely shoved a stack of dirty dishes into Daisy's hands for transport to the kitchen.

"I know you've always had my best interests at heart, Mother," Daisy said as they walked to the kitchen, hoping her voice carried a suitable amount of contrition. "But it can be a little overwhelming . . . even smothering at times. I'm not Daff or Lia; the things that interest you guys don't always interest me. You have them for stuff like shopping and makeup and . . . and that."

Daff snorted, and Daisy shot her a glare, which her sister returned venomously. Okay, so apparently Daff was more than a little pissed off with her.

"I just get a little sick of always being compared with them. And coming up short."

"You never come up short."

"Except literally, of course," Daff said snidely, and their mother gave her a quelling glance, which she returned defiantly for a second before returning to the task of loading the dishwasher.

"Daisy, I love you girls equally. And you all have your own wonderful individual strengths: Dahlia has that kind heart, Daffodil has her spirit, and you have wit and intelligence. None of those characteristics have anything to do with the way you *look*. What kind of mother would I be if I judged you on your looks?"

"Then why are you always going on about my hair and my weight and my makeup and my clothes and all of that?"

"Because, like the saying goes, I want you to be the best version of yourself you can be."

"Yes, but . . ."

"I want to hear no more about this. You girls clean up the kitchen while I go and rescue Daisy's charming friend from your father."

Daisy waited until she was out of earshot before turning to Daff, who had stopped loading the dishwasher and was now leaning against the counter with her arms folded across her chest. Everything about her stance told Daisy that her sister was *not* happy.

"Let's have it," she invited wearily.

"I can't believe you. You think you have it bad? Lia and I have been compared to you—and coming up lacking—all our lives. You've always been Daddy's favorite. He does everything with you while he merely tolerates us. And Mom is constantly going on and on about how proud she is of you. You're the doctor, the one with her own house, the independent, clever one, and you have the *nerve* to bitch about looks? Do you *know* how it feels to constantly be told that even though we're not clever like you, at least we're pretty? We've been made to feel like that's literally all we have going for us, so of course the stuff you find so shallow is important to us. It's all we have."

Daisy could feel her jaw dropping, but she was helpless to do anything about it. She felt as if the whole world had been flipped upside down. After all these years of feeling completely lacking compared to her sisters, it was humbling to understand that they had experienced the same snide comments and felt the same insecurities and doubt that she did.

"I didn't know . . ."

"What? Perfect Dr. Daisy missed something? Maybe you're not as sharp as everyone thinks?" Daff's voice had lost its edge, and Daisy offered her a conciliatory smile.

"Well, you're not as dumb as everyone thinks, so maybe there's more to both of us than meets the eye."

"I'll say. I mean, my baby sister is hooking up with big, bad Mason Carlisle. I never saw that coming."

Ouch. Not great timing, considering the revelations of the past few minutes.

"I'm not exactly hooking up with him."

"Then what's going on between the two of you?"

"It's complicated," Daisy hedged, not wanting to lie but not sure the truth was the wisest course of action here either.

"Well, then . . . *uncomplicate* it." Daisy sighed. Daff wasn't the type to just let stuff go.

"We just like hanging out together."

"Daisy . . ."

"I-kind-of-blackmailed-him-into-being-my-date-for-the-wedding." The words just seemed to pour out of her like a river, powerful, unstoppable, and completely unexpected.

"Wait. *What?*" Daff looked as stunned as Daisy felt. She hadn't expected to confess, but now that it was out she felt as if a huge load had been lifted off her shoulders. Daff grabbed hold of her upper arm and pushed her into a chair before sitting down across the kitchen table from her.

"Tell me everything . . . from the very beginning."

The story didn't take very long to relay—especially with Daisy leaving out a few of the more confusingly intimate details—and Daff said nothing until Daisy stammered to a miserable halt. And even after that she continued to remain silent for several moments. When she eventually broke the silence, it was to say something so foul Daisy actually blushed.

"That rat bastard motherfucker," Daff said. "I'm going to hang him from the ceiling by his tiny, tiny balls."

"Whoa, Daff. I'm the one who coerced him into this."

"What? No, not Mason . . . although he's not entirely innocent in all of this either. I meant Spencer. How dare he? How dare he try to hit on me, while devaluing my sister at the same time? Who does he think he is?"

While it was flattering that her sister was so outraged on her behalf, her absolute fury was a little overwhelming, and Daisy needed to rein it in before Daff unwittingly revealed the whole humiliating incident to their parents.

"Daff, you need to calm down. I have it under control."

"Yeah, and while I'm proud of you for having the stones to extort the asshole into being your date, are you *sure* this is the course of action you want to take?"

"Auntie Ivy," Daisy replied succinctly, and Daff winced. "Auntie Gert, Auntie Helen, and Auntie Mattie. Every single time I see them, I hear about how lucky our parents are to have me to take care of them in their old age."

"Ugh. I always get the pinched cheeks and a reminder that I should find a man while I'm young, because my looks won't last forever and I won't be able to look after myself when I'm old and alone."

"And then there are Shar and Zinzi and their little minions. Mason was amazing last night. He made me feel so special. And preferred. Please don't tell anyone; it won't be for long, and Mason is . . . well, fully on board. I wanted to back out last night, but after the Shar incident he practically insisted on going ahead with it. He's a nice guy, Daff."

"Even nice guys can hurt you, Deedee."

"I know that, but the beauty of this entire situation is that he's already hurt me, so I'm immune to him now."

"That makes no sense."

"It does. I fell for his act once, and I was burned before he could do too much damage. Now, even though I'm constantly exposed to his charm and good looks, I'm armored against it. It's kind of like chicken pox."

"Daisy, I love you, but for an intelligent woman you're frighteningly naïve sometimes. That man is sex on a stick, and *nobody* is ever entirely immune to that."

"I am," Daisy said, while trying not to think of those delicious, drugging kisses she had conveniently left out of her confession. Some things were too personal to talk about. And besides, it wasn't ever going to happen again, so there was really no point in talking about it.

Mason really liked Daisy's parents. Millicent was a delightful lady who seemed elegant and unapproachable at first but was instead a warm, loving woman who clearly adored her family. And he had always known that Andrew McGregor was a stand-up guy. When Mason was about ten he had found a kitten on the side of the road; the little ginger thing had been malnourished, probably riddled with ticks and fleas and definitely mangy. Mason hadn't known or cared anything about that; all he'd seen was an animal in need of love and care, one that would love him back, and had lost his heart almost instantly. He remembered walking to Dr. McGregor's practice, the cat swaddled beneath his thin jacket. It was the end of the day, and the receptionist had looked irritated and tried to send him away. Mason had kicked up a fuss, and the vet had come out to see what the commotion was about.

Mason remembered Dr. McGregor's kindness, how gently he had taken the cat from Mason and examined it. The gravity in his voice as he explained that the kitten was very sick and in a lot of pain and the best thing Mason could do as its owner was to let it go. Mason had been only ten, but he had understood the concept of death, had known the cold, hard truth couched beneath the man's kind euphemisms, but the cat was his responsibility, and as such he had to do right by it.

He balked when Dr. McGregor had tried to send him out of the room and instead cradled the tiny kitten in his arms as the vet did what had to be done. Afterward, he'd allowed the man to take the cat from him, knowing that he couldn't bury it at their house because the neighbor's dogs would probably dig it up. And when Mason offered up the few cents he had in his pocket as payment, Dr. McGregor had left his dignity intact by accepting the money and shaking his hand.

He wondered if the man sitting across from him even remembered that encounter. He must have had so many patients over the years that one small boy with a sick cat couldn't have been very memorable. And yet, the same encounter had altered Mason's life irrevocably. Before that adults hadn't treated Mason as much more than a nuisance; they had never seemed to *see* him. Dr. McGregor had not only seen him but had made him feel respected and important. It had made him want to be more than just a worthless kid from the wrong side of town. When he reflected on it now, he understood that Andrew McGregor's treatment of him that long-ago day had been the first step on his journey toward the man he had become.

"So, Mason, how do you feel about our daughter?" Millicent McGregor suddenly asked, and Mason choked on his coffee, despite having expected the question long before now.

"Millie, Daisy says they're just friends," Andrew McGregor said, his voice gently chastising.

"That's what *Daisy* says; I would like to hear what Mason has to say," the woman retorted. She looked sweet and harmless, with a benign smile on her face as she cuddled Peaches on her lap. She was stroking the dog rhythmically but kept her eyes trained on Mason's face, watching him like a hawk. The unflinching stare was a jarring contradiction to that sweet smile. Mrs. McGregor definitely had a core of steel, if that look was anything to go by, and Mason sensed an ambush.

"I like her," he replied smoothly after a long and measured pause. "And I'm working on getting her to like me back."

"Why would you have to work at getting her to like you? Seems to me she likes you already," Dr. McGregor inserted, and Mason swallowed as he heard the edge in the man's voice, even though he was still smiling benevolently. He was starting to feel like he was being worked over by a professional interrogation tag team. He was almost tempted to respond with his name, rank, and number.

"Like me in the same way," Mason said and then nearly bit off his tongue at the dumb answer.

"And what way is that, dear?" Millicent asked, leaning forward slightly, her smile becoming a little less benign and a lot more sharklike.

"A lot."

"What's that?" the older man prompted.

"I like her a lot. She likes me less . . . I'm working on resolving the disparity."

"And how do you plan on doing that?" Millicent asked sweetly, and Mason shrugged. They were playing a canny game of good cop/good cop, and it was freaking him the hell out. Good cop/bad cop, even bad cop/bad cop, he could handle, but this was something else entirely.

"You know, the usual way."

"I'm afraid I don't know," the woman said, taking a sip of tea. "What, pray tell, is the usual way?"

"Flowers and stuff?" Jesus, he sounded like an amateur. So much for having Daisy's back. He was coming apart like a wet tissue under the tiniest bit of duress.

"To what end?" The male voice was almost jarring after Millicent's catlike purr, and Mason barely stopped himself from starting.

"I'm not sure I know what you mean," he hedged.

"What will you do after you get her to like you *a lot*?" How the hell was he supposed to answer that question? He had no intention of marrying Daisy or getting into a serious relationship with her. He wanted to have sex with her, sure, but even that wasn't in the cards, and if it were, it wasn't exactly something he'd tell her parents. So where exactly was this fake relationship supposed to go?

"I don't know." He finally opted for honesty. "It's much too soon to tell. We've only just started going out."

Bizarrely, that answer seemed to please them both, and they sat back with relaxed smiles as if the last couple of minutes hadn't happened at all. Daisy and Daff chose that moment to return, and it was all he could do not to glare at Daisy for abandoning him to her ruthless parents.

They all immediately noticed the difference between the two younger women when they entered the room. They had clearly resolved the tension between them and were a lot more relaxed in each other's company, but Mason was getting all kinds of sidelong death glares from Daff. And he immediately knew the reason for them. Daisy had clearly blabbed their secret to her sister.

Goddamn it.

Luckily the after-dinner coffee didn't last too long, and because it was a work night, the evening ended soon after. Mason was relieved to say good-bye to the smiling older couple and their malevolently frowning oldest daughter.

"Tell your brother I'll be seeing him *really* soon," she hissed into Mason's ear under the pretext of giving him a hug, and he winced. Spencer wasn't going to be too thrilled to have the object of his desire pissed off with him. He said nothing in response to Daff's words and instead moved on to kiss Mrs. McGregor on her cheek and shake the doctor's hand.

He walked Daisy and Peaches to her tiny Renault coupé—she had insisted they come in separate cars—and leaned in to give her a kiss on her cheek, putting on a show for the still-watching family. Peaches, snug and secure in Daisy's arms, growled a tiny warning, but Mason ignored her.

"You *told* Daff?" he asked on an angry whisper.

"I couldn't help it. The occasion called for honesty."

"While I was tasked with sitting in that tiny room with your hard-core parents, undergoing a grueling interrogation, you simply caved at the slightest hint of pressure?"

"Tiny room? The family room is huge."

"Don't change the subject."

"And don't be silly; my parents aren't hardcore and don't interrogate people!"

"Shows how much you know. Any government organization anywhere in the world would be lucky to have Dr. and Mrs. McGregor do their interrogations for them." They were both smiling, keeping up the pretense for her family, while they had their hushed conversation.

"You're being ridiculous," she scoffed, and he glared at her.

"You're having dinner at my place tomorrow night. I'll pick you up at six thirty."

"Fine!"

"Fine."

⚊⚊

"I like that young man," Andrew McGregor said as he watched his daughter say good-bye to Mason.

"He seems nice enough. A little rough around the edges but decent and sincere."

Daff said nothing, merely watched her sister lean into Mason while they had a hushed conversation. She was beyond pissed off with that idiot Spencer Carlisle for his role in this debacle. If—no, *when*—Daisy got hurt because of this crazy plan, Daff was going to have that blockhead's guts for garters. He'd never been the sharpest tool in the shed, but he had always been almost charming in his clumsy attempts to pursue her. Using Daisy to get to her was just an unforgivable breach of the unwritten rules of their longstanding non-relationship. He pursued, while she rebuffed or ignored, and everything was right in the world. He had stayed away while he was with Tanya as was proper, and Daff had known he would start trying again after the breakup. But she hadn't known he would do so at the expense of her sister's feelings.

Mason wasn't exempt from her anger either, but she felt a bizarre sense of betrayal mixed in with her fury at Spencer, and boy was he going to pay for this.

─━

"Hey, Dr. Daisy. I hear you got a new boyfriend!" The enthusiastic words were offered as a greeting when Daisy swung by the local grocery store after work the following evening. She just smiled at the cheerful cashier, who was ringing up her wine. "Mason Carlisle. He's so handsome, hey? You're a lucky lady."

Daisy made a noncommittal sound. The woman hadn't exchanged more than the usual polite pleasantries with her before now, so this show of camaraderie was unusual to say the least. She'd been dealing with similar comments all day—some tactful and some not so tactful. It was ridiculous how quickly rumors spread in a small town like this. Nearly everybody, from the janitor to the receptionist at the practice to her patients' owners, had mentioned her "new boyfriend." For Daisy, who was used to being overlooked, it was an uncomfortable experience to be so unceremoniously thrust into the limelight. She really hadn't expected everybody to take *this* much interest in her love life. It was getting really tiresome and emotionally draining.

She paid for her wine, the enthusiastic encouragement of the cashier still ringing in her ears, and hurried home before she could be accosted by random people on the streets wanting to know about her relationship with Mason.

─━

"Coop, *quiet*," Mason admonished his barking dog. Cooper had dashed for the front door before the doorbell had even rung, and now his nose was buried at the bottom of the door as he tried to get a whiff of their visitor, his tail frantically waving like a surrendering flag.

Mason opened the door and grinned at Daisy, who was peering up at him through her wet lenses, her hair a frizzy mess around her face and her nose and cheeks pink from the cold. She looked frazzled and completely out of sorts, if the irritated frown on her face was any indication.

"Hey." He dropped a kiss on her cold cheek—partly in case anybody happened to be passing by but mostly because he wanted to—and stepped aside to let her in. Cooper, who had been happily sniffing away at her feet and legs, making little whines of approval, suddenly yelped and comically leaped away from her to duck behind Mason's legs.

"You brought Peaches, didn't you?" he asked, looking for the little fluff ball but not seeing her. Daisy opened her coat to reveal the contented-looking pooch nuzzled up against her breast, and Mason felt a surge of envy for the lucky dog.

"I didn't want to leave her alone again; she's been on her own too much over the last few days. I hope you don't mind?"

"Nah. Gives Coop a chance to overcome his irrational fear of her." He aimed a disgusted glance down at his trembling dog, who was still hunkered behind Mason, tail tucked between his hind legs.

Daisy put her weird little dog on the floor, and Peaches delicately started sniffing around the room, totally ignoring Cooper in the process. Daisy escaped from all the accoutrements of winter—handing her scarf, beanie, gloves, and coat to Mason in the process. She smelled fantastic, and the sexy little black dress she wore beneath the coat emphasized her lush curves rather magnificently.

She was looking around his foyer curiously, her eyes darting to and fro as she took in every detail. Mason was rather proud of the house, which he had designed—and later decorated—himself. Other people's opinions rarely mattered to him, but he found himself wanting her to like his home. Rather desperately, actually.

"This is lovely," she finally breathed after an interminable amount of time had passed. "I'm not going to lie, I've been curious about this house ever since they started building it. I think most of Riversend has been."

The house was built on a large hill overlooking town and offered magnificent views of the ocean. As schoolboys, Mason and Spencer had often trekked up the hill and sat in the exact spot the house was now, smoking cigarettes and watching the people in town as they went about their business. Back then they had taken pleasure in denigrating the hardworking citizens of Riversend, had pretended to be hard-asses even though both had an unacknowledged desire to be accepted and considered equals. They had been rebels because it was easier to be bad than considered the poor kids in need of charity. So they had stolen to eat, and when they were older, they had both found other ways to get by and eventually climb out of the rut they had been born into.

Buying this forgotten tract of land and later building his home here had been Mason's way of finally laying those old feelings of inadequacy and desperation to rest.

Daisy was happily poking around his living room, making appreciative sounds as she ran her finger along the furniture.

"It's so cozy in here. Warm and masculine," she said with a smile, and Mason looked around the room in an attempt to see it as she saw it. The house was his take on a traditional log cabin with a peaked roof. It wasn't very big and featured an open-plan living and dining space with a large, separate modern kitchen. A guest bathroom was tucked away beneath the staircase. The sizable loft upstairs housed his bedroom and master bathroom. The high-vaulted ceiling gave the impression of space and airiness. He had a few tall windows downstairs, but his favorite feature was the wall of windows in the loft. It felt like he was sleeping in a treehouse, and he could see for miles without lifting his head from his pillow.

Daisy had moved toward the huge stone hearth and was warming herself in front of the crackling fire.

"Make yourself at home," Mason invited. "I'll be right with you, just putting the finishing touches on dinner."

"I'll help," she said, turning toward him. "I want to see your kitchen."

"It's just a kitchen," he said.

"Don't care, I want to see it anyway."

"Fine, you can have a sip of tea while I finish."

"Okay."

He led her into the kitchen and was gratified when she oohed and ahhed over his marble finishes and redwood cabinets. Peaches had followed them into the kitchen and was happily pilfering Cooper's food from his bowl. Of the bigger dog there was no sign.

"It smells really good in here," Daisy said as she clambered onto one of the tall barstools at the breakfast bar. It wasn't an easy task for her, and she revealed a delectable glimpse of soft, pale thighs before she managed to get herself situated.

"I like that dress," Mason said with a wicked grin.

"You do?" He sent her a warning look, and she flushed. "I mean, thank you. I've only worn it once before. At my grandmother's funeral."

Mason snorted, then felt guilty for laughing, but seriously the woman had no real idea how to gracefully accept a compliment.

"Sorry about your grandmother."

"The funeral was five years ago; I'm actually surprised the dress still fits."

It probably hadn't fit *quite* so snugly five years ago, but Mason had reason to be grateful for the fit now. Her cleavage looked amazing in the thing.

"It fits great," he said. She opened her mouth to say something else, but he forestalled her by lifting his forefinger to silence her. "Just say thank you, Daisy."

"'Thank you, Daisy,'" she repeated impishly, and he rolled his eyes. "Lame."

"I know," she said, laughing.

Daisy watched Mason move around his kitchen with effortless ease. He looked so at home in the large room with its wholly masculine granite and wood fittings. The whole house was dripping in testosterone. The furniture big, solid pieces made up of gorgeous wood. Everything fit perfectly into the rough-hewn log interior that boasted both finesse and aggressiveness in its finishes. The wooden floor was adorned with luxurious shaggy rugs, and the living room furniture boasted sturdy but comfortable upholstery. Even the drapes were carefully chosen to be both aesthetically pleasing and durable. The place was a fascinating study in contrasts. It was obviously designed and decorated by a man, but one who enjoyed the finer things in life without compromising his masculinity one iota.

He was wearing faded jeans that molded his butt and thighs lovingly; the denim looked well worn and white at the seams. He also had on another flannel shirt, sleeves pushed up to his elbows to reveal those strong arms, with veins roping over his large hands and up over his forearms. The top three buttons of the shirt were undone to reveal the strong, tanned column of his throat.

"I hope you don't mind taking your tea in a mug," he said, and she snapped back into the present, hoping that she hadn't been visibly mooning over him. "I don't do froufrou little teacups."

"That's fine," she said.

"How do you take it?"

"Milk. No sugar." He grunted in response, and she barely managed to keep her grin in check as she watched him plonk a tea bag into a mug, splash hot water in after it, followed by a drop of milk. He unceremoniously thumped the mug down in front of her, with the tea bag still immersed, before turning away to stir the merrily bubbling pot on the stove top.

"Thanks." She toyed with the tea bag tag as she searched for something to say. "Smells like curry in here."

"Yeah. I hope you don't mind spicy food."

"Not at all. The hotter the better."

"I like a woman who can handle a little heat," he told her, shooting her a sexy little glance over his shoulder. Daisy fought back a blush and rolled her eyes at him.

"Stop twisting everything I say. It's childish," she admonished, and he chuckled.

"I've spent most of my life around a bunch of testosterone-fueled guys, Daisy. It doesn't make for a very refined—or mature—sense of humor. Fart jokes, sex jokes, and ti—uh—*boob* jokes, that's pretty much the extent of it." He was delightfully unabashed by that fact. But Daisy didn't believe a word of it. He had a well-rounded sense of humor—she'd seen evidence of it, heard it in the wry note that sometimes crept into his voice when he spoke.

"Who's being self-effacing now?" she scoffed, and he fully turned to face her, shock evident on his face. "Ah, you don't often have people calling your bluff, do you? The humble, 'aw, shucks, I'm just a blokey bloke' routine must have fooled a few people in the past, am I right?"

"A fair number." He lifted his shoulders, still keeping that sharp, intelligent gaze pinned on her, as if he were scrutinizing a very interesting bug beneath a microscope. It was starting to make her uncomfortable. "But not you, I suppose?"

"You didn't get to university while you were in the army, but I'm guessing you did at a later date," she said, adding a questioning lilt to her voice.

"After going in to business with Sam, I took a few business management courses."

"A few?"

"I hold a master's degree in business administration," he informed her casually, turning back to the pot. He continued to speak over his shoulder. "I started taking online courses in business administration while I was modeling and then studied full time for a year after that while Sam was getting the business off the ground. I went back to studying part time once the business was fully functional. Sam and I were divided between management and fieldwork for a long time before we finally got the hang of things. I preferred being out in the field, and he enjoyed the management aspect more, so I was the guy who trained new recruits, kept their asses in gear, and Sam schmoozed the clients. It was win-win, until I decided to get out completely."

"Why did you leave?"

"It wasn't my scene."

"It took you seven years to figure that out?" She took a sip of her tea and wrinkled her nose. She had left the bag in too long.

"We were successful. It seemed foolish to not want that success. But as the years passed, I just became more and more . . . I don't know . . . discontented, maybe. I was a good close protection officer, but it could be mind-numbingly boring at times, not quite what most people imagine. No gunfights and chasing bad guys down dark alleys. In the end it wasn't a career, it was a job, and it's not what I want to be doing anymore."

"And you're still trying to figure out what you really want to do."

"Yes."

"You don't want to use that MBA for anything?"

He stirred the pot for another second before holding the wooden spoon aloft, his free hand cupped beneath it to avoid spillage, and took the few short steps that brought him to the other side of the island.

"Taste," he prompted, lifting the spoon to her lips. She blew on it for a second before taking hold of his wrist to keep his hand steady and closing her lips over the spoon. The spicy heat of the sauce burned her lips and left a trail of fire down the back of her throat as she swallowed, and she opened her mouth to fan her tongue frantically in an effort to ease the discomfort. Her eyes watered as she grinned up at him.

"Whoa! That is *spicy*," she panted, and he frowned.

"Too spicy?"

"Just add a dash of yogurt to temper it a bit," she suggested, and he nodded, stopping by the double-door refrigerator to grab a carton of yogurt on his way back to the stove. He stirred a spoonful of the stuff into his spicy stew before taking another taste test and nodding to himself.

"Better," he muttered. "In answer to your question: I don't think I'm cut out to be a businessman. I didn't enjoy the tedious management aspect of the job at all. Hated the meetings, the haggling over prices and contracts, the legalities and bureaucracy . . . none of it appealed to me. I'm more of a get-your-hands-dirty kind of guy."

"So what do you enjoy doing above all else?"

"There is something," he said, the words seeming to be conceded with a great deal of reluctance.

"What?"

"I designed this house. It was the most rewarding thing I've ever done. I worked with an architect to get it all right, of course, but everything in here was my vision," he said. "And that got me thinking about architecture. I've always enjoyed drawing houses and buildings; I'd look at a building and automatically 'fix' what I considered to be flaws in the design. Take Chris's restaurant, for example; he had the location picked out years ago, but the original design for the place was just wrong. I was kind of horrified when he showed me the initial blueprints. It was all steel and glass and didn't suit the setting at all. When he saw my reaction, he challenged me to do better. I picked up a napkin and started sketching, and what I drew is pretty much what you saw. I mean, I don't have the technical know-how—he still had to go back to his architect to fine-tune the design—but I'm a fast learner."

"You designed Chris's place? Mason, it's absolutely beautiful. You have genuine talent," she enthused, and he averted his eyes. But if the slight flush along his cheekbones was any indication, he was flattered by her praise. "So why not go for it? If your past projects are any indication, you'd be brilliant at it."

"I don't know, it seems a little late to be making huge career decisions like that." He shrugged.

"Nonsense, time will still pass, and ten years from now you could either be an architect or a guy filled with regret because he never took the chance."

"Maybe," he said noncommittally. He smiled and propped his elbows on the granite top of the island and leaned toward her. "But enough about me. How was work today?"

Daisy was frustrated by the change in subject. Mason could see that. Well, that was too bad, because he was done talking about himself. She had this easy way about her, a manner that lulled a guy into thinking he could confide in her and tell her anything. Next they'd be sitting around braiding each other's hair and talking about their love lives. He shuddered at the thought and turned the focus back on to her. Right where it should be.

"It was okay, nothing too traumatic, just the usual stuff. Fifi needs to be spayed, Rover keeps scratching, Fido is limping. Bread-and-butter cases, my dad calls them."

"Do you see a lot of traumatic stuff?"

"Not usually, but things can get a bit hairy at *Inkululeko*. When people live in appalling conditions, it's hard for them to take proper care of their pets. Even though they try their best with the resources they have. That's why the clinic is so vital to their community."

"Isn't it dangerous? There's a lot of crime in that area." The thought had occurred to him before, but since he had properly gotten to know her, the idea of her placing herself in danger truly pissed him off. And quite honestly, scared the bejesus out of him.

"The community is so grateful for the service we provide that they serve as our protection. And we've even had a few of the shadier types bring their dogs in for medication and treatment. We've been treated with nothing but respect."

"There are always those who want to ruin things for others," Mason pointed out, keeping his voice mild even though he was desperate to urge her to beef up security for her clinic. Even one guard. Mason could organize it. Still, he knew that he didn't have a right to be concerned over her safety, and he for damned sure had no say in how she ran her clinic or where she conducted it.

"It's fine. We have ample protection. The clinic is very busy, and there are always people about. Perfectly safe."

Mason kept his own counsel but wondered how soon he could arrange a visit to the clinic and assess the situation himself.

"Anyway, I think the food's about done. I've already set the table, so if you'd like to wander into the living area and have a seat, I'll bring everything out."

"Nonsense, I'll help," she dismissed. She glanced around for the dogs and couldn't spot either of them. They were both terribly quiet, so at least they hadn't killed each other.

"Where are the pooches?" she asked, and Mason cast a disconcerted look down at the floor.

"No idea," he responded. He went to the doorway and looked into the living room and then chuckled quietly before waving Daisy over to come and see. She hopped off the barstool and tried to squeeze into the doorway next to Mason, and he took hold of her elbow and tucked her against his side so that the top of her head was nestled beneath his armpit. She tried to ignore his heat and his gorgeous scent while looking to where he was pointing. Peaches had claimed Cooper's huge dog bed. The small dog was sleeping soundly, curled up into a tiny, fluffy ball while poor Cooper sat on the carpet, about six feet away. He was staring at Peaches with his head cocked and his adorable face rumpled into that concerned, baffled expression that only retrievers seemed able to achieve.

"Oh, poor baby. That hardly seems fair, I'll get my bossy little diva out of there before the situation deteriorates."

"He won't hurt her," Mason whispered, his breath ruffling the hair above her ear. "He's just trying to figure her out. In the meantime, he'll let her walk all over him until he knows how to deal with the situation."

"But it's his house, and Peaches has just taken over."

"*Women.*" Mason chuckled, and she slanted him a glance.

"And what's that supposed to mean?" He just grinned and cheekily stole another one of those unexpected kisses from her.

"Grab the wine while I bring out the food." Still reeling a little from the kiss, Daisy was a little slow on the uptake until he stepped away to put a bottle in her hands and then put his hands on her shoulders to physically turn her until she was facing the kitchen door again.

"Off you go," he said before swatting her lightly on her butt. She gasped and nearly dropped the bottle in surprise. Another unrepentant grin before he headed for one of the cabinets to remove a few serving bowls.

~

"Oh my God, that was so good," Daisy moaned later. "I can't believe I finished all of it. Between this and all that bread at Chris's yesterday, I'm never going to fit into that stupid bridesmaid's dress."

She stared down at her empty plate in dismay; every last bit of curry sauce had been wiped up with the buttery homemade roti, which had been served as an accompaniment to the saucy lamb vindaloo.

"Glad you enjoyed it." Mason smiled at her over the rim of his wineglass.

"Where did you learn to cook like that?"

"A woman I dated, Vashti. This is her recipe."

"Oh?" Daisy tried to keep her voice casual but failed miserably. "How long were you with her?"

"A year or so. She wanted more, and I didn't have any more to give." He twirled the wine stem between his thumb and forefinger, a thoughtful look on his face.

"I see."

"Do you?" he asked, a cynical tilt to his mouth. "Women always say they understand, but they never truly do. So what do you see, Daisy?"

CHAPTER EIGHT

She stared at him for a long while, giving the question the gravity it deserved.

"I see a man who enjoys the company of women but prefers not to get too attached to them. Falling in love makes you vulnerable, and I see a man who doesn't like having any vulnerabilities. I see a man who's never really content with what he has, no matter how perfect it seems, and is always searching for something newer or better."

He drained his glass and put it down on the table carefully.

"All that?" he mused. "From what? Just three days' acquaintance?"

"Well, we have been on a 'getting to know you' intensive crash course." She forced the flippant words past her dry throat and took a sip of her own wine to ease her hoarseness somewhat.

"I suppose we have. Shall I tell you what I see when I look at you?"

"Oh, please don't." The words were soft and pleading, and Daisy was ashamed by how unevenly they tumbled from her lips. "I didn't mean to offend you, Mason."

"I'm not offended," he said, emptying the rest of the wine into his glass and draining half of it before continuing on. "Just impressed by your remarkable powers of observation."

He said he wasn't offended, yet there was something about the stiffness of his shoulders and the cadence of his voice that told her that her comments had touched a nerve. She cursed the glass of wine that had loosened her tongue and futilely wished her words back.

"I also see a man who has gone out of his way to help a complete stranger save face in front of her family and friends," she tacked on desperately, and he smiled, a cold, cynical movement of his lips that was a terrible caricature of his usual smile.

"You could argue that my motivations are completely self-serving," he pointed out.

"I don't see how they could be. You're only doing this because you allowed your conscience and guilt to get the better of you."

"Yeah? Or maybe I'm doing it because I want to fuck you senseless, and this is all a means to that end."

Daisy gasped, his mocking words slamming against her fragile defenses like boulders. Why would he say something like that? It was heartbreakingly disappointing to discover that he was just like everybody else after all and Daisy was the butt of yet another stupid male joke she couldn't even begin to comprehend.

"That's not very funny," she fumed, and he shrugged, hooking an elbow over the back of his chair and leaning back indolently.

"I'll say not," he agreed easily. "I've been a walking hard-on for days."

Daisy felt her cheeks heating at his words, and she glared at him, absolutely furious.

"You don't believe me," he said, his face and voice revealing absolutely nothing.

"Of course I don't believe you," she snapped. "Mason, on Friday your brother had to practically beg you to talk to me. And today you're telling me you want me . . . *sexually*?"

───

Mason tried to bite back a grin at the quaint phrasing and the hushed way she said *sexually*, like the word was dirty and forbidden. He shouldn't have said what he did, but her wholly accurate assessment of his personality had sent him into defense mode, and he had lashed back with a truth that he knew would make her uncomfortable. He had also known she wouldn't believe him for a second. Still, to have that knowledge confirmed was annoying as hell. He wanted her to believe him, tell him she wanted him back, and then he wanted them to go upstairs and have hot, raunchy sex. The kind that was wet and steamy and dirty and left you wrung out and strung out afterward.

"That's exactly what I'm telling you," he said, injecting a healthy dose of sangfroid into his voice. He didn't want to scare her off completely.

"Well, I'm telling you I don't believe you, and I told you before, I don't appreciate being the butt of someone's stupid joke."

This again. He should have known she'd think he was having a bit of fun at her expense. The fact that she knew that Spencer had practically forced him to speak to her on Friday didn't help his cause either.

Mason knew he was foolish to actually verbalize his desire. Better to stick to the "rules," no matter how crazy they seemed.

"Sorry I upset you," he muttered. "I guess I overstepped a little."

"A *little?*"

"A lot." His admission mollified her for a moment, and she took another gulp of wine.

"I should probably get going," she said.

"You haven't even had dessert yet."

"I've lost my appetite."

"Look, I'm really sorry about what I said. You just . . ." He shook his head and figured a strictly edited version of the truth would probably be his best defense here. "I didn't like what you said. About me. It hit too close to home. I often feel like an ungrateful bastard because just when something seems perfect, I find a way to deliberately fuck it up. Vashti seemed perfect for me—gorgeous, intelligent, funny—but when she started talking about moving in together, I called the whole thing off. Said I didn't love her."

"*Did* you love her?" Daisy asked breathlessly, and he shook his head.

"I don't know. Maybe. It felt like I should. I cared about her." He didn't know why he was revealing so much. He was telling her stuff he'd never actually even acknowledged to himself. It was unsettling. "How do we ever really know if what we're feeling is love?"

She shifted her gaze, and the deliberate furtiveness of the movement caught his attention.

"What about you?" he asked. "Have you ever been in love?"

"No."

"So much certainty," he observed. "Your ex-boyfriends couldn't have been very noteworthy."

"You could say that." She was hiding something. He could tell from her rigid posture, her averted eyes, and the tension that radiated from every pore. He didn't like it. What if she still carried a torch for some past lover? The thought of her in love—whatever the hell that meant—with some undeserving bastard didn't sit well with him at all. What if it was some guy in town, someone she saw every day? How the hell would she get over him if she saw him all the time?

"Are you still in love with one of them?"

She looked startled by his question. "No. I just told you I've never been in love. Why would you ask me that?"

"You're hiding something," he pressed, and she threw him a disbelieving glare.

"And *that's* the conclusion you've leapt to?" Her color was high, her eyes huge as they scowled at him over the rims of her glasses, and even her curls seemed to crackle with annoyance. He beat back a smile; she looked like a hissing kitten.

"So what are you hiding?"

"Nothing."

"Daisy."

"It's none of your damned business."

"Yes, it is. I'm supposed to know this shit. I haven't been here for thirteen years, everybody else knows your business, and they'll know when you've kept something from me, and I don't want to be blindsided with the news that you were once involved with a groomsman at the wedding or something." It was a paper-thin excuse to pry into her business, but it made her pause for thought.

"I wasn't," she said, and he clenched his teeth in frustration.

"It was an example."

"Mason, there is nothing you need to know, no nasty surprises that will be sprung on you unexpectedly. Okay?"

"You can't be sure of that."

"I can." She pushed her chair away from the table and got up, clearly dismissing the topic. Frustrated, Mason rubbed his hand over his short hair and squeezed the nape of his neck in an attempt to ward off an incipient headache. God, she was infuriating.

She started to stack empty plates and dishes, and he sighed impatiently.

"Leave it."

"It's no problem . . ."

"I said *leave* it," he growled, and she jumped, nearly toppling the growing stack of dishes in her hands. She pursed her lips and carefully placed the crockery back on the table.

"I'm not in the mood for dessert, and I have an early start to the day tomorrow, so I think I'll go. Thank you for dinner. It was really delicious." She could barely meet his eyes, and Mason sighed, admitting defeat. Daisy McGregor was a tough nut to crack, and frankly, it wasn't his job to crack her shell. He was just along for the very short ride, and then he'd be out of her circle of acquaintances and friends again. The thought made him feel somewhat melancholy, but that was the reality of their situation.

"I'm sorry for prying," he said, watching as she pulled on her coat and called Peaches to her. The little dog was still curled up in Cooper's bed, while Cooper was lying in front of the fire. He hadn't taken his eyes off the small intruder, seeming simultaneously confused and intrigued by her. When Peaches didn't even lift her head to acknowledge Daisy's summons, Mason snorted and strode toward the bed to scoop the dog up with one hand. Peaches growled and bared her sharp little teeth at him, but he lifted her to face level and growled back, which shut her up immediately. He handed the dog to Daisy, who tucked her beneath her coat again, before grabbing her bag and heading for the front door.

Mason beat her to it and had the door unlocked and opened seconds before she got there.

"Thanks again for dinner," she said, meeting his eyes reluctantly.

"No problem. Tomorrow night? Dinner at MJ's?"

"I have plans." He could tell she was lying but didn't call her out on it.

"Let me know if they fall through or change."

"Yes."

He leaned down to kiss her good night, but a firm hand on his chest stayed the movement.

"No."

"Somebody could be . . ."

"There's nobody out there," she interrupted, impatience lacing the words. "It's after nine, cold and wet. And this is the only house up on this godforsaken hill. Why would anybody be out there?"

Chastened, Mason shoved his hands into his pockets.

"Good night, Mason." It sounded like good-bye, and he hated that.

"I'll see you soon." And that was a goddamned promise.

The week flew by. Work kept Daisy busy, and, in an effort to avoid Mason, she volunteered to help with some of the last-minute wedding stuff. He called every day. He had her mobile number but rarely contacted her on it, leaving messages with the receptionist at the practice. She knew he was doing it to keep up the pretense and was grateful for that. He even sent flowers the day after their dinner. The bouquet arrived in the middle of the day, when the surgery was teeming with people, and everybody heard the deliveryman ask for Daisy. It was both embarrassing and flattering.

Now, late Friday evening, she was seeing off her last patient—an impeccably groomed Pekingese with an eye infection—when Mason strode into the reception area. Both Lucinda—their receptionist—and the Peke's owner, one of her mother's country club cronies, gaped at him.

He smiled when he saw Daisy. A beautiful smile that told her—and everybody else in the room—that he was happy to see her, that he had missed her, that he was focused on her alone and had eyes for no one else. And it nearly had her completely fooled.

"Hey," he murmured, his voice low and intimate but loud enough for Lucinda and Mrs. Cage to hear. "I missed you." He lifted his hand to the nape of her neck and tugged her toward him for a kiss. A very thorough kiss.

Daisy felt a little out of sorts afterward; she was barely able to string together a coherent thought and wholly incapable of actually formulating words. He had his forehead pressed to hers, his hand still at her nape, and when he spoke she barely registered his words.

"Daisy?" There was infinite patience in his voice, and irrepressible amusement in his eyes.

"What?"

"I asked what you're doing tonight."

"I have plans."

"Can I join you?"

"You wouldn't like it."

"I don't care. I want to spend some time with you." Her lips twitched; he was laying it on much too thick.

"Well, then, since you put it that way, I suppose it would be okay if you joined us."

"Us?" He looked surprised, and she grinned. Of course he thought she'd just been making these plans up in an effort to avoid him.

"Mom, Lia, Daff, and I. Dad is taking a rare evening off and heading to Ralphie's with some of his golfing buddies, but a man's opinion is always welcome. So everybody will be thrilled to know you're joining us." She relished the flare of panic she saw in his eyes and kept her smile sweet and beatific.

"What exactly will you be doing?"

"We're still having problems with the seating arrangements, if you can believe that? Just a week left, and it's a shambles. I swear it's worse than a logic puzzle."

"I'm great at puzzles; I'll get it done," he said confidently, and Daisy tried not to roll her eyes.

"And we're assembling the last of the welcome bags."

"What are those?"

"Little gift bags for all the guests."

"We're getting gifts?" He sounded boyishly excited by the idea, and she laughed.

"Yep."

"So does this evening of hard labor include dinner?"

"It does."

"Great. Pick you up or meet you there?" He was being optimistic in even asking, and she laughed.

"Meet you there. Six thirty on the dot. Lia gets hysterical if anybody's late. She's gone full bridezilla over the last few days . . ." She paused before adding, "Do *not* tell her I said that."

"Cross my heart and hope to die," he promised, holding a dramatic hand to his heart, and another laugh bubbled up in Daisy's throat. He was just so charming, and she had missed him. Which was odd, considering she barely knew him and hadn't spent more than a few short hours in his company.

"I'll see you then." He dropped another kiss on her lips and then glanced around and did a little double take as if he were noticing the other two women for the first time. He grinned at Lucinda. "Hey, you must be Lucy. Sorry for hassling you so much this week. But my little Dr. Daisy has been almost impossible to pin down." He sent her such a smoldering look that all three women gasped at its potency.

"It's nothing," Lucinda—*Lucy?*—dismissed, going beet red when he smiled at her again.

"Sorry for the delay, ma'am." He smiled charmingly at Mrs. Cage, and the woman pursed her lips.

"Just be more mindful of your sweetheart's working hours next time, young man," she admonished with very little heat in her voice. Wow, he was good. Mrs. Cage could be impossibly crotchety at times.

He gave them all a cocky grin before exiting the building. The room instantly felt bigger and emptier without him in it, and Lucinda sighed into the silence.

"Well, Daisy. That young man certainly looks like the best and worst kind of trouble, doesn't he?"

She could say that again.

⌒

"This is impossible," Mason growled as he glared at the seating chart stuck onto a whiteboard in the middle of the kitchen. Daisy was surprised by how very seriously he was taking this seating business. He looked like a military strategist planning to go to war. Within ten minutes of arrival he had the chart streamlined and color coordinated. It was both impressive and uncanny. Now, an hour later, they had hit the same brick wall Daisy's family had been slamming into for weeks. "Why can't we put the Goldsteins at the same table as the Redwoods?"

"Because Mr. Goldstein and Mrs. Redwood had a *thing* about twenty years ago, and Mr. Redwood has been gunning for Mr. Goldstein ever since," Daff explained gleefully, and Mason's brow lowered.

"I suppose that makes sense," he conceded thoughtfully. "I'd probably want to kill the guy too if he'd slept with my wife."

"Oh, Mr. and Mrs. Redwood weren't married at the time," Lia supplied helpfully.

"What?" Mason practically yelled. "The guy is pissed off because his wife had a *sex* life before they were married? What the fu-uudge?" He caught himself just in time and cast a guilty look at Millicent McGregor. The older woman turned away and hid a grin from him, but Daisy saw it and barely bit back her own snicker. He had been trying to be super polite all evening, but the seating chart was taking its toll on his good humor too.

"Okay, so then put the Redwoods at this table." He pointed to one of the little circles on the chart, and all three women hissed collectively. "What? What's wrong with that?"

"Mrs. Redwood had a relationship with Mr. Abernathy. Mr. Redwood has been trying to put Mr. Abernathy out of business since then, and both men hate each other's guts."

"Well, then, put the Abernathys and the Goldsteins at the same table; the enemy of my enemy is my friend, right?"

"Can't." Lia shook her head regretfully. "At the time Mrs. Redwood was having her thing with Mr. Goldstein, she was also sleeping with Mr. Abernathy. The men got into a massive fight over her, and they haven't really spoken since." Mason sighed but said nothing. Just pointed to another table, and all three women winced.

"Mrs. Redwood slept with Mr. Abbot and—"

"Mr. Redwood wants to murder him," Mason finished Daisy's sentence wearily, and she smiled at him sympathetically. He stood up from the round kitchen table and paced back to the whiteboard, glowering at it intently. The women remained seated.

"Okay." He cracked his neck and shook his arms as if he were limbering up for a fight and reevaluated the chart. "Let's approach this differently—who *didn't* Mrs. Redwood sleep with back in the day?"

The pause was so long and significant that Mason groaned and threw up his hands in disgust.

"Jesus." He glanced at their mother. "Sorry."

"Why not just give them their own table?" he asked.

"That wouldn't be right; they'd feel excluded." Lia was ever sensitive to everyone's feelings, no matter what the cost.

"Why did you invite them at all?" Daff asked Lia. "Mr. Redwood doesn't get along with anybody, and Mrs. Redwood drinks and flirts with every man within her radius." Lia glowered at her. It was an argument that kept resurfacing every time the frustration levels hit boiling points. Daisy groaned and buried her head in her arms on the table, while their mother tried to keep the peace. Mason just kept his gaze fixed on the board.

"Who is Kenna Price?"

"A cousin," Daisy said, propping her chin on her forearm and watching as he shifted Kenna's magnetized name strip off to the side.

"And her plus one?"

"Her partner, Trudi." The plus-one card also moved off to the side.

"What about Martin Mikkelstone?"

"One of Clayton's old university friends," Lia supplied, intrigued.

"He also has an unnamed plus one," Mason pointed out.

"Clayton said Marty will definitely bring a girl, but that's yet to be confirmed."

"And the guy is young, unlikely to have slept with Mrs. Redwood?"

"I wouldn't be so sure," Daff muttered grimly.

"Daffodil," their mother chastised, wearily.

"What? The woman seems to go through legions of men. I would be shocked if she's not a cougar too."

Daisy, still with her chin on her forearm, released the other arm and started twirling the curls at her temple.

"Katinka Van Buuren is also bringing a plus one, her mum if I'm not mistaken," Daisy pointed out, and Mason grinned at her, before moving Katinka's name with its plus one off to the side.

"I don't know why we didn't think of this before." Daff shook her head as she watched Mason move a couple more names to the side. "It's so simple."

"If you stare at a problem for too long it starts to seem insurmountable," Mason said. "Add the pressure of a deadline into the mix, and it becomes damned near impossible."

"I'm not sure what's going on." Lia shook her head in confusion.

"Mason is cobbling together a table of young singles and their plus ones and foisting the Redwoods off onto them." Daff chuckled.

"We've been trying so hard to place them with their contemporaries, when the simple fact is, they don't get along with any of their contemporaries," their mother mused.

"But that will throw the other tables off balance," Lia despaired.

"We'll figure it out," Mason soothed. "Don't worry. Once the Redwoods are sorted, everything else will fall into place."

An hour later they all stared at the completed chart in awe with Mason looking just a tad smug. Lia gasped, clutched her hands to her chest, and burst into tears.

It was almost comical the way Mason's eyes widened in horror at the sight of her tears, and Daisy, used to Lia's recent uncharacteristic crying jags, allowed herself a moment's amusement.

"What's wrong?" he asked Daff, sotto voce, and Daff rolled her eyes.

"Hormones. She's totally PMSing, and she's been an emotional powder keg for the last few days." Mason blanched.

"I didn't need to hear that," he muttered and then looked even more horrified when Lia launched herself at him and buried her face in his chest. His eyes landed on Daisy's face, and he mouthed a desperate *what do I do?* Daisy bit her lips to stop herself from laughing and mimed a hugging action. His arms closed around her trembling sister's form, and Daisy immediately regretted encouraging him to hold her. Lia looked so right in his arms. Her petite, perfect femininity wrapped up in his strong, masculine embrace. He lowered his head and murmured soothing little words into her ear, and she sobbed even louder.

"It's just we've been working so hard," she sobbed messily. "I thought we'd never fix it. *Never.* Thank you, Mason." Most of what she said was complete gibberish, but she managed to convey the crux of it.

"You're welcome," he said, patting her back awkwardly.

"I'm sorry, I'm a complete mess," Lia apologized and stepped away from him, and he released her immediately.

"I'd probably be a wreck too if I knew I'd almost definitely have my period on my wedding day," Daff cheerfully supplied. She continued, ignoring both Lia and her mother's horrified gasps. "I don't know why you didn't just go on the pill. You wouldn't have had to worry about this."

"Why must you always be so horrible?" Lia moaned and fled from the kitchen. Their mother threw Daff a disgusted look and rushed after her middle daughter.

"Do you have to constantly remind her of that?" Daisy sighed, and Daff shrugged.

"She's been a total pain for weeks. We've all been working our butts off trying to get this perfect for her, and all she's done is mope, cry, and screech."

"She hasn't been that bad," Daisy admonished.

"Please, you haven't been around for most of it. The other day she screamed at Dad because he forgot to go for his final tuxedo fitting."

"Screamed at him?"

"Screeched like a harpy. It was insane; I thought she'd burst that little vein in her temple, it was bulging so much. Mom actually forced a Valium down her throat and made her go to bed for the rest of the day." Daff shook her head as she recalled it.

"Probably nerves," Mason suggested.

"Maybe she's having doubts about Clayton Assmonton the Third?" Daff grinned, and Mason's eyes narrowed speculatively.

"You don't like him either?"

"Either?" Daff repeated as she glanced at Daisy. "Daisy's been spilling family secrets, has she?"

"It's not a secret that I dislike him," Daisy muttered defensively.

"It is from Lia."

"So's the fact that you don't like him."

Daff sighed. "Yeah, but she's so happy."

"She doesn't seem happy to me," Mason said, and both women stared at him in surprise.

"Like you said, probably just nerves," Daff said with a frown.

"Are you sure?"

"I mean, these are trying circumstances, of course they're going to stress her out," Daisy murmured.

"She's your sister, you know her best. I'm just saying, the woman I saw here tonight isn't very happy at all."

And it wasn't Mason's place to comment at all. Why was he involving himself in the McGregor family politics? It wasn't like him, but he found himself genuinely liking all of them, even the constantly acerbic Daffodil McGregor, and, from what he could tell, their soon-to-be-married sister was completely miserable. But they were so busy trying not to offend her by revealing how much they disliked her fiancé, neither of them had noticed how sad she seemed.

"So where are these welcome bags we're supposed to stuff, and are we allowed to take home any damaged or surplus goods?" he said, trying to lighten the mood, but both Daisy and Daff looked thoughtful and concerned.

"I doubt you'll want to take anything home." Daff laughed. "They're disgustingly boring. Bottled water, handmade soaps, scented candles, tiny bottles of Advil, and one bottle of liqueur. *Artisanal*"—she spat out the word like it was poison—"candies and cheeses all labeled with the happy couple's smiling faces, names, and wedding date. Super lame."

"I think it's a lovely idea," Daisy defended. "The weekend itinerary will help orient guests, the water and snacks are practical, and you know how expensive hotel minibars can be."

"I've never actually been to a wedding; is it always this . . . involved?" Mason asked, taking a sip of the beer Mrs. McGregor had kindly furnished him with earlier. He pulled a face; it was flat. He'd been so preoccupied with the seating arrangements he hadn't touched it in over an hour.

"Never?" Daisy asked as she got up to get him another beer. He took it with a grateful smile, his eyes lingering on her tired face. She looked absolutely exhausted.

"Never," he affirmed. "Busy day?"

"Hmm, emergency op on a bull mastiff. Poor thing was hit by a car." Mason winced.

"How's he doing?"

Her eyes went bleak, and he knew the answer before she spoke. "I tried my best, but the damage was catastrophic."

Mason set his beer bottle aside and gestured for her to turn around. He was standing with his butt braced against the granite countertop next to the fridge, and he widened his stance slightly to accommodate her. When she didn't move, he put his hands on her shoulders and turned her so that she was facing the kitchen table where Daff was watching them with a hooded gaze. He pulled her back against him until the small of her back nestled against his crotch. He settled his hands on her neck and proceeded to knead, massaging down toward her shoulders and back up to the tight muscles in her neck. Daisy groaned and relaxed into him, her spine melting against his abdomen and torso.

"I'm sorry about the dog," he whispered into her hair. He felt hot, much too hot, and that immense heat just rolled off him and enveloped her. He felt her breathing quicken when the hotness hit her.

"It's part of the job."

"Yeah, but it can't be easy." He heard his words slur and was amazed he could form a coherent sentence with her this close and with him so turned on.

"It isn't. Some days it just feels so much worse than others. We also had to put down an elderly cat and a sick puppy today. The mastiff was the last straw."

He dropped a kiss on the nape of her neck, adoring the soft, scented cove. He concentrated on the knot that had formed there, digging his thumbs in and loving the contented little moans she made in response.

He was hard—of *course* he was hard—and trying his damnedest not to grind against her. There was no way she didn't feel his erection prodding against her back, but she refrained from acknowledging it, probably best with her sister sitting there glaring at him like he was the worst kind of monster. Which was fair enough, considering what she thought she knew about him.

"No need for pretense here," Daff said, her voice dripping with disdain, and Mason felt Daisy tense against him as she recalled where she was. He sent Daff a malevolent glare; surely the bitch could see that Daisy was upset after her traumatic workday?

"Your sister is distraught and exhausted, why not allow me to comfort her?"

"I don't need any demonstrations of your fake relationship, Mason," she sneered. "We all know what this is about. Save it for some other gullible patsy."

Daisy slipped out of his hold, and Mason held on to her arm to keep her in front of him until he got his raging hard-on under control.

Daisy understood the silent command immediately and remained where she was, but she tugged her arm out of his hand and maintained a slight distance between them. His body mourned her absence, and his mind raged against it.

When he had himself back under control, he stepped out from behind her and stared at her averted profile until she reluctantly lifted her gaze to meet his.

"You should go home and get some rest. It's late, and you have the clinic tomorrow." The thought of the clinic still sent cold shudders down his spine.

"It's not that late," she protested, glancing at the digital display on the microwave. "Not even nine thirty yet."

"Daisy . . ."

"Oh my *God*, you're not the boss of her," Daff snapped. "You're not her boyfriend or fiancé or husband. Stop trying to tell her what to do."

"Daff," Daisy's voice was equally short. "I can speak for myself!"

"So vocal with me, aren't you, Daffodil?" Mason injected lethal amounts of ice into his voice. "Why aren't you this outspoken with your sister's douche-bag fiancé?"

"Because that's an actual relationship, and prying could do a lot more harm than good. You don't have anything remotely similar with Daisy!"

"Enough!" Daisy barked. "I've had enough from both of you. Daff, stop interfering and back the hell off!"

Her sister's eyes widened, and Mason fought back a grin at the look of sheer incredulity on her face. Their baby sister had claws, and none of them seemed to actually know it.

"And as for *you*," she seethed, turning that temper on him. "Thank you for everything you've done tonight, but just stop offering personal insight and suggestions into a situation you know nothing about. It's none of your damned business."

Stung, Mason knew he probably had the same shell-shocked look on his face that Daff currently did.

"I think I will go home. Tell Mom and Lia I'll see them tomorrow afternoon. Good night."

Before either could react, she had whirled out of the kitchen and was gone. Moments later they heard the front door slam and her car start up.

The silence stretched into minutes, and Mason finally looked at Daffodil, who was eyeing him speculatively.

"Why *are* you doing this? You didn't have to agree to her foolish plan."

He didn't owe her an explanation, but he could see genuine concern for her sister mixed in with the curiosity.

"I honestly don't know. Your sister is compelling and convincing and cute as hell; it can be hard to resist her."

"Seriously?" The disbelief in her voice rankled, and he scowled at her.

"What is *up* with everybody in this town—even her own family— underestimating her and overlooking her?" he growled. "Why don't you stop being such a bitch to me for agreeing to help her with this? And take a good hard look at yourself and everybody else who made her feel that she needed to go to such extreme lengths to avoid humiliation at her own sister's wedding."

"I don't like you, and I don't like what you and Spencer did to her."

"I don't like what we did either, and that's partly why I agreed to this."

"Seriously, Mason . . . you hurt her, I'll castrate you."

He gave her a grim little smile before nodding.

"Noted."

Mason's Jeep created deep ruts in the mud as he drove the dirt road to *Inkululeko* the following morning. He needed to see the clinic's setup for himself, needed to reassure himself that Daisy was safe and that her clinic was secure.

The mobile clinic was parked in a clearing close to the informal settlement, and as he drove up, he was surprised by the incredibly long line snaking its way out from the covered entrance. There had to be at least a hundred to two hundred people—and their assorted animals— waiting. There was no way Daisy and her father could help all these people between eight a.m. and one p.m., which was what Daisy had said the operating hours were on a Saturday.

It was a gloomy day, but the people were happily chatting with each other, some were carrying umbrellas, others wore raincoats, and a few just had plastic bags covering their heads. The settlement was visibly impoverished, but the people in line were cheerful and had an obvious sense of community. Dogs of all sizes were tethered with leashes or makeshift rope harnesses, some obviously ill, others looking bored or nervous, others still picking fights. There were a small number of cats hugged to chests, chickens clucking happily in cages, and even a few cows, horses, and donkeys.

He was filled with a renewed sense of admiration for Daisy now that he could see what she had created. These people needed this service and were grateful for it. But on the outskirts of all this organized chaos there were a few others lurking. Looking tough, acting tough, and obviously up to no good. He knew the type, had seen them in many guises all over the world. But she saw no danger, saw only the happy community. But in his experience, the ones looking for trouble knew when to pick their moment, and it would be when Daisy or her father were at their most vulnerable. There were so many spots on the isolated dirt road that led up to *Inkululeko* that could be ideal for an ambush, and his stomach churned at the thought of Daisy getting into that kind of trouble.

He stepped out of his Jeep and walked toward the clinic. The people in line prodded each other and pointed at him. He was obviously out of place with his big car and his expensive clothes. He kept his stride loose and unthreatening, nodding and smiling at some of the people who made eye contact. When he saw a familiar face at the entrance of the clinic, he grinned.

"Hello, I know you, don't I?" It was the pretty young waitress from MJ's.

"Yes, I'm Thandiwe," she said with a cheerful smile. "I'm the unofficial receptionist for Dr. Daisy and Dr. Andrew at the *Inkululeko* pet clinic."

"Fantastic."

"I want to be a vet too," she confided, and Mason felt a pang as he recalled a similarly impoverished young boy with the same big dream. He trusted this self-possessed young woman had what it took to achieve her goal.

"You learning a lot from the Doctors McGregor?"

"So much," she enthused, and his smile widened. "Are you here to see Dr. Daisy?"

"I am, but I have a couple of questions for you first if you don't mind and if you can spare the time?" He cast a look at the long line.

"A little time. I won't process the next patient until after one of the doctors finishes with their current patient."

"How . . ." He wasn't sure how to delicately phrase it. After all, she lived here, and he didn't want to offend her. "I was a little worried about Daisy when I heard about this clinic."

"You want to know if it's safe?" She was a straightforward young woman; he liked that about her.

"Yeah."

"It's safe *here*," she emphasized. "But I worry about them when they drive home. My brother has a taxi, and he sometimes follows them to the main road just to be sure they get there safely, but he's not always available. Most people here don't have cars, and while they would like to do something similar, they can't. There's a lot of expensive medical equipment in this clinic. And some people might think that it's easy money to be made." Which just confirmed his worst fear.

"Thanks, Thandiwe," he said. "Do you think Dr. Daisy will have time for a quick hello?"

"I think we can squeeze you in between the mangy cat and the chicken with the club foot." She grinned, and he felt his lips stretch into an answering smile.

"Much appreciated."

Daisy waved Mrs. Matabane and her sick cat off with a smile. Yet another case of mange; sadly it was prevalent in the township, too much dust. But luckily, Isaac, the battle-scarred tomcat, didn't have a bad case and looked to be on the mend. He needed to be neutered, and she had begged Mrs. Matabane to consider it, explaining that it would cut down on his wandering and fighting as well. The elderly lady had promised to think about it. The mangy animal reminded her of young Thomas and his dog, Sheba, and she wondered if she'd be seeing the friendly child today. He hadn't dropped by on Wednesday, and she hoped he'd come around today.

She looked up with a friendly smile as the next person entered the mobile clinic and had a moment's confusion as she stared at the tall, broad figure silhouetted in the doorway.

"Mason," her father called, his voice warm and welcoming. "What brings you by?"

"Just thought I'd have a look at the clinic; I've been thinking of making a donation and wanted to see it for myself first." Mason's voice was equally jovial, and Daisy's eyes narrowed. This was the first she'd heard of a donation—not that it wouldn't be welcome and appreciated—and it was just a little suspicious for him to suddenly show up. What were his real motivations?

"Well, feel free to have a look around while we work. It's a bit cramped in here, though." The clinic was the size of a standard RV and boasted nearly everything an actual veterinarian's office would, but there was very little room to maneuver, especially with Mason's larger-than-life presence making everything seem Lilliputian in scale.

"I wish one of us could show you around, but we're a little swamped today," her father said apologetically. He had his hands on a small black dog with only one eye. The dog's owner was staring at Mason askance, obviously annoyed to have his consultation interrupted.

"I wouldn't expect that, sir. I'll have a snoop around myself, and I hope you won't mind if I waited around a bit and maybe drove back into town with you?"

"That would be fine with us, won't it, Daisy? And you can come around the house for a late lunch."

"I'd enjoy that." He grinned at Daisy, and she kept a straight face, sure he was up to something. He leaned over her stainless-steel examination table to drop a kiss on to her cheek.

"You're looking quite sexy in your white coat, Dr. Daisy," he whispered wickedly, his breath fanning against her cheek and his voice low enough for only her to hear. Daisy felt herself going bright red and fought to keep her breath even as he nuzzled the sensitive skin next to her ear before he retreated.

He nodded to her father and started whistling a jaunty tune as he stepped out of the clinic.

"Boyfriend?" The owner of the black dog—a wizened elderly man in a dapper plaid peaked hat with matching coat—asked her father.

"Yes, that's Daisy's boyfriend," her father said.

"Ey ey ey! You tell him he must pay big *lobola* for Dr. Daisy, she's a good girl. Twenty, thirty cows maybe," the man cried, causing

Daisy's blush to deepen, and her father chuckled. *Lobola* was a traditional bride price, and it was still a common practice among certain tribes in the country. Thirty cows by any standard was a pretty hefty price.

"That many, hey?" her father mused, and the old man chuckled.

"She is a useful daughter."

"I agree," her father said with a grin.

"We're not getting married, Mr. Mahlangu. So there's no need for *lobola*." Her protestation fell on deaf ears as her father and Mr. Mahlangu continued to discuss her worth in cattle. She gave up and summoned her next patient. Soon all of *Inkululeko* would think she was dating Mason too. Talk about a situation getting more and more ridiculous.

Mason escorted them back to town as promised. What he had done all morning while waiting for them to finish was anyone's guess. She didn't want him to have lunch with her family; things were already problematic enough, especially with her mother and Lia singing his praises after his "help" last night. Both had contacted her after she got home to thank her for bringing Mason, to say how wonderful he was and how happy they were for her. And yet, the reality—and inequality—of their deception ate at her more and more each day. The man had her entire family, with the exception of Daff, wrapped around his little finger while she had barely exchanged a single word with his brother.

The guilt, fear, and frustration continued to wrap around Daisy like an ever-tightening shroud, and she couldn't wait for the next two weeks to just be over.

"Why did you *really* come out to the township today?" Daisy asked Mason hours later, after what seemed like an endless lunch. The family had tactfully retreated while she walked him to his car to say good-bye.

"I really want to make a donation to the clinic," he said sincerely, and she lifted a brow, waiting. His lips quirked. "*And* I wanted to see how safe it was."

"I told you it was fine," she said, aggravated that he had deliberately ignored her. *Again.*

"I don't think it is," he said.

"It's none of your business," she flared, infuriated, and he brushed her cheek with his knuckles. The infinitely tender gesture made her pause.

"On the contrary, it *is* my business. I know more about danger than you ever could. Trust me when I tell you it's a disaster waiting to happen. I can protect you; please let me." It was hard to resist him when he was so obviously sincere about wanting to keep her safe. It made her feel . . . cherished. And she *hated* that. *Hated* that he made her feel so special, when it was all just pretend.

"You don't have to."

"I *want* to."

"Mason, your performance needs extend only so far," she said, forcing a laugh into her voice. "As method acting goes, this truly exceeds all expectation, but it's really better to keep things superficial. Just enough to make it credible."

He swore, the expletive ripe and vicious, and she jumped in fright.

"Fuck that, Daisy! This is your life we're talking about. It has nothing to do with this stupid game you're playing with your family."

"Why do you care?" she whispered, and he reeled back as if she had hit him.

"Why do I care?" he repeated in disbelief. "You're an unbelievable piece of work, aren't you? What kind of prick do you think I am?"

"Mason, I didn't mean . . ." He made a slashing motion with his hand, shutting her up.

"You want 'credible'? Fine. Here's something for your family to speculate over." He grabbed her face between his palms and planted his hard, angry mouth over hers, painfully grinding her lips against her teeth before gentling the kiss. His tongue plunged between her lips and stroked the roof of her mouth, and she groaned and willingly acquiesced to his touch. She locked her hands behind his neck; his hair had grown just enough for her to run her restless fingers through. The intensity of the kiss was both shocking and welcome, and it allowed Daisy a brief moment of respite from her usual turbulent thoughts. A peace within which there was nothing to do but enjoy his closeness, his scent, and his taste. She was dangerously close to allowing him to breach her defensive walls again. It was a sobering realization and one that finally drove her out of his embrace. He resisted her retreat, his hands refusing to release her until she pulled her head back and her lips away from him.

"Stop." The word was breathless, husky, and reluctant.

"I want you." The words were hoarse and sounded like they'd been tortured from him.

"You don't. You *can't*," she protested.

"Why the fuck not?" She flinched, but his gaze remained fixed and unrepentant.

"This isn't how this was supposed to go," she whispered. "You're not supposed to want me; I'm not supposed to like you. It was all supposed to remain neat and clinical."

"Where do you come up with these bullshit rules?"

"They're not *my* rules. They're the dictates of modern society. You're supposed to be with someone like Shar," she burst out desperately, and he reared back in horror.

"You would wish a bitch like that on me?"

"Daff or Lia, then; you're supposed to be with someone like them."

"Will you stop trying to foist me off on to your friends and family? Shar's a malevolent bitch. Your sisters are both completely insane, and they bore me to tears."

Mason wasn't sure why he was trying so hard to convince her that he wanted her. He considered it for a moment—the dull throbbing in his groin punctuating his every thought—and concluded that he was trying so hard because he *was* so hard. There was no logic to desire; it simply happened, sometimes between the unlikeliest of people. And it was occurring in spades between Mason and this contrary armful of femininity.

It would be better if she continued to believe that he didn't want her. But, consequences be damned, he was tired of fighting his powerful attraction to her. And he now found himself wishing it weren't so damned difficult to convince her of his sincerity, even while he knew that it was his reward for approaching her under false pretenses that first night. He was paying for that dumb move in spades. She didn't give her trust easily, and he wasn't sure how to earn it back.

"Good-bye, Mason," she whispered, finality in her voice, and bowing his head, he admitted defeat.

For now.

CHAPTER NINE

"I can't believe you're actually going through with this," Spencer said, shaking his head. Mason looked up from his duffel bag and glared at his nonplussed brother. The other man was dog sitting for the weekend and was there to pick Cooper up.

"Did you expect me to back out at the last second?" He shoved his shaving kit into the bag and followed it up with his brush—not really needed after he'd shorn his hair again last night—and aftershave. The expensive stuff.

"Well, yeah."

"Why would I leave her in the lurch like that?" Mason glared at him.

"She forced you to do this. It was a sad and desperate attempt to get a guy like you to go out with her, and I doubt she'd be surprised if you bailed on her."

"I'm going to say this once only, Spence, slowly so that it'll penetrate even *your* thick skull."

"Hey."

"I like her, and after this farce of a weekend is over, I'm going to ask her out. For real. Got that?"

"You're going to ask her out?"

"And she's going to say no," Mason predicted bitterly.

"Sometimes I don't get you at all," Spencer complained.

"Yeah? Join the fucking club."

⌒

"Miss me?" The flippant question was the first thing Mason asked when Daisy climbed into his car just before midday. She smiled at him, keeping her expression painfully polite in an attempt to prevent him from seeing just how very much she *had* missed him. She hadn't seen him since that afternoon at her parents' place. He'd called her at work, sent her flowers, and kept up the pretense of their fake relationship, even while Daisy had barely put any effort into it herself. She scrupulously avoided her family as much as possible to evade any questions about the nature of her relationship with Mason.

The only person she could speak to with any honesty was Daff, and that wasn't ever pleasant or reassuring because of her sister's tendency to overdramatize and make everything about her.

"It's not my place to miss you," she said rigidly, and he removed his sunglasses specifically so that he could roll his eyes at her.

"Get that stick out of your ass, Dr. Daisy. It's going to be a long journey, and I'd prefer it were a pleasant one."

He had a fair point, and she tried her best to look chastened.

"Maybe I missed you a little," she conceded, and he grinned broadly.

"I missed you too." He pushed his sunglasses back up his nose, and Daisy drank him in furtively. He had cut his hair again, the waves that she had enjoyed just a week ago ruthlessly shorn away to leave only short spikes in its wake. He was wearing an open-necked white dress shirt, with those faded jeans she liked so much. She really *had* missed him. Everything about him: his irreverent sense of humor, his laughter, and his insightful observations. The way he tilted his head slightly when he was listening to her, as if her every word was interesting. He glanced around and raised a quizzical brow.

"No Peaches?" She shook her head.

"She's staying with Lucinda this weekend. What about Cooper?"

"He's with Spencer." He watched as she clicked the seat belt into place.

"What does Spencer think about our so-called blossoming romance?" It was something she had been meaning to ask for a while. He shot her a chagrined look.

"He guessed the truth almost immediately."

"Jeez, if Spencer could guess, then I don't know how much chance we have of convincing everybody else," she said with a wince.

⚡

"What are you trying to say about my brother?" Mason's tone was inadvertently defensive, and her eyes widened in alarm.

"Oh my gosh, I'm sorry, that sounded worse than I intended; I just mean that he doesn't strike me as very—"

"Intelligent? Who's guilty of judging by appearances now, Daisy?" he chided, genuinely disappointed in her, and she exhaled impatiently.

"I was *going* to say observant. Your brother's intelligence has never been in doubt. The man owns a successful business; he completed a master's degree, for heaven's sake. You and he are very much alike." A curl of warmth unfurled in his chest, an unfamiliar feeling that he couldn't quite identify, but it made him want to puff out his chest and grin like an idiot.

"How so?" he asked softly.

"You know how," she said, rolling her eyes. "You're both good look-ing, really smart, and determined to succeed. You're basically the com-plete package. Thanks for making me spell that out, mister. Like your ego isn't big enough as it is."

Pride. That was what he was feeling. Pride that this wonderful woman saw him in such a flattering light. He couldn't help it; the grin broke free and his chest expanded just a little.

—

"You think I'm hot and clever with a great package? Dr. Daisy, you're such a flatterer." His words were teasing, but Daisy could see a spark of sincere appreciation in his eyes. Something told her that Mason was even less used to honest compliments than she was. It was an astonishing revelation, and it completely melted her heart.

"Ready?" he asked, and Daisy nodded, suddenly feeling inappropriately ebullient as if she wasn't on her way to orchestrate the biggest deception of her entire life.

—

It was a six-and-a-half-hour drive to Morgan's Bay in the Wild Coast on the national highway, and they had long periods of silence followed by spurts of lively conversation. They debated about everything from politics to religion. Sometimes the arguments were less topical and about favorite movies, music, and even reality shows. They were also playing an ongoing, cutthroat game. The winner was the person who had spotted the most red cars by the end of the journey. It got hilariously ugly and argumentative really fast. Especially when they were driving through the tiny towns en route to their destination.

"Why doesn't that one count?" Mason asked heatedly, as they were passing through yet another small cluster of shops and homes that posed as a town.

"It's parked," Daisy said smugly, and he shot her a look so incredulous she could read it even through the sunglasses.

"Bull*shit*," he snapped. "That wasn't a rule when we passed through the last town and you called out three *dozen* parked cars."

"I didn't," she denied smoothly. It had only been three. "You're driving, so I don't blame you for not being one hundred percent focused on the game, but there's no reason to make stuff up."

"That isn't a rule," he maintained.

"Well, it should be. In fact, I think it is. Now."

"You're such a *cheat*. Fine, whatever, no parked cars. You were the one earning the most points on parked cars anyway, so it's no skin off my nose!"

"Great. So that's twenty-three to you and thirty-five to me." He swore under his breath and shook his head.

The game continued.

On long, isolated stretches of road, when there were hardly any other cars, they talked about other more personal topics, and Daisy found herself confiding things she had never admitted to another soul.

"I was convinced unicorns existed. I was embarrassingly persistent about it," she confessed. "Up until the age of twelve I was determined to prove their existence. I was so gullible, and the Internet didn't help. There are so many 'true accounts' of unicorn sightings, unicorn fossils, unicorn videos on YouTube, and grainy 'found' images. I was going to be the person to definitively prove that unicorns were an actual animal species. I thought it was a legitimate branch of research."

She shook her head wryly and a little sadly as she recalled it.

"It added to my reputation as the 'weird, *other* McGregor sister.' In fact, I think that's probably what started it. It didn't help that I was a plump, frizzy-haired misfit without a single friend and that it looked like a unicorn factory had exploded over every item I possessed. We're talking clothing, bags, books . . . I even had a frickin' unicorn Alice band." Mason winced at that revelation.

"At some point your mom *had* to have said something, right?"

"You've met my mother, of course she said something. She was absolutely appalled. At first, for about five seconds, she thought it was adorable. Until it became an obsession. I was a mouthy brat about it too. If she threw anything out, I'd whine to my dad about it, and he saw nothing wrong with it. Told my mother I was just being creative and creativity should be nurtured and not stifled. So every time after that, whenever she said anything about my unicorns, I'd throw those words back at her: *'You're stifling my creativity, Mother!'*

"God, I was such an obnoxious brat. I knew my dad would take my side, he always did, and I think that's when my mother and I started drifting apart." She sighed and then laughed bitterly. "All this time I blamed the country club while I'd been pushing my mom and sisters away for years. Always aware of how different I was and practically blaming them for it."

"There's nothing wrong with being different, Daisy."

"But I shoved it in their faces, and then when I realized how far out of reach they were, it was difficult to breach the gap."

"But not impossible. They love you and you love them. And you're not the same bratty, unicorn-collecting kid anymore."

"Nah, I collect caterpillars now," she reminded him.

"Yeah, I remember," he said with a grimace. "I've been meaning to ask, why caterpillars? Why not butterflies?"

"Butterflies are boring," she said. "They've already achieved the pinnacle of their existence. Caterpillars are beautiful and yet still have so much potential locked inside them. Weird, I know."

"Maybe a little weird, but fascinating too." And telling. Of course she collected caterpillars; a psychoanalyst would have a field day with Daisy and how she dealt with her many insecurities. Even her hobbies were a reflection of her self-doubt.

"Think about it, inside every single butterfly or moth there's a contented little caterpillar," she muttered smugly.

"Don't you mean there's a butterfly waiting to emerge from every caterpillar?"

"Meh, I prefer my interpretation. So much more fun to think that every pretty butterfly was once a fat, greedy little grub." She chuckled wickedly, and he laughed at the pure malice in the sound.

"What were you like as a boy?" she asked, changing the subject abruptly.

"Pretty much what you'd expect. Spencer and I got into all kinds of trouble; luckily it was all petty shit that didn't have life-altering repercussions."

Daisy recalled something her father had said.

"Did you vandalize Mr. Richards's store?"

"No, but I know who did." She poked him on one hard bicep when he didn't elaborate.

"Well?"

"Timmy Jr. did it."

"Mr. Richards's own son?" Well, *that* was news.

"Yeah, the little bastard figured Spencer and I would be blamed, and he was pissed off with his dad about something and trashed the place." He shook his head in disgust. "The cops questioned us for three hours, and we were only thirteen and fifteen at the time. We both had solid alibis that night, though. Our mother was in hospital, and we didn't leave her side until she died."

She had forgotten their mother had passed away at a relatively young age and was ashamed she hadn't asked him about his parents before.

"And the police kept you in custody, despite your mother dying?" She was horrified by the callousness of the adults in that situation. He pulled a face.

"We were the bad kids in town."

"That makes no difference," she seethed. "You were boys who had just lost your mother."

"It was a long time ago, Daisy." He had an amused tilt to his lips, but she could see the tension along the firm line of his jaw and knew he wasn't as unaffected by the memory as he was pretending to be.

"And your father took care of you after that?" she asked, diverting the topic slightly.

"If you can call it taking care of us. He managed to stay out of jail until Spencer turned eighteen, which kept us out of foster care, but he wasn't exactly interested in raising us. When he had money he saw to it that we had food, but when he didn't he told us to figure something out. We became pretty good at shoplifting. Always food. Never anything else. We had standards, and we always wanted to be better than our circumstances permitted. The day Spencer turned eighteen the old man took off and we never saw him again. I guess I'm grateful he stuck around, but that's about it."

"You were still underage when Spencer left for college," she suddenly realized, horrified.

"Yeah, but the house, old and dilapidated though it was, was ours, so I had a roof over my head. I also had two jobs at the time. Enough to keep myself clothed and fed and the water and heat on. Spencer sent money home too."

"Why did nobody intervene? Where were your teachers, the counselors? Other adults?" He had fallen through the cracks, and nobody had known or cared. It brought tears to her eyes, and she tried to hide them from him, knowing he wouldn't like anything resembling sympathy or pity.

"I kept a low profile. Good grades, stayed out of trouble, and if anybody asked I said my dad was back. Spencer didn't want to leave me, he wanted to drag me to Grahamstown with him, but he would be living in a sponsored dorm, and having me there would have broken the rules and possibly resulted in him losing his scholarship.

"We nearly came to blows when he insisted on staying. In the end we both knew our prospects would improve if he got a degree. The plan was he would get his degree and after he finished I would get mine. Well, that was *his* plan. I'd already started looking into the military. He nearly blew a gasket when I told him I was enlisting."

He spoke matter-of-factly, as if he were talking about someone else, and she found the disconnect telling. He had completely disassociated himself from the boy who had shoplifted to stay alive, who had spent two years completely alone. It had shaped him into the man he was, but it was no longer relevant to his present. Yet Spencer embraced that same past by giving all those motivational speeches. And while she thought the town's troubled youth could learn a great deal from Mason as well, she understood that he was a more private person who didn't open up as easily. Public speaking was not for him.

They were quiet for a long time after that, speaking only to add to their respective red car tallies.

Three hours later, after a long nap and quick food and fuel stop in Port Elizabeth, Daisy took over the driving and Mason was stretched out in the passenger seat, watching the green scenery pass by. After a while he seemed to grow bored with that and turned to watch her while she drove.

"Will you please stop doing that?" she finally snapped after a few minutes of relentless staring. "It's unnerving."

"Stop doing what?"

"Staring at me."

"I wasn't."

"You blatantly were," she gasped. A little offended by the lie.

"How do you know my eyes aren't closed?" It was a valid question, since he was still wearing his sunglasses.

"I just know!"

"I was counting your freckles," he finally admitted, and she gave him a horrified look. He pointed out the windscreen. "Eyes on the road, Daisy."

"You were *what?*" she gritted out, after diverting her eyes back on the road.

"Counting your freckles . . . and I'm a little irritated with your interruption. You made me lose count. I like how they congregate on your nose and then kind of carelessly scatter across your cheekbone like drunken little soldiers, just a few here and there. Do you know that some fell out of line and randomly landed wherever the hell they wanted? Little rebels. There's one just below the corner of your lip, looks a little lonely down there, but it hasn't fallen as far as this little guy here." He reached out and brushed his thumb over the sensitive skin of her throat. "What is it doing *all* the way over there? I think this one is my favorite."

"Stop counting my freckles and try to get some sleep," she whispered, not at all sure what to make of this.

"That's what I'm trying to do; it's like counting stars, only so much prettier." His words were starting to slur, and she refrained from commenting. A gentle snore a few minutes later alerted her to the fact that he'd dozed off, and a quick glance in his direction confirmed it. His head was lolling forward slightly and his beautiful lips were slightly parted. She forced her eyes back on the road and sighed, already missing his lively companionship. She was in deep trouble here. The man was proving to be much too irresistible.

━━━

"Daisy," her name was whispered directly into her ear, and Daisy startled awake and blinked in confusion.

"Wha—" Why was it so dark? She turned her head, and her lips brushed against Mason's stubbled jaw. He backed away quickly.

"We're here," he announced, and she rubbed her eyes.

"Already?" she muttered incoherently.

"Yeah, the last two hours flew by." He had taken over the driving again after just an hour, and Daisy had reluctantly relinquished control of the beautiful car back to him. But she'd been tired after her half day at work and was happy to let him do the bulk of the driving.

"Your hotel is fifteen minutes away," she said apologetically. "I'm sorry, it's the closest one I could . . ."

"Don't worry about it, Lia sorted something out for me."

"What?" Her sleep-muddled brain wasn't functioning properly, and she was still trying to process his words when he stepped out of the car and opened the passenger door for her.

"Come on, sweetheart," he coaxed, taking hold of her elbow gently.

"You're staying here too?"

"I am," he confirmed. He stopped at the boot to unload their luggage while a porter happily stacked the bags onto a trolley.

"I thought it was full."

"It's been taken care of," he said as he shepherded her into the hotel reception area, the porter following behind them. They were welcomed by a warmly smiling desk manager.

"Good evening, you're here for the Edmonton-McGregor wedding?" The attractive and polished woman's smile widened at the sight of Mason, who smiled back casually, flashing that killer dimple at her.

"Yes," Mason responded smoothly before Daisy could offer a reply. "Daisy McGregor and Mason Carlisle." The woman's glance slid over to Daisy, and her smile faltered very slightly. Daisy knew her hair had to be a total mess and her T-shirt was wrinkled after the long drive. As if sensing her discomfort, Mason's hand slid beneath her hair to cup the nape of her neck. He squeezed slightly, his thumb and forefinger massaging her nape soothingly. The woman efficiently went about the check-in process, and despite Daisy's muffled protest, Mason offered his own credit card for the security deposit. When she tried to offer hers to cover her own room, the woman smiled and said it wouldn't be necessary. The desk manager lifted a couple of welcome bags from behind the desk and handed them one each. Mason grinned at the sight; he had never actually got around to helping them fill the bags.

"I finally get to see what's in these," he said, prodding Daisy with a conspiratorial elbow. His humor was infectious, and she returned his grin with one of her own.

"Please note that dinner will be served between seven and nine thirty tonight. Details for tomorrow's itinerary will be found in your welcome bag."

"Thank you," Daisy said, reaching for the keycard the woman held out to her, while Mason took the one in her other hand.

"It's on the second floor," the manager supplied. "Most of our rooms are reserved for wedding guests this weekend."

"Thanks," Mason said, before hooking an arm around Daisy's waist and leading her toward one of the elevators. The porter told them he would wait for the next one, and after the doors slid shut, closing them into the little glass-walled box, which probably had stunning ocean views during the day, Daisy looked down at her card.

"I'm in room twenty-three. You?" He didn't bother looking down at his card, shoving it into the back pocket of his jeans instead.

"We're in the same room, Daisy," he informed her.

"*What?*" The word was practically screamed, and he grimaced. She shrugged out of his hold and turned to face him, crossing her arms over her chest. He looked down at her tightly folded arms, furious face, and tapping foot and seemed to be fighting back a grin.

"You look pissed off," he noted—his voice and face a study in blandness—and she gasped.

"Of course I'm pissed off," she gritted out through her teeth. "I told you we wouldn't be sharing a room!"

"I figured it would be best if we did."

"I can't believe you did this. I can't believe . . ." The elevator pinged and slid to a stop at the second floor, and Daisy's mouth slammed shut as the doors opened to reveal Lia and Clayton on the other side.

"You made it," Lia said with a relieved smile. Mason and Daisy stepped out, and Lia hugged them both effusively.

"Mason, I don't think you've met my fiancé," she said, turning to Clayton, who stepped forward with an oily smile that sent a shudder of distaste down Daisy's spine. He held out a hand to Mason.

"Clayton Edmonton the Third," he said jovially, and Daisy very determinedly kept herself from rolling her eyes at the characteristically arrogant introduction.

"Mason," the big man at her side supplied succinctly, completely without artifice. He dwarfed Clayton, who was only about five eleven. Mason just looked so much more masculine next to Clayton's urbane smoothness. Mason's big body was honed by years of physical activity and combat, while Clayton had the polished look of a man who spent too much time perfecting his body in a gym and no time at all using that body for anything other than leisure activities.

"So you're dating our Daisy, are you?" he said with a sickeningly paternal smirk. "I don't recall her ever dating anyone before."

He leaned down and planted a kiss on Daisy's lips, and she pulled her head back, feeling violated by the overly familiar embrace. He'd never kissed her on the mouth before, and it completely repulsed her. She was suddenly grateful to have Mason by her side.

She glanced up at Mason and noted the frown on his face as he took in the way Clayton's hand still lingered on her hip. He didn't seem to like it and deliberately slid his arm back around her waist and tugged her out of Clayton's hold until she was tucked securely against him.

"Join us for a pre-dinner drink?" Lia asked with a strained smile. Daisy looked at her a little closer. Her sister looked pale and exhausted, not exactly the picture of a beaming bride-to-be. Daisy tried to dismiss it as stress and nerves, but something in Lia's eyes told her this was different.

The second elevator pinged, and the porter exited, dragging the luggage cart behind him.

"We've literally just arrived," Mason said, indicating toward the porter. "We're going to freshen up, rest a bit, and join you all for dinner."

"Okay, we'll see you later, then; I think you were the last of the weekend guests to arrive—although we do have wedding-day-only guests coming on Sunday, of course—so there'll be a full house for dinner tonight. Mason, you'll be joining us at the family table, of course," Lia said.

"You're babbling, sweets," Clayton said patronizingly, and Lia's smile faltered.

"Sorry about that; it's the excitement," she said, her eyes strained. "Anyway, we'll see you later."

They entered the elevator, and Lia waved as the doors slid shut. Mason dropped his arm from around Daisy's waist and took her hand in his. They turned to follow the porter, who was already waiting at their room door.

Mason took Daisy's key card from her to open the door and helped the porter offload the cart before tipping the friendly young man and sending him on his way. Daisy, in the meantime was nervously eyeing the large, luxurious suite, with its panoramic floor-to-ceiling corner windows and its gigantic bed.

"How long has Edmonton been so handsy with you?" Mason's voice, coming from right behind her, startled Daisy.

"Uh, what do you mean?" She stalled, and he moved to stand in front of her and look down at her grimly.

"You know what I mean, Daisy. He had his greedy paws all over you."

"It wasn't that bad." She shifted uncomfortably.

"Has it been worse?" His voice was dangerously quiet, and she lowered her eyes.

"I thought it was my imagination," she revealed, her voice emerging on a tiny whisper. He was standing so close to her that she could feel his every muscle tense.

"Explain."

"He's been a little overly . . . familiar."

"And you're letting your sister go through with this wedding?" He sounded so absolutely incredulous that Daisy was both gratified that he believed her and ashamed that she hadn't trusted herself enough to talk to at least Daff about how she felt around Clayton.

"Daisy, why the hell didn't you say something? Tell me what that fucker has done to you; I need to know exactly how badly I have to hurt him."

"It's not like that. I mean, he's made me feel uncomfortable; he makes these awful comments about my body but makes it sound like advice or affection. He has patted my butt on occasion, seemingly a casual, friendly touch—but his hand always lingers *just* that fraction too long—and when I confronted him about it, he said he wasn't interested in me in *that* way. I'm 'not his type' after all, and maybe I'm jealous of what my prettier sister has." Her eyes flooded with tears, and she tried to keep her face averted to prevent Mason from seeing them.

"How has none of your family seen this? I took one look at the situation, and I could tell you were uncomfortable around him and that he was much too familiar with you."

"They don't see me the same way you do," she admitted, a tear streaking down her cheek and finally, *finally*, she was able to recognize that Mason *did* see her as different, as special, as pretty and interesting and every other really wonderful thing he had called her in the past. "I'm just Daisy. I don't attract that kind of male attention."

A single tear, and he was undone. Mason watched it trail down one round cheek and tremble on the edge of her jawline before it lost the battle with gravity and fell. He didn't know where it landed, he was too busy drowning in those sad, drenched gray eyes.

"Daisy," he groaned, reaching up to knuckle some of the stray curls out of her face. The soft, springy tendrils wrapped around his fist, and he unclenched his hand and combed his fingers into her thick hair, loving the feeling of it under his palm. His other hand moved up to cup her cheek, and his thumb moved to wipe away the last trace of that tear. "Angels shouldn't weep."

It was a silly thing to say, whimsical and uncharacteristic, but it made her smile, and that made him feel less foolish. Her small, soft hand came up to cover his.

"Thank you."

"What for?"

"Believing me." Her words infuriated him, made him want to take on every single person in the world who had ever made her feel worthless and unattractive. Starting with Daisy herself. He unwound his hand from her hair and reached for her glasses, removing them and tossing them onto a nearby dresser in one quick movement.

"Hey, watch it, I didn't bring a spare pair," she squeaked. He glared down at her, silencing her instantly, and he smothered a grin. He loved the slightly unfocused look in her eyes when she wasn't wearing her glasses; it was cute. She looked like a little fledgling owl about to leap from the nest for the first time.

"How blind are you without those?" he asked, and she blinked, a slow, sleepy little blink.

"I'm not blind," she said indignantly. "Things are fuzzy and out of focus, but I can see you clearly."

"Good, then watch this—" His mouth was on hers before she had a chance to respond, and instead of the protestation he was expecting, she sighed and sank into the kiss, as if she'd been longing for it and wanting it as much as he. Her lips parted, and before he could make his move, her tongue was in his mouth. It nearly sent him to his knees.

His hand went to the back of her head, pulling her closer as his tongue finally won their duel and ravaged its way into her mouth, seeking, asking . . . *taking*. She tasted heavenly, and her flavor was like a drug in his bloodstream; he craved more of it even as he drank it from her.

He backed her toward the inviting king-size bed, never lifting his mouth from hers, and she allowed it, her hands burrowing under his T-shirt, while she backpedaled until the back of her knees hit the bed. She lost her balance and fell onto the bed, taking him with her, and he landed partially on top of her, one hand braced on the mattress for balance and the other trailing down from her face toward her chest and then her breast. He cupped one of the temptingly soft mounds, testing its shape and weight in the palm of his hand, wishing there were no layers of clothing between them.

She arched herself into his hand, obviously wanting more, and he reluctantly left her breast, ignoring her moan of despair, to trail his fingers down her waist until he found the bottom edge of her T-shirt. His hand crept beneath the cotton, craving the heat of her naked skin against his, but she moved before he could touch her, writhing out from beneath him and breaking contact with his mouth. Gutted, he watched as she struggled to sit up and peer at him through those big gray eyes with their massively dilated pupils. Her mouth was swollen and red, her breathing out of control, and he could see her hard nipples straining against the confines of both her bra and T-shirt. She swallowed and licked her lips causing him to groan.

"Are we . . . are we going to . . . f-fuck?" The word made his cock swell more, even while he winced at the crudity coming from that pretty mouth.

"Daisy," he reprimanded shakily. "Such language."

"Learned it from you," she reminded him.

"Unlearn it; euphemisms suit you more," he murmured, while he reached out to trail his finger over her naughty, kewpie doll mouth. He leaned over to nuzzle the sensitive spot below her jaw, and she tilted her head to allow him greater access.

"Well? Are we?"

"Hmmm, I'd say so," he whispered. "But when we have more time. For now we're going to do some seriously heavy petting. You up for that?"

Daisy considered the question and looked into his strained face; his eyelids were heavy, making him look sleepy, but she wasn't fooled, he was hyperalert, his entire body radiating tension. She glanced down and could see him straining at his zipper and knew with absolute certainty that this man wanted her. Wanted *her*! Daisy McGregor. It was a heady, powerful feeling, and she craved more of it. She wanted him, and she wasn't going to fight it anymore. Why not just enjoy this? Mason was a great guy, but he wasn't the man for her. He was just the man for now.

"I am," she finally said, after a long, fraught silence. He groaned, his arms gave way, and he collapsed onto the bed on his back. He raised his hands to cover his face, and she admired his strong, beautifully veined and muscled arms. She could see the bottom edge of a tattoo peeking out from beneath the rolled-up sleeve of his shirt, and it thrilled her to know that she would soon see that tattoo. And so much more.

"Thank God for that," he muttered into his hands before he reached for her and tumbled her over his broad chest for another long, deep drugging kiss. "Come on, angel, let's get this pesky T-shirt off you."

She giggled, and together they fumbled like two teens as they tugged at and finally tore her T-shirt before dragging it up over her head. Daisy felt self-conscious as she was revealed to him for the first time. She was aware that because she was half slouched over him, her love handles were showing and her tummy was pooching, everything was too soft and nothing like his tight perfection. And he was staring, a lot . . . fixedly. She was certain that he'd never before been to bed with a woman who was less than perfect and now started to feel uncomfortable beneath that piercing regard. Until he spoke . . .

"Hello, old friend, we meet again." His tone was rough and filled with admiration. Daisy followed his gaze down to her chest and laughed when she saw that he was staring at her bra. The same lacy pink bra from that afternoon in her house.

"Stop it," she chuckled, and he shook his head.

"Do you know how often I've fantasized about you in this pretty pink thing?" His words were gruff and his tone a little reverent. He reached out and ran his finger over the flesh above the scalloped lace edge of one of the cups. Her nipples went harder at the subtle caress, and he left a trail of goose bumps in his wake. His mouth followed his fingers and she hissed at the contact, all humor forgotten.

He continued to nuzzle her through the lace, edging closer and closer to the hard, tight bead at the center of her breast. She cupped her hands around the back of his head, trying to guide him there, but he seemed to have his own ideas, moving away from that breast to nuzzle at the other one.

"Mason, please," she begged, and he looked up at her, those beautiful green eyes slumberous and heavy with desire. His bottom lip looked fuller, his breath was hitching in his chest, and she could see he was as affected as she was.

"Please what?" he asked in a whisper.

"Touch me."

"Where?"

"You know where."

"Tell me what you want, Daisy," he encouraged, and she swallowed and moved her own hand down to cup her breast.

"Here. Touch me here," she said, and he made a satisfied sound in the back of his throat. It sounded like a purr.

He sat up and dragged her into his lap. After wrapping an arm around her waist, he took her hard nipple gently between his teeth, abrading it against the lace of her bra and the edge of his teeth. Not hurting, just making it hypersensitive before sinking his mouth over it and suckling hard.

"*Oh!*" Her back arched over his arm as the electric sensation shot through her entire body. But he wasn't done; he had moved to the other breast, and the same treatment yielded the same results. Daisy, who had only ever orgasmed by her own hand, felt dangerously close to coming without even removing her jeans. Every stitch of clothing set her nerve endings on fire, and she needed to get rid of it all; she needed to feel his heat against her.

"Take it off," she sobbed, and he lifted his head, his eyes gleaming down at her.

"What?"

"Everything. I want it off."

"Bra first, I think," he said in a ridiculously measured voice. How could he sound so in control when she could feel his hot erection grinding against her bottom? He reached behind her, deftly unclasped her bra, and sent it flying across the room, before moving his eyes down to her chest. She heard him whisper a little prayer of thanks as he took in the sight before him.

"Too big," she muttered self-consciously. He didn't seem to hear her as he cupped one of the soft, naked mounds, testing the weight in the palm of his hand.

"You bite your tongue, young woman," he chastised after a couple of moments of sheer reverence. "These beauties are perfect. They're nowhere close to too big. They fill my hands with room to spare."

"That's because you have great big mitts for hands."

"Yeah? Well, you know what they say about guys with big hands," he reminded her smugly, and she laughed. Daisy had never dreamt she'd be comfortable enough with a man that she could laugh so freely while sitting topless in his lap. But this was Mason, and he'd always been marvelous at putting her at ease.

"That's big feet," she corrected.

"I have big feet too . . ." he said, then paused for a beat before adding, "and you should see the size of my cock."

He captured her laugh with his mouth, and things got serious very quickly. She started tugging at his shirt, and he happily obliged her by pulling it off and sending it in the same direction as her bra. She moaned in appreciation when she saw his beautiful hard chest. Just a sprinkling of hair, tanned and taut, but with way too many scars marring all that smooth, perfect skin. He had an intricate Celtic band tattooed around one bicep, sexy and mysterious looking, and his other arm was embellished with a stunning geometric quarter sleeve from shoulder to bicep. A true work of art. And climbing up his right side, from hip to just below his pectoral, was a stark black tree bared of all its leaves. There were gnarled initials and numbers printed randomly on some of the branches; at first glance they looked like part of the tree. And it was this gorgeous, haunting tattoo that she wondered about the most.

His modeling shots must have been Photoshopped, because none of these scars and tattoos had been present in a single pic, which was a shame because this was a warrior's body and it was beautiful and she wanted to kiss every single scar; she wanted to lick his abs and suck his nipples, trace his tattoos with her tongue . . . She abruptly understood that everything she *wanted* to do was highly achievable in this moment and started on the licking and petting and sucking seconds later. He allowed it, his breathing becoming more labored with every sweep of her tongue and every tiny kiss she bestowed at random spots on his skin.

"If you're going to kiss me, angel," he suddenly muttered hoarsely. "Do it properly, okay? I don't think I can stand these sweet little butterfly kisses . . . they're designed to drive a man insane."

He cupped her face and brought her mouth back up to his, kissing her hotly and flipping her onto her back until he was positioned between her thighs. They were both still wearing their jeans, and as he began to grind against her, the double layers of denim became a major hindrance. He swore impatiently and tore at the buttons of his jeans and, following his lead, she struggled with hers too. They both managed to shimmy out of their denims at the same time; Daisy's were completely kicked off while

Mason's were bunched around his ankles. Neither cared, and he was back at her mouth in seconds with penetrating kisses that made her lose her reason. His hands were busy at her breasts, plumping and thumbing at the nipples until she thought she would lose her mind.

Her hands dug into his back and then his buttocks when he started up that deep grinding again. This time, with only her lacy, damp panties and his cotton boxer briefs between them, the sensations were way more intense. She could feel the long, thick outline of his hard penis as he sawed against her damp furrow, the tip brushing against her clitoris with every forward stroke.

She bent her knees and thrust herself up against him, wishing that she could have more, and as if sensing her desire, one of his hands left her breast and crept down over her belly and under her panties, his thumb finding her with ease. His mouth was now at her nipple, sucking strongly, the way—she'd discovered—she loved it.

Daisy opened her thighs even wider, and he took it as an invitation to further liberties, his long middle finger attempting entry into her slick channel. He got only knuckle deep before she came like she never had before. She clenched tightly around that intrusive finger for one long, long moment, before she released. The spasms repeated again and again, while Daisy's back arched and she sobbed into his neck, her nails buried in his back, her ankles crossed around his buttocks.

One of her hands moved down between their tightly locked bodies, and he shifted slightly to accommodate her and then gasped in utter shock when she pushed his briefs down and took him in hand.

"Daisy, wait, you don't have t—" The desperate words faded into a deep groan of satisfaction as—after only one untutored stroke of her hand—he came. Hard and fast and copiously. He shuddered and spent every last drop all over their bellies and her still-stroking hand.

For an endless amount of time, neither of them moved, and then, as if by unspoken accord, they both flowed into a tangle of arms and legs. They were breathing heavily, hot and wet and literally steaming as their body heat hit the cooler air.

Daisy's head was resting on one of Mason's hard biceps, and his arm was curled so that his hand could idly toy with her hair.

"That was fucking amazing," he muttered after he finally caught his breath, and Daisy made a contented little sound of agreement as she snuggled closer. She had both hands curled against his chest with her nose buried in the hollow of his throat and was drifting off to sleep, while his one hand played with her hair and his index finger of his other hand traced lacy patterns across her back.

"Are you falling asleep?" he asked, his voice brimming with amusement.

"Tired."

"What about dinner? Should we order in?" He sounded disgustingly keen, and she smiled sleepily.

"No. Wake me up; family will be waiting." He sighed, his chest heaving beneath her hands.

"It's nearly seven."

"Just a quick nap. We can be late." She snuggled closer, feeling not even the slightest bit self-conscious at her nudity, and fell asleep seconds later.

⌐

Mason watched her sleep, a pang of . . . *something* in his chest. God, they hadn't even shagged, but it was still the most amazing sex of his life. He wasn't sure how the hell that worked; all he knew was that little Daisy McGregor had rocked his world with her irresistible mixture of charm, innocence, and lethal sexiness. He knew he should move, get a damp cloth or something to at least wipe some of the stickiness off their bodies, but he wasn't sure he *could* move, and right now the damp discomfort was preferable to letting Daisy go.

She looked so peaceful, he didn't want to disturb her, but as the minutes ticked over and their bodies cooled, he sighed and regretfully conceded to the inevitable.

"Daisy," he singsonged softly into her ear and smiled when her forehead puckered slightly. "Daaaisy."

"Hmm?" Grumpy girl. Clearly early mornings weren't the only times she hated having her sleep interrupted.

"Come on, angel. Open your eyes." A deep sigh and another moan.

"Wha—?"

"It's time to get cleaned up," he told her and watched as awareness returned to her eyes. She went bright pink as her natural shyness inserted itself firmly between them. Understanding that this was all a bit over-whelming for her, he dropped a kiss on the tip of her delightfully freckled nose and eased away from her, allowing her the space she needed.

"You can have the bathroom first," he said, and she dragged a pillow to her chest and slid off the bed, keeping the cushion firmly in front of her but completely unaware of the fact that the full-length mirror behind her showcased her smooth, naked back, nipped-in waist, and generous bum and thighs to perfection. Her tiny little pink panties rode low on her hips, low enough to just tease a glimpse of the shadowy cleft between the delightful mounds of her behind.

"I won't be long," she promised, keeping her eyes downcast, which was probably a good thing because he was hard as a steel pipe again and not doing a damned thing to hide that fact. He wanted her, and she would have to adapt to that fact very quickly because he was done retreating. He would deal with the fallout if it meant having her in his bed for however long this lasted.

CHAPTER TEN

Daisy sagged against the bathroom door and took a deep breath before dropping the pillow and shakily making her way to the sink. She was a mess, literally and figuratively. She couldn't quite believe what had just happened. And she couldn't bring herself to regret it at all. This was all new to her, and she figured Mason would be a phenomenal teacher. But that didn't mean years of shyness and awkwardness around the opposite sex would simply disappear after one—admittedly amazing—sexual experience with the guy.

"Just go with it, Daisy," she whispered, as she stared at her reflection in the mirror above the basin. "Enjoy it while it lasts."

She took a long shower, her nerve endings still alive with sensation, her body feeling completely alien to her. Throbbing and sensitive and *ready*. After she got out of the shower, she dropped the towel and stared at herself in the full-length mirror next to the huge tub. It wasn't something she usually did. She tended to avoid looking at her naked body, hating every pound of extra fat, every bit of jiggle, any hint of cellulite . . . but now she wanted to see. Wanted to inspect and list the so-called imperfections. This body, which she had practically despised for so many years, had just given her more pleasure than she had ever believed possible.

She looked at the thighs, too round, too plump . . . without any gap at all between them, the tummy—not flat and abtastic, instead soft and rounded—but not as hideous as she had once thought. Her breasts—she reached up to cup one and hissed when the sensitive nipple immediately tightened in her palm—they weren't perfect little apples; they were big, round, and overt. Her nipples were positioned high and gave a false impression of pertness, but the mounds themselves were bottom heavy and sloped gently down into a full curve.

She saw it all and automatically cataloged each and every flaw and then stopped and realized that Mason had seen all of this too, in a brightly lit room. He hadn't seen any flaws; he had seen a desirable woman. The woman in the mirror wasn't perfect, but she was . . . okay. She was somewhat ordinary with her curly brown hair, her freckles, and her pale skin; she had curves, and maybe they were a little fuller than was currently acceptable, but they emphasized her waist and gave her a pretty decent hourglass shape. She had cellulite, a double chin, and too much junk in the trunk, but right now she looked vibrant, happy, and even a little sexy.

"Is this a private party or can anyone join?" She jumped guiltily and looked to where Mason stood framed in the doorway, watching her watch herself.

He had on a fresh pair of briefs and that was all he wore. He came to stand behind her and eyed her reflection in the mirror. There was nothing but sincere appreciation and desire in his gaze. He was so tall her head only reached his chest; he wrapped his strong, hard arms around her and spread one hand over her stomach and the other replaced her hand at her breast. His dark skin contrasted starkly with her paleness, but the most striking thing about the way they looked together was that he made her seem tiny.

Beneath his huge hands, everything about her was small. His hand spanned the stomach she spent way too much time angsting over, making the extra weight look like nothing. And he was right; he was able to cover her breast with room to spare. She watched as he bent down to nuzzle his favorite spot beneath her ear and smiled and leaned against him. She loved the feeling of his taut body behind hers. She had never felt more fragile or more protected.

She turned in his arms and rubbed herself up against him voluptuously; his hot skin against her breasts felt simply amazing, and she was almost embarrassed to hear herself purring like a cat at the delightful sensation of the sparse hair on his chest grazing against her hard nipples.

His hands had come to rest on her butt and he was kneading the flesh there appreciatively before dragging one hand down to her thigh and lifting her leg so that he could rock his erection against her nude femininity. They moaned, and he leaned down to kiss her hungrily, his tongue mimicking the thrusting of his hips.

Things were starting to get out of hand when Mason groaned and reluctantly freed her mouth.

"We don't have time, Daisy," he whispered regretfully, while still rubbing himself up against her. "Christ, this is hard."

"Yes, it is," she giggled, and he growled, before nipping her bottom lip.

"Behave." He dropped her thigh, and Daisy wobbled unsteadily. He grabbed one of the luxurious white hotel robes from behind the door and stuffed her arms into it.

"Cover yourself up, you shameless hussy. Stop trying to tempt me with your charms. Now go get dressed while I shower."

She saluted smartly, just like he'd taught her, and he winked before ushering her out of the bathroom and shutting the door behind her. It reopened seconds later, and he tossed her pillow at her before closing and pointedly locking the door again. Daisy hugged the pillow to her chest and did a happy dance around the room before the fizzing in her veins settled down long enough for her to finally get dressed.

"You know you're going to have to talk to Lia about Edmonton, right?" Mason muttered somberly in the lift forty minutes later.

"Yes."

"Preferably before he touches you again," he continued dangerously. "He lays another finger on you, and all bets are off. You'll have to wind up explaining why her fiancé will be eating through a straw for the rest of his days."

"Mason, don't do or say anything until I've had a chance to talk with Lia or Daff, okay?"

"No promises."

"Mason."

"Daisy, if he touches you, I'm going to kick his ass. There's no debating that. He has been gaslighting you for months, making you doubt yourself and your instincts. Fuck that guy; he lays a hand on you, I'm breaking it."

They stepped out of the lift, and Daisy turned to him and reached up to cup his jaw and tug him down for a kiss. His stubble tickled the palms of her hands, and she moved her hands to the back of his head to the soft, fuzzier stubble of his hair.

"My hero," she whispered after ending the kiss, and he smiled at her before claiming another quick kiss.

"And don't you forget it. Now come on, we're already late for dinner."

❦

They were twenty minutes late, and everybody was already seated when Mason and Daisy walked in. Daisy paused for a second, suddenly intimidated by the sheer number of people they were attempting to fool with their ruse, but Mason took her hand and tugged her toward the family table. She followed meekly, smiling and nodding as she went along, but not really making eye contact with anybody. She could see the speculation and blatant disbelief on some faces and immediately started panicking.

Mason's arm crept around her waist, and he dropped a kiss on her cheek before whispering, "Relax and smile. You look like a deer trapped in the headlights."

"I don't know what I was thinking," she hissed. "This was a crazy idea. They all know."

"Calm down, angel," he whispered. He lifted her hand to his lips and planted a kiss onto her knuckles before acknowledging their table with a warm smile.

"Hey, kids, how was the drive up?" Dr. McGregor greeted with a smile, and Mason extended his hand to the older man.

"Uneventful, but the scenery was stunning," Mason supplied, shaking her father's hand firmly. He bent to drop a kiss on her mother's cheek. "Mrs. McGregor, you're looking ravishing this evening."

Her mother actually blushed and waved aside his compliment, even though everybody could see she was flattered by it.

Mason helped her into an empty chair next to Daff and took the one on Daisy's right. Daisy was aware of her great-aunts staring at them curiously and smiled at the older ladies shyly.

"Hello, Aunties."

"Daisy, aren't you going to introduce us to your friend?" Aunt Ivy, the oldest and scariest, asked, staring down her regal nose at both Daisy and Mason. How she managed to stare down at people when she was only four foot eleven in stature was a mystery.

"Mason Carlisle, these are my great-aunts. Ivy, Gert, Helen, and Mattie," she introduced them from oldest to youngest, and Mason turned his charm on them.

"Ladies, I'm very happy to meet all of you." His smile was polite with just a hint of roguishness, and the ladies all seemed to unbend a little.

"Nice to see Daisy bringing a gentleman friend to a family event," Gert, the sweetest of the four, said in her tiny Minnie Mouse voice.

"We all thought she was one of those lesbians," Mattie offered in her usual blunt way, and Daisy winced. Mason's left hand crept beneath the table to squeeze her thigh reassuringly.

"I assure you, ma'am, that is very much *not* the case." He sounded just the teeniest bit smug. Daisy slanted him a horrified look that he met with a wink.

"Well . . . good." Mattie, for once, seemed at a loss for words and eyed Daisy speculatively from beneath her formidable gray eyebrows— those things hadn't been waxed or shaped in *ever* and always reminded Daisy of hairy white caterpillars.

Daff slanted her a sideways glance before muttering, "Remind me to implement a similar plan for the next family event. I don't think I've ever seen her so effectively silenced before."

Daisy took a sip of wine to hide her smile.

Mason was chatting with her father, and Daisy took the opportunity to have a look around the large family table. Everybody was present, the aunts, Daff, her parents, Lia, Clayton, and *his* parents and younger brother, Carson. One big, happy family, she thought caustically.

Clayton and Lia were sitting almost directly opposite her and were involved in a whispered, seemingly heated conversation. Daisy elbowed Daff, who grunted in pain and glared at her indignantly.

"What do you suppose is going on with those two?" Daisy asked, ignoring her sister's annoyance. Daff glanced across the table discreetly.

"Don't know, but they've seemed out of sorts all evening. Definitely something's up. I was thinking of taking Lia aside later to ask her about it."

"I've been thinking about what Mason said the other day," Daisy confided, and Daff nodded.

"Me too. The guy's an ass, but he made a good point. She hasn't been herself lately."

"He's not an ass," Daisy defended, and Daff's eyes flashed with annoyance before sharpening as they took in Daisy's flushed face.

"*What* have you done?" she asked on a loud whisper.

"Don't know what you're talking about," Daisy said, before attempting a subject change. "This soup is fantastic."

"How would you know? You haven't even tried it yet," Daff rejoined, and Daisy glared at her.

"It *looks* fantastic."

"Daisy, you have stubble burn all the way down your neck," Daff whispered, shocked. "It's unmistakable!" Daisy clapped a hand over her neck, knowing exactly which spot Daff was referring to because it had been tingling since her shower. "Daisy McGregor, what have you been getting up to with that man?"

"Stop it, you sound like Nana," Daisy hissed, and Daff grimaced before glaring at her.

"Don't deflect."

"We're not talking about me right now; we're talking about—"

"What are you two talking about so seriously?" Their mother's voice interrupted the whispered exchange, and they both sat up straight beneath everybody's curious regard.

"Soup!"

"Burns!"

The words emerged simultaneously, and the sisters peered at each other wryly.

"Uh . . . soup burns," Daff improvised quickly, and Daisy threw her a disgusted look.

"Specifically how hot soup can scald your soft palate and/or tongue if you're not careful," Daisy added with what she thought was admirable poise.

"Yep. So, *soup burns*." Daff nodded. Daisy could hear Mason snorting softly beside her, and she kicked him softly. He gripped her knee, his fingers tightening in warning when she drew back her foot for another tap. His hand lingered, sliding farther up her thigh, creeping up under her skirt. Daisy gasped and clamped her knees together, effectively trapping his hands between her thighs. She could tell from the slight smirk on his nearly impassive face that he wasn't exactly dismayed by the turn of events.

"What an odd thing to be discussing," Aunt Gert squeaked, and the other aunts sent her frankly disbelieving stares, since nobody else had fallen for the blatant lie.

"Anyway, so who will be going horseback riding tomorrow morning?" Daisy asked with false cheer, deliberately changing the subject and trying not to think of Mason's warm hand resting so docilely between her thighs. The horseback ride on the beach was one of the events Lia had arranged for some of her more adventurous guests.

"I intend to be too hungover to even contemplate getting up at such a disgustingly early hour," Daff said. The ride was at dawn, and Daisy secretly agreed with her sister that it was much too early to be up.

"Daff, you can't be hungover, I'll need my bridesmaids to be ready by nine," Lia piped up. Were her eyes red-rimmed? Had she been crying? Daisy couldn't tell for certain in the dim light of the restaurant, but it certainly looked that way.

"Crap, I forgot about that," Daff groaned. Daisy had as well. Lia had organized a spa session followed by a champagne brunch for her bridesmaids. Clayton and his groomsmen as well as some of the other men would be playing golf.

"Mind giving me my hand back?" Mason whispered, his lips brushing against her ear as he spoke. "Not that I have any complaints about its current situation, you understand, but people may start to wonder why my hand is under the table. And probably jump to wholly accurate conclusions."

Aghast at the possibility, she opened her knees immediately, and after one last little pat of her thigh, he moved his hand back to the table to pick up his knife.

"I hope your *soup burns* aren't too bad," he murmured wickedly. "You're going to need that tongue later."

She groaned; the man was irreverent and incorrigible, and she was starting to adore him. He made her want to throw caution to the wind and just be very, very bad. It was a giddy sensation. Entirely uncharacteristic for her, and she *loved* it.

Dinner wasn't quite the ordeal Daisy had been expecting; the aunts were effectively muzzled by Mason's appearance, but Daisy knew it was only a matter of time before they regrouped and started firing on all cylinders. For the most part it was a pretty casual, low-stress evening.

Casual and low stress until Daff decided that she needed to go to the bathroom and that Daisy really needed to go too. Her sister's crazy eyes and not-so-subtle head jerks toward the powder room aside, Daisy played along because the "chat" was inevitable.

She excused herself, and Mason—who was having a very serious conversation with Aunt Mattie about the British royal family's security details—gave her an absent nod. She reluctantly trailed after her sister's slender figure and admired the way Daff's sexy sheath dress clung to her perfect body in all the right spots. The same dress on Daisy would look borderline indecent, what with her abundance of curves. She smiled quietly to herself as, for the first time since puberty, she didn't feel a pang of envy. Her sisters had often told her she was lucky because she had breasts, a booty, and a small waist, and she had always dismissed it as them being kind to the "fatty" in the family. She no longer felt like the "fatty." She felt voluptuous, sensual, and she walked with an enigmatic smile on her lips and an extra sway in her step because she knew Mason would be staring at her butt as she left the room.

She wasn't blind to the other appreciative male glances coming her way either, and it made her feel empowered and sexy and in control.

She wasn't used to so many eyes on her, but for once she didn't hunch her shoulders in an effort to fade into the background. She owned her femininity and threw it down like a gauntlet.

Take me or leave me, but this is me, and here I am!

"Okay, what the hell is going on between you and Mason Carlisle?" Daff asked after a cursory glance around the powder room to confirm its emptiness. Daisy said nothing, going to the mirror to check her appearance. She was annoyed to note that her hair was coming out of the bun she had forced it into. Everything else still looked fine, and the pretty blue silk chiffon cocktail dress—one of several new items she had purchased for this weekend—looked nice too. It was a little bustier than she was used to—it felt weird to look straight down into her cleavage—but she was glad she'd bought it. It had a form-flattering sweetheart bodice, with tapered ruched straps, and flared from the natural waist into a deceptively simple circle skirt. The floaty skirt merely skimmed her body as it fell to her knees, but it kissed her curves when she walked, flowing beautifully with her slightest movement. The saleswoman had been genuinely enthusiastic in her recommendation after she'd seen Daisy in the dress. And the spark of desire in Mason's gaze when he'd clapped eyes on her had made it worth the while and the expense.

"Hey, you look *really* hot tonight, so stop admiring yourself in the mirror and answer my question," Daff said, folding her arms over her chest and glaring at Daisy.

"That's between Mason and me," Daisy said casually as she tried to tuck her hair back into the bun.

"*Daisy*, don't get too involved with him. You're going to get hurt."

"He's done nothing to hurt me so far."

"You mean *other* than acting as his brother's wingman at the hen party?" Daisy flushed at the reminder.

"Nothing since then."

"Because he feels guilty? Daisy, you blackmailed him into being your date; there's no way in hell this ends well."

"Blackmail implies coercion; he wasn't coerced. I wanted to back out, but he insisted we do this."

"Just watch yourself around him. This isn't real . . . don't convince yourself that it is."

"*Why* can't it be real? Because no man would be truly interested in the *other*, ugly McGregor sister?" she asked, the old doubts resurfacing with a vengeance from where they'd been lurking just beneath her fragile new layer of self-confidence.

"Daisy, *no*! Look at you, you're beautiful. Stop denigrating yourself. I just want you to find something genuine, and while Mason puts on a great show, it's all fake. Don't forget that."

"How can I?" Daisy asked bitterly. "When I have you around to constantly remind me?"

"Daisy . . ." Her sister looked both remorseful and unapologetic at the same time. How was that even possible? Daisy shook her head and held up her hand to forestall whatever Daff wanted to say next.

"Leave it for now. I'll take your words under advisement. Thanks for your concern. I'd like to get back to my fake date now, if you don't mind."

She turned and stormed out of the bathroom with Daff hot on her heels. Both women unaware of the fact that the corner stall snicked open after they left and a grinning Zinzi Khulani stepped out, her phone already in hand to text her friend the juicy bit of gossip she had just learned.

~~~

"What did she do to piss you off?" Mason asked, while he politely helped Daisy back into her chair.

"I don't want to talk about it," Daisy said, trying to hide her trembling hands as she fought to get her temper under control. Daff, in the meantime, summoned the waiter over to order a whiskey sour, which she tossed back immediately before demanding another one. Lia looked both concerned and disapproving but didn't say anything, keeping a strained smile on her face when Mrs. Edmonton leaned over to speak with her.

Daisy tried to take in great big gulps of air in an attempt to get her anger and hurt under control. She was aware of Mason looking at her with a concerned frown, but she forced a smile for him even though he knew her well enough by now to be able to tell when she was faking it.

She watched as some of the younger couples started making their way to the tiny dance floor, laughing and looking carefree as they started to sway together. She knew most of them and envied their ease and self-confidence.

"Dance?" he asked quietly, and she shook her head.

"No. Don't dance, remember?"

"We could try to break the chicken dance curse?"

"I thought you didn't dance either," she reminded him, and he grinned. She forgot her self-pity party for a moment and tilted her head as she ran her speculative gaze over him. "*Why* don't you dance? You never told me."

"Hmm, I said it was second-date material, if I recall correctly, which means I should have told you at MJ's. My bad."

"We're not really dating, and if we were, MJ's was our first date, not our second."

"Yeah? Howdya figure that? What about Ralphie's?"

"That was . . . that wasn't a date," she spluttered. "It was a con job."

"We talked, we laughed, and I bought you a drink. It was a date."

"You didn't buy me a drink."

"I'm sure I offered to buy you—" He broke off what he'd been about to say and tsked before wagging a censorious index finger back and forth in front of her face. "Stop distracting me. I asked if you wanted to dance."

"I already answered."

"We don't have to dance in here," he said, his voice a low, sexy rumble. "We could go out onto the patio. We'd still be able to hear the music from there."

Daisy glanced longingly at the huge glass wall and doors that led out to the hotel's private terrace overlooking the ocean. It was a chilly evening, and none of the other guests had ventured out.

"I wouldn't mind getting some fresh air. Maybe just a walk on the beach or something instead of the dance?"

"If you promise to save your first dance at the wedding for me."

"Only if you tell me why you don't dance," she countered, and he grinned.

"You've got yourself a deal. Now let's get out of here."

Daff anxiously watched Mason smoothly making excuses before taking Daisy's hand and leading her through the tables toward the exit. Daisy didn't look back. She had been pointedly avoiding eye contact since their earlier chat in the powder room. Daff stifled a sigh and tossed back another drink, ignoring the weight of Lia's disapproving stare. She could perhaps have handled the conversation a little better, but she didn't trust Mason Carlisle.

The guy was much too dangerous for her baby sister. He was also sickeningly good looking, which meant she automatically distrusted him. Guys like him toyed with women, they never settled down, and Daff was terrified that Daisy was in way over her head, that she would fall for him—if she hadn't already—and get her heart broken.

More and more people were starting to head to the dance floor, and a lot of the older people—her parents and aunts included—were leaving. Daff had another drink and kicked herself for not bringing a date. She hadn't wanted to be saddled with one of her many loser guys for an entire weekend. Her options for a decent date were severely limited. Her ex-boyfriends had all been dumb, good-looking assholes—kind of like Spencer Carlisle—and any guy she carted along to the wedding would have expected more than she was willing to give. She was so sick of the lot of them, of the boring sex, the meaningless conversations, the casual disregard. She'd sworn off men for a while and she wasn't going to break her fast just for Lia's wedding. Especially not when her sister was marrying yet another worthless jerk.

Daff had a reliable bullshit radar, and she was usually really good at picking the assholes apart from the good guys. It was a useful skill to have, just a shame she wasn't ever attracted to the good guys. Clayton Edmonton III was a definite asshole. In fact, he was a rare breed, a kind of hybrid douche hole. She didn't know *why* she disliked him; she only knew that she did, and her instincts were usually spot on. But talking to Lia about it was nearly impossible. She cast a discreet glare toward her middle sister, but Lia was listening to Clayton blow hard about something. She looked perfectly miserable, and Daff knew she was going to have to talk with her sister tomorrow. Try to get through to her one last time. If this was how she looked two days before her wedding, how happy could she expect to be in the years to come?

Mason Carlisle was harder to read than most men. At times he seemed like a stand-up guy, and on other occasions he set off her asshole alert so loudly that it nearly deafened her. And Daff trusted her instincts; they hadn't let her down yet. Daisy thought she had it all under control, but Daff knew it was a train wreck waiting to happen. The only problem was, her youngest sister had a stubborn streak a mile wide, and she only grew more intractable when she felt like she was being pushed into doing something she didn't want to do.

It wasn't easy being the oldest, Daff thought, starting to wallow in a well of self-pity. She got up, swayed a bit—stupid four-inch stilettos—and wobbled toward the exit. The waitstaff was taking much too long to bring her drinks, best to find the hotel bar. Thankfully Lia didn't notice her leave; her sister could be more preachy than Auntie Ivy sometimes, and it was tiresome.

When she found a quiet spot, she leaned against a wall for balance—how much whiskey was in those sours anyway?—and fished her phone out of her suddenly cavernous clutch.

She closed an eye to focus a little better before finding the number she was looking for. There it was, excellent! It rang and rang and rang and . . .

"Hello?" The deep male voice on the other end sent a thrilling little shiver down her spine.

"You're such a prick, you know?"

"Daff?"

"You know my voice," she purred happily.

"Of course I do, why wouldn't I?"

"Because you're an a-a-asshole."

"Are you drunk?"

"Yesh! No. Wait. Don't change the subject." Pesky man.

"Okay." He was starting to sound amused. "You were saying I'm an asshole. What did I do to earn this label?"

"You hurt my sister."

"Lia?"

"No, I have two sisters, you dick! And that's your problem; you don't see her or treat her with respect. I hate that about you."

"This is about Daisy?" His voice had gone flat, all amusement gone.

"So you *do* know her name?" She was proud of the sarcasm laced through that question.

"I don't know what you've heard, but . . ."

"I heard . . ." She lost her balance and fought to right herself with as much dignity as she could. Thank goodness he couldn't see her. "I heard that you thought it would be a good idea to use your jerk brother to seduce my sister while you tried to chat me up."

"I didn't ask him to seduce her," he protested indignantly. "Just distract her a little, pay her some attention. I didn't think it would do any harm."

"How did you expect her to feel when she found out?"

"She wasn't supposed to find out," he gritted out.

"But she did."

"Yes, and she turned the tables rather nicely, don't you think? Don't underestimate your sister, Daff. She seems well able to take care of herself. She certainly has my brother wrapped around her little finger. In fact, I think he's the real victim here. She blackmailed him into going to the wedding with her, and she's performed some kind of freaky voodoo on him because he's completely irrational when it comes to anything Daisy related. I don't know what the fuck she's done to him, but I don't like it!"

"He's going to hurt her even more than he already has, and it's *your* fault."

"Well, I think *she's* going to wind up hurting him . . . and yeah"—he sighed deeply—"it's my fault."

"As long as you recognize that."

"It's your fault too, you know," he murmured, and her brow furrowed into a scowl.

"How? How can this *possibly* be *my* fault?"

"If you'd even once given me the time of day, maybe I wouldn't have had to rope Mason in to play wingman."

"So I'm just supposed to pay attention to every guy who tries to chat me up? How typical of a man to think that."

"Maybe if you weren't *constantly* sending me mixed signals I'd be a little clearer about where I stand with you!"

"Oh, please, you're seeing things that aren't there."

"Yeah? Why did you drunk dial *me* of all people, Daff?"

She paused to think about that for a moment.

"Because I'm a little too wasted to text you," she finally decided.

"That's not what I meant, and you know it. Why me at all? And how do you even have my number, come to think of it? I don't have yours."

"You want to know where you stand with me, Spencer? *Nowhere.* There has never been, nor will there ever be, anything between us. Stay away from me in future and don't fuck with my family again!"

"Gladly," he seethed. "I've had more than enough of having to deal with manipulative, psychotic, raging bitches. Tanya was bad enough, and I'm definitely questioning what I ever saw in you."

Stung, she allowed him the last word and hung up before she said something she'd regret even more. She wasn't nearly drunk enough to be immune to that scorching indictment of her character. Especially not from him. Spencer Carlisle was a dumb oaf, but he'd always been a sweet dumb oaf. That's probably why this entire situation bothered her so much. He had disappointed her. She pushed herself away from the wall, and after fleetingly considering her original course of action to find the bar and drink herself into a stupor, she decided that she'd rather fall into bed and forget this entire day ever happened.

It was colder than they expected, but the air was calm, the sky was clear, and a huge, creamy full moon was just rising over the ocean. It was a beautiful evening, and it seemed a waste to let the cold chase them back inside. Mason bundled Daisy into his suit jacket, and it dwarfed her, falling to just a few inches above her knees, while the sleeves ended well past her fingertips. She looked like a little girl playing dress-up in her dad's jacket, and Mason, as usual, thought she was absolutely adorable.

They were barefoot on the beach; Mason had his socks off and his trouser legs rolled up, and Daisy had forced him to turn around while she tugged off her pantyhose and shoved them into her bag. He had taken laughing peeks, telling her she was being ridiculous because he already knew what she looked like naked.

Now they were walking hand in hand, shoes dangling from their fingertips. The sand was freezing cold beneath their bare feet, but neither minded much. They were content to listen to sounds of the whispering waves, the high-pitched calls of the night birds, the distant echoing cries of the southern right whales that migrated here to calve in winter. With Daisy's hand tucked into his, it felt like the most perfect moment of Mason's entire life.

"So why don't you dance?" she asked, breaking the peaceful silence. But Mason didn't mind, because if there were anything more beautiful than the silence, it was the sound of her husky voice.

"Because I don't want to embarrass everybody else on the dance floor with my awesome moves," he said complacently and was gratified when she laughed in response.

"Seriously?"

"Yep. That's it. The whole story, true as God."

"And this is what you would have told me on our second date, if we were, in fact, dating?"

"It's *supposed* to impress you."

"I am impressed," she said, and he could hear the laughter bubbling away beneath her words. "I'm impressed by the size of your ego."

"You're obsessed with size, aren't you? I told you not to worry; everything's well in order," he boasted, and Daisy laughed outright at that. He let go of her hand, and she felt the loss keenly until he draped his arm over her shoulders and tugged her closer so that she was tucked beneath his armpit and sharing his body heat. She put her own arm around his trim waist for better balance.

"You always smell so great," she murmured.

"So do you." His chest rumbled beneath her cheek when he spoke, and she sighed in contentment, feeling small and safe and protected in his hold. They continued to wander slowly down the beach.

"Aren't you cold?" she asked when a sharp gust of frigid wind flirted with the hem of her skirt and sent goose bumps up her thighs.

"Nah, I've been trained not to be as affected by the weather. Extreme heat and extreme cold don't bother me too much."

"Did you see a lot of combat?" she asked, tentatively broaching a subject she'd been curious about for a while.

"I saw my share," he said after a long pause. "When I was just a kid during the Iraq War. I'd barely finished basic training before I was shipped out. Then again later, after I was more of a specialist, shall we say? We were required to do some stuff I'm not at liberty to talk about. Nothing pretty."

"Tell me about your scars; were you ever badly injured?" He stopped walking and turned to face her, and even in the pale light of the moon she could see his look of surprise.

"People hardly ever ask me about that. Top three things I usually get asked: how many people I shot and/or killed, how many bombs I've diffused, and have I ever flown a helicopter. Some folks really seem to have a Hollywood vision of war in their heads," he said with a wry shake of his head, before continuing. "Nobody ever asks me about injuries. They figure, I'm alive, have all my limbs, so I must have come through it all unscathed."

"I don't care about the other stuff. I mean, I care about the people you may have shot and/or killed but only because I worry about how it must have affected you."

"It was seven years ago; I'm over the worst of it."

"Are you?"

"I . . . I've learned how to deal. It's no longer a problem."

"But it was?"

"Daisy, everybody who has seen combat suffers from varying degrees of PTSD. I had my moments, I still have the occasional lapse—one loud, misplaced bang could see me diving for the closest cover—but they're few and far between now. I've—what's that phrase? The shrinks love it. Ah, yes, I've reintegrated."

"You still haven't answered my question," she pointed out, and he sighed, linking his hands behind her back and pulling her toward him until they stood chest to torso.

"I was shot twice and got winged by shrapnel in the IED explosion that killed Quincy. I'm afraid I have a road map of scars on my lower back; it's not pretty." Daisy had seen the scars on his chest and arms, but she hadn't seen his back yet. She looked up into his beautiful face and felt sorrow at the anguish he must have felt. He claimed it was long ago and no longer affected him, but his eyes told a different story.

"I'm glad you're okay," she said.

His lips quirked, and he bent his head to claim her lips gently. The kiss was the slow-burning kind; it started with a tiny spark and built into a small, flickering ember when his lips nudged hers apart. That ember leisurely escalated into a shy, hesitant flame when his tongue met hers. She gasped at his touch and opened up even more for him, adding fuel to the flame until it grew stronger and bolder. Her hands went up to circle his neck, and her bare toes pushed her up as far as she could go in an effort to get even closer. The flame, now blazing and building into an inferno, threatened to rage out of control when his hands found her breasts through the slippery material of her silky dress.

"Daisy," he groaned. "Let's go back to our room."

"Yes," she encouraged. "Please."

He stepped away from her and grabbed her hand.

"How fast can you run?" he asked urgently, and she giggled.

"Not very."

"Not good enough."

They made it back to their suite in under ten minutes, and Mason had her out of her clothes about a minute later. He swore reverently while she stood in front of him, trying not to be self-conscious about the fact that she was completely naked while he was still fully dressed.

"You're so fucking gorgeous," he growled, his eyes hot and intense and embarrassingly, single-mindedly focused on her breasts. He looked into her blushing face and smiled tenderly at whatever he saw there. "I'm going too fast, aren't I?"

"No, it's fine," she said, sounding unconvincing even to her own ears.

"It's just I've wanted you for so long. Come here, angel." He held out a hand, and she took it and stepped toward him without hesitation. "I'm going to kiss you, all over. I'm going to run my hands and tongue and teeth over every single inch of your beautiful body." The promise was shakily given but brimming with sincerity, and Daisy felt an embarrassing rush of liquid warmth between her thighs at the prospect.

"But . . ." he qualified regretfully. "Not now. I don't think I'll last very long the first time, Daisy."

For some reason she found his words so much more flattering than the admiring looks, the touches, the kisses, even the huge, rampant erection straining against his zipper. He didn't think he'd have much self-control around her, and that was just the sexiest thing any man could ever tell a woman. At least, that's what Daisy thought, and that knowledge emboldened her. She took another little step closer until her hard nipples were grazing against the expensive cotton of his shirt, one of them catching against a tiny mother-of-pearl button. She moaned at the sensation; her breasts and nipples were so much more sensitive than she'd ever known, and she nearly wept in relief when one of his hands moved up to cup one of her breasts, kneading it gently before plumping it up and holding it to his mouth. This time he wasn't playing around, he mouthed it, aureole, nipple, and all. The intense suction nearly brought her to her knees, and her legs buckled, but he caught her and *carried* her to the bed. The movement was so smooth and effortless she didn't have time to automatically protest that she was too heavy. She was on her back, legs spread wantonly, while he nestled between them, still fully clothed, sans only jacket, socks, and shoes. It was crazy, hot, and sexy, and Daisy loved it! He was at her other breast now, which led to more incredible suctioning, his mouth like a scorching, delicious vacuum, his tongue teasing the aroused tip mercilessly. Daisy raised her knees and planted her feet on the bed, using them as leverage to push her aching center against his hardness. She rubbed against him, wanting him to thrust back, wanting his heat against her wetness. His hands were everywhere and nowhere. Why weren't they where she needed them to be? Her hands were tugging at the buttons of his shirt, wanting to rip them off in an effort to get his skin against hers. He pushed himself up, big and beautiful as he knelt between her legs, and without any consideration for the fabric or the expense of his dress shirt, he just unbuttoned the top two buttons, grabbed the back of his collar, and tugged it over his head to toss it aside.

Finally she had access to his big, beautiful chest, and she went for one of his nipples like an aggressive cat, embarrassing even herself with her ferocity. She licked, bit, chewed, and worshipped before lavishing the same treatment on the other one. Mason allowed it, groaning appreciatively while she pleasured him. His hands had traveled down to her hips and were angling them upward to better receive his hard grinding.

"Jesus." He had no breath left, and the word was strained. "I'm not going to come in my pants like a kid again."

His hands moved down and found her hot and dripping.

"You're so wet," he moaned before his index and middle fingers located her melting channel and sought entry. His hips mimicked the slow thrust of his fingers, and he groaned appreciatively.

"Shit, you're so tight, angel." The pumping motion of his fingers inside her stole Daisy's breath, and her back arched as she rode the sensation. It was unfamiliar and a little uncomfortable, but combined with his stroking thumb at her hard clit, it was unbearably pleasurable.

She was still fighting to breathe, her mouth open, her eyes pleading with his as she felt herself climbing to the inevitable peak of her climax. Her chest heaved as she sucked in a tiny amount of air without releasing what she already had trapped in her lungs.

He bent over her, his fingers still working deliciously between her thighs, and put his mouth onto hers.

"Breathe," he urged, whispering into her mouth, supplying her with some of his own oxygen, which served as a catalyst for her to finally exhale on a sob. "That's a good girl. Now come for me."

"I can't," she cried, her body strung as tightly as a bow, teetering on the very edge, needing something more, something to send her toppling over the precipice.

"You can." He changed the angle of his fingers, and she screamed when his talented digits brushed against an area so sensitive it nearly sent her off the bed. He held her ruthlessly in place. "There it is."

"Oh my God," she keened as, with another stroke, combined with a flick of his thumb, she came. Hard. It was much more intense than any climax she had ever given herself, than even the one he had gifted her with earlier that day. It was so powerful she felt sure she blacked out for an instant. He was murmuring soothing nothings into her ear and easing his fingers out of her tightly clenched womanhood. She was painfully sensitive, but he was unbelievably gentle. She was slick with her own moisture and felt the dampness spreading beneath her into the duvet. It embarrassed her a little despite his huge, smug grin.

"Flawless," he purred before starting to kiss his way down her body. Still shell-shocked, she was absolutely electrified when she felt the first flick of his tongue on her still-spasming female flesh.

"Do you know how perfect you are down here, Daisy?" His voice was hoarse. "Pretty and pouty and pink. Absolutely beautiful."

She sobbed when he lowered his head and went back to work, and before she knew it she was coming again.

CHAPTER ELEVEN

"Like that?" he asked, before kissing her, and she tasted herself on his lips. It was a shocking and unbelievably erotic experience.

"It was too much," she said between desperate gulps of air.

"I have more of that for you," he promised. Daisy was both excited and terrified at the prospect. He fumbled with his belt buckle, and she reached down with trembling hands to help him, but he gently brushed her hands aside.

"This would last longer if you didn't touch me," he said. "Next time you can have your wicked way with me, but right now, I'm so primed that if you touch me it'll be over in seconds."

He shoved his pants down past his hips and knelt in front of her, his thighs spread as he sheathed himself in a condom. She couldn't get over his masculine perfection, everything tight and hard and beautifully muscled. And he was right to be smug; he was intimidatingly big down there. His penis was hard and thick and long and looked a little terrifying to her inexperienced gaze. At the same time, she could appreciate the elegance of the way it curved upward to kiss his belly. So perfect in every way, from the tight, lightly furred sac, up the veined length, to the deep-pink, plum-size glans. She was desperate to touch and taste, and she silently vowed that the next time she would be calling the shots.

His eyes were feverish and his face strained, and he took one long look at her, seeming to recognize the admiration in her eyes for what it was. He gave her a naughty grin before palming his erection and giving it a long, leisurely stroke from balls to tip and back again. She groaned, and he chuckled, the sound strained before covering her, bracing his elbows on either side of her for support. He kissed her thoroughly and reached down with one hand to line himself up at her entrance and ease into her.

"Christ." His voice broke on the word. "You're so tight, babe. Relax for me, okay?"

She tried, she really did, but the unfamiliar thickness, so much more than his fingers, was making her tense up.

"Daisy, please," he muttered. "I don't want to hurt you."

"I'm trying," she sobbed, feeling immediately inadequate. He stopped moving, allowing her time to adjust to his size, and she could tell from the taut strain on his face that it was taking a great deal of self-control for him not to move. He started kissing her again, taking her mind off his intimate invasion as he played with her tongue and moved down to her breasts, laving them with attention. It worked, and she relaxed in tiny increments, starting to enjoy herself. He rocked against her, easing more of himself into her with every tiny movement of his hips, and Daisy moaned when his shaft brushed against her swollen clitoris.

He was making soft, desperate little sounds in the back of his throat, and he was starting to drip with sweat. He looked like he was under a massive amount of stress, and Daisy tried to help him, lifting her pelvis to meet his thrusts.

"I can take more," she promised, and he took her at her word. She tensed up, but when he didn't move again, giving her time, she relaxed and dug her fingers into his tight butt to urge him on even further. Finally, after what felt like years, he had his entire length buried inside her, and when the stretch and burn faded, she moved her hips experimentally. Mason breathed a heartfelt prayer and dragged himself nearly all the way out, undoing all his hard work, before thrusting home again.

"Oh." The exclamation was a sound of revelation, as Daisy finally understood what he'd been working so hard to achieve. Another thrust, and his tip brushed against that same internal spot that had driven her crazy earlier.

"OH!" The exclamation was louder and a little more enthusiastic this time. Mason was utterly focused on her pleasure, and, recognizing what she liked, he kept hitting that spot with every subsequent thrust.

"Oh! Oh! Oh! Oh my *God!*" Daisy's orgasm was unexpected, massive, and once again a thousand percent better than the one that had come before.

Mason shifted her knees until they were braced against his chest, changing his angle as he lost any pretense of gentleness and simply pounded away at her. She had another orgasm in seconds, and it was as she was clenching around him that he groaned—the sound loud and long—and shuddered, his head dropping to her chest, completely vulnerable in her arms for that brief moment.

He moved her knees to the side and quickly discarded the condom, tossing it into a wastebasket next to the bed, before spooning behind her and holding her tightly against him while they both trembled through the shattered remnants of their orgasms.

Their bodies cooled down slowly, and the chill air started raising goose bumps on Daisy's skin. Mason reached for the duvet cover and tugged it over them, before snuggling behind her again.

"Are you okay?" he asked after nearly a half an hour of comfortable silence.

"Hmm."

"I didn't want to hurt you. You were tighter than I expected." There was a questioning lilt to his voice, and she turned around to face him.

"I'm kind of new to this," she admitted, and he forked his hands through her curls, pushing them out of her face so that he could see her expression better.

"How new?" he asked softly.

"I've never really done this before." He looked unsurprised and ran a knuckle over her cheekbone.

"Never?"

"Not even once."

"So your ex-boyfriends were even dumber than I suspected."

"Mason . . . I've never had a real long-term relationship with any-one." And wasn't that just the saddest thing ever? How humiliating to reveal that to him. "I know that makes me a bit of a freak."

He snorted.

"Yeah, I was just thinking that the guys in Riversend are the freaks. How could they not have seen what was right under their noses all these years? And what about college? I mean, isn't that what students usually get up to? Parties, drinking, and lots of indiscriminate fucking, right? How did you get left out of all that?"

"Is that what you got up to at college?"

"I was a grown man. Getting laid wasn't my number one priority."

"It wasn't mine either. By the time I got to college, all my insecuri-ties were pretty much set in stone; I didn't think any of the boys would be interested in me. I got through my studies by keeping my head down and staying on the fringes of everything. Nobody saw me. It was partly my own fault; I was happy enough to remain invisible. And when I got back home it was just more of the same. Until I walked into a bar two weeks ago and there you were."

"Daisy, I'm not . . ." He sounded uncomfortable, and knowing exactly where this was leading, Daisy nipped it in the bud.

"Yes, I know, you're not my Mr. Right or whatever. But today I decided that you're Mr. Okay for Now. I've decided that my shell is getting boring, and I'm a little sick of it, so I'm branching out. Trying new things. And you're a pretty good teacher. I mean, what was that thing you did earlier? I've given myself lots of DIY orgasms, but nothing of that caliber."

He was quiet for a second as he processed her words, obviously trying to figure out if she meant what she was saying.

"Uh." He cleared his throat, deciding to go along with it. "I guess you never found your G-spot when you were diddling yourself."

"Oh, so *that's* what that was," she whispered reverentially, and he chuckled. "I guarantee it'll be a part of my self-pleasuring repertoire from now on."

She felt him hardening against her thigh as her words turned him all the way on in an instant.

"Why don't you show me how you mean to include it, and I'll give you a few pointers on how to improve your technique?"

"You'd do that for me?" she teased, and he laughed.

"Damned straight I would."

"Okay, but only if you show me *your* technique. I've always been curious about male masturbation. Maybe I can help you out?"

"*Jesus.* Yes and please."

It was the last thing either of them said for a very long while.

An obnoxious buzzing sound interrupted Daisy's sound sleep, and she groaned. She felt warm and comfortable and snuggled deeper under the covers, her foot automatically searching for Peaches's comforting weight at the end of her bed. Instead she collided with a warm, masculine shin, and memories of the night before came flooding back. She went very still as she tried to orient herself. They were spooning, his crotch at her butt. One of her feet was trapped between his knees, and he had an arm curled beneath her head and the other slung across her waist, his hand cupped over her stomach. She automatically sucked it in, and he chuckled knowingly, his chest shaking against her back and his breath teasing the hair at the nape of her neck.

"Too late, I've seen everything there is to see," he said, his voice a sexy morning rumble that made her want to climb on top of him and have her wicked way with him again.

She didn't respond to his teasing words, simply let out her breath and relaxed.

"In Iraq I had this company commander, a very distinguished older guy." God, his morning voice was gorgeous, deep and with just a bit of gravel. She could listen to it all day. "He had a collection of classic movies. Whenever we got any downtime, tedium would set in pretty quickly, and we'd all get into one another's stuff. E-mails were read and reread, books were swapped around, games, cards, everything you can think of to stave off boredom. We often had movie nights, and when we ran out of the newer stuff, our commander would break out his movies. The old guy had a thing for fifties bombshells. He had Marilyn Monroe flicks, Sophia Loren, Jayne Mansfield . . . I remember the first time I saw Marilyn Monroe—I was about twenty at the time—I thought she was the perfect woman. Killer body. I printed out a picture of her in this white one-piece swimsuit—she was just standing on the beach with the wind in her hair—and kept it in my wallet. I hit the jackpot with you, Daisy; you're a dead ringer for Marilyn."

Daisy snorted at that, even while battling a pang in her heart at the thought of a young man, with no loved one back home, having to keep a picture of a long-dead movie icon for comfort . . . and probably other stuff.

"I look nothing like her; I'm not even blonde."

"I meant your body. All these sweet curves. I mean, luckily *these*"— he cupped her breasts—"are a bit more substantial. And you have a plumper, rounder ass than hers." Was he really comparing her body to Marilyn Monroe's and finding hers more desirable? That was both sweet and a little unbelievable.

"Wait, so all the stuff we did and when I had my mouth on your—*there*—last night, you were imagining I was your bow-chicka-wow-wow dream woman?" she asked without any heat, confident that he had been entirely focused on her—Daisy—last night.

"Hell no. That was all you, angel. And for someone who's never given a blow job before, let me tell you, that was a fuckin' stellar performance."

The annoying buzzing sounded again, and he reached for his phone and swiped the screen.

"*Why* is your alarm going off at this god-awful hour?" she asked, irritated.

"Thought I'd go for a predawn run on the beach, watch the sun rise. Want to join me?" he asked, nuzzling the back of her neck, while his hands started to roam. She sighed and relaxed into his embrace, pushing her behind up against his hardening erection.

"Do you *really* think I'm the jogging type?" she asked, and he made a noncommittal sound.

"I figured you weren't, but it would be rude not to ask, right?"

"Trust me, I won't think you're rude if you never ask me again. But are you sure you want to go for that run? I can think of so many other more interesting forms of exercise." Encouraged by the burgeoning hardness against her butt, she reached back and took hold of his solid shaft, and he sucked in a gasp of air. Happy with his reaction, she gave a long stroke and felt him go even harder.

"I'd love to, but you're new to this, and I could tell after our last time that you were feeling a little stiff."

"No. *You're* feeling a little stiff," she corrected, and he laughed.

"Who's twisting whose words now, Daisy?"

"Apparently that's what happens when you spend time with 'testosterone-fueled guys,'" she countered, continuing with her languid stroking, and he groaned, the sound loaded with appreciation.

"I'm trying to do the right thing, Daisy. I'd make love with you all day if I could, but you need some proper rest. Go back to sleep, and when I get back we'll take a bath together."

Daisy knew he was right, now that some of her grogginess had worn off; she was starting to feel aches and pains all over her body. He'd given her a heck of a workout last night, had twisted and turned her body in so many unfamiliar ways, she was shocked she wasn't a human pretzel this morning.

She gave him one last stroke before releasing him, and he moaned—a soft, disappointed sound—before moving away from her and getting out of bed. She immediately felt cold without him and bundled the bedcovers even closer, snuggling down and watching sleepily when he switched on the bedside lamp and started rummaging through his bag. He was walking around the room unabashedly naked and still massively aroused, and she admired every taut muscle that worked as he tugged on his briefs—*boo*—over that still-straining erection, then his drawstring workout pants, socks . . .

Her eyelids were unbearably heavy when he got around to covering up that beautiful upper body, and by the time he pulled on his beanie and fingerless gloves, she was fast asleep. She didn't know he stood watching her for a long moment before he left, didn't feel his hand brush through her hair and stroke her face, and never knew that he leaned down to kiss her lips before he grabbed his iPod and headed out the door.

There were a few people on the beach despite the early hour, some dog walkers, a jogger, a young couple doing yoga, and—of course—in the distance a small group of people on horseback, some of Lia's more enthusiastic wedding guests. Mason sucked in a few breaths of the crisp air, filling his lungs with the fresh coldness and holding it there before releasing it slowly.

God, he felt amazing. Completely invigorated. His entire body was buzzing on a natural high after last night's intense sex, and his chest gave a weird little leap every time he thought of the woman he had left sleeping back in his hotel room. He did a few long, satisfying stretches, easing the kinks out of his neck and back before adjusting his earbuds and starting up his running playlist. He began at an easy lope, allowing his muscles to warm up before increasing his pace. He didn't jog, he ran, faster and longer than most average joggers. For Mason running was about maintaining his high fitness level and increasing his endurance. He had an alarm set on his iPod to remind him when to slow his pace and settle into a cooldown run. Without the alarm he could run for hours, especially when he got lost in his own head.

He was just starting to feel the burn when he crossed paths with the horse-riding party. A few hands raised in greeting, and he raised his own to acknowledge them—happy to let it go at that and continue on his run—but when someone angled their horse to intercept his path, he was forced to stop. He looked up to the rider and felt a surge of irritation when he saw it was the groom. He kept running in place to indicate his eagerness to get going again, but he tugged an earbud out to hear what the hell the asshole was saying.

". . . want to join us?"

"Sorry, what?"

"I said while the bridesmaids are at the spa and having their brunch, we're heading to the golf course to play a few holes. Want to join us?"

Mason hesitated, not at all in the mood to spend time with the man.

"You *do* know how to play golf, right? I know it probably wasn't part of your lifestyle growing up. Or when you were soldiering. But it's just swinging a club at a ball; it takes a bit of finesse, but you'll get the hang of it."

Right. Mason's competitiveness sprang to the fore, but he kept his expression neutral.

"Don't mind if I do. I don't have any clubs, though."

"You can borrow mine, Mason," a familiar masculine voice offered, and he noticed, for the first time, that Dr. McGregor was also in the group. The man gave him an encouraging grin. "I've decided to spend the morning relaxing with a good book."

"Thank you, sir. I'll take good care of them."

"Oh, I'm sure you will," the older man said. "You can pick the clubs up at ten, room twenty-six."

"Uh, thanks." Mason nodded, appalled to realize that Daisy's parents were just a few doors away from where he had very thoroughly corrupted their youngest daughter last night. Jesus, what if they'd been right next door? He and Daisy hadn't exactly been quiet. Who *was* next door? It would undoubtedly be someone they knew. *Christ*, what if it were one—or more—of the old ladies? The thought sent a shudder down his spine. He was so preoccupied by the horrific thought that he barely acknowledged the riders as they filed past him.

He absently started running again, but his peace of mind had been thoroughly shattered by the thought of one of Daisy's naïve old aunties hearing the unmistakable and loud sounds of their lovemaking last night.

He tried to clear his thoughts and focus on his running, but the morning had been well and truly ruined.

Daisy was still sound asleep when Mason crept back into the room just after sunrise. The room was bathed in the warm dawn light, and she looked beautiful as it painted her skin with an unearthly glow. How could he ever have thought she was plain? He drank in the sight of her kiss-swollen lips, so plump and tender he longed to claim them again; those pretty freckles splashed over her nose and cheeks; her lashes long and thick against her pale skin, the perfect frame for those clear gray eyes. Every inch of her was stunning, and he wanted to spend the entire day just staring at her in wonder.

━━

"Daisy." The familiar, cajoling voice penetrated her sleep and brought a smile to her lips. "It's time to wake up, angel."

She sighed and stretched languidly, opening her eyes to stare up into Mason's beautiful green gaze. His eyes dropped to where the sheet had fallen from her breasts, and instead of covering up, as was her first instinct, Daisy arched her back slightly and watched the fire ignite behind those eyes.

"Stop flashing those gorgeous things at me," he admonished sternly, and she smiled sleepily, pulling the bedcovers up far enough to just cover her nipples.

"How was your run?" she asked, pushing herself into a sitting position.

"Shit. I couldn't stop thinking about who was in the rooms on either side of ours."

"That's a random thing to be thinking about."

"Daisy, what if it's your aunts? Unless they're stone deaf, there was no way they wouldn't have heard our lovemaking last night. You're quite the screamer." Daisy battled a blush and tried not to read anything into the fact that this was the second time he'd referred to their sex as "lovemaking."

"Daff is in twenty-four, and one of Clayton's friends is in twenty-two."

"Christ, not *Daff*. She's not much better than your aunts," he groaned, and she laughed.

"What's the time? I have to get ready for this spa thing," she said, unable to disguise the reluctance in her voice. "I don't know how or when to tell Lia about Clayton. She's going to be so hurt. What if she blames me? Or hates me? Or—worse—doesn't believe me? It'll do irreparable damage to our relationship. I wish I could talk to Daff about it first, but she's so pissed off all the time lately. Half of it is because of what she knows about us, but the other half . . . I don't know *what* that is."

"You have to try, sweetheart, or watch your sister make the biggest mistake of her life tomorrow."

"She may wind up doing that anyway, despite anything I have to say, and I don't know if I can stand up there and pretend to be happy for her after I essentially tell her that her fiancé is a . . . a . . ."

"A prick?" he helpfully supplied.

"And more," she said fervently. He smiled sympathetically and sat on the edge of the bed. He toyed with one of her feet through the covers as he weighed what he wanted to say to her.

"I can't help you, Daisy, I wish I could. Whatever you do is ultimately up to you."

"I know. Sorry for getting you mixed up in all the family drama. You were just here for the free food and drink," she recalled wryly, and he chuckled.

"This is much more interesting. Now, I've already drawn a bubble bath if you're interested in joining me."

"For just a bath?" she asked with a pout, and he narrowed his eyes.

"No time for anything else, missy," he said sternly. "So you behave. I have to meet the asshole and his buddies for golf."

"You do? When did that happen?"

"Saw them on the beach this morning."

"And you're up for that?"

"Not really, but he was being such an arrogant douche, I figured it'll be nice to take him down a peg or two."

"Mason . . ."

"In an entirely sportsmanlike, nonconfrontational way, of course."

She wasn't sure she believed him, but she let it slide.

In the end, there was enough time for a very hot session in the huge tub, leaving more water on the floor than in the tub. Afterward, relaxed and very satisfied, they helped each other dry off.

"Tell me about this tattoo," she invited, running her fingers over the branches of the gnarled bare tree on the right side of his torso. His nipples beaded, and he flattened a hand against hers to prevent her from stroking even more.

"The tree represents my years in the military. The letters and dates represent lost brothers and the dates they fell."

There were so many initials, and a lot of them shared the same dates.

"It's a beautiful gesture," she whispered, and he shrugged.

"It was the least I could do." His tone and body language told her that the subject was closed for now, and she kissed his chest just above the highest branch. He continued to towel her off before pausing.

"Jesus," he suddenly swore, and Daisy, still contemplating that stark, poignant tattoo and what it represented, jumped at his vehemence.

"What?"

"You're full of bruises."

"I am?" She twisted around to get a look at herself in the mirror and saw the dark-blue and -purple bruises mostly on her butt and thighs. There were a few smudges on her arms as well.

"Why didn't you tell me you bruised so easily?" He sounded horrified.

"Well, I had no idea that I did."

"Does it hurt?" He touched one tentatively, his face tight with remorse.

"Not at all. And before you ask, no, you didn't hurt me when we were having sex either. I didn't even feel these when they happened. We were both carried away. I mean, I don't know how to tell you this, but you have a few scratches down your back as well."

"That's nothing. It's already an ugly, scarred mess; a few scratches won't make a difference." She gasped at that and poked a stern finger into his hard, naked chest.

"Your body is gorgeous, every delectable inch of it. And tonight you're telling me what your other tattoos mean and we're going to catalog all your smaller scars. Got it?"

"Don't try to distract me. I'm not touching you again until after these fade." His face grew stormier with each new bruise he found. He was seriously pissed off with himself for bruising her.

"You're being silly." She stepped out of his hold, taking the towel from him. "And just so you know, you have a bruise too. A huge one. On your neck."

Mason turned to face the mirror, and sure enough, he had a massive hickey just above his collarbone.

"God, I look like a teenager," he groused, and she smiled, looking so damned pleased with herself that he immediately didn't mind the mark.

"I've never given anyone a hickey before."

"And you're never giving me another. One is your limit," he warned, and she nodded, still looking smug. His eyes drifted back down to those ugly bruises marring her beautiful skin, and he felt like a savage for putting them there. He couldn't recall ever marking anyone like that before, and he knew it wasn't just because she had sensitive skin. He'd been seriously out of control with her. He needed to cool down, be gentler. And that was always his intention until he got his hands on her. Then all bets were off.

They got dressed; Mason pulled on a pair of gray cargo pants, canvas shoes, and a navy-blue Henley before turning to her with his arms outspread.

"Golfy enough?" he asked, and she shook her head.

"You look much too sexy in that getup. My father probably has a plaid-shorts-and-shirt combo you can borrow." He looped his arms around her and dropped a kiss on her neck.

"*Sexy*, huh?"

"Don't you dare fish for compliments, Carlisle," she warned, and he hugged her close for a moment before letting her go with a lighthearted tap on her rump.

"You look pretty hot yourself," he said, eyeing her appreciatively, and Daisy flushed. She glanced down at her simple white shift dress—another new purchase—pink cardigan, and scuffed tennis shoes. She looked like a librarian, or maybe somebody going to Bible study group. *Hot* was not the adjective she would have used, but Mason's gaze was sincere, and she was going to simply accept and enjoy the comment.

They parted ways in the hallway, Daisy stopping to knock on Daff's door while Mason stopped a few doors farther away to pick up the golf clubs. She felt a pang of loss as she watched him walk away and wished she could spend the morning with him.

Daff yanked the door open and thankfully distracted her.

"Oh my God, you look awful," Daisy said. Her sister had black circles under her eyes, her hair was a mess, and she looked as pale as a Goth. "Are you sick?"

"A little hungover. And sleep deprived." Daff glared at her before taking her hand and dragging her into the room. "You and Mason weren't exactly quiet last night."

"You heard us?" Daisy whispered, dismayed.

"I'd be surprised if the whole hotel didn't hear you too. You guys were pretty damned vocal. What the hell, Deedee? One minute you're telling me there's nothing between you, and the next you're shagging each other's brains out?"

"It just kind of happened."

"You're not the type of woman these things 'just kind of happen' to."

"What's that supposed to mean?" She was immediately offended, and Daff rolled her eyes.

"You're the good one, that's what I mean. *I'm* the one who usually makes the dumb life choices and winds up in bed with the wrong guys."

"Well, sometimes being good is boring. Mason and I are both consenting adults, and we had fun. He made me feel sexy and raunchy and—"

"Stop. For the love of God! I don't need to hear any more."

"Maybe you do," Daisy insisted. "Do you know that I've never had a real relationship?"

"I . . . did *not* know that," Daff admitted reluctantly, the wind leaving her sails. "You're really private sometimes, and I always assumed there were guys at college. You always talked about guys."

"I was embarrassed. I felt unattractive and unwanted. Mason makes me forget that I'm the sad girl who never had a boyfriend in high school and never dated in college. The twenty-seven-year-old virgin who had no prospects of ever changing her status."

"You were shy," Daff said heavily. "I didn't realize it was that bad."

"I was shy, and I thought I was boring and ugly and fat."

"But you're not."

"I'm beginning to see that," Daisy said with a smile, and her sister sat down heavily, staring up at her contemplatively.

"You look happy and confident and really goddamned sexy," her sister mused, and Daisy's smile widened as she sat down in the other chair.

"I feel all those things too."

"So maybe Mason isn't a total douche bag."

"Not even a partial douche bag."

"But, Daisy . . ."

"It's nothing serious. We're just having fun. I think I'm entitled to a bit of no-strings fun."

"Are you sure?"

Was she? She had no option but to be sure. After this weekend with Mason, they would go back to normal. There would be no reason for them to inhabit each other's worlds anymore. She felt a huge pang of regret at the thought. She didn't want to lose him, but every time that rogue sentiment surfaced she quashed it by reminding herself that he wasn't hers to lose.

"Daff, we need to talk about Lia," she said, deliberately changing the subject. Her sister, alerted by the absolute seriousness in her voice, sat up straighter, her eyes sharp.

"What's going on?"

It didn't take very long to lay out the sordid little story in its entirety. Daff remained absolutely quiet while Daisy spoke of her discomfort around Clayton, about the innuendos, the subtle sexual harassment. And by the time she stuttered to a halt, Daff was pale and there were lines of strain on her forehead and around her lips. She didn't speak for the longest time, while Daisy watched her anxiously, fearing repudiation, laughter, or anger. What she got was a shuddering sigh as her sister dropped her face into her hands.

"Daff?"

"Oh, Daisy," Daff whispered, looking up to meet her gaze. Shockingly, her eyes were wet, and Daisy wasn't sure what that meant, until Daff got up and knelt on the floor next to Daisy's chair. Her sister reached out and pulled her into a hug, and Daisy exhaled the breath that she'd been holding on a relieved sob. "*Why* didn't you tell me sooner?"

"I thought I was imagining things. He's *really* good at making you think you're mistaken. I was so relieved when Mason asked me about it. I thought I was going crazy. I don't know how to tell Lia. What if she hates me?"

"If she still wants to marry him after hearing this, then I'm sorry to say she's an idiot who totally deserves to marry that . . . that . . ."

"Asshole?" Daisy supplied, using Mason's go-to word.

"Motherfucker!"

"Right."

"Come on, Deedee, let's go talk some sense into our sister."

Mason was soundly trouncing Edmonton and his toadying buddies on the golf course, and their earlier jovial mood was turning distinctly sour. They were on the seventeenth hole, and Mason was well below the course par, and Clayton was three shots behind. Most of the other guys were so far behind Mason's score they had no chance of catching up.

Mason had managed to maintain a relatively pleasant façade for the majority of the last two hours, but nothing he had learned about Clayton Edmonton had done anything to shift his opinion of the man. He was an arrogant prick who spoke down to people he thought were his lessers—a group that included caddies, a couple of his groomsmen, and, of course, Mason.

Mason watched critically as the man lined up his shot. He hated golf, but he had learned to play back when he and Sam had started up the business. Sam had told him it was a good way to impress potential clients. Later, when they'd had more than a few famous golf pros as clients, they'd been forced to attend charity golf functions, and sometimes the clients preferred they keep a low profile, which meant caddying or joining the game. Mason had gotten really good at the sport, even though he had never developed a fondness for it. Just another hazard of the job as far as he was concerned.

He was grateful for the experience now, though. It was satisfying to watch Edmonton lose his cool. The man was starting to miss easy shots and swearing like a trooper. Losing that urbane edge that he so carefully cultivated.

"So you're here with the *other* sister, right?" Grier Wentworth Patterson—the best man—suddenly sneered. It was the first time the man had deigned to speak to him in over two hours, and considering the not-so-subtle nod Clayton had just given him, it was a ploy to distract Mason from the game.

"None of the guys wanted to partner with her for the wedding," another bright spark added. Mason couldn't remember this one's name, but he had clearly been overindulging a bit on the beer because he was more merry and bright-eyed than the occasion warranted. "We drew straws."

Mason cast an eye over the group; it was only Clayton and his six groomsmen. Despite what Mason had been led to believe, there were no other wedding guests present. He was the only outsider, which is why he had been quite content to just play his game and ignore them for the most part. But now his blood was starting to boil.

"Her name," he said, going through Andrew McGregor's very well-stocked golf bag and taking his time selecting the heaviest driver, "is Daisy. The next fucker who fails to use it *will* regret his memory lapse." He kept his voice level as he withdrew the golf club and buffed the head meticulously. He looked up at them only after he'd finished polishing it to his liking and was pleased to note that several of the guys looked a little uncertain after his pleasantly voiced threat.

"Come on, man," Clayton said heartily. "You can't expect us to believe you're *serious* about her? You've dated supermodels, actresses . . . a *princess*, for Christ's sake. Daisy isn't exactly your usual type."

Don't hit him! The voice was like an alarm inside Mason's head, but he could feel his fists clench as the bastard continued to just vomit a ton of shit.

"I mean," he was saying, "I can see the appeal, kind of. I've always wanted to fuck a fat chick."

Don't HIT HIM!

"I mean, I wouldn't want to be *seen* with her in public. But I figure it'd be a novelty to fuck a fattie. More cushion for the pushin', as the saying goes."

DON'T HIT HIM! It was becoming a mantra. A strident, unwelcome mantra.

"Right?" Edmonton continued to spew. "I suppose you're an adventurer, willing to try anything at least once. I've always wondered about that one. The repressed ones are dynamite in the sack, right? Am I right, bro?"

Seriously? *Fuck this guy.* The rage inside Mason went quiet as his visual range narrowed until all he saw was his target: the braying ass in front of him. He inhaled slowly, feeling as lethal as he ever had on the battlefield.

He exhaled, hauled back, and slammed his fist into the bastard's midriff, reaching out to grab the front of his preppy polo shirt in his other hand. Edmonton was bent over and wheezing for breath, and Mason leaned in, ignoring the man's flinch, to speak close to his ear, his voice pitched low enough for only him to hear. "I know what you've been doing to Daisy, Edmonton. If you ever touch her again, I swear to God you'll be shitting your own teeth for a week. Got it?" He thumped the still-gasping man on his back with his free hand before shoving him toward his groomsmen.

"If *any* of you so much as breathe wrong in her direction," he said, his voice quiet and seething with fury, lifting his gaze to include the rest of the shocked little group, "I'll show you exactly how many ways there are to fuck someone up without leaving a mark. Am I clear?"

Hasty nods.

"Great," he said, dusting his hands and rolling his neck. He glanced at a still-wheezing Edmonton and smiled, a cold baring of his teeth that had been known to scare people shitless. "Walk it off, asshole. You'll be fine."

He picked up the bag from where it had fallen and inspected the clubs for any damage. Luckily everything looked in order.

"I'd say this game is over, wouldn't you? Let's never do this again."

He sauntered to his golf cart and tossed the bag into the back and drove off without looking back. One punch hadn't been enough, but if he stayed any longer he'd probably wind up maiming or killing the man. Mason had deliberately given him just that love tap of a punch because if he unleashed all the fury he felt on the man, Edmonton wouldn't be getting up from it. Best Mason remove himself from the situation before the temptation to do worse overcame him.

He definitely needed a drink.

CHAPTER TWELVE

It was practically impossible to get Lia alone that morning. By the time Daff and Daisy got to the spa, all the other bridesmaids were there already, and Lia refused to let her sisters draw her away from the rest of the group. So Daff and Daisy went ahead with the weird mud wraps and nail treatments, the facials and hot stone massages. There was an awkward moment in the change room, when everybody else had seen the bruises on her skin, despite Daisy's attempts to keep them hidden. But Daff had eased the moment by making a silly joke about Mason obviously being a wild man in the sack. Everybody had laughed uncomfortably, and Daisy had hastily dragged on a robe to hide both her body and the bruises from everybody's prying eyes.

The spa wasn't so bad; in fact, if it weren't for the rather urgent need to speak with her sister, Daisy would have enjoyed the experience a heck of a lot more. She wasn't one for spas and stuff, but after the rigors of the night before, the treatments had definitely relaxed and rejuvenated her. In fact, she might well do this more often, especially since it resulted in smooth skin, pretty nails, and an all-over feeling of general well-being.

It was equally difficult to talk to Lia during brunch, and Daisy could see that Daff was becoming similarly frustrated. It didn't help that Zinzi and Shar were being even more bitchy than usual. They kept making snide little comments and giving Daisy pointed sidelong glances and blatantly giggling behind their hands like gossiping schoolgirls. They weren't usually so overt, but this morning it was evident even to the rest of the group. The two tended to keep their bitchiness hidden from Lia, but Daisy could see her sister was starting to notice their lousy behavior. Daisy had bigger concerns than Zinzi and Shar, and she happily ignored their rudeness.

"Lia, I'm serious, we really have to talk," Daisy whispered to her sister for what felt like the hundredth time that morning, and Lia, her face pale and pinched, finally snapped.

"What?" she shouted, the sharp edge in her voice silencing the entire group of women. "For God's sake *what*? What's so important that you can't just let me enjoy this morning?"

Daisy cast an awkward glance around the room of avidly staring women and sent a pleading glance at Daff, who made her way toward them.

"Not here," Daisy whispered miserably. "It's a private matter."

"I'm a little busy today, in case it's escaped your notice."

"It's about Clayton," Daff gritted out, losing her patience.

"This again?" Lia wasn't even attempting to keep her voice down, and the other women were all painfully silent. "Why won't you two accept that this wedding is happening and just be happy for me?"

"Lia, we can't discuss this here," Daisy said calmly. "Please can we talk about this somewhere a little quieter?"

"*No!* Nothing you say will make me change my mind!"

"Not even the fact that your bastard fiancé has been sexually harassing Daisy?" Daff finally yelled, and Lia's eyes widened as they sought Daisy's. Daisy could do nothing but return her stare with a wide, fixed gaze, horrified that Daff had simply blurted it out like that in front of the entire group.

A muffled laugh suddenly broke the silence, and all heads swung toward Shar, who had her hand up over her mouth in an attempt to stifle her horrible laughter. Zinzi sniggered as well, while the rest of the women stood around in awkward uncertainty.

"Oh, I'm sorry." Shar giggled. "It's just that . . . *come on*, are you guys really going to go with that? Clayton's been hitting on Daisy or whatever? Clayton? And *Daisy*?"

It was Daisy's worst fear come to life. The laughter, the disbelief . . . the scorn. Some of the other women were now eyeing her speculatively as well, and Daff stepped forward to intervene, but Daisy had finally had enough. She held up her hand to prevent Daff from interceding and took a step toward Shar.

"You know, Shar," she said conversationally, "you really are a malignant cow. I don't know *what* I've ever done to deserve your scorn. Quite frankly, I no longer care. I spent way too much time trying to figure it out, and I'm done. Sometimes people are just born mean. You and Zinzi are rotten to the core, and since your opinion means nothing to me, I no longer care about why I became the target for your schoolyard bullying. My sisters and I are trying to have a private conversation, so if you don't mind, we'd very much appreciate it if the rest of you could—"

"Why should Lia believe your pathetic little stories, Daisy?" Shar interrupted with a haughty little smile. "You're clearly jealous of her and what she has with Clayton. I mean, you couldn't even get a date to your own sister's wedding, could you? You had to blackmail poor Mason into being your date, didn't you? If you could lie about something like that, I'm willing to bet you're pathetic enough to fabricate horrible stories about Clayton too."

Daisy felt all the blood drain from her face at those words and swayed slightly beneath their impact.

"And if you're wondering how I know that, it came straight from the horse's mouth," Shar supplied smugly, and Daisy felt lightheaded as the words sank in. Why would he tell anybody? What possible reason could he have to tell? "We had quite a laugh over it. Poor, desperate

Daisy, showing up here with that stud on your arm, and all the while the man is here against his will. It would be laughable if it weren't so—"

"Enough!" The sharp command came from Lia, who looked pale and pissed off yet remarkably poised at the same time. "Shar, consider our friendship over. Same goes for you, Zinzi. You have no right to speak to my sister like that. Daisy's right, you're *both* malignant bitches, and I think it's best if we never see each other again. Now, if the rest of you don't mind, my sisters and I need some privacy. Please excuse us."

She and Daff moved to flank Daisy, and she was vaguely aware of each woman grabbing one of her elbows and leading her out of the private dining room. Daisy wasn't sure where they were taking her, but she was just so relieved to get out from beneath all those mocking gazes and away from Shar's vicious diatribe.

"Daisy?" It was Lia's voice, sounding very far away.

"Shit, she looks like she's going to faint." Daff sounded anxious.

"I'm not going to faint," Daisy denied, shaking her head.

"Drink this." Lia shoved a glass into her hand, and Daisy took an obedient sip before dragging in a pained breath and exhaling it on a cough.

"What the hell is that?" she asked, suddenly back in the sucky present. It looked like they were in Daff's room.

"Brandy. They always give it to people in the movies," Lia explained when her sisters both leveled disbelieving looks at her. "You looked like you needed it for the shock."

"Why would he tell her?" Daisy asked, her voice breaking.

"So that thing about Mason was true?" Lia asked, and Daisy nodded, too afraid to speak in case her voice failed her entirely. Her chest hurt. Why did it hurt? Was she having an anxiety attack? Something was wrong with her heart; it wasn't working properly, it felt wrong. It felt . . . broken.

She lifted a hand to stifle a sob, but it escaped nonetheless.

"But why?" Lia asked in confusion, and Daisy shook her head.

"Long story," Daff spoke for her.

"And the stuff about Clayton?" Lia asked hesitantly. Before shaking her head in irritation. "I don't know why I asked that. You wouldn't lie about something like that."

"You believe me?" Daisy asked in a wobbly voice, and Lia frowned.

"Of course I believe you," she said, sounding shocked that Daisy would even think she wouldn't.

"I'm sorry," Daisy whispered, and Lia hugged her.

"Deedee, you have nothing to be sorry about. I'm the one who brought him into our lives."

"I should have trusted you and spoken about it sooner."

"Maybe. It doesn't change the fact that he did what he did."

"You seem remarkably okay about this," Daff pointed out, and Lia shrugged.

"I am. I've been having . . . doubts anyway. I've been fooling myself, but the truth is, he's just not a very nice man. He's hypercritical about everything from what I eat to what I wear to whom I speak with. He even . . ." She paused, looking ashamed, before sighing and continuing. "He chose my wedding dress. All that dress-hunting business was just a ruse. He had a dress preselected and I pretended to 'find' it."

"You took us to four separate shops," Daff reminded indignantly, and Lia smiled tiredly.

"I just wanted to try to pretend I had an actual choice."

"Are you heartbroken?" Daisy asked softly, wanting to know how that felt. Wanting a basis for comparison. Lia thought about her question for a moment before shaking her head.

"No. I'm relieved. I thought I loved him. I wanted so desperately to love him. He seemed perfect. But, oh my God, the ego. Everything was always about him. And he was incredibly selfish in bed."

"Yuck. TMI. Seriously between this and Daisy last night, I—" Daff broke off abruptly when Daisy burst into tears. "Shit. Deedee, I'm sorry."

"It's just . . . I think—I think *I'm* heartbroken. But how can I be heart-broken? You have to be in love to have your heart broken. Isn't that how it usually works?" God, she was a mess. And this wasn't even about her. Her sister's wedding was in a shambles, and she could think only of herself.

"Everybody knows now. I feel so stupid and humiliated. I don't understand why he would tell her."

"Are you sure it was him?" Lia asked, and Daisy shook her head and buried her face in her hands.

"I don't know. He's always seemed contemptuous of her; I don't see him deliberately telling her, but how else would she know?"

"What are you going to do?" Daff asked and Daisy lifted her face to stare at her concerned sisters resolutely.

"Deal with it."

"And what about you?" Daff directed the question at Lia, who shrugged.

"Mom and Dad are going to be so disappointed," she said, regret adding weight to her words.

"They'd be more disappointed if you wound up marrying a man you don't love," Daff said.

"But they went to so much effort. *Look* at this place; it cost the earth. And all the guests; they've all lost money. How can I possibly repay everybody?"

"The people who love you want you to be happy, and the guests got a nice relaxing weekend at a beautiful venue for their trouble. Time to be selfish and think of yourself, Lia."

"Then I suppose I have a wedding to cancel."

~

"Hey, angel." Mason smiled when Daisy walked into their suite ten minutes later. He looked totally relaxed, kicking back on the sofa with a well-worn paperback facedown on his chest. "How'd it go?"

"The wedding's off," Daisy told him, without any inflection in her voice. She kept her gaze carefully averted as she opened the closet and dragged out her suitcase.

"No shit. So you told her? How'd she take it?" He sounded concerned, and Daisy flipped open her suitcase and scanned the interior intently, happy for the task because it allowed her to keep avoiding his gaze.

"The wedding is off. How do you think she took it?" She walked over to the bureau where she had stored a couple of T-shirts and her underwear and withdrew the carefully folded clothes and carried them over to her case.

"She's okay with you?"

"Uh-huh." She began to carefully place her clothing back into the case and—from the corner of her eye—she could see his body language change subtly.

"What are you doing?" he asked. His voice had a lethally soft edge to it.

"Packing."

"Why?"

"No more wedding, so there's no need for this farce to continue." She was happy that her voice and hands remained steady, but she still couldn't meet his eyes, not even when he got up from the sofa and came to stand right beside her. He was much too close. Close enough for her to smell his cologne, to feel his body heat, to hear his soft breathing.

"So we're going home?" he asked quietly.

"I think it's best if *you* went home. Today. I'll catch a ride back with Daff."

"What's going on? Why are you being like this? Has someone upset you?"

"I'm releasing you from our agreement," she said, with barely a wobble in her voice, and Mason swore before taking hold of her elbow and turning her to face him. The movement dislodged the tears that had been brimming in her eyes, and he swore again as he watched the twin silvery tracks scorch their way down her cheeks.

"*Who* made you cry?" His quiet voice promised retribution to anyone who had dared hurt her, and the hypocrisy of it just made the silent tears flow faster. "Daisy, tell me what happened."

"Everybody knows," she said on a broken whisper. "Everybody knows. I'm a laughingstock, a pathetic object of scorn and pity. How ridiculous is that? An entire wedding is being called off, and the only thing people will be talking about is the fact that Daisy McGregor blackmailed a man into being her date."

"*What?*" He sounded horrified. God, could he really be this good of an actor? Daisy didn't know what to think, what to believe; all she knew was that it would be best if he left. Everything between them had happened way too fast; she'd been too caught up in the fantasy of what could be to accept the reality of what was. And the reality was that they would never work. She had allowed herself a brief moment of "what-if," but that was over now, destroyed by the truth that she'd seen in Shar's eyes. She and Mason didn't work. And they never would.

"I need you to *leave*."

"Daisy, me leaving would be the wrong move," he said, his hands tightening on her elbow. "It would just confirm whatever the hell people are thinking. I should stay, make them doubt whatever it is they heard. We should keep up a united front."

"Why are you doing this?" Her voice was as fractured as her heart, and she clamped her trembling lips together in an effort to regain a modicum of dignity and control before she spoke again.

"I'm doing this because I care about you," he confessed hoarsely. "Because I don't want you to go through this alone. Because I want to show them that nothing about what we have is fake."

"*It's all fake!*" At the end of her tether, her voice rose sharply until she was practically screaming. The volume shocked both of them, and she inhaled deeply before speaking again. "I want you out of my life, Mason. This little sideshow is over."

"Daisy."

"Permanently out of my life, do you understand?"

"No!" he yelled back. "What the fuck is going on?"

"Did you tell Shar about us?" She didn't know why she even bothered asking. She could no longer deny the truth. Mason was a good guy. She didn't know *how* Shar had learned the truth, but it wasn't Mason who had told her. All Daisy knew was that the question would drive a wedge between them, and she desperately needed to put some distance between them. She needed him to leave because it was time for Daisy McGregor to get back to the real world. The words dropped between them like lead, and Mason took a horrified step back from her.

"What?" His voice was soft and lethal, and she couldn't read his expression at all, but something in his eyes sent a shudder of sorrow down her spine. She swallowed and calmly repeated the vile question.

"Did you tell Shar about us? She knows every detail, and I certainly didn't tell her."

"Shar?" The woman's name sounded harsh on his lips, and Daisy winced when she heard it. "You think I told fucking *Shar* about our arrangement?"

He dropped her elbow and stepped away from her, and Daisy felt the loss of his body heat keenly, even while she despised herself for her neediness.

"How the fuck can you think that? How can you think that I would hurt you . . . *you* of all people, like that?" His voice hitched, and he swore softly before turning away from her and striding to the closet to grab his duffel and his garment bags. Daisy stood frozen and watched as he efficiently repacked the duffel bag within mere minutes, every movement of his beautiful body looking stiff and furious. When he was done he strode to the door, turning to face her only after he had opened the door.

"You need to grow up, Daisy. You're still way too hung up on shit that happened when you were in high school. You've allowed petty teenage crap to cloud your vision of yourself and affect the way you live your life. Call me once you've grown up." He paused before shaking his head irritably. "On second thought, don't call me. I'll have moved on from this *situation* by then."

Daisy didn't have a response to that. She felt immeasurable loss at the thought of never seeing him again.

"And you may want to find out who the hell really told Shar about our agreement," he advised, his tone harsh. "Because it sure as hell *wasn't* me." He slammed the door behind him, and Daisy released the shuddering breath she'd been holding and sank down onto the bed as her legs gave way. She curled up into a ball, feeling wounded and broken as she tried to keep the tears at bay. She hugged a pillow to her chest; it smelled like him, and her throat ached as she continued to fight her tears.

The door opened, and for a wild moment she thought it was Mason returning, but it was Daff, the spare key card in her hand.

"Mason stopped by my room on his way out," she said softly. "He gave me this and told me you needed me."

Oh God. There was no holding back the tears after that, and—thanks to Mason—Daff was there to hold her and comfort her.

"Mason? What are you doing back so soon? Isn't the wedding tomorrow?" Spencer stepped aside, and Mason stormed past him furiously, pausing only to greet his ecstatic dog.

"Lia called it off," Mason told his brother, and after another affectionate hug for Cooper, he made his way to the kitchen and straight to the fridge. "Is this all the beer you have?"

"Yeah."

"We're going to need more."

"There are a dozen beers in there," Spencer protested, and Mason glared at him, before taking both six-packs out of the fridge and carrying them into living room. After placing the beers on the coffee table, he sat on the nearest lounge chair and then shook his head.

"That's not enough beer."

"What the fuck, man? What happened? And what do you mean Lia called it off? Like the whole wedding?" Spencer sat down too and reached for a beer.

"No, only the ceremony and the reception and the bit where they throw the bouquet," Mason retorted sarcastically. He was in a seriously black mood, and the long, lonely drive back hadn't exactly helped. "Of course the *whole* wedding."

"But why?"

"Because her fiancé is a piece of shit."

"So you and Daisy came back early? Isn't there a lot of crap to take care of? I would have expected Daisy to want to stay and help with that."

Mason grabbed one of the beers and popped the tab. He took a long, thirsty drink before feeling ready to answer his brother's question.

Daisy.

He was furious with her, but beneath the fury was an underlying feeling of hurt and betrayal. Yes, she had hurt his feelings, and he felt like a pussy for even admitting it to himself. He was pissed off that she'd had so little faith in him, and right now he couldn't even think about her without wanting to break something. He drained the rest of the beer and then crumpled the can in his fist, before thumping it onto the coffee table and reaching for another.

"Whoa, easy on the beers, Mase," Spencer cautioned, still working on his first can. Mason ignored him and had half of his second beer consumed before talking again.

"Daisy didn't come back with me. She told me to leave."

"Oh." There was a wealth of confusion in the sound. "And you're angry about that?"

"She thinks I told Shar about our . . . arrangement."

"Did you?"

"Fuck off, Spence."

"So you didn't?"

"Of course I didn't. But apparently Shar knows, and the only other people who knew about the whole stupid scheme were you and Daff."

"I don't talk to Shar," Spencer hastened to assure him. "Or rather, Shar doesn't talk to *me*. Ever. I'm not classy enough for her."

"And I can't imagine Daffodil McGregor telling anybody, so I have no clue how Shar managed to find out about it. Did you speak to anybody else?"

"No. Of course not."

Mason moved on to his third can of beer, his mind in turmoil. He wasn't sure how he felt any more; all he knew was that he would miss that crazy armful of neurotic femininity more than he cared to admit. She was funny, intelligent, insanely sexy, and sweeter than any other woman he had ever met, and he felt like he'd lost something unique and special. Hard as it was to admit, no amount of beer would fill the hole she had left in his heart.

—

"Daddy, have you ever seen that car before?" Daisy asked one Saturday afternoon on the way back from their clinic day.

"What car, sweetheart?" her father asked absently, keeping his eyes on the road.

"Behind us." She had her eyes on the rearview mirror, checking out the dark sedan with its tinted windows directly behind them. "I've seen the same car on our last three visits to *Inkululeko*."

"That's nothing to worry about," her father said with a smile. "They've been escorting us to and from the clinic every week for the last month."

"What?" The word was a whisper, and she doubted that her father even heard it.

"Mason insisted. It was part of his donation to the clinic." Mason had made an outrageously generous donation to the clinic, enough for them to buy new equipment and a bigger mobile clinic. He had also sponsored a full scholarship for Thandiwe's current and future studies. The girl was ecstatic and enthusiastic about the future. "In addition to the money, he insisted on providing security for as long as we needed it."

"We don't need security," Daisy insisted, feeling a little lightheaded that he had actually gone ahead and done this. It was more than a month since the wedding and at least six weeks after he had first brought up the need for security.

"I feel better knowing that they're there. They're very discreet. You haven't even noticed them until recently, and they've been escorting us on our last eight visits."

"Why would he do this?" Her father's eyes flicked from the road to her face and back again.

"He's a good man. And he cares about what happens to you."

"You once thought Clayton was a good man too," she pointed out. It was a low blow and she knew it, but her father took the hit with nothing more than a smile.

"I never thought Clayton was a good man, but I had hope that Dahlia saw something in him that I didn't. I trusted her good judgment, and in the end my trust was warranted."

"I suppose it was nice of Mason to arrange this," she said quietly.

"More than nice, I think."

"Maybe."

"Daisy, I don't know what happened between the two of you . . ."

"Yes, you do, Daddy. Everybody knows it was all fake. We were pretending to be a couple."

"You like him, he likes you. No pretense there," he said with a shrug.

"No, he did what he had to because I forced him." Her father laughed at that, the sound so genuinely amused that Daisy was a little offended by it.

"Sweetheart, you can be difficult and stubborn and a little crazy at times, but nobody on God's green earth, especially not a lightweight like you, can force a man like Mason Carlisle to do anything he doesn't want to do."

"I blackmailed him."

"He came to that wedding because he wanted to," her father dismissed.

Daisy didn't respond to that, but her eyes drifted to the side-view mirror, and she watched the other car for a long moment. Mason had been out of her life for a month; she hadn't seen him or heard from him at all in that time. And she knew it was her fault; she had leaped at the excuse to drive him away. At times she was sure she'd made the right decision, but then at other times—like right now—doubt crept in and she wondered if perhaps she hadn't made the biggest mistake of her life. She often wondered who had really told Shar about their scheme. Not that it really mattered anymore; the damage had been done. But she was still curious.

Straight from the horse's mouth.

How could Shar possibly have found out about their deception unless she had heard it from one of the parties involved? Could it have been Spencer? He was the only other person who knew about it.

"I'll tell you what I told my brother," Spencer said, when Daisy went by his house later that evening to pose the question to him. "It wasn't me."

"Mason asked you about it?"

"He's been trying to figure it out too." He handed her a beer, not offering her a choice, and she took it with a nod. Beer wasn't her drink at all, but he was trying to be civil.

"Daisy"—Spencer's grave face mirrored his tone of voice—"I deserve your doubt and your ill will. I haven't been . . . kind to you, and I'm very sorry for that. I've treated you badly in the past, but I want you to know that the night I asked Mason to distract you while I chatted with Daff was only because I wanted a chance to speak to her and she's always been very protective over you. So I—stupidly—thought if she saw that you were happily preoccupied, she'd be more open to relaxing and talking with me. Mason was reluctant to go through with it, not because he had anything against you but because he's a good guy and he thought it might hurt you if you found out his interest wasn't genuine." He shook his head. "It was a stupid, ill-advised, and flawed plan. And it failed miserably . . . for me. Mason, on the other hand, my brother liked you from the beginning. And this entire fucked-up situation has messed him up more than he's willing to let on. He's miserable."

"He is?" Daisy hated the thought of Mason being miserable. Especially if she was the cause of it.

"Do you know that he punched Edmonton?"

"What?"

"He didn't tell me about it; I heard it from one of the guy's groomsmen. Apparently Clayton was spouting off some shit about you, and Mason punched him and warned the groomsmen if they ever mentioned your name again he'd lay a world of pain on them."

"*Oh.*" Daisy's hands went to her mouth, and her eyes flooded with tears. Nobody had *ever* done anything so sweet and romantic for her before. Mason had always been kind, gentle, and protective of her. And Daisy had simply thrown it all away because of her own stupid insecurities. Mason was right; she was so hung up in the past, in what people *used* to think of her, that she'd allowed it to color her vision of the world and herself. And then he'd come along and had seen something completely different, and because his image of her didn't gel with hers, she had dismissed it as fantasy. As part of an elaborate act.

What a fool she was.

The following afternoon Daisy nervously rubbed a damp palm over the denim of her jeans before lifting her hand to ring Mason's doorbell. There was a faint answering bark inside. The barking grew closer and closer until she could hear Cooper just inside the door. She cast an anxious glance around. Mason's Jeep was parked outside, but she couldn't see his bike or BMW and she wondered if he was out. The possibility filled her with both relief and disappointment. She needed to apologize and to know if they could still have something real between them. She hoped so, because she had stupidly—and against every ounce of her better judgment—gone and fallen in love with the man.

Cooper was still kicking up a fuss, and when she heard Mason command him to be quiet, her heart started up a frantic rhythm in her chest, and for a fraught moment, she insanely considered dumping her peace offering and making a run for it. But then it was too late, the door swung inward, and there he was, staring down at her from his great height. And he was really . . . *dirty?*

Her eyes fluttered over him. He wore a pair of dirt-streaked jeans, boots, and a ripped T-shirt. His clothes and face were streaked with grime and sweat.

Daisy blinked and wondered if she were dreaming because he looked like he had just stepped out of one of her favorite erotic fantasies. She licked her lips, searching for something to say, more than a little wrong-footed by his appearance.

"Uh . . . you're really dirty," she pointed out, wincing at the inadvertent sexual ambiguity of the statement. Instead of jumping all over the unintentionally provocative words, as he would have in the past, he shrugged, causing the muscles in his shoulders and chest to flex impressively.

"I'm busy," he said, his voice flat and unencouraging.

"So this is a bad time to talk?"

"What do you want, Daisy?"

"To talk," she said again.

"I figure we've said everything that needed saying," he muttered.

"May I come in?" she asked doggedly. He sighed, the sound impatient and explosive, and stood to the side. He held on to the door, while his body shifted to allow her to pass him, forcing her to duck beneath his arm in order to gain entry. He smelled wonderfully earthy, of soap and good, healthy male sweat. None of that expensive, sexy cologne she liked as much. He slammed the door behind her once she was inside and brushed past her as she bent to pat Cooper, who was greeting her with a happily wagging tail and a grinning face. She followed Mason into the kitchen, where he twisted the cap off a beer and took a long drink. He lowered his arm to stare at her and, unlike his brother the day before, refrained from offering her one.

"I brought you something," she said shyly, holding up the wrapped package in her hands. He didn't respond, which forced her to elaborate. "It's a bacon, cheddar, and zucchini bread. Freshly baked."

"What do you want, Daisy?" he asked again, his voice so cold it sent a shudder down her spine.

"I wanted to apologize. I know you didn't tell Shar about us."

"Who did?"

"I'm not sure."

"I'm shocked you changed your mind without definitive proof," he sneered, and she carefully placed the bread onto the center island and braced her hands on the countertop.

"I knew you didn't almost from the beginning, but I was freaking out a little about us, you know? It was all a little overwhelming, and

274

maybe I jumped on the whole Shar thing as an excuse to—to drive you away." She was babbling, she knew she was, but his face was just so cold and impassive. It was making her nervous. "Anyway, I should have spoken to you about my fears. I shouldn't have dealt with it the way I did."

"No, you shouldn't have."

"Mason, I'm truly sorry."

"Fine." He took another sip of his beer, before looking at her again. "You're forgiven."

"I was wondering if maybe we could try again?"

"Try what again?" God, this was really hard. This Mason was a far cry from the warm and easygoing man she knew. He was cold, callous, and calculating. But she knew the other Mason was in there, and it was up to her to find him and appeal to him.

"Us."

"We're not an *us*. There's never been an *us*."

"I would like there to be."

"Yeah?" He slammed his bottle down on the counter between them and leaned toward her, his entire body vibrating with tension and unmistakable fury. "It's not going to happen. Go play your high school games with some other idiot, Daisy. I've done my time. You don't know what you really want. I was your first fuck, and you think that means something, don't you? Little Daisy with her teen dream fantasies about the perfect boy. The one who will love her just the way she is, right? That's what you want from me? I'm through role-playing. I won't be your fantasy man—the guy too impossibly perfect to exist in real life."

"I don't want that," she denied. "I made a mistake, and I'm sorry. But I wanted us—"

"There's that word again," he sneered. "Get it through your head, Daisy. There's no fucking *us*!"

"I love you." It was a desperate cry, and she knew saying it was a mistake.

"You don't love *me*. You love some fictional being. You've only ever been with one guy, Daisy. How can that be love?"

"And when did *you* suddenly become such an expert on love, Mason? You who once asked how we'd know if we were ever really in love? You're always looking for the next best one, right? Because the one you're with is never good enough. I suppose holding you to a higher standard was a ridiculous pipe dream, wasn't it? Yes, I've only ever had one lover, and maybe it makes me naïve and stupid and ridiculous to think that I'm in love with him."

"Maybe?" The haughty sarcasm in his voice proved to be her undoing, and she blinked, forcing back her tears, before straightening her spine and meeting his mocking gaze head-on.

"Anyway," she said softly. "I wanted to apologize. For *everything*. And to thank you for what you've done for the clinic. I won't bother you again."

She picked up the bread, and he made a sound in the back of his throat. When she threw him a questioning glance, he shook his head, his face still that awful blank mask.

"Leave it." The barked command was unexpected, and Daisy carefully put the bread down again.

"I'll see myself out." She didn't wait for his response before she turned and left.

Mason remained still as he listened to the quiet sounds of her departure, a soft whispered good-bye for Cooper in the hallway, the snick of the front door handle being turned, a slight soughing sound as the rain-swollen wood of the door resisted her initial attempt to tug it open. The wind rushing into the hall, carrying the faint scents of wood smoke, wet leaves, and soil all the way into the kitchen, and then finally the door closing. Her car door opening and closing, and the engine of her small car firing to life. He didn't move, even when Cooper padded into the kitchen to sniff out some snacks, didn't move until the sound of her car was finally swallowed up by distance and the rising wind . . . and then when he *did* move, it was slight. Just a release of tension, his muscles relaxed—shoulders slumping—and his head bowed as he stared down at her offering on his kitchen counter.

"Jesus." A prayer? A plea for help? An exclamation of regret? Even Mason didn't know. All he knew was that he had hated seeing her, hated speaking with her, hated hearing her say those *fucking* words. She didn't have the faintest idea what love was. What being in love felt like. How could she? She hadn't really lived her life. Hadn't experienced enough of the wrong people to know when the right one came along. Because if all these years of coming close to falling in love had taught Mason anything, it was how to recognize the real thing when it came along.

～

"You two are getting on my nerves," Daff complained Friday evening two weeks later. They had enjoyed dinner at the farm, and the sisters were all three crunching their way through a gigantic bowl of popcorn and watching reruns of *Friends*. "So you lost your boyfriends, whatever, it's not the end of the world."

"He was my *fiancé*!"

"He wasn't my boyfriend!" Daisy and Lia exclaimed at the same time, and Daff rolled her eyes.

"Like I said, *whatever*. You're getting off your asses tonight, and we're going out."

"There's nowhere to go in Riversend," Lia grumbled, and Daff pinned her with a no-nonsense glare.

"Get changed."

"I have nothing to wear, and your clothes won't fit me, so don't even suggest it," Daisy warned. "Besides, if we go out and run into

Shar tonight, I'm going to hit her. So it's probably best if we just stayed home."

A week ago, Daff—sick of Daisy's moping around—had confronted Zinzi regarding where Shar had obtained her information about Daisy and Mason. The woman had confessed to a simple and uncomplicated case of eavesdropping. The news had sent Daisy into an even worse spiral of despair when she comprehended how completely she had authored her own destruction. How positively and irritatingly Shakespearean.

"We won't run into Shar; her husband dragged her away on some gross four-week-long seniors' cruise. Rumor has it the old guy bought a boatload of Viagra before he left. She's going to *hate* it." All three of them took a moment to enjoy the thought of Shar trapped on a prolonged cruise with senior citizens and her horny ancient husband, before Daff snapped back into bossy mode. "Go home, get changed, we'll pick you up on the way."

"I really don't feel like—"

"You're going. *Both* of you," Daff interrupted Daisy.

"Fine, but only because I'm really bored," Daisy relented. She wasn't bored. She was just apathetic and sad. Really, really sad all of the time. It frightened her, this deep and abiding melancholy; she couldn't remember ever feeling this way before, and she wanted it to end. She wanted to wake up one morning and feel lightness in her soul, and contentment and happiness in her heart. She wanted to turn around and greet Mason with a smile and a kiss and be grateful for what she had. But all of that seemed so far out of reach that just thinking about it made her plummet even further into complete and utter misery.

She hungered for just the sound of his name, and she heard it often. Her father spoke of the work he was doing around town, donating money and resources, and his own manual labor, toward renovating some of the more faded landmarks. Thandiwe said he'd come into the school to speak with the students. Daff mentioned him now and again, she'd seen him at MJ's, Ralphie's, and out in Knysna at a popular local night spot, a different woman on his arm each time. Even her mother and Lia spoke of him, of how he had called after news of the broken engagement had spread through town, to ask if they were okay and if they needed anything.

The only person who never saw him, or heard from him, was Daisy. And she knew that it was deliberate. He was avoiding her; maybe she had embarrassed him with her declaration of love. Who could blame him, really? She was a total stranger to him, and a few weeks of fake dating couldn't change that fact. So why couldn't she accept that reality and move on?

Maybe because, despite all those warnings and reminders she had given herself to the contrary, it hadn't felt fake at all.

Ralphie's. Great. Of course it would be Ralphie's; there was literally nowhere else to go. Daisy sighed and reluctantly climbed out of the car, pulling her too-short and too-tight skirt down surreptitiously. She was trying new things, and this skirt was part of the wardrobe that she had bought a week after Mason had so roundly rejected her. Tight, black, and a smidgeon too far above knee, it clung to her hips and butt a little too lovingly. She'd combined it with a sparkly black scoop-necked top, black stockings, and shoes that were an inch too high. She left her hair wild and loose, and for the first time appreciated the carefree look it gave her. Daff had done her makeup, telling her the outfit called for smoky eyes and "fuck me red" on the lips. Daisy wasn't so sure about the red, but it did make her lips look plumper, which wasn't a bad thing, she supposed.

They were slammed with that familiar wall of heat and sound when they entered the door . . . and greeted by a cacophony of enthusiastic wolf whistles. Daisy's first instinct was to take a step back and allow her sisters the spotlight, but after just a second's hesitation, she stepped forward in unison with them and greeted the crowd with a vivacious grin. The male eyes scanned all three of them with equal amounts of appreciation, and it felt quite . . . liberating.

The whistles and catcalls drew his attention, and Mason lifted his gaze from their deep contemplation of his beer to the commotion at the front door and froze.

"*Christ,*" he swore shakily, and Spencer—who sat with his back to the door—watched him in concern.

"What?"

"What the fuck is she wearing? She's going to cause a riot in that getup!" Spencer glanced over his shoulder, and his eyebrows climbed to his hairline, before he added his appreciative whistle to that of the adoring male crowd.

"Hellooo, Dr. Daisy," Spencer growled, and Mason's brow lowered.

"Hey! Stop staring at her like that."

"I can't help it; that skirt is killing me. And that top does great things for her ti—"

"*Don't* say it!" Mason interrupted viciously, and Spencer turned his gaze back to his brother.

"What?" he asked, all innocence. "She's hot."

"I know that," Mason said. "I don't know how none of you saw that before. Why does she have to shimmy her way into a skirt that ends just below her ass cheeks for you to see it now?"

That skirt was way too high, and it took every ounce of willpower Mason possessed not to march over there and throw his jacket over her to cover her up. She hadn't spotted him yet; she was still smiling—God, what was that shade of red on her lips? It should be illegal!

"I have to go," he said, getting up and reaching for his wallet. He had successfully avoided her for weeks, trying to get back into the dating game but finding every woman who Spencer set him up with unappealing and boring. He needed just a little more time before he was able to face her without saying or doing anything stupid. Just a little more time to get his shit together.

"You can't keep avoiding her forever, you know?" Spencer predicted, and Mason shrugged.

"No clue what you're talking about."

"I think I'll ask Daisy to dance," Spencer said, and Mason snorted.

"Good luck with that; she doesn't dance."

"Well, that definitely looks like dancing to me," Spencer said, and Mason's head flew up. Just in time to see Daisy shimmying against some douche bag in a plaid shirt and jeans. The guy looked like Christmas and all his birthdays had come at once, and then, as Mason watched, she did it . . . She actually pulled a few chicken dance moves and then laughed at herself for doing it. Her laughter was so contagious that it invited her partner and everybody else in the immediate vicinity to join in, and when she leaned into the guy to whisper something in his ear, Mason felt his blood boil. When the guy tipped his head back to laugh and started doing the chicken dance too, Mason knew that she had "confided" her so-called dance weakness to him.

He felt outrageously betrayed by that, like she had taken something that was theirs alone and shared it with the masses. And it was crazy, irrational thinking like that, which meant he had to get out of here immediately.

"*Mason!*" Shit. Lia had spotted him. Her screech could be heard over the noise and music, and Daisy's head snapped around and her eyes found him immediately. Not hard to do when he was standing up and obviously watching her. He couldn't tear his gaze from hers, and she never broke eye contact as she leaned toward her partner to say something to him, before battling her way through the crowd to make her way toward Mason.

He couldn't move, not even when Lia got to him first and gave him a hug and a kiss. He responded automatically, keeping his eyes on Daisy. Always Daisy. Forever Daisy.

And then she was there. So close. Too close . . . And he was vaguely aware of Spencer and Lia discreetly edging away from them to allow them as much privacy as they could get in a place like this.

"Mason." That was all she said, and he nodded, before forcing her name out. A name he had futilely forbidden himself from even thinking over the last few weeks.

"Daisy."

"It's so nice to see you." She put a hand on his shoulder, and he tried not to flinch from her touch. She went up onto her toes and attempted to brush her lips across his cheek. He didn't bend down to meet her halfway, and instead her mouth grazed his neck, and he tensed even further.

She removed her hand, and he mourned the loss of her touch.

"You're dancing," he pointed out, desperate to keep everything casual. Just a couple of acquaintances, reacquainting themselves.

"Yes. As you so kindly pointed out, I've spent way too much time mulling over the past, so I figure it's time for a change, right? Time to grow up and try new things."

What new things?

"Your skirt's too short," he said, and she bent backward and craned her neck to try and see her own butt.

"You think so?" she asked, sounding remarkably unconcerned, where before she would have gone into spasms of doubt and insecurity over it.

"Your ass is hanging out."

She laughed at his words, still much too lighthearted. "Well, you always said I have a nice bum, so I'm showing off my best asset. No pun intended." Her voice was light, inviting him to share the joke, but he found himself incapable of even smiling right now, and her smile faded while the laughter died from her eyes. And Mason immediately felt like a prick for extinguishing that inner light. "Are you still angry with me? Won't you forgive me? I know I was wrong to use Shar's bitchiness as an excuse to end things with us. And in the end, it was *literally* all my fault." Daisy laughed bitterly. "Do you want to hear something hilarious? It was *me*. I'm the one who told Shar about us. Zinzi overheard Daff and I talking in the powder room. And that's where Shar got all her information! I'm so sorry, Mason."

"Don't," he said gruffly. "Don't keep apologizing. You have nothing left to apologize for."

"We were friends," she said, her voice mournful. "And I hate losing your friendship."

"We weren't friends," he growled. "You told me that once, remember? We were never merely friends, Daisy."

"Then what were we?"

"Nothing." But that was a lie, and he shut his eyes before admitting the truth. *"Everything."* When he opened his eyes it was to see her back as she walked away, never having heard his truth.

CHAPTER THIRTEEN

Daisy cast a nervous glance around her and conceded that she had made a stupid error in judgment in coming to *Inkululeko* on her own so close to sunset. Thomas had been relieved and happy to see her and had gratefully accepted the antihistamines she'd brought for little Sheba. The boy had called her at the practice, distraught because his dog was sneezing and vomiting nonstop. Symptoms that had developed practically overnight. Daisy promised to come and see Sheba after work, and one look had confirmed some kind of allergy. She had given the dog a shot, told Thomas how to administer the antihistamines, and advised him to bring Sheba into the clinic on Wednesday for a checkup.

Now, it was fully dark as she slowly drove through the maze of dilapidated shacks, and she uneasily acknowledged that most of the people staring at her were unfamiliar, none of the friendly faces she usually saw at the clinic. It was Monday evening and nobody knew she was here; her father had been busy with his last patient when she'd left, and Lucinda had taken a half day.

She breathed a sigh of relief when she took the corner and left the settlement behind, but the dark road back to town yawned threateningly ahead of her. The poor condition of the dirt road made it impossible for her to drive at a speed that would have made her feel a little more comfortable, and as she crept her way forward, the only light on the road coming from her headlights, she cursed herself for her stupidity. She looked down to search for her phone, her intention to tell someone where she was, and when she looked back up it was to see several armed men step onto the road in front of her car.

She wasn't about to stop and sped up, but her tires spun on the gravel, unable to find the required traction, and the car fishtailed dangerously.

Oh my God, this can't be happening!

Mason cursed when the annoying frickin' ringtone that Spencer had programmed onto his phone jerked him from his work on the Ducati Diavel Walkaround that he'd been endlessly tinkering with for weeks.

He grabbed the phone with one greasy hand—it read "unknown caller," which annoyed him even more—and uncaring of the smears he left on the screen, put it on speaker.

"Carlisle," he grunted, grabbing a cloth.

"Mr. Carlisle?" The voice was female, hesitant, and familiar.

"Yeah, it's Mason Carlisle." He reached for a rag and wiped his hands.

"It's Thandiwe Modise."

"Thandiwe? What's wrong? Are you okay?" he asked, immediately on alert.

"I'm fine, but you told me to let you know if I heard of anything that could be threatening to the clinic or Dr. Daisy. I'm worried; she came to the township this evening—"

"*She what?* Alone?" Mason could feel his blood start to boil. What was wrong with the foolish woman? How could she go out there on her own after hours on a Monday evening?

"She brought medicine for a boy's sick dog. I heard that there might be some trouble. We're worried. Some of the *tsotsis*"—thugs—"were seen following her."

"Is she still there?" Mason felt a chill settle over him as his heart thudded sluggishly in his chest.

"I'm not sure."

"If she is, keep her there, don't let her leave. I'm on my way." He hung up before she had a chance to respond and grabbed his jacket. She'd better be okay. Better be safe and well and whole so that he could shake some sense into her before wringing her little neck.

He took the Jeep and broke the speed limit to get to the dirt road that led to the township. He was halfway down that road when he saw the commotion up ahead. A large crowd of people, cars and lights everywhere. A panicked sound broke free from his tight throat, and he stopped the Jeep and nearly fell out of it in his haste to get to the scene. There was shouting, a lot of angry shouting, and he shoved his way through the crowd, desperate to find Daisy. Where was she?

"Daisy!" He couldn't contain himself anymore and shouted for her, and the crowd quieted, finally spotting him. "Where's Dr. Daisy?" he asked, sensing no threat from them.

"Mason?" He nearly went to his knees at the sound of her voice and turned on wobbly legs to find the crowd parting to let her through, Thandiwe supporting her. His eyes drank in the sight of her; her clothes were a mess, her face was tear streaked, and was that a fucking *bruise* forming on her jaw? He tensed, feeling a murderous rage settling over him like a cloak. He was going to *end* the mother-fuckers who had hurt her.

"Oh God, are you bleeding?" he asked—spotting the bright splash of red on her dress. Her eyes dropped to her side, and her hand automatically clamped over the spot.

"Just a little," she admitted, her voice sounding shockingly weak. He made a harsh sound in the back of his throat and made his way to her, wrapping a gentle arm around her waist. She leaned against him, trembling violently, telling him that she was hurt, shocked, and terrified without saying a word.

"Who did this?" he asked, his voice lethal, and an old, familiar-looking man stepped forward.

"We caught the *tsotsis* and we called the police. We warned them many times to stay away from the doctor and clinic, but they think we're just old men or women. They think we're weak. They don't care about our words, but we showed them." There were murmurs of agreement in the crowd.

"Mr. Mahlangu and everybody else saved me," Daisy whispered. "They came out and risked their lives for me."

"*Who* did this? Where are they?" Mason asked single-mindedly.

"Dr. Daisy is hurt, and you should take her to the hospital," Thandiwe advised calmly. "The police and ambulance are on their way, but you'll probably get her there faster."

It was all the distraction Mason needed, especially when Daisy sagged against him even more, and all thought of retribution fled as her well-being became his number one priority. He lifted her into his arms and carried her to the Jeep.

"I'm too heavy," she protested.

"You're in enough shit as it is," he warned frigidly. "Don't add to it by talking crap."

━━━

Daisy snuggled closer; she was cold, hurt, and in shock and so relieved to be in his arms again. She could tell that he was livid, but she had never felt safer.

She shuddered as she recalled those terrifying moments after she had left the township. Her car had spun out of control, and before she'd known it, she was off the road and being dragged out by vicious hands. They had ransacked the car and taken money, torn her jewelry from her, and when she had fought back, one of them had hit her. Another had pulled a knife out and cut her . . . She sobbed at the thought. They would have done more, so much worse, but the taxies and old, broken-down cars had shown up, and the shouting had started. So many wonderful and brave people had come to her aid. Thandiwe had pulled her aside, while the crowd had proven that when good outnumbered evil there was no way evil could prevail. Before she knew it, the young men—boys, really—had been tied up and shoved to the side of the road. And then, mere minutes later, Mason had shown up. She had never been happier to see him.

He settled her into the passenger seat of the Jeep, and she watched him through a haze of tears, his grim profile a black silhouette against a dark background. He was angry. And it showed in his sharp movements as he maneuvered the Jeep back to the main road into town.

"Why are you bleeding?" he asked harshly, speaking for the first time in minutes.

"One of them cut me," she confessed. The car veered, and his head swung to face her.

"They stabbed you? Oh Jesus, why didn't you say something? How bad is the bleeding?"

"I said cut, and I meant cut. It's not a penetrating wound. It's a slash," she said, forcing calmness into her voice. He was on the verge of panicking, and it wouldn't do to spook him further.

"How the fuck would you know that?" he asked angrily.

"I'm a doctor, remember? I may treat animals instead of people, but I do know the difference between a serious wound and a superficial wound."

"Does it hurt?" His voice was too restrained, too mechanical, for lack of a better word.

"A little," she lied. It hurt like hell, and it was still bleeding sluggishly, which told her she'd probably need stitches.

The thought of her in pain was unbearable, and Mason gritted his teeth and drove even faster. God, he could kill her for being so damned stupid.

"You're angry," she said, her voice timid. He shot her a disbelieving glare but refrained from responding to that obvious statement. "I'm sorry I inconvenienced you."

"Daisy, shut up," he advised steadily. "I'm not willing to get into this with you now."

Thankfully, she listened to him, but only because she was in pain. He could tell because of the way she held herself, like she was afraid to move. He was an expert at pain and the coping mechanisms people implemented to deal with it.

They got to the small local clinic less than five minutes later, and he leapt out to find a doctor and a wheelchair. He called Spencer and asked him to contact Daisy's family before rushing to be by her side again.

The doctors forced him to stay in the waiting room while they wheeled her into the ER, and all Mason's pent-up rage at Daisy and the bastards who had dared to hurt her made him want to break something. He started pacing, prowling up and down the length of the room like a caged animal as he attempted to calm his raging thoughts. Part of him wanted to rush back to *Inkululeko* and beat the offenders to a pulp, while another—much bigger—part of him wanted to stay here and just never leave Daisy's side again. He wanted to wrap her in cotton wool and keep her safe from everything and everybody.

"Mason!" He turned just as Daff stepped into the waiting room followed by Lia, their parents, and Spencer. "What happened? How is she?"

"Your sister decided that it would be a good idea to go into *Inkululeko* after dark and without an escort," he enlightened them shakily, and Dr. McGregor swore furiously. "She's fine. A few scrapes and bruises and a nasty cut, but the residents came to her rescue."

"Oh, thank God," Lia whispered; she was weeping quietly and hugging her distraught mother.

"Oh my God, that *idiot*," Daff snapped, and Mason nodded.

❦

"Finally we agree on something," he said drily before resuming his pacing. He was aware of the concerned discussions around him, and when they started talking about who would stay with Daisy tonight, he stopped pacing to face them.

"You should probably be aware of the fact that the only place she'll be staying tonight is at mine," he stated uncompromisingly, leaving no room for argument in his voice.

"The last time you saw her, you told her that you didn't even have a friendship," Lia reminded, and Daff glared at him.

"And that means you don't get to have a say in her well-being right now," Daff added.

"Look, I was trying to do the right thing. She thinks she's in love with me, but she's not."

"How do you know that?" Spencer asked him curiously. His brother remained removed from the group, just sitting quietly in the corner and waiting.

"Because I was her first"—Mason's eyes shifted to her listening parents and felt his face warming slightly—"uh, first boyfriend." What a stupid word that was. Puerile and pointless, he was neither a boy, nor a friend. "Nobody falls in love with their first significant other."

"Nonsense," Mrs. McGregor stated decisively. "I did."

"As did I," Dr. McGregor added. Mason looked at them in blank surprise.

"You did?"

"We met in high school, fell in love in our senior year, and got married after Andy finished medical school," Mrs. McGregor stated, and her husband nodded fondly.

"Don't be so quick to discount her feelings, son. You once told us you were working on getting her to like you in the same way you liked her."

"Daisy and I were . . ."

"I know, pretending. Right?" Mason nodded. "And yet you seemed sincere. Now you tell me she says she's in love with you. Seems to me you finally got what you wanted. Don't see what the problem is."

"I—I . . ." The ER doctor walked in, and Mason had never been so relieved to see another person in his life. He was still completely thrown by Daisy's parents' easy acceptance of her so-called feelings for him and more than a little stunned by her father's interpretation of what he believed Mason's words had meant so many weeks ago.

"Daisy will be fine," the doctor assured them. "I've administered a mild sedative to help combat the shock. She had a deep laceration on her left side, which needed several stitches; a few nasty bruises; and whiplash, but I'm happy to release her tonight. She needs a couple of days' bed rest for the blow she received to the head—but luckily it's not a concussion. I do recommend she seeks counseling for any PTSD she might suffer. She's currently being interviewed by the police, but as soon as they're done taking her statement she's free to go home."

"Daff, I'll need you to bring Peaches to my place later. I don't want Daisy to worry about her," Mason commanded, and the woman gave a disbelieving little laugh.

"Listen here, Mason, you can't—"

"Daff, do as he says," Andrew McGregor interrupted firmly.

"But, Daddy . . ."

"He'll take good care of her, *won't* you, Mason?"

"I'll make sure she gets enough rest." Mason nodded. His response was met with four exasperated faces and one amused one. "What?"

Daisy was hugged and fussed over by her family, but she was very much aware of Mason just standing in the doorway watching them all. Why was he still here? She would have expected him to make his escape by now. Spencer was there too. The man came into the room to give her a kiss and tell her he was glad she was okay, before saying his good-byes and leaving. But Daisy was too overwhelmed by her family to give much thought to Spencer's unexpected appearance.

Her father was giving her a gentle lecture on the irresponsibility of her actions, which she humbly accepted because everything he was saying was true. Her mother constantly asked her if she was okay, patting her hair and stroking her face as if she had to have her hand on Daisy at all times. Lia fussed over her bruises, and Daff insisted on seeing her stitches.

The rest of the room went quiet while Daisy unbuttoned her dress to show them her wound. Even though it was covered with waterproof dressing, the size of the bandage around her torso made them all gasp in horror. Daisy was thankful that they were spared from the sight of the actual wound—a long, vicious-looking cut that curved up from her hip to just a couple of inches below her breast. She had been shocked by the size of it and grateful that it had required only a few stitches. It could have been so much worse, and she was so grateful to the people of *Inkululeko* for saving her.

Daisy's eyes lifted to where Mason stood in the doorway. He was staring fixedly at the covered injury, his eyes burning and his jaw clenched. When he looked up to meet her gaze, she was shocked by the raw emotion she saw swirling in those beautiful green eyes of his. He looked furious, but he also looked . . . anguished.

His lips thinned, and he cleared his throat, breaking eye contact with her.

"That looks huge; you're going to have a badass scar," Daff stated, trying to sound cavalier but defeated by the wobble in her voice and the haunted look in her eyes.

"I think it's time Daisy gets some rest," Mason recommended gruffly, and Daisy was stunned when her family seemed to defer to him. They all hugged her and filed out of the room.

"Wait, why are they leaving?" Daisy asked after a moment's shock. "Who's taking me home?"

"I'll get your stuff, and then we're leaving."

~━━━

Five minutes later they were back in his car and once again stewing in grim silence. This was getting a little old. If he didn't want to talk to her, he should probably stop acting as her self-appointed protector. It was bizarre and confusing.

"Why are you turning here?" she asked in alarm when he turned onto the path that led up to his house. "I'm tired; I want to go home."

"You're staying with me tonight."

"I can go home and Lia or Daff can stay with me. I can't leave Peaches alone overnight."

"Peaches is here, Daff brought her, and before you say anything, she packed a bag for you too."

"But *why*?"

"Somebody needs to keep your ass out of trouble."

"And you think you're the man for that job?" she asked incredulously. He didn't reply, merely stepped out of the car and rounded the front to open the passenger door for her. When she stubbornly refused to move, he sighed impatiently.

"If you don't get out, I'll pick you up and carry you to the . . . fuck it, never mind." He slipped one arm behind her back and the other beneath her thighs and very carefully lifted her out of the car.

"Mason, I'm too . . ."

"If you say 'heavy' again, I'm going to drop you on your butt," he promised grimly, and she prudently shut her mouth. He carried her to his front door without breaking a sweat and carefully lowered her to the doormat while he reached above the doorway and lifted down a key.

"That's so unsafe," she observed, and he let out a sharp laugh.

"Says the woman who just drove into a township alone at night?"

"*Touché.*"

The dogs were both going crazy, and when he opened the door, Peaches made a beeline for her while Cooper happily greeted Mason. He patted his dog affectionately before moving to pick up a wriggling Peaches just as Daisy was leaning down to get her.

"You want to bend down with those stitches? And you wonder why you need a minder?" He handed her dog to her, and she glared at him before limping her way into his house, while murmuring little love words to Peaches. She spared some love for Cooper too; the bigger dog seemed more relaxed around Peaches, so maybe they had come to some kind of canine truce in the short time they had been left alone together.

"Are you hungry?" Mason could see Daisy was exhausted and—despite her defiant front—in some serious pain. He should probably just have let her family take care of her, but—and even though it had seemed like the wisest course—he just couldn't stand the thought of not being with her right now. He was angry with her, sure, but he also wanted to cling to her with every fiber of his being. Just hold her close and never let her go.

"Not right now," she said. "I just need a really long shower." He nodded.

"The bathroom's upstairs; I'll help you." He settled a hand around her waist, taking Peaches and putting the dog back on the floor in the process. She went rigid beneath his touch and stepped deftly away from him.

"I'm sure I can manage."

"I told Daff to put your bag on the bed."

"You only have one bed, don't you?" she asked wearily.

"Yeah."

"Are we sharing?"

"I—" He should have thought about this earlier and felt like an idiot for never considering the obvious flaw in his plan. "I can take the sofa."

"Hmm." She sighed tiredly and started to drag herself up the staircase, leaning heavily on the banister. Mason followed her closely, worried that she'd lose her balance.

"Stop hovering," she snapped uncharacteristically when she finally got to the top. "It's annoying." Her gaze started to rove around the loft. Mason was happy with the airiness he'd achieved in this space; from the tall, panoramic windows to the skylight and the gigantic bed, everything just felt roomy yet at the same time—because of all the wood—cozy and warm. The loft overlooked the living area of cabin, but if one glanced up from below, the tucked-away aerie could barely be seen.

"Shower's through there." He pointed toward the frosted-glass double doors leading to the massive full bathroom and clenched his hands to prevent himself from reaching for her as she limped her way toward it. "I'll get some dinner on. Your appetite may come back a little later. Call if you need me."

She didn't respond, and he reluctantly turned away and left her to it. The dogs were stretched out on their tummies in front of the cold hearth, facing each other with their wet noses touching. Coop looked smitten but confused, while Peaches looked smug.

"You too, huh, boy?" Mason said in quiet sympathy. "Trust me, it won't get any easier. She's going to drive you completely crazy."

Neither dog acknowledged him, and he left them to it.

Nearly an hour later, Mason stepped out of the kitchen and listened for any signs of activity from upstairs. The shower wasn't running, and the light was on, but everything was silent.

"Daisy?" No response. Concerned, he rushed upstairs only to halt on the landing. She was stretched out on her side, wrapped in nothing but one of his massive towels, fast asleep. His eyes tracked over her bare skin, inventorying every little scrape and bump and bruise. The mark on her jaw was now a livid purple and was starting to swell.

Her knees were badly scraped; had they dragged her? A sob caught in his throat at the mere thought of it. Finger marks on her arms and around her wrists, a massive bruise on her left thigh, all of which made him feel physically ill. But none of them compared to the sizable knife wound that he knew was hidden beneath that massive dressing. He had nearly thrown up at the sight of it and had hated himself for not being there to protect his woman. The terror she must have felt. It killed him to know that she now understood what that kind of fear felt like.

She was trembling, he suddenly saw, and her skin was pebbled with goose bumps. She must be freezing. He dragged a comforter over her, but the shivering didn't stop, so he kicked off his shoes and dragged off his clothes until he was wearing only his boxer briefs and climbed in behind her. He tugged her carefully back against him, telling himself he would hold her just until she warmed up. But even after the shivering stopped, he couldn't bring himself to let her go. He didn't think he would ever have the strength to let her go. He fell asleep resigned to that fact.

He awoke hours later, the house still ablaze with light, and he groggily reached for his phone to check the time. It was just after two in the morning. He got out of bed, careful not to disturb Daisy, but she didn't move at all, and he headed downstairs to switch off the lights and check on the dogs. The pooches were both curled up in Cooper's big bed and lifted their heads to watch him approach.

"You show your girlfriend how to use the dog door, boy?" he asked quietly, and Cooper's tail thumped against the wooden floor. He checked that there was enough water in the bowl for them and went to the kitchen to store the soup in the fridge.

After making sure the house was locked up and everything was switched off, he headed back upstairs. Daisy hadn't moved at all, and he watched her for a moment, contemplating the sofa downstairs before deciding that he would risk her wrath in the morning, and climbed in next to her once again. This time she sighed and snuggled closer to his body heat. Content, Mason allowed himself this moment of peace and fell asleep again in moments.

Daisy was warm and comfortable and reluctant to open her eyes. A small, niggling part of her brain told her that waking up would bring way too many problems. She wanted to stay in this happy, peaceful moment, where everything was perfect.

A light snore surprised her into opening her eyes. The sound had not come from her. And with full consciousness came pain and memory. There wasn't a single part of her body that didn't hurt, and she groaned. The glorious source of heat all along her back tensed, and she knew immediately who it was.

"You okay?" his sexy morning voice asked in concern.

"Achy," she said, and the large hand resting on her thigh squeezed gently. He sat up, careful not to jostle her, and she looked up into his grim, unsmiling face in confusion.

"What happened to the sofa?" she asked.

"The bed was more comfortable. I'll get you some coffee." He got up before she could stop him, and she flushed when she saw he was wearing nothing but a pair of white boxer briefs . . . and an impressive morning erection. He didn't acknowledge it, but he made no attempt to hide it either, keeping his gaze level and his face impassive.

She pushed herself up, wincing when her stomach wound tightened and pulled at the stitches.

"Gently," he snapped. "You don't want to tear those stitches."

"Okay, nurse, I just forgot about them for a second. And where the hell are my clothes?" The latter as she realized that she was stark naked beneath the covers.

"You were wearing only a towel when I found you last night. It probably came off during the night." Despite that impressive hard-on, he managed to look remarkably unaffected at the idea of her nudity.

"Mason, why am I here?" she asked quietly, and he tensed.

"You needed someone to take care of you."

"You know as well as I do that my family would happily have done so."

"I needed to be sure that you were okay."

"And now that you're sure? Should I go home today?"

"Who says I'm sure?"

"I'm bruised and a bit achy, but I'm fine," she pointed out, and he glared at her.

"Well, I'm not fine!" he snapped furiously. "I'm nowhere near fine. You scared the hell out of me, Daisy, and the least you can do is stay put while I—while I . . . get over that fright."

"This is a lot of concern for someone who isn't even a friend," she pointed out with what she believed was impressive logic, but he didn't look impressed at all. He still only looked mostly pissed off.

"I'll get you that coffee." He turned away from her and headed downstairs, while Daisy sighed before gingerly getting out of bed and going to the bathroom. She grimaced at the sight of her reflection in the huge wall-to-ceiling mirror. She looked like death warmed over, so pale that the bruises stood out in stark relief against her flesh. She examined the waterproof dressing over her stitches carefully, but there were no signs of bleeding beneath it, so they had managed to survive the night intact.

She glanced around the bathroom for a robe or something but saw none. Mason definitely wasn't a robe-wearing kind of guy anyway. She had used up all the towels last night and had no idea where he kept the spares. She should have brought a change of clothing in here with her and cursed her lack of foresight. She had no choice but to head back into the loft—naked—for her overnight bag.

Mason was back, a cup of coffee in one hand. His eyebrows rose to his hairline when she stepped out of the bathroom, and she could see his Adam's apple bob as he swallowed.

"What are you doing?" he asked carefully, and she tried not to roll her eyes at the suspicion in his voice.

"Seducing you?" She barely stifled a grin at his horrified expression.

"Oh, baby, you look like you were hit by a truck," he responded softly, his voice laced with both regret and sympathy. He looked uncertain about whether he should take her seriously or not.

"So, not sexy?"

"You're always sexy," he whispered. "Clothed, nude, bruised or not. You're the sexiest woman I know."

"Such a blatant lie," she said, taking the smallest of steps toward him.

"I've never lied to you. Not once."

"Never?" she asked. "What about the time you said we weren't friends?"

"We weren't."

"So what were we?"

"More than that. Always more."

"More? How much more?" Her question seemed to snap him out of whatever daze he seemed to be in, and he shook his head.

"Get dressed, angel, and enjoy your coffee," he said, putting the mug on a nightstand. "I'll grab a shower. And we'll talk afterward."

When he finished his shower, he entered the room to find Daisy cuddling both dogs on his bed. She was fussing over them and speaking to them in that annoying voice she always seemed to adopt with Peaches.

"Don't talk to Cooper like that; he's not a baby," he protested, heading to his closet to drag out some clothes and dropping his towel without concern to get dressed. He was aware of her eyes on him at all times and did nothing to conceal his ever-present Daisy-induced erection from her.

After he was dressed, he turned to face her, and she was watching him with unflinching admiration in her gaze and a dreamy smile on her face.

"I like your body," she said unabashedly, and he fought the grin that threatened to surface. But he couldn't fight anymore, and it escaped, which seemed to delight her, if her answering smile were any indication.

He sat down on the edge of the bed and just watched her until she shifted uncomfortably.

"I'm angry with you," he said matter-of-factly, and she sighed heavily.

"I know. I shouldn't have let the Shar thing—"

"No," he interrupted impatient. "Enough about fucking Shar. This has nothing to do with Shar or your sister's aborted wedding. It has to do with the danger you placed yourself in yesterday."

"I'm sorry."

"You can't do shit like that, Daisy. You can't risk yourself like that. There are people who care about what happens to you. People who would be devastated to lose you."

"I know," she said in a small voice.

"*Do* you? Do have any idea how many people would suffer if you got hurt or—or died?"

"I know it would destroy my family," she admitted.

"Not just your family," he grated out. "Other people too." Her eyes were glued to his face, narrowed speculatively as she watched him carefully.

"Do you understand what I'm saying?" he asked, and she bit her lip before shrugging.

"Why did you say we weren't friends?" *Why did she keep harping on about that?*

"Because I don't see you as a friend."

"You don't? Well, then, you once asked me if I wanted to know what you saw when you looked at me. So I'm asking you now, if you don't see me as a friend, then what am I? What do you see when you look at me, Mason?"

Mason ran a shaky hand over his head and lifted his eyes to hers, hoping she could see everything he wanted to say in them, hoping she understood, even if he made a mess of his reply.

"Everything," he grated out. "I see my whole fucking world, Daisy. I see all my days, my weeks, and my years. Every season of my life. All spent with you. I see everything I want, need, and desire all wrapped up in you."

⸺

Well, then.

Daisy ambidextrously petted a dog on each side as she looked at Mason. It was that or throw herself at him and caution to the winds. But she wanted no misunderstandings, no take backs, and no outs this time. There was way too much at stake.

"Do you still think I can't possibly love you?" she asked seriously, and he swallowed.

"I don't see how you could," he admitted hoarsely. "I was your first lover, our entire relationship was built on a lie, and you've known me for mere weeks. You don't have enough experience to know for sure."

"Well, how do you ever really know if what you're feeling is true love?" she asked, throwing his own quote back at him, and he smiled grimly.

"You know when you have basis for comparison. You know when everybody else pales in comparison to The One . . . I know because I can't think of a single reason I found anybody else attractive or interesting or beautiful before you. I know because I love you so much that the thought of not having you love me in the same way hurt so much that I would rather have let you go than accept anything less from you."

"So you'd let me walk away, even though you love me?" And how absolutely wonderful it was to know that he felt that way about her. But Mason was a stubborn man, and she would not allow him to throw away their future because he had some crazy idea in his head about how much experience she should have before she could possibly genuinely be in love with him.

"No. Not anymore. Not after last night. You've had your chance to escape, Daisy. Now you're stuck with me."

"Even though my love might be childish and temporary?" She couldn't resist rubbing that in, and he winced.

"Look, maybe my opinions are a little extreme and dated and seem silly to you—"

"*Maybe?*" Oh, that felt good. And he grinned, allowing her the delicious retribution.

"I've been a prick."

"Yes. You have. But guess what?"

"What?"

"I love you anyway." Oh good, she got a slight, patronizing smile in response to her proclamation this time. The man really was irritating. And stubborn. "So are you willing to stand aside and allow me to gain the experience required before I'm properly able to decide whether I love you or not?"

There was a flicker of panic in his eyes at her question, and Daisy left the dogs and crawled into his lap.

"Whom should I start with, do you think? Kevin, the guy I met at Ralphie's the other night, was really nice."

"You know his name?" He seemed really shocked by that fact.

"Of course, I danced with him, after all. You know what a big deal that is for me."

"I hated seeing you dance with him," he confessed reluctantly. "I felt like the chicken dance was our thing."

She shuddered delicately at that and nuzzled his neck.

"The chicken dance should never be anyone's thing."

"You make that ass-jiggle bit look sexy."

"Mason, you're really going to have to start believing me when I tell you I love you," she said seriously.

"Tell me why you love me."

"I've always been shy. For years I've remained happily curled up in my shell in public, in private, with family or friends. I don't think anybody ever really saw me. I don't think even *I* saw the real me. But something weird happened around you. Even on that very first night when you were being a good little wingman . . . I opened my mouth and I spoke and I laughed and I engaged. You looked at me and saw Daisy. You helped me find myself, and I liked the person I found hiding in that shell. Even after I learned you were just talking to me as a favor to Spencer, there was just no going back to meek little wallflower Daisy. How can I not love you for that?"

"That's gratitude, Daisy." She gritted her teeth at his so-called logic.

"You're incredibly irritating," she seethed. "And I still love you. And when you're obnoxious, I love you too. When you're so arrogant, I feel like there's no way a room could possibly contain your ego . . . I inexplicably *still* love you. If being in love with someone isn't about loving them even when they're being complete assholes, then I don't know what it is."

That made him smile. A big, generous, gorgeous smile that filled every inch of her soul with joy.

"That's more like it."

"What?"

"I love you when you're crazy and irrational and contrary as hell."

"I love you when your language is foul enough to strip paint from the walls, when you brag about the size of your penis, and when you wake me up at ungodly hours of the morning!"

"Yeah, well, I love you when you bitch about getting up, speak to your dog in that annoying voice, and cheat at car games!"

They stared at each other for a beat and started laughing.

"So I guess you love me," he said.

"And you love me."

"Looks that way."

"So now what?"

"I have a few ideas," he whispered, lowering his head to kiss her. "Firstly, I have to ask, Daisy McGregor . . . will you be my girl?"

"Oh yes, please."

"And you won't go running around and putting yourself in danger at every turn?"

"That happened *one* time," she retorted, exasperated.

"Once was more than enough." He shuddered, his hand reaching up to stroke the bruise on her jaw. "You have to understand, you're my life's blood, Daisy. It's terrifying. Everything that happens to you happens to me. Every offence, every insult, every hurt, I carry it with me too. So promise me you'll take care of yourself."

"I promise. No more putting myself into dangerous situations. But I'm not stopping the clinic."

"I wouldn't dream of asking you to. I just want you to be careful."

"I can do that."

"And you'll go fishing with me?"

"Possibly," she hedged.

"Camping?"

"Maybe."

"Hiking."

"Probably." He gave her a look, and she rolled her eyes. "Fine, I'll do some of that with you. But you'll owe me. We're talking ballets and symphonies and chick flicks." He winced.

"We'll compromise," he said quickly. She kissed him, and he opened his mouth to her, allowing her to take what she wanted from him, before lifting his head to continue the negotiations. "And you'll bake more of that delicious bread for me?"

"You liked it? I wasn't sure you'd eat it."

"I was pissed off, not an idiot. Of course I ate it. It was fan-fucking-tastic! I expect more of the same. Also cakes and pies."

"Done! I wish we could seal our deal with some sex," she said wistfully, and he choked on a laugh.

"Absolutely not. You've just been stabbed."

"Sliced."

"That doesn't sound the slightest bit better. My point is, you're hurt and bruised and stiff." She wriggled in his lap.

"You're stiff too," she pointed out, and he groaned.

"You're going to have to work on your raunchy jokes, angel. You can't keep falling back on that one."

"We can do other stuff," she pouted, and he hugged her closer.

"We have plenty of time for the other stuff. Because you're mine now, Daisy McGregor, and I plan to love you and have my wicked way with you for many, many years to come."

"Promise?"

"Easiest promise I've ever had to make."

EPILOGUE

ONE YEAR LATER

Daisy and Mason's engagement party was in full swing but, despite the festivities around her, Daff circled the room restlessly feeling out of sorts and a little bit moody, like a shark cruising the shallows looking for a potential victim. She spotted her prey just a couple of feet away and made her way to his side. He was a big bastard, topping her five foot seven height by at least seven inches. Massively built with shoulders that could block out the sun, he was easily twice her size, but all muscle. She knew he kept fit, always out playing rugby, swimming, cycling, and surfing. While his brother had a lean elegance to his gorgeous body, Spencer was all brute force.

"Stop fiddling with that tie," she said when he tugged at the length of fabric. "You've done enough damage."

"What do you care?" He glared at her from beneath that fall of black hair. He looked like a beast, hulking, menacing . . . His hair fell over his eyes, a wild, sleek mane. It was kind of thrilling how savage he seemed at times. No wonder he always messed up flirting with her; he had all the finesse of a stampeding bull.

"Fine, if you want to continue looking barely civilized, then by all means, fiddle away." She continued to stand beside him, sipping her bubbly while he wavered for a few seconds before his hand discreetly went up to touch the knot of his tie, obviously checking if it were as bad as she'd implied.

"So your brother finally popped the question," she said, her eyes going to the happy couple dancing in the middle of the room. They were so damned perfect together. Daff couldn't fathom that kind of yearning for anybody. It wasn't something she had ever aspired to, and she hoped never to actually feel anything remotely similar. How terrifying that would be. And yet . . . sometimes it physically hurt to see them together. She was pleased for Daisy; her sister deserved all the happiness in the world, and Mason made her ecstatic, but looking at them made Daff feel . . . lonely.

"I think he started asking her about six months ago. She finally said yes," Spencer corrected, and Daff grinned. The couple's relationship had been anything but ordinary, so the news didn't surprise her in the slightest.

"And you're the best man?" She framed it as a question, and he nodded.

"Well, since I'm the maid of honor, we'll be partnered and expected to *do* stuff together. I just wanted to be sure you were okay with that?"

"Why wouldn't I be?"

"We haven't really been on good terms."

"I hadn't noticed. You don't exactly feature prominently in my life." Ouch. That hurt.

"Right. Anyway. Bygones?"

"If you say so." He shrugged. Feeling foolish, Daff walked away and wished she'd never approached him in the first place.

"I can't resist it," Daisy whispered, and Mason grinned.

"Try," he said for the sheer hell of it.

"You know I can't."

"This time, I'm sure you can."

"No. I'm seriously OCD about it."

"Then go for it," he said and stepped away from her. And she went for it. In the middle of "Lady in Red," she slowly formed beaks with her hands, and did a couple of arm flaps followed by a sexy little butt wriggle. Before she could finish with a clap, Mason took her hands and pulled her back into his arms, laughing heartily as he did so.

"Oh, babe, I love you so damned much."

"Yeah, you do," she said contentedly, and he kissed her.

ABOUT THE AUTHOR

Natasha Anders was born in Cape Town, South Africa. She spent nine years working as an assistant English teacher in Niigata, Japan, where she became a legendary karaoke diva. Now back in Cape Town, she lives with her opinionated budgie, Oliver; her temperamental Chihuahua, Maia; and her moody budgie, Baxter. Readers can connect with her through her Facebook page, on Twitter at @satyne1, or at www.natashaanders.com.